ANNA BURKE
SEA WOLF

Bywater
BOOKS

Ann Arbor
2021

Bywater Books

Copyright © 2021 Anna Burke

Print ISBN: 978-1-61294-201-8

Bywater Books First Edition: July 27, 2021

Printed in the United States of America on acid-free paper.
Cover design: TreeHouse Studio

Bywater Books
PO Box 3671
Ann Arbor MI 48106-3671
www.bywaterbooks.com

For Tiffany,
and for Faith, my little sea wolf.

"It is with great satisfaction that we give the council the report that the mutineer, Miranda Stillwater, was summarily executed this evening in accordance with statute 617A of Archipelago Naval Law. Any threat to the stability of our great experiment is a threat to our very survival, not just as a nation, but as a species. Today that threat was once again held at bay. This victory belongs to all citizens of the Archipelago, and we now declare the official end to the Stillwater Mutiny."

Milo Korevich, Representative of Orion Station
June 5, 2509

"As we mourn our losses and celebrate our victory, remember what we fought to protect: the Archipelago is all that stands between humanity and anarchy, and those who would see us fall would do well to remember that we carry the seeds of civilization in our holds."

Josephine Comita, Admiral of Polaris Station
September 5, 2513

"Archipelageans are full of shit."

Orca, First Mate of *Man o' War*
Every *Fucking* Day

.

North

Captain's Log
Captain Miranda Stillwater
Man o' War
February 23, 2514
5°06'46" N, 50°01'02" W

Increased blooms have kept us subbed more than usual to spare the filters. The toxins from the algae alone could end us if they get into the drinking water, and while Rose has kept us clear of the worst of it, the crew misses sunlight. Our sonar screens are white with noise. Jellyfish everywhere. My scars burn. These mindless, ravenous sacs will outlast us all.

Fuck 'em.

Chapter One

There is no such thing as true north. This was the first thing they taught us about navigation in Fleet Preparatory Academy. Or rather, true north existed, so long as we bore in mind that the exact location shifted with the poles. I remembered the lesson the same way I remembered my first whiff of hydrogen sulfide: bitter, rotten, the poisonous truth beneath the fragile crust of logic that sustained everything I knew.

This gave me nightmares for years. I dreamt I stood on the bridge trying to chart a course, but my inner compass spun and spun, unable to settle, unable to align, and I'd wake up in a cold sweat to the sound of my own voice chanting the only words that had ever brought me any guarantee of clarity: *north, east, south, west*.

I missed those nightmares. These days, my dreams were full of blood.

Coordinates spooled out of my fingers as I stared at the charts, taking stock of our location and the distance between us and the coastline we'd agreed to map for Admiral Comita. I could see the course we'd take: a meandering thing, avoiding the treacherous shallows with their sunken cities while we searched for signs of mineral deposits and other anomalies that might one day be of use. Secret coves where sonar couldn't penetrate, signs of other pirate fleets, a host of dangers known and unknown that could end an unwary navigator and her crew. The ocean pulsed. Each minute shift of the current tugged at my blood as the iron in my veins adjusted to crosscurrents and cardinal points. I was quicksilver. I was light. I was a compass needle, singing to the poles.

I sank into the work. Beside me, Miranda flicked through a notebook, checking inventory and periodically crossing something out with a pen. A sheaf of partially transcribed whale song lay on the table between us. The shorthand flickered in and out of my focus as I pictured the charts before me in three dimensions. Danger above, danger below. Miranda's knee brushed mine as she turned another page.

So easily distracted, I scolded myself as my attention drifted to her instead of my work. Sunlight limned the strong lines of her fingers and blurred the thin scars spanning the backs of her hands. I traced them, sometimes, when she was drifting into sleep, half-believing there was meaning in their patterns.

I knew better. Miranda was an unlikely oracle, and in the three months I'd spent sleeping beside her, I sometimes felt like I'd come no closer to understanding her than I had my first day on the *Man o' War*. Other times, she seemed as familiar to me as my own breath. She sensed my gaze and favored me with a crooked smile, lifting one of those scarred hands to brush my jaw.

"Trouble?" she asked.

"Just you."

Her low laugh echoed in my chest as she turned the page of her notebook and made a mark by one of the columns. I refocused my attention on the charts. Admiral Comita, my former superior officer, hoped to find new deposits of minerals and iron ore close enough to the shore for Archipelago Station drills. She'd commissioned our help—albeit grudgingly. Thinking about how close we'd almost come to death at her hands still churned my stomach. I'd never be able to prove whether or not she'd meant us harm. Some days I wondered if not knowing was worse than the betrayal itself. Miranda had shrugged off my attempts to lure her into speculation.

"Does it matter?" she'd asked.

"How could it not?"

"We'll always be a liability for her. Trusting her will never be an option. Let it go."

The distant sound of running footsteps shattered my concentration. I forced myself to exhale, then inhale again as I listened for the ship's alarm bells. Five seconds. Ten. Thirty. I willed the footsteps to mean nothing. Quiet moments with Miranda during our days were as rare as whales themselves, and the tenor of my thoughts felt too much like foreshadowing.

The footsteps faded. Children, maybe, chasing a cat around the upper decks.

Coordinates welled once more. The Archipelago stations would be drifting south this time of year, closer to the African coast than the curve of South America, where we currently sailed. A week away if not more, depending on the dead zones. Far away from Admiral Comita and Archipelago stations.

More footsteps clattered on the grates. I set down the thin sheet of bioplastic.

"Should we be worried?" I asked my captain.

"Hmm?"

"What are you reading anyway?" I reached for the transcript, but she folded it in half and slid it into her notebook.

"Just a scout's report. Nothing relevant."

I was still learning the code Miranda's ship used to communicate with scouting vessels and other mercenaries over long distances. The ancient whale recordings were haunting to listen to, but I could only pick out the most basic sequences. Translators had a shorthand for the calls—because translating them directly into the language most of us onboard spoke was, apparently, too simple—but none of the looping symbols on Miranda's paper made any sense to me. Comita didn't use whale song. Archipelago code relied on sonar clicks adapted from dolphins, which translated more efficiently into binary.

"Sounds like something's going on out there," I said as raised voices followed the footsteps.

She made no move to investigate. "There's always something."

"Captain Stillwater, are you hiding?" I pushed the charts away and propped my chin on my fist.

"A good captain doesn't hide. She practices elusion."

"I see. And who are you eluding?"

"Right now? Everyone but you."

"That was almost sweet," I said, reaching out to tug the collar of her shirt.

The alarm bells clanged.

"Neptune's balls," said Miranda. She sprang for the door. I pushed back my chair and bolted after her onto the catwalk outside, which overlooked the unfinished open interior of the midship where a garden would be on Archipelago vessels, and shoved past a woman carrying a load of laundry.

"Watch it," she shouted at me over the sound of the bell. I didn't bother reminding her I was second mate and could shove who I liked. Chances were high she'd challenge me to a boxing match I'd lose, and Miranda was already half a flight of stairs ahead of me. The added muscle I'd put on during training did little to compensate for the fat I'd lost on *Man o' War's* feeding regimen. I remained slight and unimposing.

Cats scattered out of my way as I took the stairs to the bridge two at a time. I still hadn't gotten used to the sheer number of cats on this ship. Back home on the Archipelago, cats were carefully regulated, but here the healthy rodent population sustained their swollen numbers.

The hatch to the bridge stood open in Miranda's wake. I rounded it and collided with Orca, who stabilized me with what might have been a punch to the midsection or a helping hand. Odds were even either way. The red eyes of the orcas tattooed on her arms glared at me from her biceps, and the shells and bones in her braids clinked as she shook her head at me.

"What's wrong?" I asked when I regained the ability to breathe. Miranda stood in a cluster of frowning crew members, staring at the instrument panel. Blue water shifted past the thick plex of the helm. Glittering shafts of late afternoon sunlight filtered through the several meters separating us from the surface.

"Breach in the portside bulkhead," said Orca. She patted me on the back as I coughed, which did not help my winded lungs. The first mate had an estranged relationship with gentleness.

"Orca, take the helm." Miranda's order scattered the sailors around her, and her long braid whipped through the air as she turned away from the ocean.

"But—" said Orca.

"Now. Rose, with me."

Orca opened her mouth to argue, but settled for a curt nod when Miranda raised her hand to cut her off. Only the slant of her eyebrows conveyed the frustration she otherwise concealed.

Miranda set off for the stairs at a jog. I kept pace with her and tried to read the severity of the situation from the set of her jaw.

"How bad?" I asked.

"We've lost the first deck, but engineering sealed the storage rooms before they flooded."

"Did everyone get out?"

Miranda slowed to allow a flustered young man herding a group of children into a crèche to pass. "We've got a work crew trapped in one of the storage rooms."

Hiding from enemy sailors in a ballast tank. The feel of water rising over my head, only the sound of my breathing in the oxygen mask keeping me company through the dark hours. I chewed on the inside of my cheek as the memory faded, ashamed at how relieved I felt that I was not trapped with the work crew.

Tubes filled with bioluminescent algae shed their bluish light on the landing to the engineering level. Miranda gripped the hatch and rotated it, and, as always, my lips dried at the sight of her muscles tensing with the effort.

"How large is the breach?" I asked.

"We're about to find out." She held the hatch open for me and I entered a world of chaos.

"Seal the fucking door," someone shouted as Miranda locked

11

us in. Whoever it was had not bothered to look up to see who had entered, and under the circumstances I doubted Miranda would take umbrage.

The giant pipes that filtered our water and cooled the engines wrapped around the room, and access to the bulkheads was partially obscured by the control panels monitoring our systems. I saw a familiar head of curly hair emerge from behind one, followed by an order shouted in Harper's clear voice. Admiral Comita's daughter knew her way around an engine room.

"Captain," she said as we approached. Sludge streaked Harper's coveralls, and a smear of something green marked the brown skin of her cheek. "We're not totally screwed, but the pump is jammed, and something gave on the portside valve. We need to bring the ship to the surface."

"You." Miranda stopped a passing engineer. He pocketed his wrench and came to attention. "Tell the first mate to bring the ship up."

"Miranda," I said as he took off. "We're in a dead zone."

"All vents are sealed," said Harper. "And we don't have a choice. We'll need to pump it manually, unless you want to say hello to Davy Jones. CO2 scrubber on the algae tanks gave out, too. No air in, no water out."

"What do you need?" Miranda asked.

"I need her topside and I need divers," said Harper, looking around at the crew of people at her disposal. "Plus a new valve."

I ran through the inventory of what we'd brought from Polaris Station before we'd departed three months ago: new algae cultures for the biolights and printers; seeds; parts to upgrade the dilapidated technology that kept the ship afloat; minerals; vaccines; antibiotics. We were running low on all of them, though the algae, at least, was capable of reproducing.

"Do we have a valve replacement?" I asked Harper.

"If we don't, we won't be able to sub without risking the rest of the ship," she said. "I don't trust the pressure locks on the inner doors."

Miranda met my eyes and waited.

"If we can't sub in a dead zone . . ." I trailed off, running the calculations. Submerging the ship kept us safe from storms and waves and hydrogen sulfide, not to mention the toxic algae and swarms of jellyfish that clogged our filters. I would never have taken us under a dead zone if I'd thought this was a risk. Then again, mitigating risk was my job—I should have considered all eventualities. I cursed myself and felt for the currents, closing my eyes. The pull of the Northern Equatorial was weak, but if we could get out of the North Atlantic gyre, we'd find cleaner waters. That, at least, was in my power. I visualized the charts I'd been staring at just minutes before, orienting myself in the earth's magnetic field. Dead zones lay inside the gyres, contained by the currents—with a few exceptions. Luckily for us, this was one of them. If we could use the nearest current to get out of this zone, we'd stand a chance.

I opened my eyes. "I can get us out."

"Good." Miranda touched my elbow—a light brush, fleeting, but enough to calm me. "Let's see the breach."

Harper shooed a tech away from one of the control panels. The indicator for the portside aft bulkhead was lit up in red, and more red flashed from the storage level below us.

"I ran a systems check last week and nothing showed up." Harper's brows furrowed as she tapped commands into the ship's ancient computer. "Which could also mean we're having a problem with diagnostics. I'll run another check manually once we get this sorted out. The crew is in L7. They've got two hours of air, max, assuming they were able to seal the door in time."

"What kind of mess are we looking at?" Miranda asked me.

"We're going to be surfacing in the middle of a swarm." I sensed the pulsing pull of the jellyfish field above. "And we'll lose any jellies we can harvest for the squid tanks once the algae gets in."

"Lovely. Not only will we get stung, we'll get poisoned," said Harper.

"We'll deal with that later."

I ran calculations while Miranda and Harper discussed the likelihood of making repairs before a storm boiled out of the sky.

13

In a worst-case scenario, once the crew got to safety, we could let the level flood again if we needed to sub and repairs could not be made in time. I reached for the currents again. Nothing indicated a brewing hurricane, but that didn't mean a squall wouldn't whip up out of nowhere.

"...can't send a diver out in this," Miranda was saying. "Not at dusk."

"We don't have a choice." Harper turned away from the panel and I jerked my attention back to their conversation.

"It's feeding time."

Miranda, of course, would know all about the things that rose from the depths to feed on jellyfish at night, lured by the promise of the only reliable non-algaeic food source in the seas. I didn't like thinking about the days she'd spent drifting, buoyed by Portuguese man o' war, and left for dead by Gemini Station. The scars on Miranda's skin gleamed in the low light of the engineering hold.

"Then we'll send out spears to keep off the squid. I need that valve fixed, Captain."

"Parker, get a diving team together," Miranda said. A massive woman in hemp coveralls looked up from her work and nodded with a grim smile. Miranda didn't need to tell her to take spears. Parker's eyes flickered over to me, and I stiffened. There were still members of the crew who would never forget where I'd come from, and all the antibiotics and Polarian tech in the world weren't going to change their minds. I couldn't let it matter. Not everyone needed to like me, but I needed to keep them alive—even the people who might wish me dead.

The ship groaned. I felt the vibration through the thin soles of my shoes. Harper turned back to the panel, keyed in a command, slammed her fist down on it, and cursed.

"It's frozen."

"What does that mean?" I asked.

"Who the fuck knows? The wires shorted, total system failure, the—" Her mouth slackened, and her eyes narrowed as she followed her thoughts in silence. "Rose."

"What?"

"We need to get the ship back to Polaris."

"We're a week out at least," I said.

"Why?" asked Miranda.

"Because if this means what I think it means, we don't have the right parts."

"Make do without," said Miranda. "That's what we do out here."

Harper bit her lip. "But—"

"Print a new part. We've got the bioplastic."

"I need metal."

"Print a plastic part for now, then," said Miranda. "We won't make it to the Archipelago."

Harper nodded reluctantly. "We'll still need a replacement soon. I'll have someone check the hold for metal scrap once we get it drained."

"Good." Miranda surveyed the room. "Keep us stable."

"Yes, Captain."

I hung back with Harper as Miranda strode off.

"You okay?"

"You know how I said I wanted to be chief of engineering?" Harper wiped at the smeared algae on her cheek with a dirty sleeve. "I've changed my mind. I want to be a hydrofarmer."

"No, you don't."

"No, I don't." She grinned as adrenaline lit her eyes and the challenge ahead brought some of the life back into her face. Disaster was her drug of choice. "Shouldn't you be figuring out how to keep us alive?"

"That's your job," I said. "I just tell you all where to go."

"And when to go fuck ourselves. If we survive this, you owe me a drink."

"How do you figure?"

"Rose," Miranda said from across the room.

"Your captain calls."

Harper made a lewd gesture with her tongue and shoved me away. I trotted toward the hatch, shaking my head, reassured by Harper's ability to joke in the middle of a crisis.

15

Someone finally turned off the alarm as we climbed the stairs back to the bridge. My brain cleared as the claxon faded.

"We need a contingency plan," Miranda said, nodding to a passing cluster of sailors.

"Like what?"

"A place to stay surfaced."

"We could head for the nearest station."

"You know as well as I do what kind of welcome we'd get from the Archipelago," said Miranda.

"Polaris is close enough—"

"We're not going to Polaris."

"There's nowhere else, unless you want to take the ship into the coast, and that's suicide."

"Not the coast."

"Which leaves Polaris." I stopped on a landing, forcing traffic to swerve around me. Her eyes, blue-black in the hold, met mine.

"We could make for the islands."

"Miranda."

"It's what, a day or two closer?"

"Depending on the currents, yes, but we need decent material. There's no guarantee we'll find that on Paradise," I said, stumbling over the name of that island, "and then we'll have twice as far to sail. It isn't logical."

"We can't trust Comita."

"No, but I trust Archipelago supplies."

"I said no, Rose." She softened the command with another swift touch to my elbow. "Chart a course."

Back in the chart room, I pulled out the binder corresponding to my captain's order with fingers slick with sweat. Miranda returned to the bridge to help Orca keep the ship stable while I sat alone with my coordinates and the taste of dread metallic in my mouth. Miranda's decision risked crew and ship, and her refusal to listen didn't make sense. I was her *navigator*.

Maps blurred as I visualized currents and dead zones. We were a two-day journey from the Caribbean islands, which was a distance I was more than happy to maintain. We didn't belong on—or anywhere near—land. Especially not land marked by our recent past. I felt bodiless, floating, as I once again saw the pirate Ching Shih's bloodstained sword at Admiral Comita's feet, followed by Miranda's assurances that Ching had been taken care of—neutralized, killed.

I wanted to believe my captain. I wanted to forget about the prisoner we'd dropped off on Paradise's foreign shore, the slender body hooded and alone, and I wanted to forget, too, my own fear. I couldn't think Ching's name without needing to throw up.

Pirate queens and mutineers and admirals. Who the fuck was I in the middle of this?

The course was easy enough: follow the current, stay out of the swarms, and pray for fair weather. No doubt Miranda was currently barking orders to deploy the tie-downs which would keep our possessions from hurtling across holds and rooms, preparing the ship for troughs and waves and wind. In the hold, our trapped sailors would do their best to conserve their air. I'd learned the tricks myself in fleet preparatory. Deep meditation. Measured breaths. Counting, three breaths per minute, first flushing the lungs, then steadying. Panic killed underwater, but if I couldn't get us to safety, we might all die anyway.

I returned to the helm at a walk. The ship boiled around me. Children were shepherded into crèches—not so different from the nurseries of my home station—while their parents lashed down anything that could move. In the hydrofarms, technicians would be draining the pipes and deploying algaeic foam to shield the roots. Kitchens would secure utensils. The laundry would seal the water tanks. Everywhere, people prepared for a disaster I was somehow supposed to avert as second mate.

"Jelly," Orca said by way of greeting. The bones and shells in her braids clinked as she looked up.

"Where's Miranda?"

"Back in engineering."

Of course. The captain went where there was trouble, and it was not my place to wish her here with me when she was needed elsewhere.

I fed Orca the coordinates and the disturbances I'd calculated, and she adjusted our trajectory. Already I felt the list of the ship as the pumps purged water from the other ballast tanks. We'd be lucky if we even managed to surface.

A monster of a man entered the helm. My face split into a smile as Kraken sought me out, the tentacles tattooed on his bare chest and arms rippling as he moved. His shaved skull wore the mask of his namesake, and within it his brown eyes crinkled at the corners.

"Orca," he said in his deep voice as he pulled me into a one-armed embrace. "Tell Mere I'm diving."

"Tell her yourself."

"I can't disobey an order I don't hear."

"Why are you diving?" I asked him, fear contorting my heart into a misshapen lump of cortisol and dilated vessels.

"Parker's dive crew is down a man."

I craned my head back to see his face. He squeezed me and let go.

"Miranda will be pissed," said Orca.

"Then let her piss. You know as well as I do they'll be safer with me out there."

Sweat prickled my armpits as I thought about Kraken and the engineers swimming in the murky waters near the surface with the threat of jellyfish from above and squid from below. This was my fault. If I hadn't taken us on this route, then the valve might have broken in clean waters, and we could have sent divers out safely. Kraken shouldn't have to risk his life for my mistakes. Pulse pounding in my throat, I said, "I'll come too. I can at least keep a lookout."

"Like hell you will," said Orca and Kraken simultaneously. I shoved aside my relief.

"But what if—"

"—you get eaten? Yeah. Then we're stuck with the captain,

which is the only reason I haven't tossed you overboard," said Orca. "Besides. We need your freaky navigation shit here."

"I've given you the coordinates. You don't need me to—"

"You're staying," said Kraken. "You're more use to the ship here."

"Bring back some calamari," Orca told him as he headed for the door. To me, she said, "Don't be a fucking idiot. You're not a diver. You're a liability."

"You always know exactly what to say to make me feel better."

She showed me her teeth. I couldn't quite call it a smile.

The ship rose through the water as the ballast shifted, the compressed air generated by the algae tanks forcing brine back out into the ocean. We listed farther to port. The crew gritted their teeth and adjusted their stances as the first tendrils of the swarm came into view through the plex. Yellow and purple sacs followed as the lower ranks of the swarm rode the current. Their transparent bodies moved with lazy purpose, the edges rippling as they pulled in water, then expelled it, bells hung to ring into the deeps. I wondered if Miranda had retreated to engineering to escape this view.

I still found it beautiful. Sunlight lit the upper ranks of jellyfish with reds and liquid purples that shifted with the blues and greens of the sea. The tentacles caught the light and sent refractions down to the bells of the jellyfish below. For all that they had the potential to damage my ship, and for all that they had marked my captain with their indifferent malice, there was an elegance to their motion that entranced me.

"Hey." Orca jabbed me in the side with a finger and I snapped myself back to attention. "Any way we can scatter them?"

Something rumbled through the deck, shrill with the sound of shearing metal. The ship shuddered.

"The fuck—" Orca said.

I ran for the hold.

Harper screamed into the steam of the engine room as I shut the hatch behind me. Her voice sounded raw as her orders fought to drown out the horrible sound of something crumpling. I slipped

19

in a pool of condensation, righted myself, and grabbed her arm.

"Pressure tear," she said when she saw me. "We've got to get the crew out of there. The storage rooms are breaching."

I imagined water pouring into the hold, jellyfish drifting, hunted by the predators who followed them, and our sailors trapped there in their midst. "How many people do we have down there?"

"I sent Jeanine and a team to do some repair work in L7. They should have time to get out. Unless . . ." Harper's eyes widened in horror.

"Unless what?"

She bared her teeth as another shudder shook the hold, then sprinted toward the etched map of the ship hanging below the busted console. "The system's down, but . . ."

Again, she trailed off.

"Harp, where was the breach?"

Steam screamed in the pause before she spoke. "L7."

"They'd still have time to get to the hatch before it sealed. Right?"

"They have three minutes."

Less, now.

"Do these doors open from the inside?" On *North Star* each hatch, provided the airlock functioned, had an override code for crew in emergencies like this one.

"Tia," Harper shouted at a passing engineer. "Override on the hatch doors?"

Tia shook her head.

Irascible Jeanine, always handy with a wrench and a quip. I held my breath. On a good day I could hold it for more than two minutes. We'd know if they made it out of L7 when my lungs gave out. Harper took in my stilled chest and expression of concentration.

"Screw that. Come on." She pulled me toward the hatch to the stairs.

Our footsteps echoed in the comparative silence as we pounded down. The lower storage bays were usually empty of

20

personnel save for a few guards. Several cats streaked past. Five guards clustered around the airlock at the base of the staircase, staring at it with rigid expressions.

"Who are we waiting on?" Harper asked them as she skidded to a stop.

"Two of your crew, one medic—"

The medic in question tumbled into the hatch on the far side of the airlock with his arms full of supplies. A guard opened the hatch on our side and yanked him out. Brine soaked his clothes from the waist down. There was no sign of Jeanine.

"How fast is it coming in?"

"Fast." He panted to catch his breath. "Must be huge. Whoever's in there—"

A wall of water hit the airlock's window. Harper keened deep in her throat as it frothed over the far plex. I couldn't even summon a curse. Curses were inadequate against the ocean's fury.

"Get a dive team," said the medic.

"They're all deployed." I'd never heard Harper's voice so empty of life.

"If they got into a room in time and sealed it—" But the medic stopped. There was no way to seal the rooms effectively enough to make a difference. Not without a dive team on the way.

"How long will it take them to repair the valve?" I asked Harper.

"Too long."

"Then we find someone else. We've got other tanks."

The medic shook his head in resignation and answered before Harper could speak. "Not with the debris you'll find in there, and if it filled this fast, there'll be worse than debris. You need a team, not a solo diver, or you'll just have more bodies."

The froth darkened as the water level rose against the plex window.

Harper's fists clenched. "I'm chief, and I say we send someone. Jeanine wouldn't leave anyone in there."

"I'll go," said one of the guards. "I know the layout."

"You're not a diver," said the medic. I considered throttling him. Time slipped away with the air. Jeanine had been one of the first to welcome me aboard the *Man o' War*. Her cutting humor and shrewd observations were not always warm, but she cared about her ship and her crew and had risked her life for both. For her to die like this was unthinkable.

"We don't have time to argue this," said Harper. The emergency oxygen tank in its plex case mocked us. "Fuck it. I'll go."

She yanked open the case and began fumbling with the straps. I remembered a tug and the sensation of floating as the *Man o' War* rushed over me, and then the stars bright and hard in the ship's wake. The memory shone with brutal clarity. Fitting—it was refreshed regularly in my nightmares. Cold sweat slicked my skin.

Harper did not stand a chance in the maelstrom beyond the door. Her swimming had only ever been passable, and in the darkness without protection or light she'd be easy food for squid. I, on the other hand, had been the best swimmer in our fleet prep class and could navigate blind. My throat closed over the words I knew I had to say.

"Rose?"

My hand rested on hers, I realized. I tried to speak again. When I'd offered to dive with Kraken, I'd known they would refuse. This was different. Visions of hanging at the bottom of a rusty ladder with Annie looking down assaulted me. Black water. Black sky. The diving knife strapped to my thigh and the weight of the empty tank on my back.

North. South. East. West. There was only one choice I could live with. "Let me."

She tried to shrug me off, but I tightened my grip.

"Harp."

I could see her running the calculations in her head. We didn't have time. Jeanine didn't have time, and Harper knew it. The cold, brittle look that crossed her face told me everything. She knew what needed to be done, and she was commander enough to swallow her conflicts of interest.

"Move fast."

"I always do."

She secured the tank to my back and nodded at the guard nearest the airlock. He opened it. I stepped through and placed the mask over my nose and mouth.

My resolve wavered as I faced the second hatch. Beyond could be anything—metal sharp as light, hunting squid, jellyfish, and mangled material that could tangle and trap me. Someone else could go in my place. I did not need to risk my life. This wasn't really my fault. As navigator, I'd had no way to predict an equipment failure. Guilt was dumb. I was dumb. This whole damn—

The hatch opened.

Chapter Two

Water exploded. I braced myself behind the open door, waiting for it to fill the airlock before I faced the torrent. Seconds ticked by. The water level rose, and within it, as I'd feared, I saw a few luminous bodies. Their bells caught the light from the hatch window. My skin tensed in anticipation of pain. I felt for the pulse of their bodies in the brine, then slid out the door, wishing I had a suit and fins as I eased the hatch shut and cranked the handle. Biolight barely illuminated the water beyond. The hallway gaped like a broken mouth and jellyfish floated in its midst, mindless, drifting, their tentacles brushing the walls in search of prey. I swam as close to the ceiling as I could. Up here, only their bells touched me, not their tentacles, and I could see anything else that might mistake me for a meal.

The tear lay out of sight, and without seeing it I didn't know the scope or the size of the predators to expect. I knew, as did every child of the sea, that squid could squeeze through spaces impossible for vertebrates. They stalked the horror stories we told each other as children. *Don't swim in the pools at night*, we whispered. *They can reach out from the shower drains and break your ankles.* My mother had worked in the eel beds on Cassiopeia Station, and I used to worry she'd be eaten—or worse, that I would be as I helped her, swallowed by alien mouths.

These fears came back to me now as I kicked through the darkening water. At least this time I was fairly certain anything I encountered would be a manageable size, instead of the monster I'd battled with Orca and Kraken months ago. A jellyfish turned in front of me, and a glistening strand of stinging cells skimmed my arm. Pain seared. I bit down on my mouthpiece in lieu of cursing, and swam on, my body tingling with the stinging cells clinging to my skin.

Most of the storage rooms were sealed. One, however, had ruptured in the pressure change, and debris floated in a cloud ahead of me. Barrels bobbed amidst the jellyfish, labeled with numbers and letters that made sense only to the people in charge of inventory. I could not guess at their contents; I only knew each barrel blocked my view of the hallway ahead.

The current stabilized as I rounded a corner. I paused, holding on to a light tube, and felt the settling weight of the ocean. Nothing rushed. Nothing spurted. Everything hung, suspended, trapped in the body of my ship. Only the jellyfish moved. I felt their lazy motions in ripples and electric static, and as my eyes adjusted to the murky light, my fear evaporated. Clicks and groans were the only sounds. My breath came evenly. I treaded water with deliberate strokes. The cardinal directions sang in my blood, louder here than on the crowded bridge. Ahead, a dark shape jetted toward a luminescing bell and enveloped it in a snarl of tentacles. The squid was no bigger than a housecat. Not a threat. I pushed off the wall and swam past.

My position as head navigator did not require me to spend much time in the lower levels. I was familiar with engineering only because Harper worked there. Harper had found a following among her work crew once she'd revealed her enthusiasm for moonshine. I tried not to begrudge her the ease with which she'd settled in. Nobody had cut her loose from the ship to drown. Nobody had beaten her black and blue. Nobody called her fleet scum, for all that she was more Archipelago fleet than I was.

A barrel thudded into the back of my head as I misjudged a

stroke. This was not the place for self-reflection. Water distorted distance, and the debris field forced me to alter my trajectory as I swam down hallways and stairwells. One of the stairwells had an airlock that hadn't flooded, and seawater pummeled me to the floor in the ensuing tumult of displaced air and held me down until the pressure stabilized. The next level, however, was just as flooded as the one above, and so I continued on—albeit more bruised than I had been before.

As I rounded yet another corner in the increasing black, a squid made a dive for my hand. My fist closed instinctively. The beak scraped across the back of my knuckles, and I curled my body in on itself as I fumbled for my knife. It wasn't a large squid. Its body looked bluish, though it was hard to tell, and lights pulsed down its mantle as it retreated a few feet to survey me.

Fucker, I thought at it, hoping it was alone and not part of a pack. Luck like that, however, didn't come my way often, and so I inched backward until the wall met my spine.

The second squid appeared as I adjusted the air tank on my back. It hovered behind the first, appraising me with wide round eyes. I bared my teeth around my mask. This would not be how I died.

Lights pulsed down their sides. The shifting colors suggested language, nuance, an intelligence determined to find its way into the soft meat of my body. I edged along the wall with my knife hand ready.

The third squid hit me from below. I felt tentacles close around my leg as the beak tested the resiliency of my pants, rearranging my hamstring muscle in the process. My knife sank into its head, and the skin parted with a rubbery ease I did not have time to contemplate as the other members of its pack made their moves. One went for my knife arm.

The other went for my face.

I felt the give of my mask as its powerful body ripped the tubing from my mouth. Spluttering, I bit into the tentacle and screamed in a stream of bubbles as its beak raked down my cheek, sending my blood into the water along with a cloud of ink. The squid on my leg released me—hopefully to die—and I scrabbled at the squid around my head and neck with my other hand. Slippery flesh slid against my fingers. My lungs ached. I needed air, and the squid on my knife arm was twisting my bicep against my humerus with vicious intent. The tentacle in my mouth writhed as it tried to get away. I bit down harder. If I let go, I would try to breathe, and water would flood my lungs as it had flooded my ship.

The squid doing its best to remove my bicep released me without warning. In relief I dropped my knife, then cursed—freeing the other squid from my teeth—and lunged after it. I kicked toward the bottom of the hall with my lungs crackling and sparks dotting the edges of my vision before I realized my head, too, was free, and jammed the breathing apparatus back between my teeth. That first breath of air blinded me. Oxygen raced through my veins as I forgot about my attackers. When I recalled my predicament several breaths later, closing my hands around the hilt of my knife, I found myself in a fog of ink.

Neptune, no.

I swam back to the ceiling with slow kicks, my leg and arm aching and my face leaking red around my vision, and passed over the cloud and down the hall with a tight rein on my panic. Only one thing would have distracted the squid from wounded prey, and I had no desire to meet any more predators.

Sure enough, when I looked over my shoulder, my enemies were engaged in a battle for their own lives as an even larger squid shredded the one I'd wounded. Humboldt hybrids—vicious and ruthless in their pursuit of their own kind. This, I reminded myself, was why divers went out in groups with spears instead of six-inch knives. Praying my blood didn't draw any more unwanted attention, I pushed on through the swarm.

The door to the room where the crew were trapped opened at my touch. Bioluminescent algae swirled in the water, which meant the light tubes must have shattered, and I paused in the doorway to feel for life. Blue light arced from each steadying sweep of my hands and feet and clung to the fine hairs on my arms.

Something moved in the corner. I jerked my knife out before

me, bracing myself for another attack, and then kicked toward it as I recognized the shape of a human leg in the luminous clouds.

My eyes struggled to parse what the shifting light revealed. The shapes did not add up. Eventually, however, I realized there were two people huddled beneath an overturned storage crate. The crate would retain the air inside so long as they held it in place, though not enough to last them for long. It had to be mostly carbon dioxide by this point.

Rescue protocol stated you always brought along a spare tank. Otherwise, a drowning crewman might kill you both in their panic. I didn't have an extra tank. All I could do was take a deep breath, hold out my hand to get their attention, and duck into their shelter.

Jeanine's grinning skull tattoos shimmered in the reflected light as her eyes found mine. I passed her the rebreather. She fastened it over her face and took several long breaths before passing it back to me. I gestured at her companion to indicate he should take it first, and then my heart constricted. I knew him: a boy no more than sixteen, training up to be an engineer. Jeanine supported him, but no breath stirred his chest. Numbness spread from my stomach to my limbs. A child. He was a *child*.

She pushed the rebreather into my mouth. I gulped air.

"He got stung. Allergic reaction." Jeanine's tone was matter of fact, but I'd seen her in the dining hall with the boy—Dev was his name—joking and tousling his hair. I'd come too late. Had she held him, here beneath this crate, while he asphyxiated as venom overrode his system?

"What happened to your face, Rose?"

"Squid."

Jeanine nodded. She didn't ask what had happened to the ship. All that could wait. As for Dev, I sized up his frame. He was taller than me, and heavier. Dragging him back through the debris field for his family would be difficult, but I couldn't leave him here to be eaten.

"If we carry him—"

"Don't be a bleeding idiot." Jeanine sucked air to replace what she'd expelled from her lungs in her outburst. Without another word, she dove. Shock still had my limbs in its sluggish grip. She'd returned by the time I managed to convince them to move, towing the lid of the crate behind her. "We'll seal him into the crate."

Efficient. Cold. How many people had she seen die over the years, that she could react like this?

"Jeanine—"

The look she sent my way silenced me. Bioluminescence painted the scene as Jeanine tipped the crate. Bubbles erupted, briefly crowning Dev's head of black curls before vanishing into the gloom. The crate sank to the floor. Jeanine folded his body into the empty box with a tenderness that raked across my ribs more fiercely than any squid, then fastened the lid. I offered her air. It was all I could do.

A scan of the room for threats revealed the crew had been doing repair work on a maintenance panel. A length of pipe connected by a single screw floated nearby. Jeanine worked the screw free with the tip of my knife. Packages had settled back to the floor, save for a few with air bubbles trapped inside. I pried the lid off a smaller crate. Sodden bags of rice flickered in the light. The lid was small enough for one of us to carry without slowing us down, and would act as a shield between our bodies and the waiting swarms. I couldn't bring myself to look at the crate where Dev lay tucked in on himself as if asleep.

Armed with her pipe and with my knife back in my waistband, makeshift shield in hand, we traded the rebreather back and forth. The door to the hall yawned darkly. I motioned for her to stay close as we kicked off and began our swim.

Nothing remained of the squids that had tried to make a meal of me. Even the ink had dissipated, and while I saw shapes flitting in the distance, nothing attacked. I held the lid between my body and the trailing jellyfish. Jeanine swam directly above me. The magnetic field fizzled against my blood as I oriented myself to the darkness of the hall. It wasn't a far swim under normal circumstances, though admittedly there were no normal circumstances in which an entire bay flooded enough for a swim, but the hazards of floating scrap and supplies and boneless predators changed the terrain. Water displaced by Jeanine's hands rippled over the back of my neck. Glowing jellyfish drifted, menacing and aimless, and their bells hit the lid with soft thumps.

The strike came from behind. Jeanine twisted and her pole scraped against my leg as she struggled. I fought to turn as a line of stinging cells brushed my bare feet. Pain seared. I had the rebreather, and I inhaled sharply. The tank swung on my back and threw me off balance. By the time I righted myself, dropping the shield in the process, a squid the size of Kraken had Jeanine wrapped in its tentacles.

Orca, floundering in the water beneath the behemoth. Finn, lying senseless on the floor while Kraken launched himself at the squid. Diving beneath that massive body. Closing my hand over Orca's wrist.

The memory assaulted me. Ink spiraled in black swirls as Jeanine tried to drive the pole into the squid's mantle, but it had its tentacles wrapped around her torso. I could barely see her in the darkness. My knife came to my hand as I slashed at the muscular appendages, but without a clear view of Jeanine, I worried I might stab her, too.

She needed air. I grabbed hold of a limb and pulled myself closer, driving my knife into the rubbery flesh. A sucker fastened to my left forearm. The pressure burned against my skin. My knife dug into the tentacle as I sawed back and forth. Another tentacle slapped me across the face and sent me tumbling through the water. Jellyfish brushed me with pulsing strands, leaving trails of electric agony.

The floor met my feet. I pushed off again, desperate to get to Jeanine. She couldn't have much oxygen left. This time, I collided with the body of the squid. It writhed as I drove the blade into the mantle as deep as it would go. The heart lay toward the mantle's posterior, and its brain sat between its eyes. That, however, was too near Jeanine. My arm twitched as jellyfish venom fired through my muscles. I clenched my teeth on the rebreather and drove my blade deeper still.

The monster shuddered as blood poured out of the wound.

With a tangle of arms, it released Jeanine and jetted away, leaving me to catch her.

Not all the blood in the water belonged to the squid. I pressed the rebreather into Jeanine's slack mouth. She did not respond. I shook her. Performing CPR beneath the water was impossible, but I prayed to Neptune anyway. Her head, with its inked sharks, lolled against my shoulder.

I scanned her body for signs of damage and choked on a cry. Her chest was a ruin of muscle and exposed bone. The squid's beak had sliced her from sternum to belly button, and while the worst of the damage had been inflicted on her ribs, the iron in the water from her spilled blood soured my mouth. I had to get her back to the airlock.

Abandoning hope of immediate resuscitation cost me several seconds. At last, spurred on by another sting, I took back the rebreather and lifted Jeanine. Her weight bore me to the floor, and, damning the jellyfish, I swam the long hallway back to safety, each kick another second of oxygen deprivation for my burden.

Light from the airlock broke through the murk as we rounded the last corner. I pounded on the hatch while Jeanine's unconscious body slumped beside me, partially suspended in the water. It opened. The sound of compressed air fell on my ears like a lullaby.

The airlock took five minutes to drain. I knew this, and knew it could not be hastened, and yet those five minutes meant the difference between life and death. I brought Jeanine to the expanding surface and did what I could. Compressions on her ragged chest stained my hands red with her blood, and her lips were cold as I blew air into her lungs. I repeated the motions until hands pulled me up and I found myself on the wet floor, surrounded by dying jellyfish and the motionless body of my friend.

The medic took over. He shouted something, and footsteps echoed. Harper hauled me out of the airlock and away from the jellyfish, where I collapsed while she removed the tank from my back. My limbs twitched with venom. A familiar voice shouted in the distance as Harper looked me over, noting the damage to my face and the welts on my exposed skin, and then Miranda knelt before me.

"Jeanine," I said. My throat burned. Somewhere along the way I had swallowed salt water.

Miranda pulled me into her lap and held me close with a strength both tender and vicious.

"Never do that again," she whispered into my hair. "Never fucking do that again."

"I had to save her—"

"I would let this whole ship drown before I lost you."

Not the whole ship, I thought as she clutched me tightly to her. *Just Jeanine*. Her body remained still and lifeless on the floor beside me, and my hands were sticky with her blood.

My stings were treated in the infirmary by a vast, muscular, tattooed woman with gentle hands. Jeanine's body lay on a table nearby. Finn, her partner and the ship's communications specialist, sat beside her. He did not weep. He clutched her fingers in his, and his lips moved as he spoke inaudibly into the private bubble of his grief. I lay silent, feeling the venom leech out of my skin beneath the compresses, and wished myself dead.

"You did everything you could," Harper said hours later, around a mouthful of rum. I'd wanted to crawl back to my quarters and burrow deep into the mattress and my despair, but Miranda was needed on deck, and she'd refused to let me mourn alone. Instead, we sat at a bar table, drinking to Jeanine's memory.

Harper slumped with her head on Orca's shoulder. Kraken sat on Orca's other side, tossing his lucky dice into the air between sips of the bitter drink the bartender, Nasrin, kept replenishing for him.

I sat beside my captain and wondered if Dev's parents, or Jeanine's, were on ship. I'd never thought to ask. Each time I blinked, I saw her chest, splayed open to reveal cartilage and bone, and I longed to scrub the feel of raw tissue from my hands. I'd come so close to saving her.

"You got the valve replaced," Miranda said. I tried to tune into the conversation.

"Replaced is a stretch. More like patched. It won't hold up under pressure, so we can't sub very deep. Pray for calm weather."

"It won't need to hold for long. I sent out an SOS. A friend of ours is in range."

I hauled myself out of my grief-induced stupor. There was only one universal rule on the ocean: never ignore an SOS. It didn't matter the captain or who they served. Nobody left another ship to drown. Ships that broke this rule knew they would be blacklisted, and, if they ever needed help, might be turned down. Even Archipelago ships obeyed the unwritten mandate, unless, of course, they were in the middle of a war.

The news of help on the way came as a distant relief. I couldn't feel much around the inconceivable ache of our loss, but I was aware enough to realize this also meant we wouldn't need to head for Paradise island. More relief eddied at the edges of my consciousness, reaching me only in faint ripples.

"Who's the friend?" asked Harper.

"Seraphina."

At Miranda's words, Orca jerked her head up. "Seraphina? *The* Seraphina?"

"Who's Seraphina?" Harper turned her interrogation onto Orca.

"You wouldn't have heard of her, but out here, she's like . . ." Orca trailed off, clearly unsure what kind of comparison to draw to best illustrate her point.

"She's a fucking gem," said Kraken.

"Wait, is that the woman you were telling me about?" I asked Miranda. "The cultural historian?"

"Cultural historian?" Orca looked from me to Miranda, and then burst into strained laughter. "More like pleasure boat captain."

"Seraphina's business is information *and* pleasure, and yes, Orca, she is also a cultural historian." Miranda sounded almost prim in her correction. I would have found it endearing if I didn't still smell like Jeanine's blood.

Miranda's collection of books had fascinated me when I first came aboard her ship. I'd recently inquired about their origins, and Miranda had launched into a rhapsodic account of a captain named Seraphina who had made it her business to collect and document cultures past, present, and evolving. She hadn't mentioned "pleasure."

"Like a sex boat?" Harper put my question into words.

Orca's grin widened until it crossed the line from "amused" to "malevolent." "Haven't you heard about what happens when two pirate crews get together?"

Everything I'd ever heard about pirate debauchery flooded my synapses. Orgies fueled by the drugs grown from fungi in their bilges and bizarre strains of weed and algae; sporting events involving the mutilation of the losers, and sometimes the winners—in short, every vice known to humankind throughout all its ages, crammed into leaky holds full of unwashed criminals.

"She also will have spare parts." Miranda rested her hand on the small of my back. Her touch was lighter than her voice, which sounded as heavy as the ship. "And after . . . this . . . the crew could use a break. Boost morale."

"How soon can she get here?" I asked, thinking of sudden squalls.

"Six hours. Let the crew know, will you?" Miranda waited for Orca to nod before turning to me. "You should rest before she arrives."

"I'll escort her back to her quarters," said Harper, extricating herself from Orca's grip.

Miranda squeezed my hip in a silent apology that she could not escort me herself.

Harper led me, not back to my quarters, but to the room she shared with Orca. It had changed since I'd last slept there. The whale skull still hung on the wall, but instead of a sling hammock, she had a hammock bed made from hemp stretched across a metal platform. No doubt Harper had designed or commissioned it herself. The small chest that held Orca's things had been replaced by shelves built from scrap—more of Harper's handiwork—and a carpet covered the floor, woven from scrap cloth and fringed with brightly colored tassels. She even had a mirror.

"What are we doing?" I wanted to lie down in the bed I shared with Miranda and weep.

"Miranda doesn't always know what's best for you. We all need a rest, seas save us, but there's something I need you to do, first. For us. For Jeanine."

Harper pulled a few objects off the shelves, and I registered a cake of soap, a bowl of water, and a straight razor. I glanced between it and her head and backed away.

"Don't be such a jelly."

"I'm not cutting your hair. Ask Kraken. He—"

"I don't want Kraken to do it. I want you to. Please?"

"I don't know how to cut hair. And yours is so pretty."

Harper shook her head, letting her thick curls swing forward. "It will still be pretty. I just want you to shave the sides but leave the length on top. Like yours, but longer. I know you can draw a straight line."

"For *coordinates*. Not with a razor. Why are you doing this?"

"Because it will be hard to get a skull tat otherwise."

I took in her determined, red-rimmed eyes, and understood. Harper had worked beside Jeanine every day for the past few months. Jeanine's acceptance of both me and Harper had been instrumental in soothing the rest of the crew's suspicions. Beyond that, she was a friend. If Harper needed to do this to begin reconciling her grief, I'd help her.

"I'll do my best."

"You'll do fine. Here." Using her fingers and a comb, she separated the hair she wanted to keep and pinned it out of the way, leaving a tangle of curls behind. They felt heavy and soft in my hands. Each ringlet was thick enough to wrap around two of my fingers with ease, and I didn't want to see them lying on the floor, waiting to be swept into the compost bin.

"Are you sure?"

"It grows back. You might want to chop these bits off before you start in with the razor, and try not to cut me open."

"I still think Kraken—"

"You're my best friend." The edge in her voice carried echoing layers of meaning. I pulled my knife out from my belt and rubbed a strand of her hair between my fingers, wishing I could cut out the cancerous growth of loss instead.

My knife was sharp. By the end of one side of her head, however, I had to saw at the strands. "I had no idea hair could take the edge off a knife."

Harper grunted in reply. I didn't comment on the tears leaving glittering blue trails of light down her cheeks. Tufts stuck out of the side of her temples and past her ears. I set my knife down and dipped a cloth in soapy water to lather up her scalp. The number of times I'd shaved anything could be counted on one hand, but I understood the principle. Don't slice skin. Go slow. Try not to leave a bloody mess. The razor glinted in the low light of her quarters. When I set it to her scalp, she took a deep breath, and I tried not to flinch with her as the razor slid over her skin. Each small scrape freed more and more of her scalp. I wiped the shorn stubble on the cloth and chewed on my cheek as I concentrated. What tattoo design would she choose? Sharks, like Jeanine?

The sudden image of Jeanine's still face superimposed itself over Harper's.

"Careful," Harper said.

"Sorry." I stared at the bead of blood rising from her skin, pink against the foam of the soap. My pulse skittered. The razor felt heavy in my hand, more weapon than tool, and I wanted to fling it from me.

"Not a big deal, unless you leave me looking like this."

It's just a razor.

"Rose?"

The metallic taste of my own blood filled my mouth. I released my cheek, tonguing a small flap of severed skin, and tried to ground myself. Harper's fingers removed the blade from mine and set it on the shelf. Her half-shaved head dripped soap onto her shoulder, but her hands were on my arms and she was staring into my face with love and concern.

It was the worst possible thing she could have done.

Tears blinded me. I let her guide me to her bed, and I leaned into her shoulder as I sobbed again for Jeanine and all the others.

"I told you it will grow back," Harper said, her voice gentle and teasing. "I'll put some in a locket for you if you want."

I choked on a small laugh as the more egregious sobs subsided. "After John—"

She stiffened as I named the Polarian SHARK she'd killed to save me. "What about him?"

"How did you . . . how did you keep going?"

"By reminding myself he didn't give me a choice."

"And that's enough?"

"Of course not."

Would it be easier if I had someone to blame? Faulty, aging equipment had taken Jeanine's life, but I could have saved her from the squid if I'd only been faster. Smarter. Better.

"What if instead of making things better, we just make everything even worse?" I asked. I wasn't sure what, exactly, I meant. Our decision to leave Polaris? Defiance of Comita? Defeating Ching?

"Like this half-assed haircut?"

"Yeah."

She removed her arm from my shoulders and shifted to sit cross-legged on her bed. "I feel like I've done that my whole life."

"You?"

Her eyes looked everywhere but at me. "I'm the admiral's daughter. She wanted me to be perfect."

"You're brilliant—"

"She wanted another commander, not an engineer. I never cared how people worked, though. Just ships. I can fix ships. I can't fix people. And each time I tried to stick it to her, I got other people in trouble. Look at what happened to you."

"I'm not your fault. You saved me."

"Fair. But maybe she wouldn't have paid you as much attention, no matter how good you are, if you hadn't been my best friend. She might have sent someone else."

"Then I wouldn't have ended up with Miranda."

Exactly, said Harper's face, but she didn't say it. Instead, she said, "And John. He was an ass, but if he hadn't been sent to guard me, he'd probably still be alive."

"John—"

"And I'm the one who sent Jeanine and Dev down to the storage bay." Her voice broke into a sob.

"Stop." Listening to Harper beat herself up over things outside her control was too painful. It wasn't the same as when I did it, and she deserved better. She deserved to be happy. "You were just doing your job. So was Jeanine."

"Then so were you. And not even—it wasn't your job to rescue her, but you went in there anyway. You gave her a chance. We both know I wouldn't have made it even half that far if I'd dived." The self-loathing was back in her voice.

I took her face in my hands and gave her my best glare. "Since coming onto this ship, you've prevented how many major breaches?"

"I don't know."

"Yes, you do."

"At least six."

"Then that is six times you've saved us. And you saved us when you joined the crew. You know that, right? We're protected from the Archipelago because you're on this ship. Nobody fucks with Comita's daughter."

"Just Comita."

"Well, yeah."

"And you saved the entire Archipelago," she said, blinking tears out of her large brown eyes.

"That was dumb luck."

"You forget I sailed the channel with you. We could have died a thousand times without your navigation."

"I just wish . . ." I couldn't finish the sentence. *I just wish I could have saved Jeanine.* "We were so close. The squid—"

Harper wrapped her arms around me. I rested my head against her soapy skull, and we sobbed until snot and drool and salt half-drowned us.

"Gross." Harper wiped at her face with her sleeves. I did the same, sniffling. Hair-flecked soap coated my cheek.

"I don't know how to live with this," I admitted. "I was so young when my dad left, and we never really found out if he was even dead. I haven't lost anyone since. Not really. Not like this. Even the war—"

"I know." She took my hand and pulled me off the bed. "It's fucked up. But I do know I'm not walking around with my head half-shaved."

My grip on the blade was more confident as we returned to the mirror. When I finished, Harper had only two small cuts, and the sides of her head gleamed the same smooth brown as the rest of her skin. She braided the top in a loose fishtail that left the majority of her hair spilling down her back, and I couldn't help grinning despite my puffy face.

"I look fierce as fuck," she said.

"Hell yeah, you do. Orca is going to lose her shit when she sees you."

"Probably."

Miranda found me in Harper's quarters half an hour later. I raised my head from Harper's pillow at the pounding knock on the door.

"Rose?"

The door opened, and Orca and Miranda strode inside. Miranda's face was a mask of tension. It eased as she took in my presence.

"I didn't know where you were."

"I was here," I said, too groggy to make sense.

"Clearly." She held out her hand. I rose from Harper's bunk and stumbled toward her, dimly aware of Orca's gasp as she took in Harper's haircut.

"Sorry." I leaned into Miranda as we walked the short distance between rooms. "Harper needed me."

"You needed sleep."

"I needed her, too." I frowned at Miranda, the expression

39

sending a dull ache through my head. All my facial muscles were sore from sobbing.

She let out a short, frustrated exhale. "No, I'm sorry. You just scared me so much today."

"I know."

The door to our quarters opened and shut. Seamus gave a plaintive meow and immediately attempted to wind his orange way between our legs.

"If you—" she broke off. I heard the unspoken words.

"I didn't."

"I can't lose you. Do you understand that?" Desperation roughened her voice. "I just can't. I can't, Rose."

"Mere—"

"When they told me you'd gone in—"

"I was the best swimmer there. I didn't have a choice."

"You did. Don't be noble. Don't be a hero." She searched my face, holding me at arm's length. I saw the panic in her dilated pupils.

"Miranda, I had to try. You would have done the same thing."

"That's different."

"It's not."

"I'm the goddamn captain. Of course it's different."

I wrenched away from her, suddenly furious. "I do not need a lecture right now. Two people died today, and neither of them was me."

She looked, for a moment, like she wanted to argue further, but then her face softened, and her pupils relaxed their choke hold on her irises. A shuddering breath tore through her.

"Dev was just a kid."

I lay down on the bed and patted the mattress, encouraging her to sit. She remained standing.

"And Jeanine—*fuck*. I love that bitch." She took a long pull from her hip flask.

I watched the reality of the day's losses roll over her as she paced, and realized she'd been holding this moment at bay by fixating on me. Her fist collided with the wall, tearing through the canvas of her Portuguese man o' war painting. My muscles twitched as they tried to rouse my body into action, but the lassitude of grief and spent adrenaline had finally caught up with me.

"Everything is always breaking, and it doesn't need to be that way. We don't have to fucking live like this." Her shout echoed off the walls. "We shouldn't have to rely on rusted-out parts. We shouldn't have to spend half our lives wondering if we're going to die from tetanus—*tetanus*—because the Archipelago can't bear the thought of losing their monopoly on vaccine tech."

"Parts break on fleet ships, too, Mere."

"Not like this. You didn't see the breach. I just inspected it. The valve was so rusted the supports around it gave, too. That whole section of hull crumpled. Harper's patch is brilliant, but on a fleet ship we'd have spares. My old ship—"

She did not speak of her Archipelago ship. Ever. The only thing I knew about it was its name, and I'd learned that from Kraken: the *Inevitability*. An unfortunate choice, all things considered, if an accurate one. She was always going to mutiny. Even if her brother hadn't been killed in a raid, something else would have caused this infection, so long as things remained the way they were.

Inevitable. Inevitable, too, that one of this crew would die in an accident. Inevitable I'd eventually lose someone I cared for. And inevitable that I'd end up here, with her, grateful she had words for the violence in my own chest—a chest that felt as raw and as torn and bloody as Jeanine's.

"Fuck," she shouted, and then kept shouting until the words subsided into sobs and she sat on her haunches on the floor, rocking on her heels with her head on her knees and her hands tugging at her hair. I slithered off the bed and curled around her. She moaned, a wounded animal, and crumpled like her hull into my arms.

In my dreams, I walked the decks of an empty ship, looking for Miranda. The biolights burned bright blue, bluer than the sky, bluer than her eyes and almost violent in their intensity. Shadows flickered in that unearthly light. I had to find Miranda before it was too late. The certainty of my dread propelled me forward down twisting halls. No real ship would have been designed this way, but dream logic did not answer to architects. A door opened to my right. I reached for my knife; it remained stuck in its sheath as if glued.

Ching Shih stepped into my line of sight, holding Jeanine's disembodied head. Blood dripped from her severed neck and pooled at the former pirate queen's feet. A jellyfish swam in the gathering pool in denial of physics, its bell the dark rust-red of organ meat. Ching's smooth black hair hung around her shoulders. She smiled at me, the expression conspiratorial, almost friendly, save for the glint in her eyes.

"I made Miranda. Whatever little plot you think you can hatch, remember that. Your people broke her and threw away the pieces, and I put them back together. She owes who she is now to me."

Old words. Jeanine raised an eyebrow. Ching carried her by her hair, and the sharks tattooed on her skull swam in lazy circles around her scalp.

"She's not yours anymore," I said.

"Don't be naïve. We don't ever really let anyone go. You'll see. In the meantime, you forgot something." She tossed Jeanine's head. It landed with a wet thunk at my feet. Jeanine glared up at me in disapproval as she wobbled on her cheek.

"Next time, catch me," said her head.

"You couldn't save Jeanine, and you can't save Miranda. Go home, fleet scum."

Another voice spoke, one that didn't belong in my dream. I fought the cloying grip of sleep as I'd fought against the water in the hold, dragging Jeanine behind me. My last, half-lucid thought before waking was I'd always be carrying her like this, her weight buoyed by the ocean, her blood in my mouth.

Miranda shook me awake. I burrowed into her shoulder and gasped as sobs wracked my body. She stroked my back, her hands smoothing the fear away down my spine. The dread and the loss remained.

I should have known better than to hope the recurring nightmare would spare me just because I was in mourning. Jeanine's inclusion in the familiar plot twisted the knife. Miranda didn't ask what the nightmare had been about. She probably didn't need to. My vocal cords ached as if I'd been shouting in my sleep on top of crying.

Ching's dead. I repeated this, willing it to be true, and wishing I had the courage to ask Miranda for verification.

"It's time to wake up anyway. Seraphina's here."

The sailor who met us in the landing bay was nondescript in every way possible. Short, dense, dark hair. Nori-brown eyes. Stocky build. Practical clothing. Only one earring, which was little more than a glint in an earlobe. I took them for middle-aged at the earliest, and nothing about their bearing screamed "Welcome to my decadent orgy ship."

"Sera," said Miranda.

Seraphina—for that was who this must be, I realized half a second later—enveloped Miranda in a hug that lasted several seconds and made me think, irrationally, of my mother. Miranda relaxed in her embrace, and the relaxation lingered even after she withdrew, though purple circles shadowed her eyes, as they did all of ours.

"There's my favorite monster," Seraphina said to Kraken. He crushed her to his bare chest and kissed the top of her head. I blinked at the blatant display of affection, fighting the bleariness of too little sleep.

Then she turned to me.

"My navigator, Rose," said Miranda. "And Harper, my chief engineer."

"Rose." Seraphina took my hand and clasped it firmly. Her brown eyes crinkled with what appeared to be genuine pleasure to greet me. I touched the raw patch of skin on my cheek with my tongue and made myself meet her gaze. She didn't comment on my eye color, which was a nice change, and instead squeezed my hand, released it, and smiled. "Welcome aboard the *Trench*."

"That's what she named her ship? The *Trench*?" Harper asked in a low voice. Orca had stayed back with the ship as acting captain, since she was the first mate. She and the rest of the crew would have a chance to mingle with Seraphina's people once Miranda and Harper took care of business.

"There's a story she had it dragged up from a fault line, but I don't believe it," said Kraken as we followed Seraphina into the hatch of her ship. Harper hovered at my elbow. I leaned into her for creature comfort.

"You know the drill," Seraphina said to Miranda.

Miranda handed over the manifest. "No infection."

Seraphina skimmed the log. "Checks out. So, what the hell happened?"

"We blew a valve."

"Damage looks worse than that."

"And compromised hull integrity," said Miranda.

"You're lucky you're still floating. Anyone injured?"

"Two dead. A few more with minor injuries."

Seraphina touched Miranda's cheek with the backs of her knuckles and gave her a look of such profound empathy that tears sprang to my eyes. "I can send someone to do the service."

"Thank you."

"Come have a drink. All of you."

Beyond the hatch lay a hallway lit with bioluminescence in varying shades of blue and green and yellow. The effect was as calming as Seraphina's smile, but even so, I wasn't prepared for what lay on the far side of the door.

Black ocean surrounded us outside, visible through a vast plex dome. Inside, however, biolights hung around a massive garden. The entirety of several upper decks had been devoted to it, and pools lay interspersed with reeds and flowers and trees. Small glowing fish darted through the roots of the trees nearest me, and people basked in the water, some clothed, others not. The air smelled fragrant and clean, and—

"What is that?" I asked, inhaling deeply.

"Food," said Seraphina. "Are you hungry?"

My mouth watered. I couldn't place half of what I was smelling. Spices and oils and herbs drifted with the smell of flowers. My stomach had been churning with nausea for hours, but at this influx of aromas, I became aware I hadn't eaten in almost a day and that, against the odds, I *was* hungry.

"We would never turn down your hospitality," said Miranda.

Seraphina led us to an alcove hung with vining plants. A low table had already been laid, and, following the example of Miranda, Kraken, and Seraphina, I sat on the ground. I recognized the rice pots, but anything could lie beneath the other lids. Harper's hand found mine beneath the table and squeezed.

Seraphina served us the rice. Then, she uncovered the first dish. The squid had been marinated in spices I couldn't name by scent, and steam rose from the tender flesh as she forked a serving over to me. Next came a bowl of greens, sautéed in something savory, and after that, plump balls of a substance that might have been dough, but tasted sweet and unlike any rice flour I knew. I lost track of the other dishes. Miranda, Kraken, and Seraphina spoke of the ocean and mutual contacts while Harper and I filled our bellies. I still couldn't name most of the seasonings. One or two seemed vaguely familiar, as if I might have eaten them in watered-down form. I recalled the small kitchen in Miranda's quarters with a new suspicion.

"Did Kraken learn to cook from you?" I asked when I could cram no more down my gullet. I couldn't remember the last time I'd been allowed to eat more than my fill.

"I may have given him a few lessons."

"Thank you," I said, meaning it.

Seraphina settled back and uncorked a bottle of a pale green liquid. "May I serve your crew?"

"A small glass. I need them functional."

"What is it?" Harper asked. Her eyes gleamed with the curiosity of someone well-versed in potent brews. I banished the memory of Jonah Juice before it could lay claim to my palate.

"A blend of my own. It takes the edge off the unbearable."

The edge. I thought of Jeanine and blood-red seas, and drank. Miranda also had a glass, though hers, I noted, was considerably larger.

"Oh," said Harper, appreciation oozing from the syllable.

It didn't hit me like rum. Instead, a slow coolness crept through me, easing the grief and anxiety from my limbs. My head didn't feel fuzzy. If anything, it felt clearer, as if my grief and exhaustion had blinded me to the brightness of the world.

"Enjoy yourselves," Seraphina said, and nodded at Miranda. "Come find me later."

"What is this place, really?" I asked when she was out of earshot.

"Everyone needs a place to feel free. Seraphina provides it, and we, in turn, provide her. Come on." She stood and held out a hand. I took it, holding the other to my full stomach. A trailing vine brushed my cheek. I closed my eyes at the caress.

"What does she have in her nutrient bath? These greens would make the hydrobotanists on Polaris shit themselves," said Harper.

"She might tell you if you ask. Kraken, can you and Harper see to the parts before I turn you loose?"

"Course."

"What are we doing?" I asked her.

"Taking care of you."

Harper's newly shaved head drifted out of sight, dwarfed by Kraken. I allowed Miranda to lead me through the gardens. Unfamiliar plants grew all around. Most were rooted in carefully concealed hydroponics, but a few sprang from soil. I stroked a waxy seed pod dangling from one such plant. A sweet, spicy aroma clung to my fingers as I pulled away.

Miranda halted by an empty pool. Tall canes of bamboo sheltered it from view.

"Soaking pools?"

"You need it," she said, then untucked her shirt and began

to strip.

I followed suit. The last time I'd had a proper soak had been on Polaris station, back when I still wore an Archipelagean Fleet navigator's uniform. The sudden lump in my throat surprised me. I didn't miss my old life. But the pools reminded me of my childhood on Cassiopeia Station, where I'd spend hours floating on my back, feeling the ocean, convinced it was speaking just for me. The weightlessness had felt like an embrace. I'd gone to the pools for comfort during the worst of the bullying that had defined my time in Fleet Preparatory. Miranda's scars glowed in the half-light like shooting stars. How had she known this was what I needed?

Water closed over her body as she slid beneath the surface. I remained dry a moment longer, possessed by the impulse to look skyward. Several stories above me arced a clear plex roof. Wild bioluminescence pulsed beyond, and beyond that, somewhere far from my sight, real stars. I felt the north star's pull and oriented myself toward it unconsciously.

"Come in."

I couldn't decide if the pool was warm or cool, or if it was whatever Seraphina had given me to drink that made it impossible to tell. My toes, then my ankles, then my calves, breached the water's surface until I was submerged up to my chin. Water took my weight. The release of pressure drew a shallow sob from my throat.

Hands drew me closer. Water swirled through my hair and beneath my breasts, cool and soothing, and Miranda's body was warm against my back. She held me while we watched the bamboo stir in an artificial breeze. I wondered what the pools on Gemini were like, and if this reminded her of home, too.

A woman had died beneath my hands. I replayed Jeanine's last moments again. The drink slid between me and the images like a wall of clear plex. I could still see them, but the impact was somehow lessened. My fingers didn't itch with the remembered smoothness of exposed bone. I couldn't smell the sharp tang of blood. I couldn't hear my frantic breathing.

Miranda spoke in my ear. "Nobody tells you that part about command. How everything is your fault. Navigator, captain—we choose the wrong course, people die."

"I feel . . ." I trailed off, unable to encapsulate the horror of the loss into something as banal as words.

"You feel like you're caught in a storm, and no matter how deep you sub, the waves still crack the hull."

That wasn't how I felt. I felt like the storm itself, unable to stop screaming over empty water, but I understood this was Miranda's way of putting her own feelings into words and so I did not correct her.

"She and Kraken were the first people to accept me." I didn't include Annie, as her acceptance had been largely opportunistic, and had ended with me clinging to the back of the ship. Miranda had walked her for that. Attempted murder was taken seriously on *Man o' War*.

"Close your eyes."

I did as I was commanded. Miranda's hands left my waist and moved to my shoulders, working the knots in long, smooth strokes. With each, I briefly felt the stab of physical memory: swimming as fast as I could toward the hatch, trying to keep Jeanine from drowning. Salt flowed silently down my cheeks. Eventually, the memories slowed, then ceased, leaving me alone with Miranda's hands. Her fingers found the knots in my neck, at the base of my scalp, my jaw, my ribs, my arms. She didn't speak as she worked.

Seraphina's drink, whatever it was, spread with Miranda's touch, and with it came desire. At first, I fought the gathering warmth. Jeanine's body was only hours cold, I was exhausted, and the stings from the jellyfish still burned. But as Miranda loosened a muscle deep in my lower back, I couldn't repress the whine of need at the edge of my next exhale.

Her hands paused, and she pulled me flush against her.

"We shouldn't," I said.

She turned me in the water, her hands sure on my hips as she settled them over her own. Bioluminescence softened the sharp planes of her face, and the sly tilt of her mouth caught a blue glimmer. The taut muscles of her abdomen pressed into me. I felt her pulse, rhythmic and hypnotic. An artificial breeze shivered over my wet skin.

"We're alive, Rose. There's no shame in that."

"Just guilt," I said, tracing her collarbone.

"Do you remember on the trawler, when you and I were in the head, and Jeanine kept pounding on the door?"

I laughed despite myself. Of course I remembered. "You told her to go piss in the ocean."

"She was being a cock block."

"She warned me to be careful with you, after you stormed off."

"She was a loyal cock block," said Miranda with a sad smile. "Even when I didn't deserve it."

"Poor Finn." Finn, Jeanine's lover, had only gotten three months with her before this, and he'd spent at least one of those months recovering from injuries sustained by a giant squid.

"Yeah." She settled me more firmly against her. "But better him than me."

"Miranda," I said, horrified.

"I meant what I said. I will not lose you. Not like that."

I looked into her face, noting the fierce set to her jaw and the desperate fear behind her eyes, and forgave her. "You won't."

"You were so frightened, when you first came aboard. Your eyes were huge, and when I pulled out my knife . . ."

"I thought you were going to kill me."

"But you didn't make a sound when I marked you."

"Is that when you fell in love with me?" I said, half-joking.

"That's when I knew you were going to be a problem, yes." She skimmed her fingers over my ribs. "I knew you'd be hard to break."

"Did you want to break me?"

She held my eyes, and I felt the air between us charge as it always did. "Initially, yes."

A large part of me wondered what that would have felt like. Too large a part—my sense of self-preservation had never been strong where she was concerned. But for a woman who liked to find the cracks in others, she seemed staggeringly fragile as her lips curled in a coy smile. An almost claustrophobic sense of protectiveness surged through me. I wanted her to feel as safe as she made me feel. I wanted her to feel loved, protected, and shielded, for the moment, from the unbearable tenuousness of our existence.

"Do you know what I can break?" I asked, tilting her chin upward.

"What?"

"Every Archipelago record for holding my breath underwater."

Her lips flushed as she took my meaning. "Prove it."

Kissing her once, I took a deep breath and dove.

I could have stayed in that pool happily for the rest of my life. Miranda held me loosely, her hair, unbound from its braid, floating over the surface. Ripples from the rising and falling of our chests stirred the black strands. A minute shift in her breath warned me, however, that this moment of peace was about to end.

"Time to go," Miranda murmured in my ear. "As much as I don't want to."

We left the soothing buoyancy of the pool and pulled our clothes over damp skin. I kissed her shoulder blades as she slid into her shirt, savoring the way the firm line of muscle gave slightly beneath my lips. She paused her struggle with her shirt and leaned back into me. My arms wrapped around her bare waist.

The sound of approaching footsteps broke us apart. A young couple peered through the bamboo, saw us, and apologized.

"It's fine. We're leaving," said Miranda.

We walked through the gardens and into the ring of corridors and living quarters on the outskirts. Miranda seemed to know her way through the low-ceilinged halls. Biolights burbled and graffiti decorated the patched plex. Some drawings were crude, but most had an ethereal beauty that spoke of real artistry. I paused by a mural of three octopuses with their tentacles entangled like hands. The mottled flesh looked so real. When I touched it, however, I just felt paint.

Many of the doors we passed stood open. Song drifted from some, and I wished we could linger to watch the performers. One room contained a small group of older people gathered around a rotund woman with a gray cat curled in her lap. Rugs lined the floor in patterns unfamiliar to my Archipelagean eyes. The woman's low voice resonated around the room, and I caught snatches of a story told in a different tongue.

"What is this?" I asked Miranda.

"Singers, storytellers—Seraphina collects and cultivates culture."

"What language is that?"

"Arabic."

"Arabic." I sounded out the word, tasting its corners. I knew that Arabic was one of the influences on the Archipelago common tongue, but I'd never heard it spoken purely. "Do you know what she's saying?"

Miranda closed her eyes and listened. "It's an origin story. I only know a few words."

"An origin story?"

"Of how her people came to the ocean, and where they came from before that."

"Why does it matter where we came from before?" I asked. My own history was a half-formed thing. My mother's family came from all over the smaller stations, and my father was deep ocean through and through. His drifter origins were story enough for me. Why go actively *looking* for more pain?

Miranda raised an eyebrow. "History is valuable."

"History's dead weight."

"You'd toss it, then?"

I mimed throwing something overboard.

"We carry history with us whether we acknowledge it or not," said the woman with the cat. I hadn't thought she could hear us. All the eyes in the room focused on me and Miranda. Blood rushed to my face.

"Sure," I said, not wanting to argue.

51

"Where are you from?"

I shrugged. I wasn't going to tell this stranger my history, no matter how kind her eyes.

"See how it weighs on you, even when you deny it?"

"I'm not—" I began.

"She's not used to philosophical debates, Mae," Miranda said, placing her arm around my shoulders.

The woman—Mae—nodded and gave me a smile as kind as her eyes before resuming her tale. We listened to the lyrical rise and fall of her words for a moment more. The cat's purr blended with the low notes. My shoulders prickled beneath Miranda's arm. The light pressure felt heavier than normal, as if Mae's words had settled there as well.

"Come on," said Miranda.

I was more than happy to obey.

Miranda eventually knocked on a nondescript door. At the occupant's bequest, she opened it, and we entered a comfortable office. Seat cushions lay scattered across the floor in place of chairs. Seraphina sat on one with a chart spread across her knees.

"Where are you off to?" Miranda asked her as she sprawled across several cushions.

I made myself into a smaller shape and sat with my knees tucked to my chest. Odd lights danced in the corner of my vision.

"Southwest."

Deep ocean. My mind calculated a series of courses before I remembered nobody had asked me to do so.

"Calm seas then."

"And you?" Seraphina inquired.

"Depends on how repairs go."

Seraphina folded up the chart and focused on Miranda. "I'm glad to see you. They say the Archipelago will fall, soon, one way or another."

The languor left my limbs.

Miranda waved away Seraphina's words. "Ching was defeated."

"But she nearly won. Someone else will rise up, soon. Maybe you."

"I'm done with that."

Seraphina didn't look like she believed Miranda, which made her an intelligent woman. "Either way, they've scaled back trade. I could use you."

"Like you don't have raiders of your own." Miranda's tone was gently teasing, but still respectful. Seraphina radiated power with a subtlety that took me unawares. Beneath that calm exterior, I sensed a mind as sharp as Miranda's. Sharper, maybe. Which was dangerous. I fought to clear my head. Whatever chemical compound she'd given us seemed designed to lower our inhibitions. Miranda appeared untouched by it, but what if I wasn't capable of accurately gauging her mental state?

"Never hurts to have one with Archipelago ties. Keep me in mind if you . . . stumble . . . upon supplies."

"Always."

Who *was* this woman? Seraphina and Miranda discussed trade while I sat there, still half entranced by the drink. Why did she think the Archipelago was about to fall? If anything, the Archipelago now seemed poised to reclaim lost territory under Comita's influence. I tried to muster feeling about the potential collapse of my home, and blamed my apathy on intoxication. Of course I cared about the Archipelago. Of course it mattered to me if they fell. Collapse would lead to chaos. We would lose precious technology and algae strains and human life. The Archipelago was as much an ark as it was a nation; within, we carried the seeds of civilization, or so said our historians.

So I'd been taught, and yet, remembering Seraphina's flourishing gardens, I wondered.

"How long have you been below the equator?" Miranda asked as I tuned back in.

"A few months. The ships that survived the Gulf made it here if they could. Good salvaging. Surprised it took you this long to join us."

"We've been trawling the coasts," said Miranda. "Not a lot of fleet activity that way."

"May I speak plainly?"

"You always do."

Seraphina paused. Her face radiated empathy as she took Miranda in. "Ching overreached. I know what she was to you, and I know how things ended. I'm sorry."

Miranda didn't stiffen. I studied her for signs of a reaction, but she just said, "thank you," and seemed to mean it.

Another pause. Seraphina steepled her fingers and appraised Miranda over their tips. "This ship is, and has always been, a parley ground."

Miranda did stiffen now. I fought against the lingering effects of the drink and felt the change in the air currents between them.

"Your business is your business. I trust there will be no unpleasantness?" Seraphina continued.

"I don't understand." Miranda's voice was a tonal catastrophe: it managed to be both flat and stricken at once, and her attempt to modulate it raised the hairs on the back of my neck.

"You—" Seraphina's brows contracted in confusion. "I assumed you knew."

Miranda's skin was a shade too dark to pale with blood loss, but her scars blanched as she stared at Seraphina.

"Ah. You didn't." The steepled fingers tapped themselves together in a rapid dance.

"What didn't we know?" I asked, because Miranda didn't seem capable of forming syllables through her clenched jaw.

"I've extended sanctuary to Ching until she can find a ship to take her home."

The air in my lungs crystalized and broke into a thousand shards. Alveoli shrieked in the ensuing slaughter. I did not hear the words Miranda said to Seraphina. I did not hear anything until the door to our quarters shut behind us and Miranda collapsed onto a couch and closed her eyes, looking three decades older, and then the sound I heard was the quiet breaking of my heart.

Chapter Three

Seamus rubbed his head against my legs, his feline indifference to the glacial air in the room impressive. I felt frostbite forming on my nose. I couldn't think. My thoughts crashed into each other over and over again, run aground by Seraphina's words. Miranda kept her silence opposite me. Her head was bowed so low I could count the vertebrae in her neck.

This woman—my captain, my lover—had comforted me through countless nightmares, held me when I'd woken, screaming, from dreams where Ching Shih slaughtered everyone I'd ever loved before hunting me through the lower levels of the ship with her sword dripping blood. And all that time, as Miranda'd assured me I was safe, she'd known Ching Shih was alive. Worse, she'd orchestrated Ching's survival. The most haunting of my nightmares was not the bloody ones, but a dream in which I stood on the prow of *Man o' War* and watched a hooded figure be led away. It paused at the wharf and looked back over its shoulder, and then the hood was blown back, and the face beneath belonged to the woman who'd tried to destroy my world.

"She's alive?" I said, because I needed to say something.

Miranda raised her head from her hands and turned empty eyes on me. "Three months."

"What?"

"It took you three months to ask that question."

Jeanine's ghost laughed in the recesses of my skull, a reminder of the nightmare that had woken me only hours before. The effort of preventing a stream of projectile vomit from leaving my stomach gave me the illusion of calm.

"You told Comita she was dead," I said around a mouthful of bilious saliva.

"No. I gave Admiral Comita Ching's sword and *implied* she was dead. I owed Ching a life debt. She cashed it in."

"You should have told me." My voice sounded small and tremulous.

Hers was flat when she replied, "And you should have asked."

Fury pushed down nausea. "Don't put this on me, Mere. I trusted you. I believed you. I—"

"You don't trust me, though." Her voice remained expressionless. Mine, however, rose.

"I gave you my oath. In fucking blood. I gave up everything for you."

Cold stole over her features. "No, you didn't."

"I—"

Her eyes narrowed. "You left a ship where you were shit on for your heritage to be second mate on mine, years before you would have achieved the same position in the Archipelago. You still have your family. You still have your best friend. You still have your sanity. The worst thing that has ever happened to you is that someone tried to drop you off my ship, and you were rescued within minutes. Don't you dare talk to me about sacrifice."

"Miranda—"

"I owe Ching Shih everything that I am. I couldn't kill her. I thought you of all people would understand."

I stood up from the chair I'd collapsed into and backed away from her toward the door. My entire body trembled. "I never asked you to kill her. All I've ever asked of you is trust. But you can't give that to me, can you?"

Miranda's glare deepened. She drew herself upright, and I

saw sweat beading along her hairline. "You're a fine one to talk about trust."

There were several instances she could be referring to where I'd disobeyed her orders, but she didn't *get* it. She hadn't just lied to me as my captain. She'd lied to me in our bed.

"I am responsible for wiping out her entire fleet. She will *kill me*, Mere, and you didn't think I might want to know if she was alive?"

"Believe me, I'm aware of what you did."

I choked on the fist of her words. I didn't recognize the woman in front of me. Her face was twisted in a rage that made no sense. I was the one who'd been lied to. I was the one who should be upset, not her.

"What the hell is that supposed to mean?"

Miranda's jaw muscles jumped as she held back the words I could tell she wanted to launch at me. "Forget it."

"No, Mere. Say it."

She looked at me. I glared into her eyes, blue and clear and laced with the same hairline fractures that crisscrossed her body in the shape of her scars, but ran much deeper. I'd seen the damage following Jeanine's death, and I saw it again now, as if blue light irradiated her. It arrested my breaking heart mid-shatter. I was a navigator. Detecting undercurrents was my job. What was I missing? Why would Miranda lie to me about Ching? She wasn't looking at me like someone caught out in a lie. She looked like a woman haunted.

A sick feeling crept over me as I studied her, as cold and clammy as toxic fog. All the secret reasons why I'd never dared ask her about Ching stirred in my marrow.

It had never been only about Ching, though my fear of her was real enough. Ching represented a time in Miranda's life I would never fully understand, but it *had* been a part of her. It was still a part of her. Miranda had sailed with Ching, which meant many of the people who'd perished in that battle were people she knew. People she cared about.

People I'd helped the Archipelago kill.

A buzzing sound filled my ears. The room seemed overly bright, flooded with blue, and I hovered on the brink of something vast and sharp. The buzzing intensified. I squeezed my eyes shut, willing myself not to tumble over the edge, but it was already too late. Blue light bled into the backs of my eyes and turned them as purple as the exposed muscles in Jeanine's chest.

I'd been asking myself the wrong questions this entire time.

"You didn't want her fleet destroyed, did you?" I said.

Miranda jerked her eyes away from mine and stared back down at her hands, twisting the ring on her thumb—a Gemini captain's ring. Another reminder of the things she'd lost. Once, I'd floated at the stern of her ship, cut loose by a woman I'd thought was my friend. The silence of the stars that night had been a cataclysm; they were nothing compared to what I saw in the depths of Miranda's averted irises now. In my arrogance, I'd thought I'd saved her. Instead, when I'd led the Archipelago down on Ching's flank, I'd cut *Miranda* loose.

It didn't matter that I hadn't been the one to give the orders, or that, given the option, I would have offered clemency. Without the hidden channel I'd discovered through drowned Florida, the Archipelago wouldn't have been able to slaughter Ching's fleet and sink her ships. The fight would have been fair—or at least fairer—and Ching would have had bargaining power. Equilibrium might have been achieved. But, like a much younger Miranda, I'd underestimated the Archipelago's capacity for violence. Unlike that Miranda, I should have known better, for I was in love with the evidence of their cruelty.

The buzzing intensified. I hated Ching for the war she'd brought down on my people, but I remembered the revelation I had after Jeanine's death: how Miranda had fixated on nearly losing me, instead of the reality of losing two members of her crew. I remembered, and as I did, the blade fell. I'd been fixating on Ching to avoid something even uglier. By finding the channel, I'd given the Archipelago the means to commit genocide.

The vomit I'd been holding back burned my nose as I bolted for the head. Seamus hissed as I tripped over him. I clutched the plex sides of the toilet and heaved and heaved and heaved. My stomach was always one step ahead of me. My mother had called my tendency as a child to feel ill before a stressful event "your nervous stomach." This was so much more than that. It was like my body knew it was toxic, knew I brought death with me wherever I went, and now wished to rid itself of itself.

A hand settled on my back. All the muscles in my abdomen quivered with the effort of expulsion. I threw up until the only thing that emerged was rancid air, and then I leaned my forehead on the plex and sobbed.

Miranda wiped my face clean with a wet rag when I stopped convulsing. I accepted the glass of water she handed me and rinsed out my mouth, then drank, replenishing the liquid I'd lost with a diligence outside my own volition. I drank for Miranda. I sat up for Miranda. I slowly, painfully, accepted I would not die in the small bathroom in our quarters, and looked up into the face of the woman who'd lied for the same reason I'd never asked about Ching. If we acknowledged the damage that lay between us, it would open a gulf as vast and full of our dead as the Gulf of Mexico.

The cool plex of the shower stall supported my back. Miranda arranged herself cross-legged in the narrow space between the toilet and the door with her hands dropped loosely in her lap. Neither of us spoke for a long time.

"We had a plan," Miranda said at last. "Together, we'd take down the Archipelago and bring equality and stability to the Atlantic. It took four years before I realized she had another agenda. All Archipelageans were the same in her eyes. She didn't want equality. She wanted sovereignty. A nation of her own. No matter the cost. When Comita approached me, I thought I was so fucking brilliant. I thought I could play them against each other and force the treaty I'd first tried to get on Gemini. I thought, like a bloody fool, that I could make up for what I'd done to my station."

Her words did not echo in the small space, but I felt them reverberate down my body anyway.

"I didn't tell you about this before the Gulf because I did not know if I could trust you. After, I didn't tell you because I did not want you to feel as I've felt every day since they walked me. I thought I could protect you. And Ching . . ." An expression I'd never before seen crossed her face too quickly for me to read. "I could not be certain you wouldn't go to Comita, if you knew."

I saw the fires burning over the surface of the Gulf and, just below, the bodies.

Would I have gone to Comita? If Miranda had sat me down and said, "Rose, I cannot lose this woman even if she is a monster, because I have lost too many people already to this war," would I have spat in the face of her trust? I didn't think so, but I understood why she could not take the risk.

Understanding brought no comfort. Miranda and I stared miserably at each other, lost in our own private hells, and she did not reach for me.

"I think I should go," I said.

She flinched, but did not argue. I stood unsteadily and walked the short distance to the quarters assigned to the second mate. I rarely used them. I hadn't kept so much as a spare shirt in a drawer. The room still felt as if it belonged to the previous occupant, who'd died in an attempted mutiny—also my fault. I curled into my hammock and felt the ship hum around me. Hard to believe we were still docked beside the *Trench*, or that the rest of the crew, including Harper, were off enjoying themselves in Seraphina's hold.

I'd helped the Archipelago destroy an entire fleet of people. Yes, I'd been driven to it, chased into the channel by Ching's scouts, and yes, what I'd seen of Ching's treatment of our mining stations had horrified me. Ching had no right to punish Archipelago innocents for the decisions of the elite. That didn't mean her sailors had deserved their fates. A fate I'd brought down on them. I should have known what would happen. Maybe a part of me had. All this time, I'd struggled to reconcile my love for Miranda with my history and the values instilled in me by my upbringing, unaware she'd been struggling with something far greater.

My dreams that night were once again drenched with blood.

Faces floated in dark water, bloated and bruised, and even the water in the hydrofarms ran red. Dev called for me to find him while squid wearing Ching's face hunted me through the tangled ruins of my ship, Jeanine's head in their beaks. Harper panted in pain, a sword through her gut, asking me to tell her mother she forgave her while Orca crawled toward me, Comita standing over her with a knife. Behind them, Annie laughed, a rope in her hands. "I'll save you," she said, but her face was half skull and rotting flesh, and an eel peered out from the empty socket. And Miranda—Miranda lay still and silent at my feet, her scars as livid as they must have looked the day she got them, and she didn't move when I shook her. "You should have saved us," said Jeanine. "You should have saved us all."

I woke, screaming, to the feel of Miranda's arms around me and her voice in my ear.

"Easy, love."

She held me tightly as I sobbed, until the sobs turned into dry heaves and then back to sobs and finally to sleep, and when the nightmares came again, she sang to me until the fresh grief passed. Her voice was rough and sweet. It passed through me and into my bones, where it hummed with the rhythm of the ship.

"Did I ever tell you the story of how I found Seamus?"

I shook my head against her collarbone.

"This was back when I first started under Ching, after I'd recovered enough to remember who I was. I mostly helped Ching plan raids, which meant I spent a lot of time talking with drifters. This ship came in to trade—it was even smaller than our trawler—and I was in the docking bay with Kraken gathering intel. He was chatting with the captain, who looked like she was twelve, when this ball of fluff erupts from their hatch. Obviously I caught it."

"Obviously."

"And it bit me. Hard. But before I could drown it, it climbed up my arm and hid beneath my hair, hissing and biting and clawing me every time I tried to get it off. So I let it stay. He didn't come down for four hours, and I ended up with the rest of the litter before the end of the day."

She toyed with my curls as she spoke, smoothing them between her fingers and letting her nails lightly scratch my scalp, the way both the cat in question and I liked.

"I never found out why he wanted to get off that ship so badly. Sometimes I'm glad. It doesn't always matter what we're running from, as long as we get away."

"What about the things we can't get away from?"

Her lips pressed against the top of my head. "That's when we hold on to each other—and our knives."

When I woke up again, I was alone once more in my room.

Harper sauntered toward me during breakfast with her eyes half-lidded and a satisfied smirk on her lips. Her haircut looked as fierce as she'd claimed it would in the morning light. Orca trailed her, looking equally smug. I fixed as blank an expression on my face as I could manage, aware I looked like shit but desperate to keep Harper from asking what was wrong. Last night's revelations were a poison coating every inch of my insides. Miranda did not join us at the table. I did not know where she was, or if her appearance beside me last night had been a dream.

"You missed out by leaving early," Harper said as she slid into the seat beside me.

I side-eyed her, noting the rumpled state of her clothing, and forced a light tone. "Have fun?"

"More fun than you'd believe." She stretched. "Neptune, but I'm sore. Everywhere." Her wink left her meaning unmistakable.

"You're going to put me off my breakfast. What did you get up to?" I asked Kraken, turning away from Harper's lazy grin.

"You'll have to wait and see, but I promise, it's delicious."

Harper perked up. "Food?"

"Seraphina's been cultivating a new species. She discovered them last year. Easier to raise than eels, fast protein, and while they're not much to look at, they're delicious."

"When you say not much to look at—" Orca began.

"She calls them sea roaches, but I'm working on a more palatable title," said Kraken.

"Sea roaches? Like cockroaches?" Orca pushed her tray away. "Hell no."

"Juicy, tender—you won't even notice."

"I'll notice."

"You'll eat it," said Harper, "like a good girl."

"Seraphina has a library of old recipes," said Kraken, perhaps sensing an audience in Harper.

"How old?" I asked, feigning interest.

"Pre-flood. Spices you've never heard of. Plants and animals that don't exist anymore. She's been trying to recreate some of them for years. Food is culture."

"And yet, you want us to eat bugs," said Orca.

"I've eaten real roaches before." Kraken's voice lost its light-heartedness, and he seemed to grow in his chair.

Orca was undeterred. "Right, but you were starving."

"We're always one blight away from starvation."

An awkward silence followed this pronouncement. Harper broke it.

"This took a turn. Orca, shut up. You'll eat your roach and you'll like it. Can we call them Roach Roasts? Or, what about Roachellini in red sauce? Little nuggets wrapped in rice flour could be . . . Rumplings. Roach dumplings."

"Rumplings." Kraken savored the word and rubbed his bald scalp. "I like it. Or roasts."

"Vomit," said Orca, but she said it quietly and without heat.

I pulled her aside as the meal finished.

"I'm busy," she said automatically.

"Fuck that."

Whatever she heard in my voice was enough to break her concentration. The languid expression left her face as she focused on me. "You need to hit something?"

I nodded.

She led the way, not to the rings, but to a mostly empty storage room. Crates and barrels lined one wall, but the floor was larger

63

than a ring and had been recently swept. The resident cat hissed and bolted out the door before Orca shut it. Neither of us had wraps for our hands—not that wraps had ever stopped Orca from beating the shit out of me in the past. My breath echoed in my ears.

"You good?"

She meant, I knew, good to fight; there was no question about my emotional state. I could feel my face twitching as I struggled to keep from screaming, snarling, or crying—hard to say which one. She crouched into a waiting stance, and I lunged.

She let our bodies collide. The force, concussive and wonderfully solid, would have borne us to the ground if she hadn't turned at the last second and let our momentum spin me off. Stumbling, I steadied myself on the far wall and lunged again. She caught my fist in hers but didn't try to land a blow in response. I brought my leg up in a sweeping kick; she blocked that, too. The snarl won out. Her lips curled in a satisfied smile as I charged her, growling, all the finesse she and Harper and fleet prep had tried to drill into me forgotten.

I landed on my back with the wind partially knocked out of me and Orca pinning my hands over my head.

"Get me off," she said, the double entendre presumably accidental.

I kneed her in the groin. She managed to dull the worst of the blow by taking it in the thigh instead, but that was all I needed. I flung myself on top of her and battered her shoulders with my fists until she locked her hands behind my back and my legs with hers, holding me until my ribs creaked with the force and her shirt was drenched. I thought it was sweat, at first. Only after several minutes did I realize I was sobbing.

Orca didn't comfort me. Not in words, at least, or anything resembling a kind gesture. She kept me trapped against her as the fury and fear and hurt and hate ripped through me. I breathed in the familiar scent of her sweat and her hair and our enmity, and was grateful. We'd both grown and healed since that day in the ship's training room months ago, when, like today, I'd been angry and heartbroken. I'd kissed her then, and she'd been angry and heartbroken enough to kiss me back. I did not want to kiss her now. I smelled sex and Harper on her skin, and while Harper would always be my first and dearest friend, in this moment only Orca understood me.

"You good?"

This time, she didn't mean good to fight. My head pressed into her shoulder. My arms were trapped against my sides. I wanted to peel off my skin and slither away like an eel. I was the least good I'd been in my entire life.

"Did you know Ching's on Seraphina's ship?"

"Shit. No. How did that come up?" Her voice rumbled through her chest. Gradually, she released me, and I flopped onto my back beside her on the floor to stare at the ceiling.

"Seraphina told Miranda."

"I wondered what had happened to that fucker."

I doubted Orca would ever forgive Ching for commandeering *Man o' War* on her watch.

"I didn't know she was alive," I said.

Orca rolled on her side and propped herself up with an elbow. The shells and bones in her hair clinked. "Only Kraken and I knew, aside from the captain. It wasn't personal. Though, honestly, you probably should have guessed."

She never pulled her punches.

"Orca," I said, taking comfort from the heat of her body, "do you hate me?"

"What?" She blinked her gray eyes and frowned. "I mean, I hate your face, but you've grown on me."

"No, I mean for what I did."

The frown deepened. "What did you do?"

"Helped the Archipelago blow up the Gulf."

"Oh, that." She shrugged with one shoulder. "Nah."

"I committed genocide."

"Your ego," she said, miming something large, "is ridiculous. You didn't tell them to light the fucking ocean on fire, did you?"

"But the channel—"

"We'd most likely be dead if we hadn't gone through. You're

not blaming yourself for that shitshow, are you?"

"Miranda is."

Orca gripped my arm and shook me gently. "The captain knows fuck-all. She's still blaming herself for Gemini. Don't be like her. The Archipelago's been trying to off the rest of us for generations. We had shit choices, Rose."

I wanted to believe it was that easy to absolve myself.

"Look at it this way if you're going to be an idiot. I was the captain of the trawler. If you want to blame someone, blame me."

"What do we do, then?"

"About what? I've had approximately two hours of sleep. Use your words."

"About Ching."

"That's up to the captain, Rose. It always has been."

We remained docked beside Seraphina's ship. Sailors ferried supplies back and forth, and *Man o' War* periodically clanged with the sound of repairs. Harper was busy overseeing the work; Orca, presumably, was busy with the same. I hesitated outside the captain's quarters, then opened the door.

Miranda wasn't inside. I hadn't expected her to be, really, and relief brought shame alongside it. My body ached as if I had a fever, and the sick lurch of self-loathing accompanied me, closer than my shadow. I did not know what to do. I needed to talk to Miranda, and I was so afraid of what she might say. The empty room—save for Seamus, who slept on the back of a chair—felt like her. I wanted to be back in the dream of her comfort. I wanted . . . I didn't know what I wanted. I wanted Ching Shih to be dead and I wanted to rid myself of the knowledge that my actions had led to a massacre. I wanted to curl up in my bed and lie there for days. I wanted, more than anything, to be home on Cassiopeia with the mother I hadn't seen in nearly a year.

"Rose."

I startled, still in the doorway, and turned to face Kraken. His bulk offered a bulwark against which I might throw myself, but he was Miranda's man. Did he carry the guilt I now did? He'd been with me. He'd known, better than anyone, what was likely to happen, and he'd said nothing. Why?

His eyes, those warm, brown, grief-stained irises surrounded by fearsome tattoos, held mine. Kraken knew how to carry his dead.

"Captain wants us," he said, his voice vibrating on the level of whale song.

"Where is she?"

"Seraphina's. Can you pull yourself together?"

His question was delivered with a measured calm that told me everything I needed to know about my face. I nodded.

"Good."

Orca joined us in the docking bay. She arched a brow at me, and I gave her the same nod I'd given Kraken. Together, the three of us entered the plex tube connecting the ships like an umbilical. I could see the lights of the ships through the hazy bioplastic, and beyond that, dark water. Sunlight filtered through the upper levels of the ocean, but we were subbed well below the wave zone.

"Any idea what this is about?" Orca asked Kraken. He didn't respond. We all knew what this was about.

The awe that had accompanied my last visit to Seraphina's ship was a bleached memory. Her gardens did not soothe me. The smell of cooking did not rouse my appetite. I doubted anything ever would again. I closed my ears against the whispering chant of song and story. Miranda's insistence that history meant something was just another reminder our history might damn us.

Kraken stopped outside a door on the upper level. Nothing marked it as special. Just plain, gray-green plex with a simple handle, lacking ornamentation or graffiti, and unmarked by labels of any kind. It could contain anything. He opened it, and my heart thudded sickly.

The room beyond smelled like tea. I detected the slight tang of the metal teapot, and the harsh, herbal aroma of hot leaves. Smells I associated with the memory of Ching on *Man o' War*, serving tea to us while her armada floated nearby. She'd drunk rum.

Miranda and Seraphina sat at a low table in the center of the room. A plush carpet served as seating, and the walls were covered with geometric tapestries. I took these details in like water to my lungs, a passing afterthought to drowning. The third person in the room looked up at me from her cross-legged position across the table from my captain. My bowels liquified with dread.

The intervening months had not been kind to Ching Shih, former pirate queen of the Red Flag fleet. Named for an ancient pirate by those who feared her, she'd brought hell down on the Atlantic; now, hell looked like it had swallowed her up and coughed her back out. Her once shining straight hair was gone, shorn to stubble on her skull. It accented the plainness of her face and the faint lines around her eyes and mouth. Her square jaw and broad forehead, however, framed eyes that cut with a startling, cruel beauty. They were a brown so dark it was nearly black, like a kelp garden in the evening, and the shadows beneath them only cast them into sharper clarity. Those eyes looked at me and knew.

A hand pressed into my back, steadying me. Orca stood close enough the gesture was hidden from sight, and I leaned into her touch for the brief moment of contact, taking strength where I could find it. *I'm with you*, that touch said, and I was grateful for the second time that day for her presence in my life. Funny how time changed things. Once, I'd wished her buried in the Mariana trench.

"Please sit," said Seraphina. Kraken and Orca moved to comply, and I did not want to draw attention to myself, so I followed suit, folding myself into the space between them instead of the spot beside Miranda, as that would have put me directly in Ching's line of sight. And . . . because I did not trust myself. Miranda's nearness might undo the slim control I had over my emotions.

Kraken, Orca, and I made up Miranda's inner circle: spy master, first mate, and second. This was ship business. Miranda's face was a study in composure. No traces of the woman who'd broken down before me last night remained, and her hands rested easily on her tea cup.

"Shall we parley?" asked Seraphina, looking around at each

of us in turn.

"Yes," said Miranda.

"Yes," said Ching. Her voice raised a cold sweat on my skin. I'd heard it too many times in nightmares.

"Well," Ching began, taking over the conversation. "I admit I never expected to find myself in this position."

"And what position is that?" Miranda sounded pleasant, as if she were having tea with an old friend. Maybe Seraphina had drugged her.

"Needing your aid."

I counted off the cardinal points as I listened, focusing on things that made sense.

"Aid?" Miranda's voice cracked almost imperceptibly.

"Perhaps you didn't notice, but I appear to be short a ship—and an armada."

I flinched. Ching's eyes flicked in my direction, and I regretted being born.

"The navigator," she said softly. "Hello again."

"Captain Shih," I said, hiding behind fleet formality. She gave me a small and crooked smile. It was not the reaction I'd expected.

"I rarely underestimate my enemies. But you surprised me."

What could I say to that?

"There are no enemies on my ship," said Seraphina.

"Let's dispense with that illusion, Sera. But I am reasonable, and I do not believe you acted on your captain's orders, did you?"

I looked to Miranda for guidance, but she was watching Ching. Now that Ching's attention was not on her, I saw the cracks again. Her eyes devoured Ching like she was afraid she was a cloud mirage, and her lips quirked downward with the effort of suppressing her emotions.

"No," I said.

"You nearly killed your captain and your crew."

"Yes," I said again.

"But she's seen fit to keep you. I cannot object, as questionable as your judgment appears to be."

This last was directed at Miranda.

"I did not come here to discuss my navigator," said Miranda.

Why did you come, then? Ching's eyes seemed to ask, but that might have just been my terrorized imagination.

"I have a proposition for you. I need a sturdy ship and crew to get me where I need to go."

"Taking you aboard compromises the safety of my crew," said Miranda.

"Which is why I have something to offer you."

"And what is that?"

"What you asked me for years ago."

Miranda's face did a strange thing. Her lips parted in surprise, but her eyes glittered with an emotion disturbingly similar to malice.

"Why now?" she asked.

"I have nothing more to lose."

"If you'd done it years ago—"

"The outcome would have been the same. I'll tell you again what I told you before. You won't get what you want out of it. But if you're still determined—"

"Yes."

Beside me, Orca shifted, her frustration showing. So she didn't know what was going on, either. A small comfort. Kraken remained implacable.

"A small part of me hoped you'd say no," said Ching. "But you've never taken my advice. Shall we establish terms?"

Orca cleared her throat. Miranda glanced up as if she'd just remembered the rest of us were there.

"Captain, could you tell us what we are agreeing to?"

"An opportunity." Miranda's eyes slid to mine, then away. "We're taking Amaryllis home."

"Ama—" Orca began before cutting herself off.

But I knew. Ching had told me herself that Ching Shih was a title, not her birth name. Of course Miranda would know her real name.

"Where?" It took all my courage to ask the question. I did not want those eyes turned back on me.

"90 degrees south, Compass Rose."

I stared at Ching's—Amaryllis's—mouth in order to avoid her eyes, noting the chapped skin and the determined bow of her upper lip, and had one coherent thought: *What the actual fuck?*

"What the fuck?" Orca echoed my thoughts, slamming her hand on the table in what I assumed, dimly, was shock. "Nobody sails there. The water—"

"Isn't the real danger," said Ching. I couldn't quite bring myself to call her Amaryllis.

"Like hell it's not."

"Orca," Miranda said in warning.

"I'm just very confused about why you're suddenly insane, Captain."

"That is a conversation we will have later. For now, assume it is worth our while."

Orca's molars made sounds of protest as she ground her jaws, but she did not argue the point. I wished she would. Sailing into the Antarctic ring didn't make any sense. Neither did the motivation. What did Miranda want so badly she'd be willing to take Ching onboard, risking Comita's wrath, not to mention all our lives? Ching was one woman, but she was a woman who by her own admission had nothing left to lose. What if she tried to kill Miranda? Or *me*?

"Here are my terms," said Miranda. "You will grant us an introduction. You will refrain from contact with my crew as much as can reasonably be helped. You will make no attempts to exact revenge on my navigator or any of my other sailors. You will obey my orders. You will incite no mutiny."

"I'm in no position to do any of the things you think me capable of, Mere."

"Precautions."

"And here are my terms," said Ching. "I will grant you an introduction, but you will not hold me responsible for the results. My warning stands. This will not end the way you want it to."

"I never asked for anything else."

Ching briefly closed her eyes. Their lids were a dark bruise

71

blue. "Then we have a deal."

Miranda drew her belt knife, and my palm prickled. She sliced a thin line over the matching scar on her palm, raising beads of bright blood. Then she held the knife out to Ching. Orca tensed. Even Kraken stilled in his seat, eyes intent on the blade.

"Do it yourself, and do it right," said Ching. She and Miranda held each other's eyes for an interminable length of geologic time. At last, Miranda jerked her head in a curt nod and reached for Ching's overturned palm. Her left hand held Ching's wrist steady.

Orca hissed beneath her breath as Miranda's knife carved an inexorable curved line over Ching's palm, followed by three smaller lines underneath: the jellyfish sigil of the *Man o' War*. Ching made no sound. She just gazed at Miranda with something horribly like tenderness.

Miranda took my hand as we exited the *Trench* what felt like a lifetime later. I let her, aware of the blood drying in the creases of her palm. Kraken and Orca flanked us. Orca muttered to Kraken in a voice just low enough to be unintelligible, but I had a suspicion I could guess the content.

"I need to check on the hydrofarm to see what stock we can spare," Miranda said. "Orca, make the arrangements."

"Captain," Orca said, turning and blocking the hallway. "I don't trust her."

"Neither do I."

Orca's mouth thinned, but she seemed satisfied by this response. She and Kraken parted ways, leaving me and Miranda alone. I walked at her side and tried to quell the tempest in my rib cage. It was too much. It was all too much. And I needed Miranda desperately, but was afraid to look into her face, in case that silent accusation lay behind her eyes. We didn't speak until we came to the hydrofarm.

"Over here." She pulled me into the shadow of an eel tank. The strong odor of the pirate hemp crop clung to my nostrils. It was possible for us to be overheard, but unlikely. Pumps rushed water and nutrient baths over roots, and the low hum of the handheld pollination wands created the sort of ambient noise that drowned conversation.

She'd brought me to a public forum, I realized, instead of our private quarters, to forestall another fight. I pulled my hand from hers.

"Rose—"

"I don't like sailing blind."

"Then let me explain."

"Why did you mark her?" I hadn't known I was going to lead with that, but the pain in my voice was obvious even to my ears.

"It's complicated. And not something we have time for right now." At my expression, she reached for me again. I tucked my hands behind my back.

"Then what do we have time for?"

"So goddamn little." She slumped against the plex. "I didn't want any of this to come out this way. I was going to tell you everything when the time was right. I just . . ."

"I get it. I helped the Archipelago murder your friends."

Hands seized my shoulders, and she tugged me close enough to see the burst capillaries at the corners of her eyes. She looked exhausted. "Never say that again."

"It's true."

"No, it's not, and guilt will kill you."

"I led them down on her fleet."

"Yes. And I led a mutiny, but the Archipelago pulled the trigger. Not us."

"You don't really believe that, though," I said. "I know you, Mere."

Even when you feel oceans away.

And hadn't she implied blame only the night before?

"I tried to end things twice after Ching saved me. The first was because everything hurt so damn much. The second was guilt. Ching—Amaryllis—told me after the second time she found me half-drowned that if I wanted to absolve myself, death wasn't

73

going to help."

"I don't want to kill myself."

"Good. Because I'd hate to have to drag you back out of hell." She cracked a smile. "Rose, we've both made choices that led to terrible things. We're not . . . we're not innocent. But you have to remember where to put the blame."

"On the Archipelago?"

"No, actually. On our fucking ancestors. They evolved in a world perfectly calibrated for their survival, and they broke it. We're all just trying to survive. Even the seas-damned Archipelago."

Her thumbs stroked the tops of my shoulders. I wanted to believe her, but I'd seen the way she had looked at me the night before. I'd seen the accusation. I dropped my gaze.

"Ching told me once that she made you."

"I wish that were true. I'm not really something I want to take credit for. Amaryllis was there for me when my people threw me away. I owe her everything, but I made myself. So have you. And I'm telling you now that there's another option besides fighting over the last drop of poisoned water."

"Better purification systems?"

"Yes, actually." She took a deep breath and let it out the way I'd seen her do when she was preparing for a round of boxing. "Amaryllis is a sea wolf."

Chapter Four

"She's *what?*" I couldn't shout in the hydrofarm without drawing unwanted attention, but I put as much force into my whisper as I could muster.

"She's a sea wolf."

"Neptune, Mere." I shook my head, trying to clear it.

Wolf pup.

You've got eyes like a sea wolf.

Yellow-eyed drifter.

Who was your father?

A lifetime of questions assaulted me at once. Her eyes pleaded with me to listen, but I wasn't sure I could. All this time, she'd known the sea wolves were real, and she hadn't seen fit to mention it? Lying about Ching I understood, even if I hated it. This, though . . . this was different.

"This whole time, you knew the sea wolves were real. You had proof. And you didn't *say anything?*" I pulled away from her.

"Rose—"

"I don't know if I can do this, Mere." My eyes burned with unshed tears.

"Rose," she said again, cutting off my escalating thoughts. "Listen to me."

I remembered nights growing up with my pillow soaked with tears, both hating and missing my father and hating the drifter heritage he'd given me. I remembered years where it hurt to look in the mirror, because all I could see was the wrongness of my face, the lurid brightness of my eyes, golden as a cat's, wrong, wrong, *wrong*. Any justification, any answers, would have changed my life.

"Am I one of them?"

"I don't know," she said. "It's the most logical explanation for what you can do, and your eyes . . . the color is linked to genetic expression. Amaryllis didn't like talking about that part of her life, but I know that much."

"Her eyes are brown."

"Yes. It's a bit of a sore point."

I set that aside for later analysis. "You should have told me."

"How could I have told you the sea wolves were real without telling you about Ching?"

"She's either Ching or Amaryllis. Pick a name, Miranda. And you could have, I don't know, told me you knew about the wolves from someone else. Seraphina, maybe. And 'sea wolves' is a fucking stupid name, anyway."

I was shouting, now. Workers scuttled to the far side of the room.

"It's only been a few months, Rose. I'm not just your . . . lover." She stumbled over the word. "I'm also your captain. This is still so new. I can't—"

"You were worried we wouldn't work out," I said, lead in my heart and on my tongue.

"No. Yes. I was worried you'd change your mind." Her voice broke, and her fingers spun the Gemini ring round and round her thumb. "This life is hard."

"You're not exactly making it any easier."

"Rose—"

"Forget it. As you said. You're my captain. So explain to me, Captain, why I'm sailing south."

I answered the question myself as I spoke. No one sailed near the poles. It wasn't Archipelago territory, and I hadn't thought it

76

was pirate territory, either. I hadn't thought much about it at all. Keeping control of our own waters took enough as it was without worrying about other oceans. There was also increased risk of volcanic activity farther south. The melted glaciers had shifted tectonic balances, and I knew from previous records that ash periodically drifted north from the southern sky. Then there was methane, also disturbed by the plates, and squid. And—abruptly none of those things made sense as deterrents. Our dead seas carried equal risks. From dead zones to toxic blooms and jellyfish, we sailed in the soup, eking out an existence in the liminal spaces below the surface. If there was life at the poles, why weren't we taking advantage of it?

Why, unless . . .

The depth of my willful ignorance floored me. The answer had always been obvious. The Archipelago didn't sail near the poles because the poles were someone else's territory. Someone better equipped, better armed, capable of resisting annexation or conquest. Nobody in the Archipelago government would have wanted that knowledge spread, and so they quelled our curiosity and focused their resources on threats they could control, like pirates.

And even then, we were almost overrun. *Would* have been overrun if it hadn't been for my pure dumb luck.

"They're at the poles," I said aloud, my revelation temporarily outweighing her betrayal. Ching had surprised the Archipelago. We—they, I reminded myself, for I was no longer an Archipelagean—were used to pirates driven reckless with deprivation, not unified naval forces. I pictured the Archipelago charts Miranda had put in front of me during my first few weeks as part of her crew. Archipelago territory was shrinking. Part of that had been Ching, and another part the loss of surface waters to inclement conditions. Regardless of the cause, it amounted to the same thing: they patrolled less and less territory each year. What if Comita really did need us to update her charts? What if the Archipelago had no real idea about what—or who—else occupied the oceans? I'd thought our mission was mostly busywork to keep Miranda far away from the stations, concealing her role in the war. Perhaps I'd been wrong.

"Yes."

"The north, too?"

"I'm not sure."

"And you want an introduction to them? I thought they killed anyone who wasn't them, or something."

"We'll have Amaryllis. And . . . you."

"Nobody likes a half-breed, Mere. Haven't you realized that?" The vitriol that boiled up in my voice left a bitter aftertaste on my tongue. "Anyway, what do you want from them?"

She turned to glance at the curious eel lurking over her shoulder, studying it before answering.

"I want to fix things."

I recalled a conversation I'd had with Miranda shortly after we'd escaped Comita. We'd been topside, watching a distant squall and sharing a flask of rum.

"If you could design a new world, what would it look like?" she asked.

"You'd be there."

She pulled me into her, resting her chin on top of my head. "That goes without question."

"I don't know. I've never thought about it before."

"Sure you have."

I felt her words vibrate through her chin and into my skull. I asked, "What would your world look like?"

"Less tribalism. Less tyranny. Less us versus them."

"Good luck with that," I said, memories of my time on North Star *all too present.*

"Think about it." She pulled away, turning to sit cross-legged to face me. "What do we fight over? What is the one thing we all need, the source of every rift?"

"Um. Vaccines?"

"Partially. Resources. Namely biofuels and plastics, plant strains, and knowledge. If drifters and pirates had access to Archipelagean tech and know-how, we wouldn't need to raid. If we didn't raid, we

wouldn't need to hate each other."

"But there's still the issue of clean water."

"Yes. But better filters would eliminate that."

"Maybe."

"I've studied enough history to know power loves a vacuum. With Ching gone, someone else will rise in her place, and we'll do this all again."

"What are you saying? Are you going to be the next Ching?" I'd meant it as a joke, but she considered it.

"I don't deserve that kind of power."

"Does anyone?"

She smiled at me, looking for a moment like a young woman, instead of the scarred and battered captain of my ship. "Probably not."

The memory receded.

"Can it be fixed?" I asked. I wasn't just talking about our world.

"Why does the Archipelago hold sway over the Atlantic? What gives them the right to withhold resources from everyone else?"

"There isn't enough to go around."

"That's squidshit and you know it."

"Resources are limited. The mines—"

"You can still share limited resources. It's the fact *they* have those resources that matters. If the drifters and the rest of us have something the Archipelago doesn't, they'll have to treat with us. We could finally get something like equality. And if they don't, then we'll build something new."

The light in her eyes unnerved me. This was the Miranda who'd led the Gemini rebellion against the Archipelago—an idealist and a warrior. That combination, I now knew from experience, got people killed. And yet, I thought about Jeanine and Dev, who wouldn't have died if *Man o' War* had been outfitted with Archipelago-grade parts. I thought about Ching, who'd led her sailors in an attempt to upset the power balance because she, too, needed resources. I thought about small stations like Cassiopeia who were a part of the Archipelago but shared only the barest taste of its bounty. I understood Miranda's rage, but equality felt impossible. I wished I could believe in something like that. It was hard enough to have faith in the people around me, let alone an idea.

Maybe, for Miranda, ideas were easier than people.

"What if we're just not capable of equality? What if it's biologically impossible, and that's why we ended up in the ocean in the first place?" I said.

Miranda shrugged, disturbing the inquisitive eel and sending it rippling back into the weeds. "Then at least we've tried."

"Comita—" I began, but I stopped myself. Comita wouldn't want to help us equalize the power dynamics that benefited her people. She'd proven that already.

"We can deal with Comita." Something dark filtered through the blue of Miranda's eyes. It looked like hate.

"How? When she finds out we didn't kill Ching—"

"I held up my end of the bargain. Ching was neutralized. Without a fleet, she's just Amaryllis. What can one woman do?"

I looked at Miranda. One woman could do a hell of a lot of damage. All we had to do was look to our own pasts for the proof.

"Do you know what your admiral told me when we first negotiated a contract?"

"She offered you a pardon."

"No. She offered me a revolution."

I blinked. There wasn't room for more surprises in my system, but my adrenal glands made a valiant attempt to flood my body with more cortisol.

"It took me a while to figure out she was playing me. She had no intention of negotiating autonomy for Gemini, but she knew it would get my attention. Granted, I was trying to play her, too. But she won."

"And you think, what, the sea wolves will give you something you can use as leverage? Resources or whatever? Even though they like raiding anyone who isn't them? Your logic doesn't add up."

I was so sick of secrets.

"I don't think they will *give* us anything. Amaryllis made that clear. But if there is even a chance of negotiation, shouldn't we at least try?"

"Honestly? I don't know," I said. She frowned at my response. Before she could protest, I continued. "Is there anything else? Because I swear to all seven seas, Miranda—"

"That's everything."

"Do you promise?"

"I promise."

"Swear it on your ship."

"I swear it on my ship."

"Okay."

She raised her eyebrows, clearly expecting more of an argument. "That's it?"

"That's it." I didn't have any emotions left over for a fight. There were only so many betrayals, only so many times my world could be upended, before the ability to care was stripped from me. The plex felt cool against my neck. "Am I excused, Captain?"

Without waiting for her response, I fled.

"The South Pole?" Harper looked up from a steaming vent, wiping condensation off her forehead. It had taken a good ten minutes for Harper to stop swearing after I'd explained, dumbstruck, that Ching would be joining us on *Man o' War*. The vent had not survived the encounter. Harper had understandably strong feelings about Ching's methods. Her abduction by Ching's sailors had not been gentle, and ultimately had resulted in deadly violence. Much like Harper's attack on the vent. She traced her finger ruefully along the edges of the busted plex.

"Yeah."

"And these sea wolves are real?"

"Yeah."

"And she's really not dead?"

"Unfortunately not."

"It's super fucked up Miranda didn't tell you."

I let the steam shroud my expression. "Should we do something about this?"

"Oh. Yeah." She pulled a length of tape from her toolbelt and wrapped up the rent. "That will hold for now." A pause. "Fuck. What are we going to do?"

"I don't know."

"You look like a drowned ass," she said.

"Sounds about right." My stomach would probably never settle again.

"Wanna get drunk?"

Drinking wouldn't solve anything, especially the nausea. I shook my head. "I have to plot a course."

She double-checked her tape work before replying. "Miranda's breaking contract with Comita, isn't she?"

"I don't know," I said.

"She can't keep mapping and go south."

"Do you think Comita will care? We'll just get reports to her later."

Harper tapped the vent. "My mother will come after us as long as I'm on board. We could always leave, Rose. We don't have to stay here."

"You don't. I do."

"I'd protect you."

"Miranda," I said, though it wasn't an explanation.

"She just admitted she's been lying to your face for months. You don't owe her shit."

"And Orca?"

Her face fell. We were both in too deep for easy extrication. "She'd understand. Maybe. I don't know. But I can't be on the same ship as that bitch."

My chest ached with unreleased tension. I couldn't be on the same ship as Ching, either. Nor could I leave. Harper meant well, but I could never return to Polaris. Not knowing what I knew. Not with what they'd done. I hadn't mentioned the guilt I felt over the massacre of Ching's fleet to Harper. Some wounds were too fresh.

"I don't know, Harp."

She looked at me. Her eyes were rimmed red from angry

tears, but they saw me. They knew me. She tugged on my sleeve and drew me to her until she could wrap her arms tightly around my waist. Her head came only a few inches above my chin, but I heard her whisper anyway.

"She doesn't get to hurt you like this. Not again."

The scars on my body burned in response: the one on my hand, which I now shared with Ching, and the one on my stomach, from Miranda's whip. In Harper's fierce embrace, the beginnings of a sickening certainty settled over me.

I couldn't leave, but neither could I continue on as I had been, love-drunk on Miranda, blind to the disparities in our relationship. Today had been the beginning of something, and I was terribly afraid that something was an ending.

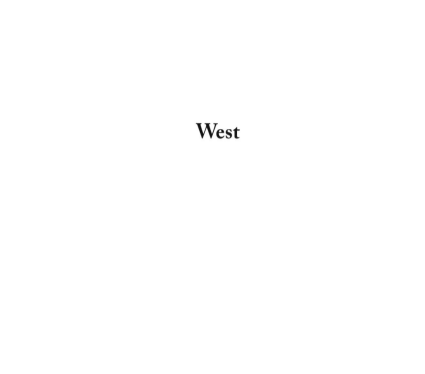

West

Captain's Log
Captain Miranda Stillwater
Man o' War
February 24, 2514
5°06'46" N, 50°01'02" W

Narrowly avoided catastrophe after a major breach to the hull. Lost two crew members—see attached casualty report—and significant supplies. We were lucky that Seraphina and *Trench* were within hailing distance and that she had the component parts we needed to replace that section of hull. See damage report for details.

While docked, Seraphina engaged in parley with Amaryllis, formerly known as Ching Shih. I—fuck. [redacted text] As captain, it is my job to see to the preservation of my crew. I cannot in good conscience bring her aboard. And I cannot leave her behind. After years of asking, she's finally agreed to grant me an audience with her people. She will take us to Symbiont. If it had been any other offer, I would have turned her down, despite everything she was to me. But I cannot turn my back on this.

It is my last chance for redemption.

Chapter Five

The chart room welcomed me into its cocoon of silence. I slid into my customary chair and stared at my hands on the table, unable to contemplate the course ahead. I needed to select the appropriate maps from their shelves. I needed—

I didn't know what I needed. My insides felt hollowed. All that remained were the cardinal points. They whispered soothingly, the magnetic field a second skin over my own.

Ching. Miranda. South.

The sea wolves did not seem worth it. What was wrong with continuing on as we had been, mapping the coasts, building up the ship, and enjoying each other's company? Why had Miranda wrecked everything so thoroughly? I wanted to be enough for her, like she was for me.

I also missed my mother. Tears slid down my cheeks and splattered on the tabletop. "Wait and see what she is made of before you make any big decisions," I imagined her saying. "Don't jump into anything."

I'd jumped all right, and I'd taken Harper with me. My relationship with Miranda played out before me like some sick film reel: Miranda, carving up my hand. Miranda, telling me I was just a tool. Miranda, walking Annie. Miranda's whip. Miranda's dismissals. Miranda's lies. Miranda's secrets. Miranda's mutiny. Did the good outweigh these stones?

She loved me, in her way. But she didn't trust me. Her secrets came out because fate had exposed them, not because she'd decided I was worthy. Yes, I understood her fears. My loyalties had been split, though she could not fault me for that. And yes, I understood a part of her was protecting me from my role in the Archipelago's slaughter, but that had not been her decision to make. How could we ever be equal if she resented me for the deaths of her former crewmates and friends?

And the sea wolves. How many people had told me I had eyes like a sea wolf since signing on to her ship? Most thought the wolves were a legend, but Miranda had known differently. Maybe I was one; maybe I wasn't—it was just another unknown in my genetic code—but regardless, Miranda knew how I'd been treated all my life for my heritage and my abilities. What had she said in our last fight? That I'd left a ship where I'd been shat on all my life to be second mate on hers long before I would have achieved that rank under Comita? If the sea wolves, whoever and whatever they were, explained my navigational abilities, I would be less of a freak. I'd sit easier in my own body. And Miranda hadn't thought I needed to know.

Miranda didn't know me at all.

And now she expected me to accept Ching Shih as part of her crew on our fool's journey to the south pole, inciting Admiral Comita's wrath, and risking everything for the faint hope that, what, our little crew could single-handedly bring about systemic change? Orca had been right. Miranda was insane.

The door to the chart room opened, as I had known it would, to admit my captain. I took in her tired face, her scars, her warm lips, and her blazing eyes. I had a choice before me. Unlike previous occasions, this time I knew the stakes.

"There you are," she said.

"I came to plot your course."

"That's why you have so many charts out. I wondered."

I did not smile at her joke. "I need to talk to you."

"I'm listening," she said.

But you're listening too late.

"We need to send Harper back to her mother," I said. She eased into a chair across from me. The bloody line on her palm had faded to a brown stain.

"We can't do that."

"Why not? If we go off the radar, Comita will try to track us down."

"We'll feed her an excuse. Sending Harper back will raise suspicions. Does she want to leave?"

"That doesn't matter."

"It isn't your decision to make."

I stared at her. The hypocrisy of her statement thrummed through my bones. I weighed a thousand pounds of anguish. "Miranda."

She flinched at the pain in her name as it left my lips.

"At least give her the option to leave," I said.

"If she comes to me and asks, I will grant it." She searched my face. "Do you . . ."

"I can't go back."

Never again would I see Polaris. I hadn't been happy there, exactly, but it had been a home, of sorts, while I served under Comita. A home I'd thrown away.

"I never meant to hurt you, Rose."

My vision blurred with more tears. I blinked them away. "What you meant to do doesn't matter. I get it. You're the captain. But I need more than that."

Her hands closed over mine and held them tightly. "I'll give you what you need."

I wanted to believe her. I wanted, so desperately, to fall into her arms and let her reassure me that everything would be fine, that we would work this out, that nothing was beyond repair.

"You can't," I said instead. "Not like this."

"What are you saying?"

I swallowed. The words were larger than my throat, and I choked on them as I tried to force them through the raw wound of my mouth. "I can be your navigator. But I can't . . . I can't be more than that right now. I need time."

Her hands remained on mine, but the warmth receded. We were frozen at the table, trapped in amber by my statement. I longed to retract it.

"Is this about Amaryllis?"

"This is about you lying to me, Mere."

"I told you—"

"And I get it. You have to make those choices, and I can handle that as your navigator. But it hurts too much like this." The tears scalded my cheeks as they ran in torrents down my chin and onto the table, save for the torrent streaming down my neck and into my shirt. A briny pool formed between my breasts.

Miranda's tear-blurred face was stricken. Her scars stood out against her skin, and once more I had the sense they were not so much scars as hairline fractures, and if I pushed her too hard, she would shatter.

"Are you ending this?" she asked.

"I just need time."

"And I need you. I've told you that." Her voice hardened, as I had known it would.

"I—"

"Are you asking me to *prove* myself to you? Because that isn't what I do. You knew what you were getting into. You know what I am."

"Miranda—"

"I've asked you, repeatedly, if you can handle being with me and being my navigator."

"And I could before I knew how much you'd lied to me!"

"Nothing's changed! And you should have guessed Amaryllis was alive."

"Don't put this on me."

"Why not? You're putting it all on me, and I'm not the only one in this relationship."

"You're the only that matters, though. That's the fucking problem." I cleared my throat to rid myself of sobs. "Don't you get it? It always comes down to your decision."

"I'm the captain. It isn't like I want—"

"Yes. You're my captain. And I thought I could handle that, but I can't handle being lied to, too."

"If you want to talk about honesty, maybe we should look at you." She yanked her hands away from mine. "Have you proved *you're* trustworthy? No. You routinely contradict my orders. You question everything. And Orca—"

"Orca meant nothing!"

"You sabotaged my relationship with my first mate."

"That's not—"

"I can't look at her without seeing you on top of her. Fuck you for that, by the way. You're the one with the boundary problems."

"So it's my fault you won't tell me anything about Ching Shih? It's my fault you can't accept I'm working to overcome years of Archipelago conditioning to be with you on this ship?"

"And I'm working to overcome years of betrayal. Forgive me if I find it hard to trust."

"I'm just asking for time. I'm not—I'm not ending this."

"Sure sounds like you are."

"Please, Mere."

Her lips tightened, and I hated the pleading in my voice.

"Take your time then. Take all the time you need. But I can't promise I'll be here when you're done."

With that, she turned and stormed out of the room, leaving me alone with my charts and the harsh sounds of my stuttering heart.

I moved my things to my room. Miranda wasn't present as I gathered up my scant possessions, and I took one of her shirts with me. It smelled like her. Seamus watched me through slitted feline eyes.

"Take care of her," I told him. He turned to groom his tail. That would have to be answer enough.

Time felt surreal as I deposited my pile of possessions in the small room belonging to the second mate. No private bathroom. No kitchenette. Just a hammock and a battered chest, a small sink, and the gray plex walls. I hated it. I tossed my clothes into the chest and shook out the blanket folded in the hammock, then laid it over Miranda's shirt, ashamed at how much I hoped her smell would permeate the cloth.

Nothing felt real. I hadn't just broken up with Miranda. She hadn't just threatened to leave. Everything that had happened over the past week had been a nightmare, and I would wake up, soon, to the sound of Jeanine's sarcastic voice and the hum of a ship that did not contain Ching Shih. Where would Miranda even put her? The brig? An empty bunk? Would she at least put a guard on her?

I had courses to chart and things to do, but I crawled into the hammock and buried my face in Miranda's shirt, wondering if I'd made the biggest mistake of my life.

Harper found me, eventually. A hand stroked my hair and I heard her whispering to someone else in the room.

"Is she broken?" they asked.

"Shut up."

Orca. I raised myself from my fetal curl and blinked out of swollen eyes.

"Captain's called a meeting," Harper said gently. "Nobody could find you."

"Do I need to be there?" I asked, my voice barely a croak.

"Yeah, baby, you do."

"What's wrong with her?"

"What part of 'shut up' is so hard for you to understand?" Harper said to Orca. Then, to me, she asked, "What happened?"

"I . . . I think I broke up with Miranda."

I didn't meet their eyes. An awkward silence fell.

Orca broke it. "That explains *her* mood."

"I don't care about her right now," said Harper. "Baby, you okay?"

I shook my head. She pulled my face into her chest and rocked me back and forth. I was cried out, but I sniffled, grateful for the comfort.

"You did what you needed to do. That's all we can do. And now you need to pull yourself together and get through this. I'll be right next to you. So will Orca."

"For whatever that's worth," said Orca.

"Okay." I extricated myself from Harper's bosom and stood. I stank like stress sweat, and my clothes stuck to my body. Harper grabbed a cloth from the small shelf by the sink, wet it, and ordered me to strip. I didn't have the energy to protest as she sponged me down. As she worked, she murmured soothing nothings, and I let her voice wash over me.

Orca averted her eyes as she handed me clean clothes. I tugged them on, splashed water on my face, fixed my hair, and took a shaky breath.

"I'm ready."

"No, you're not, but we're here for you," said Harper. And, sandwiched between them, I was marched out of my lonely quarters to Miranda's council chamber.

Miranda, Kraken, Ching, and several other ranking sailors looked up at our approach. I steadfastly did not meet Miranda's eyes. Ching—I refused to call her Amaryllis—stared at us from her seat beside Miranda. *My* seat. I sat beside Harper instead, and Orca took Miranda's right-hand chair, as befitted her rank.

I can't look at her without seeing you on top of her.

I fixated on the surface of the wooden table. I'd sat here when Miranda marked me, and through many meetings since. None had felt this painful.

"Nice of you to join us," said Miranda.

She could be such a bitch when she was hurting. Answering would mean acknowledging the gibe, so I folded my hands before me and did my best to look attentive.

"First things first. Some of you have sailed with Ching before. Some of you haven't. Some of you fought against her."

Harper swore beneath her breath and flexed her hands below the table. I grabbed the nearest and held on.

"I need you to put all that behind you."

This, apparently, was too much for Harper.

"That might be a little difficult for those of us she personally tried to have killed."

"Harper—" Miranda began, but Ching cut her off.

"You were never supposed to be harmed," said the most feared woman in the Atlantic.

"Funny how often that doesn't work out."

"*Harper*," Miranda said again.

"Let her get it out." Ching leaned forward and linked her fingers, giving Harper her full attention.

"I saw what you did to our mining stations."

"Conditions weren't exactly something to brag about when I arrived. Given time, I would have fixed that."

"Easy for you to say that now."

"True. Perhaps I should have left conditions at the mines for Comita's daughter to worry about. Tell me, had you even given them a thought before my sailors brought you in?"

Harper's face flushed purple as she tried to stand. I dug my fingers into her hand and tugged her back down. "I'll see you in the ring," she said.

Miranda interceded. "Amaryllis is under my protection. Any grievances you have against her and her past actions will be addressed through me. When not assisting, she will be confined to quarters for her own safety, and I have assigned a guard."

Good. That might make it harder for her to stab me while I slept.

"Where are her quarters?" asked Orca.

"I've had Zia's old room cleared."

I didn't know Zia, or where her room was, but I could ask Orca later.

"Secondly, we're altering our trajectory. We'll finish up mapping this stretch, send in the report, and then let Comita know we're taking an extended leave for repairs. That will buy us some time. Chief Engineer, will this be enough?"

"Conceivably." Harper matched Miranda icy syllable to icy syllable. "Completely accurate predictions are impossible where the admiral is concerned."

"We will resume the work when we return, unless circumstances demand otherwise. Navigator, Amaryllis will supply the coordinates. You will chart us a course. I understand the charts from the south are out of date. We won't know exactly what we're sailing into. That, however, won't be a problem for you, will it?"

"No, Captain," I said. I was just "navigator" now, which is what I had asked for, but it ached.

"Good. You will not need to work directly with Amaryllis, in recognition of your history. All correspondence will go through me or an intermediary. Is that understood?"

"Yes, Captain."

"Engineer, how are we on repairs?"

Harper launched into a detailed explanation of the work that had been done, and the work remaining. Following her report, Miranda grilled the rest of the assembled crew on supplies and armaments. Ching listened to the proceedings with a neutral expression until Miranda began explaining the nature of our new venture. Then, she watched the reactions unfold around the table while I watched her, looking for signs of duplicity. Our eyes met twice. Each time, I glanced away.

"With all due respect, Captain," said the man in charge of inventory, "it's a risky proposition without any guarantee of gain."

"There's never a guarantee."

"The crew is used to raids, where there's a chance of spoils."

"And they'll get a share of whatever we find."

He did not seem satisfied with her answer, but he nodded.

"And if they blow us out of the water?" asked another sailor.

"Wouldn't be the first time someone tried," said Miranda.

The questions continued until the faces around the table seemed temporarily soothed from disgruntled to mildly curious.

Perhaps this sort of thing happened all the time: Miranda appearing before them and suggesting the impossible. It took most of my concentration to prevent my face from seizing up again with tears.

The following weeks were among the most miserable of my life. The sections of coast remaining on our mapping mission were easy enough to navigate. I wished for a storm or jagged underwater promontories; anything to distract me from the crushing pressure on my chest. Harper did her best to cheer me up. I pretended it worked, for her sake.

Sixteen days after Ching Shih reentered my life, Harper and Orca dragged me to the training room. The mat squeaked beneath my bare feet as I settled into a loose fighter's stance. Harper leaned on the ropes with a better's avid interest, and across the mat, stretching her lithe muscles, Orca smirked.

"Ready?" She rolled her shoulders, shook out her arms, and held my gaze while I released a steady stream of air through my nostrils—to ground myself, not because I thought my nose might not survive the bout, though that did occur to me.

"Like it's ever mattered to you if I'm ready or not," I said.

"Fair." She leapt forward and struck out with the heel of her foot, missing my thigh only because I scrambled backward. Orca pressed her advantage. I blocked her first punch and threw my own. It went wide, and I caught my balance in time to feel her palm collide with my ribcage. Cartilage groaned. Jeanine's ravaged chest splayed across my vision. Her death hadn't gotten any easier to process, either.

"Don't feel like you have to pull your punches or anything," I said as my ribs protested against the singular abuse of breathing.

Her response came in the form of a sweeping kick that knocked my feet out from under me.

"Come on, Rose," said Harper. "You're embarrassing me."

I rolled to my side and snared Orca's ankle between my own before she could complete her coup. She hit the mat beside me.

I dove out of the way of her hasty headlock. Her fingers closed over my calf instead, but I kicked her off and bounced to my feet, panting.

She blocked my next uppercut, as I had anticipated. She did not block the left-handed strike I sent to her middle, though she deflected the force of the blow by leaping backward.

"Shouldn't you put your money where your bunk is?" I asked Harper.

"Nah. Gotta keep her on her toes. Watch your—"

The hook caught me in the shoulder. Reeling, I took three hasty steps to catch my balance. Orca sprang forward and we went down again. This time, her headlock trapped me. She pulled me flush against her as her elbow clamped around my throat. I clawed at her forearm, then reached for her head. Teeth met my fingers.

"Foul," I wheezed.

"Yeah, you do taste like ass," she said in my ear.

I kicked at whatever parts of her I could reach with my heels until she wrapped her thighs around me. Trussed and partially suffocated, I tapped out.

"You're getting better," Orca said as she released me. "Still wouldn't bet on you, though."

"Whatever." I tugged my shirt back down over my stomach and rubbed my throat.

"My round." Harper jumped the ropes and rolled her neck.

I stretched while they sparred. Orca and Harper were evenly matched, and the grunts and smack of flesh on flesh didn't seem to favor either one. Orca wore her braids tied up beneath a scarf and Harper had secured her curls in a knot that shed strands each time she lunged. Both panted past grins as they did their best to bloody each other.

"This one's for you," Harper told me as she fixed Orca in a headlock much like the one that had lost me my round. Orca wriggled out with a twist of her torso and leveled Harper with an elbow.

"Spoke too soon," I said.

"She always does." Orca pinned Harper and grinned, scuffling her arms behind her head. Harper growled, then moved her hips in a slow gyration that blew Orca's pupils. Sensing the situation devolving, I finished stretching and took my leave. The moment the door shut behind me, my lungs contracted with grief.

The halls of the ship throbbed with sound. The engine was louder than any fleet ship's, and beyond the mechanical thrum came the sounds of the crew and their families. Children screeched in games that made sense only to them, and the raucous shouts of people calling good-naturedly to each other reverberated off the walls. Exposed pipes were interspersed with stretches of murals and graffiti near the creches.

I followed my usual route from the training room back to my quarters, staring at the scuffed toes of my shoes. Fighting had eased some of the lassitude gripping me, but now it settled back around my neck. I wanted to sleep for a year and wake up in a new life.

"Navigator."

Ching's voice went through me like a spear. I jerked upright and met her gaze. Her hair had grown in a little since I'd first seen her on the *Trench*, but her eyes were still hollow, and the meat remained melted from her bones. She looked like a woman who'd lost everything. Which she had, thanks to me. The animal part of my brain screamed that my death was imminent. However, a familiar sailor stood on Ching's right: Nasrin. Her eyes never left Ching Shih, and she had to weigh at least twice what the former pirate queen did now. Nasrin also ran the ship's main bar, where she bounced her own patrons and "took no shit," in Harper's words. Ching would have to be superhuman to get past her to harm me.

"Ching," I managed to say in acknowledgment.

"Keep close to the shelf for as long as you can."

With that, she passed right by me, leaving me soaked with sweat and trembling.

Keep close to the shelf? Directly against the current? That didn't make sense. Our engines would have to work twice as hard. Sailing through deeper water was far more economical. I turned to ask her for clarification before remembering I was not supposed to engage with her directly—which hadn't stopped Ching, of course.

"Amaryllis," I said.

Her back stiffened, and her right hand gave a minute spasm. She looked back over her shoulder at me. I got the distinct impression she did not appreciate me using her given name.

"Rose," she said, her voice calmer than her body language.

"What's in the deeper waters?"

"Just take my advice, and we won't find out."

The coordinates Ching gave Miranda to give to me, which Miranda had delivered through a note instead of in person, hovered off the coast of the southernmost continent. I stared at the charts with a cup of tea in my hands and the sounds from the bridge below familiar and soothing. I spent more and more of my time in the chart room. Miranda never came here, and I could be alone, save for the occasional shout from Crow's Eye above in the crow's nest. Then, I'd climb up and see for myself what had caught his eye. Squid sometimes, or a swarm I hadn't felt in my distracted state.

Today I planned to finish up the last set of charts for Admiral Comita, but I couldn't concentrate on the task. Sailing south still felt like such a fool's errand, and for what? I'd loved Miranda's idealism once, but now it merely seemed delusional. Worse than delusional—she'd thrown away our relationship for a whale's tale. If she hadn't still clung to this hope, would she have lied to me?

I knew it wasn't that simple. Nothing ever was simple where she was concerned. But blaming the coordinates was easier than blaming myself for my own naivete. The tip of my finger traced the route we'd take.

The sea wolves. The grief living in my chest shifted, presenting me with a different, half-remembered face: my father. He hadn't been a sea wolf. I was sure of that. But if he'd been descended from them? Was the truth about my uncanny navigational abilities as simple as recessive genetics? Could my entire existence be reduced to "Oh yeah, forgot to mention your grandmother was a fucking legend?" Did my mother know? Had she lied, too? Or had he lied to her? Could anyone around me tell the truth?

Worse, what if we got there and the sea wolves took one look at me and dismissed me out of hand? What if they didn't want to claim me either?

The storyteller on *Trench* was wrong. History only hurt. It didn't have anything to teach me I didn't already know. I didn't belong anywhere or with anyone.

Sinking into self-pity wouldn't help me get any work done, but I couldn't pull myself out of it. I missed Miranda. I hated not touching her, not laughing with her as we lay in bed at night going over the day, not falling asleep to the sound of her breathing. Now, when I saw her in the halls or at meals, she gave me a cold nod. I'd hurt her, that nod said, and so she'd give me what I'd asked for: space and the cold professionalism of a captain-navigator relationship. The few times I'd called after her, she just kept walking.

At meals, she sat beside Kraken and Ching. Sometimes Ching said something too quietly for me to hear, and Miranda would smile. Once, Ching brushed a strand of Miranda's hair out of her face in a gesture that spoke of years of familiarity. It wasn't sensual or motherly or sisterly, but something in-between, and Miranda didn't even seem to notice. Ching didn't look up at me afterward and flaunt her closeness with my captain. She didn't say "I made her," as she had once before. She didn't need to. Maybe she didn't even realize she'd done it. There was coldness still between them, but it was the coldness of a relationship that ran too deep to sever. I understood, as I watched them day after day, what I hadn't fully understood before.

Ching, Amaryllis, whatever she wanted to call herself, was more family to Miranda than anyone else on this ship, save maybe Kraken. Definitely more so than I'd ever been. Miranda might not have agreed with Ching's methods when it came to the Archipelago, but she loved Ching Shih. Truly loved her. I'd been an idiot not to realize it before, or what it meant for me. If Miranda had been willing to break with Ching over ideological differences, then breaking with me over the same was inevitable. I would never come first. When I'd asked her for time, I'd been too hurt to process anything but my own heartbreak. I'd wanted a moment to breathe and lick my wounds. I hadn't meant to end things. Not really. But she'd clearly taken it that way.

This is what you wanted, her eyes said each time they met mine. *You asked for this, not me.*

I'd hoped she'd come to me. I'd hoped, like an idiot, for a grand gesture or an apology or some sign she'd be willing to change or provide proof I mattered to her, and instead she'd turned on me like a wounded cat.

"She's been hurt too often and too badly," Kraken said one evening as we walked together. "Give her time. Right now she can't see past the pain, and she can't be rational."

He'd meant to reassure me. Instead, he'd just confirmed what I already knew, and what I'd told Miranda: she would always be the only one who mattered in our relationship. What I needed was immaterial.

Being right sucked.

I shook my head to clear it and got back to the charts.

Man o' War made wake, and our new parts held. The course I'd plotted took us along the South American coastline. Ching's cryptic warning hovered at the back of my mind as I battled the prevailing current. On the bright side, if Comita ever caught up with us—*when* she did, I reminded myself, as it was always safer to assume the worst—at least we could make a case that we'd been continuing her research. Not that she would give us time to make a case. Absconding with her daughter wasn't something she was likely to overlook.

"Check that out," said a lean pilot named Reya. She tapped the sonar screen, then pointed at the view out of the plex. I left the helm, where I'd been making sure the coordinates I'd plotted matched with the ship's instruments, and joined her. The sonar screen was blank, save for variations in the seascape. A few splotches of color appeared, then scattered as the waves clarified, but I immediately saw what had drawn her interest.

To our right lay the sharp slope of the continental shelf. Sunlight pierced the water in shafts, illuminating the incline. To our left, according to the sonar, rose an underwater mountain. I reached for the currents. This deep, the water generally stayed stable, and I'd kept us subbed to avoid a passing storm. Now, though, I detected a disturbance.

"Neptune's balls," I said, pulling back into myself.

"Is it active?" Reya asked.

"Very."

Superheated water poured from the volcano's mouth. Though it was half a mile away and invisible to the naked eye, I felt the impact of the eruption in the roiling water displaced by the temperature change. We didn't want water that hot anywhere near us. Our systems were built to filter water, not to cool it, and the gasses that would escape with the heat were even more deadly.

"Adjust." I called out coordinates to the bridge and took the helm, feeling for any more surprises, like vents in the ocean floor. Surfacing wasn't an option. Waves still dominated topside, and I sensed a large swarm to the east. Ordinary terrors. Volcanoes were different. Fleet prep covered their hazards, but because the Archipelago floated in deep ocean, far away from active vents and mountains, the exercises were largely rhetorical.

"We should be far enough away, right?" asked Reya.

"We should." I tried to scrub my doubts from the words. Why hadn't I sensed this? Had it been too far away? Or had I been too distracted by my own eruptions to notice the threat? I couldn't afford to slip in unknown waters. Volcanic activity vibrated through the ship just past the range of hearing. At least in another decade or two, when the area cooled, there'd be rich mineral deposits to mine, provided we survived long enough to report it.

The wheel felt strange under my hand. I'd gotten used to inputting coordinates, and the manual override reminded me of the trawler I'd sailed with Miranda, Orca, Jeanine, Kraken, and Finn. *Man o' War*, however, was a much larger ship, and I kept my touch steady to avoid overcompensating as I took us closer to the shelf and farther away from the active blow.

"Incoming." Reya pointed at the sonar again. Shapes took form from the deeps.

"Shouldn't be a problem." I gritted my teeth anyway. The other reason volcanoes were dangerous was their propensity for attracting squid. I didn't understand it. They were normally drawn to cooler waters, but something about eruptions lured them, whether it was minerals or a food source we hadn't identified, and they didn't like intrusions. We watched them circle the ship, first on the radar, and then in front of us through the plex. Long bodies jetted past, equipped with eyes the size of plates and long, questing tentacles. Sweat poured down my back as nausea gripped me. Squid like these had killed Jeanine, and had nearly killed Orca back on the trawler.

"Get the fuck outta here," said another crew member.

I, too, wished the squid a speedy return to Davy Jones's. One plastered itself to the plex. Reya, after an initial burst of cursing, held her hand to the plastic. The sucker nearest was easily the size of her palm, and the creature dwarfed her. Crow's Eye had to be getting a real show. At least I was glad I was not in the crow's nest.

"You really fought one of these?" Reya asked as if reading my mind. I wondered who she'd heard the story from, for it varied depending on the teller. I pinched the web between my forefinger and thumb to try to ease the nausea.

"Kraken and Orca did the fighting." All I'd done was save Orca's life; she'd wielded the sword that stopped the squid from dismantling our ship.

"That's not what I heard." The squid currently latched to the plex peeled away and dove back to its lair, leaving a few of its smaller brethren to harass us as we sailed. "Orca says you held your own."

"She's just building me up so she looks better when she kicks my ass in the ring," I said, trying to inject a lightness into my tone I didn't feel.

"Sounds about right. You sure we can't head deeper? We could avoid all this." She gestured at the plex, then at the sonar.

I hesitated before answering. The coast was volatile. Every day could be one near disaster after another. Deep ocean carried comparatively fewer threats. Ching's warning made little sense. And now that I thought about it, why had she delivered it in the hall instead of passing it through the channels set up by Miranda?

Doubt gnawed like a ship's rat. What if Ching hadn't wanted Miranda to know she'd told me to stick to the coast? Possible reasons for this scenario flashed before me like the jetting squid. Maybe she had friends lying in wait. Leave it to Ching Shih to plot an ambush from afar. Or maybe she wanted to watch the ship sink, her own life be damned, in a twisted game of revenge. I'd let her get under my skin and affect my judgment, putting us at risk.

The smart thing to do would have been to go to Miranda for clarification and ask her to interrogate Ching for more information. But I couldn't.

"Mapping this shit isn't worth it," Reya added.

"I know."

The look on her face suggested she understood the subtext of my words. None of this felt worth it to me.

I'd tracked our location on the charts earlier that day, making note of measurements that differed from previous accounts. Depth readings varied drastically, and in them I read cataclysmic change. Whatever shift in plates had made them must have caused a tsunami unlike anything recorded. It also revealed the unpredictability of our course.

"I'll check the charts," I said to Reya. "We can at least avoid this sector."

My constant awareness of the ocean calmed as I directed *Man o' War* past the shelf. The drop-off yawned beneath us, and past it was open ocean. The ship's engines stopped their somewhat asthmatic chugging as we broke free of the current, and subsided into a pleased purr. I'd reassess our course tomorrow, I decided, and consult with Miranda, no matter how painful that prospect would no doubt be.

Walking back to my bunk took me past the captain's quarters. I slowed instead of hurrying as I'd done over the previous weeks and rested my fingers on the handle: not to open it, but to pretend, just for a second, I was going home.

Inside, I heard voices.

"Absolutely not," said Miranda. The words were muffled, but she'd spoken loudly. Another voice responded. I couldn't make it out. ". . . my crew," Miranda continued, more quietly, but I caught those two words. Something in her tone alarmed me. I pressed my ear to the door.

". . . willing to make sacrifices," came a voice I hadn't wanted to ever overhear coming from Miranda's rooms. My cheek felt suddenly feverish against the plex and damp with perspiration. Of course it was Ching fucking Shih. I pictured her sitting on one of the couches, elbows on her knees as she leaned forward to make her case to Miranda. *My* Miranda.

"I said no." Miranda's voice was firm and cold. Hearing it reassured me.

"You don't have anything else to offer them, Mere."

"Get out."

I jumped as I realized Miranda had just ordered Ching to leave, which would bring me face to face with both of them the moment the door opened. *No thank you.* I bolted for my quarters, whipping inside just as I heard Miranda's door open. *Safe.* But what in all seven seas had Ching said to piss Miranda off?

The following day brought us into a patch of sea calm and clean enough for us to surface. Miranda brought the ship topside and cleared the decks for recreation and dispute resolution. I stayed in the chart room, avoiding the confrontation I needed to have with my captain about our course.

"Hey, what are you doing in here?" Harper leaned in the

doorway, smudges covering her face and coveralls. "Come get some sun while we still can."

"I've got work."

"It can wait a half hour. When was the last time you breathed fresh air?"

"The air is fresher in here than it is out there."

"You're the ass that gave the all clear."

"Yeah, well." I bent back over my chart, which was a mistake. Harper grabbed a handful of my hair and yanked my head back up. Hair follicles protested.

"You need to get out of your head."

"Difficult. It's attached to me."

"Funny girl. Seriously, though. It would be good for you to get some sunlight."

"I don't want to, Harp." The words came out more harshly than I'd intended.

"Fine. Stay up here and be cranky." She paused at the doorway to look back over her shoulder. Hurt was writ across the downward tug of her mouth, and she rubbed one forearm.

"I'm sorry," I mumbled. "I just . . ."

"I get it."

"I know you're trying to help."

"I could kick her ass for you. Would that make it better?"

I pictured Harper landing her signature right cross punch on Miranda's jaw and winced. "Then I'd just feel sorry for her."

Harper scoffed and perched on the table beside me. "She's been shitty to you. Not just about Ching and all that."

This wasn't a conversation I wanted to have, but Harper continued.

"Branding you? That thing with the whip and Annie? And how she always thinks she knows what's best for you? You made the right call. I know you love her, but she needs to get her shit together. You deserve better."

"I don't know about that."

"No. You do." She put her arm around my head and pulled me into her chest, effectively smothering further protests, and spoke into my hair. "You deserve someone who treats you as an equal."

"That can't happen if she's captain," I said into the comfort of her breast.

"Sure it can. She just needs to learn how to compromise."

"As if."

"You're a catch, Rose."

I didn't feel like one. She let me go, fixing my rumpled hair in the process.

"Stay and play with your charts if that makes you happy. I'm going to get some sun and watch idiots fight. Don't say I didn't invite you."

"Wouldn't dream of it."

"And hold your ground. Make her come to you."

"Not much chance of that," I said.

"Then that's her loss."

Harper sauntered out of the chart room, leaving me to stare at the coordinates I'd plotted. The new course was shorter. I promised myself I'd run it by Miranda as soon as I had finalized the details. Despite Harper's advice, I also contemplated throwing myself at her feet and begging her to talk to me, pride and principles be damned. So what if she'd lied? So what if her needs came first? I could live with that.

Remembering I was pathetic didn't help my mood. I returned to my charts.

The blare of the alarm startled me out of my seat a half hour later. Cursing drifted down from the crow's nest. I bolted for the ladder and scrambled up, losing my footing twice in my haste. Crow's Eye, the pirate who permanently manned the post, stabbed a finger at the plex when I emerged, and I froze.

A ship. Her hull was blue-green to match the waves, and narrow, and the slope of her upper deck confused my Archipel-ago-trained eye.

"Who?" I asked.

"No fucking idea. They came out of nowhere."

"You sounded the alarm?"

"Aye."

109

"But sonar didn't pick up—"

"Exactly."

I half fell down the ladder and landed hard enough to send pain through my knees and into my hips. Limping, I raced as best I could out of the chart room and down the catwalks to the bridge. Chaos met me. Miranda stood in the center, shouting orders, and crew shoved past me as they obeyed. Reya grabbed my arm and hauled me over to the radar.

"Fucking nothing."

The screen was blank, save for the occasional expected aberration. Where the ship now floated beside us was only open ocean as far as our radar was concerned.

"Do we still have people on deck?" I asked.

Reya nodded. "The captain is ordering the hatch sealed in five."

Harper. I moved, and Reya grabbed my arm again.

"Our place is here. We've got to lose them before they blow a hole in our hull."

I struggled against her grip. "There are people—"

"Miranda's got raiders. You're our navigator."

If Harper was killed—

I stopped myself, breathing in and out to each cardinal direction. Reya was right. I couldn't do anything for Harper by charging toward the hatch, but I could help us dodge our attacker.

Man o' War shuddered and listed sideways.

"Fucking fuck," Reya shouted.

"Seal every level. Evacuation protocols for breaches only." Miranda's voice carried over the chaos. "To your stations."

Order returned as sailors flung themselves into the business of staying afloat.

"Captain," I said, coming to attention as if she were a fleet captain instead of a mercenary—which proved the effectiveness of fleet discipline in times of crisis, I supposed. "Chief of Engineering was on deck as of half an hour ago."

"Then she better get her ass back inside. You." Miranda pulled a sailor off her screen. "Go find Patrice and tell her to report to engineering if she isn't there already. She's acting chief until we

110

track down Harper."

The sailor sprinted to do her bidding.

"I need a damage report before I can—" I began.

"Manage without. We've got a hole somewhere and they've only been here ten minutes. If we don't get the fuck out of here soon—"

The ship shuddered again, and silence fell on the bridge. Miranda's lips thinned. As her navigator, I could see only one possible course, and I didn't think she was going to like it. I also knew by the grim set of her jaw she'd already come to the same conclusion.

"Bring me Finn," she said. 'We need to open communication."

Most communications took place in the closet-sized room where Finn worked, but the bridge had its own simpler system for emergencies. This counted as an emergency. Miranda dictated her message for the rest of the bridge crew to hear as soon as Finn limped in.

I'd been avoiding him since Jeanine's death. Dark circles bloomed beneath his eyes, and he'd lost weight. I'd feel guilty about that once we weren't sinking.

"Parley. Send it on all frequencies," said Miranda.

Finn worked quickly. I, meanwhile, stared at the sonar screen and tried to make sense of what I wasn't seeing. No swarms hovered to give them shelter, and deeper swarms wouldn't have given them cover this close to the surface. Something about their hull, then, must reflect or deflect our radar. I sincerely doubted they'd let me inspect it, seeing as they were doing their best to sink us, but from here I could make out a shimmering substance coating it like glass. I could also see our upper deck. The figures were too distant to make out, but the red stains on the rec area were unmistakably blood. I grabbed a pair of binoculars from a hook and searched for Harper.

None of the faces that came into focus belonged to my crew. The clothing, too, was different, though subtly so, as it was just as varied as the clothes worn on *Man o' War*. Most of the enemy sailors wore their hair in locks. All were armed. Shaking, I lowered the lens. No response came over Finn's equipment. He tried again. We waited. Still nothing.

Footsteps pounded toward the bridge door at a dead run. Reya opened it, and a ship's runner burst through and halted, heaving, in front of Miranda.

"They've taken the first two decks and breached three of the lower."

"Taken?"

"Hostages. I don't—no one—we don't have any idea what language they speak."

That explained the communications. Or, just as likely, they'd realized they didn't need to worry about parleying since they held all the cards. Miranda stared out the plex at the ship surfaced beside us. I'd never seen her look so grim.

"Some things are universal," she said. "We don't have much choice here, do we?"

I expected someone to argue or at least offer blustering bravado to keep face. Which just went to show how little I knew these people.

"Mere—" I said. Our differences didn't matter right now. Only Harper did.

"They have hostages." It wasn't an explanation, but it was all she gave me as she set off at a fast clip for the door.

"Where are you going?" Reya asked as I peeled away to follow Miranda. I didn't answer. Harper needed me. I didn't know what, if anything, my presence would do to help, but I wasn't going to sit by while she—or Miranda—got hurt. I caught up with her in a few jogging steps. She didn't stop me or tell me to go back to the bridge. Neither did she welcome my presence.

Crew lined the halls. Many had armed themselves. Miranda explained the situation to a few as we went, and those few made it their business to pass it along. Everyone was to cooperate unless the boarders turned violent, and then they were to fight like their lives and ship depended on it. We could hear the sounds of a struggle by the time we got to the hatch that led to the first occupied level.

"Do exactly as I say and stay behind me," said Miranda.

"Yes, Captain."

Heedless of the watching crew, she grabbed my collar and kissed me hard before turning the hatch door.

I reeled. My lips ached for her, but I stifled the desperate whine that welled up in my throat and followed her to our fate.

Sailors sat in bound clusters in the hall. A few lay unconscious or dead, and I averted my eyes before I could recognize them. I needed to stay present, and grief would dull that. The dead would still be dead in an hour or a day or a year. Enemy sailors barked orders at each other in a language my ear strained to recognize, or at least draw a comparison with from the languages I did know. Most Archipelageans spoke the tongue that had developed out of our founding language stock: a blend of English, Spanish, and Arabic that veered at times in one direction or another, depending on the station or the ship. This didn't sound like any of them.

Enemy sailors looked up at our arrival. A woman moved to attack, sword drawn, but Miranda held up her hands and pointed to her chest, then the ship beneath her feet. *Captain,* that gesture said.

Our would-be attacker nodded in understanding and said something to the people nearest her. A man detached himself from securing more hostages and motioned for us to follow him. I wished Kraken was with us, or Orca. Both of them would be more useful than I would be to Miranda in a fight. On the other hand, there wasn't much we could do against odds like these. Strangers filled our decks. The other ship was big, and they'd had the element of surprise. Periodically the ship shuddered again, though not from more attacks; the breached decks were just filling with water. "Just—" as if that wasn't catastrophe enough.

The number of our sailors huddled in guarded knots didn't match the census. More were either in hiding or had barricaded themselves elsewhere. I refused to consider the option that they'd been slaughtered. There wasn't enough blood. This was the only thing that gave me comfort. If our enemies had intended wholesale slaughter, they would not be wasting time keeping people under guard, which suggested they wanted what most pirates wanted: supplies, or perhaps new sailors to flesh out their crew.

A man nearly as large as Kraken greeted our party with a frown and a phrase. He had a neatly trimmed—though massive—beard, and a prominent scar beneath his right eye. I watched him take in Miranda's scars as he spoke again. Miranda shook her head and repeated the same gesture she'd made before.

A girl stepped forward. She didn't look much older than sixteen. In clear, though oddly accented North Atlantic, she said, "Greetings from the *Docile*."

Either the ship's name didn't translate well, or the captain had a sick sense of humor.

"I am the captain of *Man o' War*. I'd welcome you aboard, but you've already made yourself at home."

The girl translated, and the big man laughed.

"I've been informed you have hostages," Miranda said before he could respond. "I am willing to cooperate."

He spoke, and the girl, after a moment's pause, said, "We are glad to hear it. Nobody else needs to get hurt, as long as you give us what we want."

"May I stabilize my ship first?"

He spread his arms wide, as if to indicate it was stable enough.

"He says, 'No. That is your problem, not ours. Your hostages will remain on our ship until we've received our demands.'"

"What do you want?"

The girl rattled off a list longer than my arm, which included algae strains, tech, medical supplies, and food. My eyes widened. We'd be beggared if they took all that, and we'd have to return north immediately. I searched the faces of the enemy crew for some explanation.

Cheekbones jutted out at me. Beneath their clothing, I detected a few ribs. Not enough to suggest long-term starvation, but poor condition, combined with the scabbed-over wounds I

114

noticed on a few, helped me start putting together at least one possible explanation. This man's crew had been through rough times recently. If our roles were reversed, I knew Miranda would do the same. That didn't make me any happier about it. Much of what he demanded had come from the Archipelago. If he took it, we wouldn't be able to replace it without raiding or returning to Comita.

But goods were nothing compared to people, and he had our sailors. Even as we negotiated, if this could fairly be called a negotiation, his crew herded their captives toward the upper deck. Was Harper with them? Captive was better than dead, but in the heat of that initial assault, she would have fought tooth and nail, ready to die before surrendering, *because she was an idiot like that.*

North.

South.

East—

"Ask him about our dead," I said to Miranda.

He noticed me for the first time, and his mouth twisted into a snarl. I didn't have time to react. My arms were jerked behind me even as Miranda threw herself between me and his crew. An elbow wrapped around my head, muffling my struggles, but I heard the thud of something heavy hitting flesh, followed by Miranda's grunt.

I stopped fighting. The hold on my neck loosened enough for me to breathe, and I saw her on her knees, one arm clutching the opposite shoulder. Her arm hung awkwardly in the socket as a sailor lowered his cudgel.

"Not. Her." Miranda's words came out in a wheeze.

The girl waited for her captain to finish a string of guttural words, then translated: "He says she is one of them. We will take her, and some justice will be served."

"One of who? She is a part of my crew. Whoever you think—"

But I knew who they thought I was. No matter where I went, it was the same.

"I am not a sea wolf," I said past my choke hold.

The girl frowned, as if my words didn't make sense. Maybe

they didn't call them sea wolves, whoever these sailors were. I pointed at my eyes and tried again. "I am not one of them."

Perhaps it was even true.

The captain spat on the ground. "He doesn't believe you," she translated unnecessarily.

"She's from the Archipelago," said Miranda in rising desperation.

"We do not know what that is."

"North. Big stations. Fuck— she's just my navigator. Let her go." She turned to me as she spoke, and the anguish in her eyes undid me.

The girl and the man conversed for what felt like a geological era. At last, she said, "She will come with us, and you will hurry to get us what we want if you wish her to live."

Miranda opened her mouth to speak. I never heard what she said. A sound cracked above my ear as light burst in sparks across my vision, followed by sickening darkness.

Chapter Six

"Hey."

A cool hand on my forehead. Light. Sound. I tried opening my eyes, but one of them didn't respond, and without its twin, the other couldn't focus. Shapes swam. My stomach roiled, and I groaned.

"Good to see you, too. Are you—yes, yes you are. Here."

Rough plastic touched my cheek as I vomited. I heaved until the heaving sent black sparks skittering across my eyes and my head pulsed with a pain that made me more sympathetic toward tectonic plates. It felt like the plates of my own skull were scraping against each other.

"No, you can't pass out again. Trust me, I wish I could, too, but they want us to move."

Moving was most definitely not an option. I groaned again.

"Rose."

I recognized the voice saying my name with dim clarity. "Harp?"

"Yeah, baby, it's me. Come on. I need you to sit up for me, can you do that?"

"Ughhnn."

"I know. They got me pretty bad, too, which is why I'm not

carrying you. They're letting us go, though, so you need to sit up. They're not gonna be gentle with you."

"I. Can't see."

"No shit. Might be a good thing in case you pass a mirror."

"Are. You. Hurt?" I'd been worried about Harper. I remembered that much. Everything else was fuzzy and smelled faintly of lemon, which didn't make sense.

"Yeah, but it's okay. We're alive, and we're going back to the ship. You got hit in the head pretty bad. This is, like, the third time we've had this conversation. You gotta stay with me now, though."

"The ship." It was so hard to think. It had never been this hard to think before, had it? Why were we not on our ship? There had been another ship. Two ships, and one . . . one hadn't shown up on sonar, which was a problem because—

Harper grabbed the bucket just in time to catch a dribble of bile and saliva.

"Okay. Real slow. Don't think about anything right now except me, okay? Don't nod. I guarantee that won't end well. I'm going to put my arm around you and we're going to stand up together, which is going to be real fun for us both."

I didn't find out whether or not we had fun, as I passed out again. When consciousness next assaulted me with its sights and sounds and smells and—*Neptune's balls, my head hurts*—I was upright, though to say I was "standing" stretched the definition of the word past its breaking point. Harper panted the shallow breaths of a person in pain as she supported me. Vague shapes and noises that might have been other humans came in and out of my vision. People were speaking, but I didn't understand anything they said.

Harper hissed occasionally as we shuffled forward. I wanted to ask her how badly she was hurt, but my tongue didn't cooperate. To say each step was agony would have quantified it. Nothing about our journey was quantifiable. My ability to gauge anything fluctuated dizzyingly. The ringing in my ears and the harsh sound of our pained breathing drowned everything else out. I might have gotten sick again. I wasn't sure. Harper kept us moving forward.

It felt like a perpetual fall, and once she shouted at someone to back off, which I didn't understand, since we were now floating in a thick fog of colors and the smell of lemons.

Eventually, however, I registered a difference in my surroundings: sea air. I tried to orient myself instinctively. Nothing happened except that my head let out a new pulse of pain, and so I stopped and focused instead on putting one foot in front of the other, which I fancied I was getting slightly better at, though one of my feet drooped in a way I didn't remember.

"Please be careful with her," Harper said.

I was lifted and laid against something warm. It moved, and I moved with it. Another voice, this one not Harper's, said my name in a deep rumble. The rumble came from beneath my ear, which made as little sense as anything else. The movement was punctuated with even beats that sent spikes through my temple.

"She's concussed; don't touch her too much." Harper again.

"Put her down here." Another voice. I knew that voice. I tried opening my good eye, but then the warm bulk lowered me, and I had to focus on not getting sick as everything spun and spun and spun and—

Light turned the backs of my eyelids red. I reached up to touch my head, which throbbed horribly, and my fingers encountered stiff bandaging and hot, puffy flesh where I was used to having an eye.

"Easy on that." I turned my good eye slowly toward the speaker. He came into focus with some squinting: Finn.

"Ow." It was not what I'd intended to say. I'd meant to ask several questions in quick succession—namely, what happened, is everyone okay, and is there still an eye beneath this mess, but being conscious was growing increasingly more uncomfortable with each passing second.

"Oh, friend, don't I know." He smiled sympathetically, then added, "you might recall that I, too, have experience with head injuries and, if not, you will eventually. I wouldn't try to do too much thinking right now."

"Miranda."

"There."

I slowly rolled my eye in the direction he'd indicated. Miranda sat slumped in a chair with her head tilted to one side, asleep.

"I'll wake her in a moment. This is the first time I've seen her sleep in days."

"Days? Oh. Right." The past seventy-two hours came back to me. The attack, my capture, and the agonizing period that followed. Someone had cleaned the wound on my head with stinging iodine, and lights had been flashed in my eyes. Tests had been done to determine the extent of neurological damage. Eventually, I'd been ordered to sleep.

"Relax, kid."

"My eye."

"Will be fine. You have a nasty cut above it, but the swelling is coming down."

"Harper."

"Also fine. Broken ribs, several stab wounds, nothing lethal or infected."

"That's not fine."

"She's alive and she kept you alive. I'm going to wake the captain now. You're going to reassure her *you're* alive, and then you're going to rest again."

"Okay."

I closed my eye while Finn roused Miranda to give it a moment to recover from the strain of seeing. When I opened it next, Miranda leaned over me. She looked anguished and beautiful and ragged around every edge.

"Mere."

"Hi." She cupped my cheek and tried to smile. Her lower lip quivered.

"I'm fine. Finn said so."

"Finn's a liar." The trembling in her lower lip worsened, and something hot and wet landed on my chin.

"Finn wants to remind you that Rose needs to rest," said Finn.

"Everything's all fuzzy," I said to Miranda. "Our hull was breached, wasn't it?"

She smoothed my hair with a touch so light I almost didn't feel it. "We patched it."

"Will you still love me with only one eye?"

"Of course. And your eye is fine."

It didn't feel fine, but I decided not to mention that, as speaking ground the bones in my head together.

I was aware of Finn standing and murmuring something to Miranda, but I kept my good eye fixed on her face. *Of course*, she'd said.

"Stay with me?"

In response, she lowered herself onto the bed beside me, and I turned into her, tangling my hand in her shirt and breathing in the fear sweat and the stress and the lingering hint of hibiscus that clung to her skin. My hair absorbed her tears.

I was allowed to remove the bandage two days later—or at least, I thought it was two days. Time stretched like melting plastic and I struggled to hold on to thoughts.

"This might hurt a little. It's adhered to your skin again." Miranda sat cross-legged on the bed before me with clean cloths and a bottle of iodine. I closed my good eye and tensed as her fingers probed the edges of the bandage. I could tell whatever she found displeased her by the way she exhaled.

The first few lengths of bandage unwound easily. They'd been carefully wrapped so not to add pressure to my head, and I barely felt them save for the occasional pulled hair. The bandaging packed over the wound itself was a different matter. Miranda drizzled iodine over the cloth and picked at the edges, peeling them back with care. They must have changed the packing previously, but I blissfully had no memory of that, or else I would have known what was coming.

"Brace yourself."

"Ow." The bandage peeled away, and iodine ran into the wound and down my nose. Pain seared my vision as I squinted involuntarily, then tried to open the eye. Something had gummed it shut, but the light that snuck in through the cracks burned. Miranda slowly worked the gunk free, a process that involved equal parts holding damp cloths to my eye and glaring at the wound.

"Infected?" I asked.

"A little. I'm going to need to flush it."

"What does that—" I stopped speaking as my skin prickled and sweat sprang from every pore. My stomach clenched. She'd filled a syringe without me noticing, and cold, awful liquid flooded the inflamed skin and enraged it further. I would have cursed if I hadn't been gagging. Something foul-smelling dripped onto my upper lip. Miranda wiped it away.

"Again."

"No, please, I can't—*fuck.*" It hurt even more the second time. I gagged, choked, and screamed in a simultaneous gurgle that spiked my headache.

"Done."

I panted through the nausea and tried to muster up the strength to curse her out. All I managed was the breathing.

"It's going to be quite the scar."

"Show me."

She hesitated, but nodded. "You'll have to stand."

"I can."

I couldn't. The room spun the moment I stood, but with her help I made it to the private bathroom in her quarters and clung to the sink. Above it, small and clean and unfortunately clear, hung her mirror.

Half of my reflection was familiar. Amber eye. Messy curls. Slightly pointed chin. The other half looked like it belonged to a sea slug. Greens and blues and purples and yellows mottled the swollen flesh around the gash in my forehead. It started an inch below my hairline and split my eyebrow. The only thing that had saved the eye itself was the bone around the socket, which hadn't obviously broken, though it looked—and felt—as if it might have suffered a small fracture. My eye was an overripe tomato. The bruising continued into my cheek, and bloodshot whites surrounded the small slit of visible iris.

"If you want to keep me in the brig, I'd understand," I said, trying to joke.

"Can't. The brig flooded and we're still drying it out."

Something about her tone was too light, but I couldn't focus on it. Not with my busted face oozing and the ship spinning. I reached for north to steady myself and came up empty. I tried again. Nothing.

"Mere—"

She grabbed me as I began to slide to the ground. Without north to cling to, the world felt unknowable and all too vast, like I'd fallen off the edge of the map. Long before other people had made much of my navigational abilities, long before anyone but my mother even knew something about me was different, I'd found solace in the cardinal points. The sea yawned to every horizon. Directions organized it into quadrants, and quadrants could be measured and therefore understood. Without that, I was little more than sargassum. What if the head blow had damaged my compass? What if I never recovered?

"Stop it." Miranda's hands squeezed mine. I gazed at her through bleary eyes and tried to calm my thoughts.

"I need to lie down."

"Easy." She lowered me to the pillow and covered me with a light sheet. The painting of the Portuguese man o' war framed her as she sat at my side, still bearing the hole she'd punched through the canvas. She gazed down at me like she wished she knew how to put my broken pieces back together.

I wished I knew, too.

The knock on the door roused me from the state of perpetual half-sleep now dominating my existence.

"I'm coming in."

123

Sounds from the corridor pounced on my bruised brain as Harper let herself into my quarters. Her shuffling movements confused me until Orca came into view with Harper leaning on her arm. A crutch supported Harper's other side, and sweat slicked her face.

"Sit," I said, sitting up myself too quickly in my haste to see her off her feet. I was used to the room spinning by now, and counted out a long exhale while I waited for Harper and Orca to come back into focus.

Orca appeared unharmed. Harper, however, had clearly been beaten badly. Bruising mottled most of her exposed skin, and I remembered Finn telling me about her broken ribs as she wheezed. He'd said something about stab wounds, too.

"You look like hell," I said.

"You're not looking too sweet yourself."

"Why can't you walk?"

"Fuckers got me in the leg. I'd show you, but I'm not supposed to take the bandage off, according to this squid shit."

Orca ignored the insult aimed in her direction and looked me over. "Finn says you're concussed pretty bad."

"Thought I'd let you feel like you were smarter than me for a bit." I was proud of my comeback, but hoped I didn't need to try for more repartee anytime soon. Carrying on a conversation was like trying to hold water in my hands.

"Didn't knock any sense into you, though, did it?" said Harper. Her expression sobered. "I thought they'd killed you."

"When?"

"They dragged you in with the rest of the hostages. Your face was covered in blood, and you weren't moving and—"

Orca put an arm around Harper's shoulders. Taking another wheezing breath, Harper continued.

"I got them to leave you with me."

"How?"

"You don't want to know, and I'm not telling you. You could have died, Rose."

"Says the woman with multiple stab wounds." Another comeback. I gave myself a point.

"Stabs, schmabs. Speaking of bitches with knives, tell the captain I'm mad at her for not letting me see you until now."

"She wouldn't let you in?"

"You know she would have been here otherwise. Miranda's been . . ." Orca trailed off.

"What?"

"A nightmare. Listen, Rose." Orca leaned in and stared intently into my face. "She's neglecting her ship. I'm covering as much as I can, but she needs—"

"You promised not to stress her out," said Harper.

"This is important."

"What's important?" I asked.

"She needs to be more present. To deal with this shit."

"What shit?"

"Orca," said Harper, giving her a meaningful look.

"Just the usual. Plus, we're fucked if we don't get new supplies soon. It will take weeks for our stocks to grow back. The crew needs to know their captain cares more about them than just you. No offense."

"None taken." The thought of Miranda neglecting her crew in a time of crisis to care for me eased the pain in my head, even as I scolded myself for being selfish. This wasn't the proof of her affection I needed. I knew she loved me. I just didn't think she knew how to be what I needed. A problem for a time when my head didn't feel like an unlanced boil. "What are we going to do about supplies?"

"We're not telling you anything. You'll start plotting courses or whatever and then your brain won't recover," said Harper.

"Just tell Miranda you don't need her by you twenty-four hours a day."

I nodded carefully. "Who's navigating?"

"Reya and the rest."

"You're starting to think about it. No. Not allowed."

I didn't know how to tell Harper that no matter how I strained, the cardinal points eluded me. In their place was a yawning abyss so dark and deep it took years for light to filter through the water if it ever managed to do so at all.

"But you're going to be okay?" I asked.

"Yeah. Nothing's seriously infected, and it hurts like salt water up your ass, but I'll live."

The increased frequency of her cursing suggested it hurt far worse than a seawater enema. I didn't contradict her.

"I'll talk to Miranda," I promised.

I didn't have to wait long to make good on my word.

"That's enough," Miranda snapped at Harper and Orca as she shut the door behind her.

"You can't—"

"I damn well can. Out."

Harper's eyes flashed, and her lips curled in a snarl as she prepared to argue.

"Sure thing, Captain," said Orca. Her hand closed over Harper's wrist in a clear warning.

"No. She's not your prisoner, Miranda. I have just as much right—"

"Out."

I'd witnessed Harper Comita back down from a fight three times in my life. Two of those instances were with her mother, who, as admiral, was the embodiment of the law. I'd written the third off as an anomaly. I prayed, for all our sakes, this would become the fourth. Harper glowered at Miranda from beneath black brows. Her full lips had thinned to a gash, and the tendons in her neck stood out from her skin, shiny with sweat. She looked every inch a warrior. The moment stretched as their gazes locked. Harper was injured, but I knew from experience that wouldn't stop her. I didn't think it would stop Miranda, either.

"I'm fine," I said. "Really, Mere. It was nice to see them."

"I gave you an order, Comita."

"With all due respect, *Captain*," Harper spat, "I'm not in the habit of obeying stupid orders."

"Shut up, both of you," I said. "You're hurting my head."

As I'd hoped, they swung to fix me with concerned expressions, temporarily avoiding bloodshed. I took advantage of it. "Miranda, please. You have a ship to run. Harper can stay with me, since she's . . ." I couldn't think of the right word and gestured at Harper's battered body.

"I can spell you, too," offered Orca.

"Like hell you will. I'm not leaving you alone with her."

"Miranda, *stop*." The pleading in my voice arrested her. She seated herself on the foot of the bed and put a hand on my leg in contrition. Steel remained in her gaze.

"Harper can stay with you tomorrow if she gets the fuck out of here right now."

We weren't going to get a better deal. Orca knew it, even if Harper did not, and she half hauled Harper out of the room without looking at the captain. Miranda buried her face in her hands when the door clicked shut behind them.

"You can't do that, Mere."

"I can," she said into her fingers.

"And Orca—"

"I don't want to hear about Orca."

I gave up. My head throbbed and the room spun. Focusing on anything else took too much effort. After a while, she murmured, "I'm sorry."

I kept my eyes shut and did not acknowledge I'd heard.

The lemons, small and irregular shaped as some of them were, didn't lend themselves to stacking. My tower collapsed again. Prepared this time, Seamus lunged as the fruits rolled across the floor of the receiving room and toward the edge of the carpet.

"You'll regret it," I warned him as he pounced and sank his teeth into a yellow peel. Letting him puncture the fruit was wasteful. I promised myself I'd eat it, along with the other damaged specimens before it had time to turn.

Seamus sneezed, squinted his eyes, and backed away from the offending zest.

"Told you so."

The scent of citrus filled the air. My nose struggled to detect it, which didn't make any sense, since it smelled lemons when there were none. Its failure to register the real thing was another reminder nothing about my brain functioned the way I'd depended on it to function my entire life. I rolled the rind across my upper lip.

Behind me, the door clicked open. Miranda's footsteps fell lightly on the braided rug, then stopped. I didn't look up at her.

"Lemons?"

"Seamus hates them." I held the fruit out toward the cat. He humped his back and twitched his tail in displeasure.

Miranda sprawled on the couch and took a sip from her flask. "Bored?"

"No."

"Right. Because you're playing with lemons. My mistake."

"Watch." I piled them on top of each other, getting a stack of six before my work disintegrated. Seamus watched one roll toward him and, though his flattened ears suggested he thought it unwise, batted it with his paw.

"Do you want to try eating in the mess?"

I abandoned all pretense of being amused by fruit and looked up. The motion barely hurt; two weeks of confinement had been good for that much, if nothing else. Harper had kept good on the promise she'd made Miranda not to tax my brain, and mostly spent the hours we shared fiddling with spare parts of machinery or napping beside me. "Really?"

"It might be too soon."

"No, I'll come." I rose carefully and collected my lemons, threatening my balance with dire punishments if it failed me now. My feet obeyed with only a slight delay. The drop in the left was getting better, and the world didn't spin as wildly as it had for the first week.

I still couldn't reach north, and we hadn't spoken at all about

128

the tenuous status of our relationship.

Miranda waited while I glanced at my reflection. The cut was fully scabbed now, and the bruising had retreated. Both my eyes opened fully. Focusing was still a hit or miss, and the nausea was constant, but I needed to get out of this room. No one would tell me anything about what was happening around me, except for whatever sanitized version they thought wouldn't stress me. The fact it needed to be sanitized, however, itched more than my healing forehead. Without the cardinal points and the currents, I was worse than blind.

Miranda led me by the hand—though out of necessity, rather than tenderness—and we entered the mess hall together. Heads turned. My pulse leapt with anticipation that maybe for once they were happy to see me, until I realized the eyes leveled in our direction were sullen, not relieved.

It wasn't that I'd expected cheers. The crew had learned to accept me as best they ever would. Resentment, though, was new. Or rather, it was familiar, but not from here. *North Star* had resented me. *Man o' War* disliked me on principle, and perhaps because I'd helped raze Ching's fleet, but they didn't look at me like I'd stolen something from them. Miranda didn't seem to notice. That didn't make sense, either. Miranda was observant, especially when it came to her crew.

"Steady," she said in my ear as I stumbled. I refocused my efforts on walking.

The captain's table, at least, let out a whoop at my approach. Harper leapt up, cursed as her wounded leg buckled, and settled for waving from her seat. Kraken smiled and gave me a nod. Orca nodded too, but her eyes were on the rest of the mess hall, and I knew she'd seen what I had and was just as worried. The rest of the chiefs were more subdued in their greetings. I bared my teeth in a smile burdened beneath the work of conveying joy and simultaneously keeping the contents of my stomach where they belonged.

"You chose a good day to return," Kraken said.

"Why's that?"

"Our first batch of roasts was ready to harvest."

"Roasts?" My mind struggled to recall any conversation from before my injury, but this time, regrettably, it dredged up a discussion about sea roaches. "No."

"They're not bad," said Miranda.

"Even Orca ate them," said Harper.

Orca snorted and raised an eyebrow. "I don't turn down food. That doesn't mean I wanted to *see* them in their natural state, thank you very much. If you don't know what they look like they're fucking delicious, though."

"Fast protein, surprisingly social, and hardy," said Nic, chief of hydroponics. "I've added them to tanks that need more bottom feeders. They clean things up nicely."

"I'll get you some." Miranda left me to go get a tray. Everyone else had finished eating, probably in the time it had taken me to get to the cafeteria, which meant they'd be watching me try to keep down dinner. The prospect further spoiled my appetite.

"How do you feel?" Harper leaned across the table, wincing as the motion pinched her ribs.

"Like a half-baked squid."

"But you're walking."

"And talking," said Orca, "which, as always, is a pity."

"Shut up." Harper elbowed Orca and turned back to me. "She's missed you."

Orca shifted in her seat and let her curtain of braids hide her face.

"What's new on deck?" I asked.

They shared a brief look. It passed from Orca to Kraken to Harper and back to me, and Harper offered up a passable attempt at her usual grin. "Nothing too exciting. We were able to trade with another ship for some of what we lost, and Miranda sent out raiders for the rest. A few have already returned."

"That's good."

"Yeah."

"Where are we?"

This time, the looks that passed between them were easily

recognizable: concern, confusion, and surprise.

"You mean you don't know?" Harper asked.

I realized my mistake with a rush of nausea. My stomach had always been sensitive to stress. The concussion, however, had magnified things to unbearable levels, and I clutched it with a groan and closed my eyes. *Shallow breaths. North, south . . . fuck.* What was the point of naming the points if I couldn't reach them? I'd never had to ask for my location before. Knowing was as much a part of me as my cells, and now . . .

"A little above the second parallel at about -44 degrees," said Orca. "Which you'd know, if you weren't so busy dying all the time."

Her comment elicited a laugh from Harper, and Orca flashed me a warning look from behind her hair. *Act normal*, it read, and cold trickled down my neck. Something was definitely wrong if Orca was helping me cover up a deficiency. It hurt too much to try to parse why she was helping me, though, and Miranda chose that moment to deposit a tray in front of me. The smell of food registered—though everything still smelled faintly like lemons except lemons themselves—and I surveyed my plate. A section of hard carapace lay beside an algae patty and fresh greens. The greens tasted sharp on my tongue, and I chewed them slowly while Kraken explained how to break into the shell of the roast.

Inside, the meat was tender and sweet and salty, and my appetite returned with enough force to make Kraken laugh as I prodded the shell for remnants.

"Glad you liked it, kid."

"I don't care what they look like. That is delicious."

"You say that now," Orca said darkly.

"Council meeting after dinner." Miranda's redirection caught all of our attention. "Rose, attend only if you're functional."

"I'm functional." In truth, my head felt pulped. The noise and lights and smells of the mess hall ground my brain like fruit beneath a booted heel. Retreating to Miranda's quarters was all I wanted to do, but Orca's warning lingered. For some reason, I needed to act normal, and I had a growing suspicion I was overlooking something important. Something I should know to ask about, but couldn't remember.

Miranda's officers followed her out of the cafeteria. Kraken's bulk walked behind me, which I took comfort from, but the same murmuring rose from the crew as we passed. I tried to scan the crowd. The effort made me dizzy. Faces blurred, and focusing on any of them brought on spikes of pain. Those faces I did manage to make out didn't offer any clues.

My gaze snagged on a pair of dark eyes. Mocking lips twisted as the face turned away, and when I squinted to better make the person out, they were gone. The memory, however, left a kernel of fear.

The council meeting unfolded around me like ink in water. Words enveloped me but did not penetrate the fog in my brain, obscuring more than they revealed. Supplies. Trajectories. Coordinates. I sensed Orca watching me each time coordinates came up, and I tried to keep an interested expression on my face. Even without north in my veins, I should have been able to make sense of longitude and latitude. My fingers itched for a chart to orient myself, and my panic rose until it drowned out everything else.

What if it never came back? I traced the scars on my palm in lieu of the cardinal points. My sense of direction was what had gotten me onto Miranda's ship, had guided me since childhood, had gained me admission to fleet prep, and defined every inter-action I'd had with my peers since then. Even my name—my fucking *name*—was a reminder. I was nobody without the ocean.

". . . redirect our efforts."

"—without methane, how can we—"

". . . haven't checked in with my sources, but it isn't clear . . ."

I pressed the ridged flesh in the center of my palm until the scar began to twinge.

"The fuck is wrong with you?" Orca's voice cut through the fog. Crew stood around the table, talking amongst themselves, which meant the meeting was over. Harper and Nic were engaged in a heated debate that sounded like it had something to do with biofuel and algae. Kraken, Miranda, and the other ranking crew members argued about something else a few feet away. No one paid me and Orca any heed.

"I'm concussed."

"You know what I mean." Her gray eyes pinioned mine. "You're not working right."

"I'm not a tool."

We're all tools, Miranda had told me once.

"Listen. Are you capable of listening?"

"Screw you."

"Things have gone sideways. You need to fix whatever is busted—" she gestured at my head, "before—"

"Orca." Miranda motioned for her to join her with a curt wave of her hand.

"What's gone sideways?" I asked.

Orca's shrug was the only answer I received.

Chapter Seven

I stroked the fine hairs at the base of Miranda's neck as she stretched across our bed. Seamus purred in the hollow between her thighs and stomach, and she scratched his chin. She smelled like stress and lemons. The looping scars across her back were redder than her light brown skin, and one crept up into her hairline beneath my fingers.

"Is everything okay?" I asked her. Neither of us had drifted off to sleep.

She rolled over. Seamus grumbled and stalked to the foot of the bed, where he lay down with an air of insulted dignity. I traced the scar that connected the hinge of her jaw to her eyebrow. "Everything's fine."

"You promised not to lie to me." This was the closest either of us had come to addressing our fight.

"I'm not lying." She kissed the palm of my hand. "I have things under control."

"But there is something to control."

"There's always something to control." The grumble in her voice matched Seamus's, and I tapped the corner of her mouth. She nipped my finger. "You don't need to worry about it until you're healed."

I settled deeper into the thin mattress and let my hand fall to the sheet between us. "What if I don't heal? What if I'm stuck hiding in this room forever?"

Broken, I didn't add. *Useless.*

"You're improving."

"Barely."

"You can walk. We're having a conversation."

"Everything is hard and smells like lemons."

"That, I don't understand."

"I hate lemons."

"You used to love them. Remember that time in the garden?"

Even my broken mind could recall with vivid detail which time she meant. We'd lain in the sunshine by the plex overlooking the stern, and I'd told Miranda she was sweet. *Only you would say that*, she'd said. *I'm a lemon, Rose.*

She'd plucked one, and dared me to sip the juice from her cupped hands.

We hadn't stopped there.

"I remember," I said now, my body flushing. "Mere . . ."

"You can't see your progress because you're in it."

"I feel like I can't see anything."

Miranda turned now to lie on her back. I studied her profile and waited for her to speak, the sense of foreboding returning.

"Amaryllis is the only reason the attack stopped where it did."

"Were they her friends?" I asked.

"The pirates? No. She rallied the crew, though, and held them off the creches."

"Why would they go after kids in the first place?"

"Kids are easier to press-gang into service. They adapt. It's a pretty common practice. But . . ." She trailed off. Something was worrying her, and I wished I could put the pieces together faster.

"What?"

"I think you were right."

"About what?" I said, stunned both by the thought of pirates taking children to replenish their ranks and also by this admission.

"It was a mistake to bring her aboard."

135

I stared at her. She still had her eyes glued to the ceiling. Admitting fault wasn't one of her strengths.

"Did she do something else?"

"No. But she saved my crew's kids."

"I don't understand. I'm sorry. My head—"

"She saved them. I didn't. And she's been helping with repairs."

The spinning in my head intensified. I reached out to Miranda to steady myself and closed my fingers around her braid. It anchored me, as tugging on it anchored her when she was frustrated, but did not ease the rising fear.

Orca's comments were beginning to make sense.

"Most of my sailors crewed for her long before they elected me," Miranda continued in a monotone confession.

"But you're the captain."

"It's not like the Archipelago. We choose our captains. I serve them just like they serve me, and if I don't—"

"They elect someone else," I said.

"Yes."

"They wouldn't choose her over you. They *left* her to sail under you."

"I know."

But the timing was bad. I could see that, even if I didn't like it. The attack. The lost supplies. Jeanine's death before that, and the push to sail south into unknown waters.

"What are you going to do?" I asked.

"Keep sailing, and get to the pole as fast as we can."

"And if she leads a mutiny?"

"She won't. I have it under control." She meant it. The conviction in her voice held all the fierceness of the winter sea, but there was only so much even Miranda Stillwater could control. "You should keep staying here, though. I know we haven't . . . talked . . . about anything. But you're safest with me."

As if I could argue even if I wanted to.

Miranda brought the charts to her quarters the next day. I spread the charts on the carpet and lay on the rough weave trying to will them to make sense. Without my internal compass, I had to rely on instruments—but Miranda hadn't brought me any. I did what I could with memory and my fingers. The process made my head ache terribly, and my eyes felt like I'd held them open in salt water for hours. From what I could gather, we were miles off our initial course, and I wasn't sure why. After we'd restocked our supplies and waited for our agricultural stocks to grow back, shouldn't we have returned to the course I'd plotted? Unless it had taken longer to accomplish those things than I realized. I rubbed my temples and tried to push past the fog. The harder I pushed, the thicker the fog.

Miranda found me curled up on the carpet hours later. Charts stuck to my cheek when I raised my head to blink up at her. The look on her face unsettled me. I caught shades of pity, frustration, and fear before she cleared her expression. The hands that raised me up were gentle.

"Time for dinner."

Making the trek to the mess hall again was the last thing I wanted to do. Even getting knifed by Ching or one of her sympathizers held more appeal than sitting in that raucous room, but Miranda shook her head when I opened my mouth, and I shut it. There was a reason she was making me go, and it wasn't torture. Perhaps she wasn't as oblivious to her crew's discontent as I'd feared.

"Make any progress on the charts?" she asked as I tried to tidy my hair.

"A little." More like none, but I didn't want to admit that. "Why are we so far off course?"

"Supplies." A reasonable explanation, and the one I'd guessed. Her eyes met mine squarely. There was no reason for the suspicion, growing despite my mental fog, that she wasn't telling me the whole truth.

A theme. I wasn't telling her the whole truth, either.

"Before we got attacked," I began, choosing my words carefully, "Ching told me to avoid deep ocean. Do you know why?"

"It's pirate territory. Which we found out."

"You don't think she's working with them?" I asked.

"Wouldn't she have joined them then?"

"I . . . I don't know."

"The risk Amaryllis poses isn't like that," Miranda said, considering my concerns for a change. "She's a captain. You can't have two captains on the same ship without people comparing them. This isn't about her. It's about the crew. If they think I've dealt them a bad hand, they'll start looking for another dealer. It might not even be Amaryllis they elect."

I thought I understood her logic. By offering up a comparison, Ching exposed Miranda's leadership flaws. Still, I didn't think Ching was quite as blameless as Miranda seemed to want to believe. Stoking a mutiny seemed exactly like the sort of thing the Ching I knew did for fun.

As we walked, I practiced adjusting my focus from objects near and far until I nearly ran into a group of sailors. Miranda steered me out of danger, but the look she shot me afterward warned me against further physical therapy.

"Captain." A woman hailed Miranda before we reached the mess hall. Hallé, maybe? Definitely something starting with an *H*. She had rings tattooed on all her fingers and around her biceps, and was heavily pregnant. Miranda answered her questions while I let my brain rest.

A familiar phrase jerked my attention back to the present. Over Miranda's shoulder, I could make out a knot of sailors speaking in low, angry voices. Miranda either didn't seem to notice or was too engrossed in her conversation with Hallé to care.

". . . fucking fleet scum."

It was the only phrase I could pick out. I wished I hadn't heard it at all. Their eyes slid off me like oil spills, but they left a filmy residue clinging to my skin. Miranda broke off her conversation with Hallé with a sharp jerk of her head. I'd zoned out again, but the motion alerted me just in time to stumble backward as she shoved me aside. Something hissed by my right ear, then clattered to the ground. I stared at my feet. A knife lay there, still spinning on the scuffed floor.

"Stop." Miranda's order rang out, silencing hallway traffic. I couldn't see much past her broad shoulders, which radiated the kind of rage that should have had her crew cowering before her, but I could see enough. Sailors came to attention grudgingly, instead of with their usual good-natured alacrity. Most seemed confused about the cause. That made their reaction somehow worse.

The cause.

Slow to react even to threats apparently, my brain refocused on the knife. Someone had thrown a knife at me. Hallé stepped away with a hand to her belly. I didn't blame her. The knife could have easily hit her when it ricocheted.

"Who?" Miranda said the word in a low, dangerous voice. With one hand on the wall for balance, I leaned over to pick up the blade. Standard fleet issue several years back. Grip worn from sweat. Blade thin from sharpening and use. The fact it was fleet meant nothing; most likely it had either been traded or stolen from one of the Archipelago fleets. The fact it had almost lodged itself between my eyes was far more important. My fingers closed around the handle. One of my fellow crewmates had tried to take my life with this knife.

I reached for north. The currents whispered past the edge of hearing, but they were only so much noise. I still couldn't touch them.

"I said, *who*."

"Captain—" Hallé broke off at the look Miranda shot her.

"I will walk each and every one of you if someone doesn't answer me. Right. Now."

Listening to her voice, I didn't doubt it.

"Me." A thin man with thick, short brown hair stepped forward and into my line of sight. He didn't glance at me, and his expression as he faced his captain was grim but determined. He knew he was going to die. "Captain, this woman—"

She opened his throat. I didn't even see her pull the knife. The sailor grabbed at his neck in surprise, as if he couldn't quite believe what had happened, either. Blood welled between his knuckles.

"You know the code. A life for a life. We're done here."

The sailor crumpled to the floor. Miranda stepped over his body and pulled me after her, tucking me under her arm and lifting me bodily over the still-twitching corpse of a man whose palm, like mine, bore her mark. I moved because her grip on my body rendered anything else impossible.

Kraken met us at the door to our quarters, Orca at his heels. Word traveled fast.

"Nobody comes in," she said to Orca. She said nothing to me, but the look in her eyes was as full of anguish and rage as I had ever seen. Blood misted her cheeks and stained her shirt in a thick spatter.

"I'll protect her," said Orca.

The door shut on us. Orca locked it, pausing to rest her forehead against the frame before confronting me. I expected her to shout at me, to ask what I'd done this time. I wasn't rightly sure I knew. My broken brain replayed the scene again and again. The man. His knife. The blood. It couldn't have happened. Could it?

"Are you hurt?"

"What?"

"Are you hurt."

"Oh. No." Shaking, yes, and out of air, but unharmed. I still clutched the knife. Orca pried it from my fingers, which creaked. She helped me sit. I rested my pounding head on my knees and wondered how much of the nausea was from my injury, and how much was from the vision, burned into my brain, of Miranda exacting justice. It was the second time in my life someone I loved had killed a man for attempting to knife me. You'd think word would have spread it wasn't good for your health, I thought, as a giggle tried to pry my jaws open.

I pressed the scab on my forehead to cut off the hysteria. Pain steadied me.

"What happened?" Orca asked.

"I'm not really sure." I relayed the events in short, clipped words, not daring to give in to even the slightest bit of emotion.

"She shouldn't have killed him," I said when I finished.

"Killing him's the only smart thing she's done in weeks."

"A life for a life. I'm still alive. He missed."

"You got lucky."

"But why would he want me dead?"

"Miranda made them promises. Some she's kept, but you . . . she's a fucking idiot over you. No offense."

"It's fine."

"Before you, she fucked around, but she never put anyone above anyone else. Being her lover didn't get you anything or make you special."

"She doesn't treat me like I'm special."

"She didn't leave your side for days, Rose. Days Ching used to her advantage. The ship was barely floating. We needed a captain. And Miranda was in here, with you."

Orca didn't sound jealous or even bitter, just exhausted. As first mate, the brunt of Miranda's responsibilities, as well as Miranda's messes, would have fallen on her.

"It's not even your fault." That was more like Orca—annoyed she couldn't blame me. "You were asleep for most of it."

"Do you . . . do you know what his name was?" I nodded toward the knife.

"Luca, I think."

Luca. Dev. Jeanine. Annie. Most of Ching's sailors. My predecessor, Andre. The SHARK who'd tried to kill me to save Harper; Harper had killed him in turn. When would it end?

"What is Miranda going to do now?"

"Dunno. Kill Ching if she's smart."

"She won't do that."

"Nope." Orca kicked her legs up on the arm of the couch across from me and sprawled across it, balancing the knife on her fingertip.

"Shit." I stood fast enough to lose my balance, but caught myself before I toppled. "Harper. They could go after her, too."

"Not a chance."

"But she's—"

"She's Comita's daughter and a valuable hostage. Plus, they'd have to get past engineering, and those assholes love her. You think I'd be sitting here otherwise?"

"Right." Only Miranda and a handful of other sailors loved me. I'd hoped with time that would change. That seemed unlikely, now. "I've messed everything up."

"You should be used to that by now. Ugh, gross, don't start crying." Orca's eyes widened as mine welled. "This is bigger than you. It isn't about you. Look."

I couldn't look at anything past the sheen of tears blinding my eyes, but I suspected she was speaking metaphorically.

"They elected Miranda because she had Archipelago intel, and they admired her guts. Under Ching, she was vicious in a raid, and they thought she'd get us rich. We were going to retake Gemini and open trade with the rest of the ocean—"

"Wait, what?"

"That was the plan, for a while anyway. But it didn't happen. Ching wanted more than Gemini. She wanted to burn the whole thing. That was too much for Miranda, and they fought about it constantly."

"Right." I was following, despite the pain the effort caused me.

"But all the crew can see is that she keeps putting off delivering them the safety they wanted for their children. We're still living on Archipelago sufferance. Chasing the sea wolves is Miranda's thing, not theirs."

"Are they going to mutiny?"

"Maybe." She seemed so blasé about it. I wiped my eyes and sat back down, staring at her. Blasé, or just past caring?

"What happens then?"

"You definitely die. I probably die. Miranda probably dies, too."

"They'd kill her?"

"You think we'd go down without a fight?"

"The code, though. If they ask for a vote of no confidence—"

"Ching isn't interested in a bloodless coup. There will be blood,

Rose. There always fucking is." She closed her eyes. The shells and bones in her hair fanned across the couch.

"What do we do about it?"

Orca tapped the blade of the knife against her thigh. "You need to get better, like yesterday. She has to stop worrying about you and start focusing on the ship. And we need a target that's more interesting than the sea wolves. Something richer. Then we can go chasing whales."

"Like the Archipelago?" I said, because there was no other target rich enough to warrant the risk.

"Exactly. What's that station on the southern tip?"

"Crux."

"Whatever. They're close enough for us to hit a supply ship."

"Comita—"

"Isn't here. Ching is."

I sank back into the chair and thought of blood congealing on the floor and Luca—whose name I hadn't known until a moment ago—cooling somewhere while his family said whatever words they needed to say before he was sent to the compost.

"Orca," I said with my eyes closed.

"Still here."

"We need a backup plan."

"Way ahead of you. Kraken's been stocking one of the smaller ships in the bay for a few days now."

"I thought you said you'd put up a fight."

"I didn't say that was the only option I was considering."

"Miranda won't leave her ship."

"Probably not." The pause extended so long I thought she'd finished speaking. "But she might, for you."

Miranda returned several hours later, Kraken at her heels and more blood on her face. It wasn't hers. She paced the room while Orca, Kraken, and I waited for her to clear her thoughts enough to speak.

"I know what you're going to say," she said to Orca.

More pacing. Orca didn't reply.

"But it's done. She's here. We're here."

"Walk her," Orca suggested.

"That will make things worse," said Kraken.

"How could it get worse?" Orca leaned forward. "They don't have anyone to put up besides Ching. If she's dead—"

"We're not walking her," Miranda said.

"Mere—"

"There are lines."

"She crossed one today by having one of her people try to off our navigator," said Orca.

"She didn't order that. It isn't her way."

"Right. They do it without her needing to ask. How is that better?"

"Because they're right." Miranda's shout surprised us all into jumping backward. "Tell me, honestly, that I deserve to captain this ship."

"Miranda—" Orca began, but she couldn't seem to bring herself to say anything else.

"In the last month, how many dead?"

"You couldn't control that," said Kraken.

"If I'd just sided with Ching, the crew would be fat as cats and living on the Archipelago right now, and they know it."

"There's no guarantee of that, either," said Kraken.

"Pretty good odds, though."

"So maybe you've fucked up a few times," said Orca. "Fix it."

"Yes. Brilliant. I'll just 'fix it.'"

"Or you could keep shouting about it. Bet that will help."

"First mate—"

"You can't say 'Oh, poor me, I'm the worst captain ever' and then pull rank." Orca and Miranda now stood face to face, fists clenched, and I wondered if anyone planned to intervene.

"I'm trying to—"

"You're not trying to do anything, and you sure as salt aren't taking any of our advice. If you were, Ching wouldn't be on this ship."

"We need Ching."

"*You* need Ching," said Orca. "Let it go. Forget about Gemini. We've got a good thing going out here. A good ship. We can go back to how things used to be. Take a ship in a raid and give it to Ching. The crew who want to follow her can go. She can get back home on her own wind, or not, and it won't matter to us."

"That's a fair point," said Kraken.

"You're *missing* the point. I'm not spending the rest of our lives chasing after scraps when we don't fucking have to."

"Maybe we do." They all turned to look at me. Rubbing my temples, I tried to rally my thoughts. "There's always someone with a bigger ship willing to take things from you."

"Rose—"

"You grew up on Gemini." Now I was shouting. It hurt. I didn't stop. "I know what happened, and I'm sorry, but Gemini is a well-off station compared to Cassiopeia. We weren't much better than drifters, and we were a part of the Archipelago. We didn't have enough ships to even think about revolt."

"What's your point?"

"My point is that you don't really know."

Orca and Kraken looked from me to Miranda. Kraken's vast shoulders were slumped, and Orca gave me a tiny nod, encouraging me to continue.

"What don't I know?"

"What it's like to have nothing."

"I lost every—"

"Exactly." Words skittered away from me as I pulled them into coherence. I snatched a few back. "You know what you lost. They don't. They want it because it looks nice from a distance, but they'll settle for less because it's what they know. It's what I know."

Miranda's mouth hung open as if I'd slapped her. She swung her gaze to Kraken for support.

"She's right, Mere," he said.

"Maybe a little dramatic, but yeah," said Orca.

"So because my crew grew up half starved, I should let them settle for more starving? Is that what you're asking me to do?

Because if that's the case, then you elected the wrong bloody captain." She seemed to have forgotten, in the heat of her anger, that this was exactly what she feared had occurred. "Other suggestions?"

"Raid again," said Orca.

"We just won a raid."

"*You* didn't. You were here with Rose. Lead the assault, remind them why they chose you, and they'll get over this. Give Ching a ship. We can find the sea wolves without her if you still want to, or with her—but keep her on a different ship."

Miranda yanked on her braid so viciously I thought I could hear her hair follicles screaming. She said, seething, "Kraken?"

"It's a solid plan." It had probably been his plan to start with. It had more nuance than I wanted to give Orca credit for on her own.

"Fuck you all."

She collapsed onto another chair and glared at us with bloodshot eyes. "And fuck Luca."

Grief and rage roughened her voice. I wanted to go to her and take her in my arms, but not with Orca and Kraken watching. She didn't allow herself to be soft in front of other people.

Except she had. She'd shown a softness for me, which was where this had all started going wrong. I half wanted to laugh at the irony. I'd hated how cold she was toward me on deck, but she'd been right. Coldness, brutality—these things were necessary.

They shouldn't have to be.

Thinking like that, though, would set me back on the path we needed to leave, and I'd meant what I said. I wasn't sure there was a better way to find.

Chapter Eight

Harper knocked on the door. "Rose? It's me."

I unlocked the door. "Do you have it?"

She edged away from me. "Are you sure this is a good idea? The doctor—"

"The doctor isn't Archipelago trained. She probably doesn't even know what she's talking about. Give it here."

"You have no idea what's really in this."

"I know it will make me more functional, and I don't have a choice."

"It will allow you to push yourself when you should be resting."

"Someone almost knifed me yesterday, Harp. I can't stay in this room forever, and I need . . ." I lost my train of thought. "Seas. Just give it to me."

Harper removed her hand from her pocket slowly and uncurled her fingers. A jar of plant matter lay inside. "Do you have a pipe?"

"What?"

"This isn't home. They actually smoke it."

"How do they light it?"

Harper whipped a minuscule contraption out of her pocket and flicked it. Blue flame danced at the tip before extinguishing. Methane.

"I don't have a pipe," I said, belatedly answering her question.

"I'll loan you my spare."

"Spare . . . what the hell, Harper?"

She grinned. "There's an art to fitting in, Rose."

"Like sacrificing your lungs?"

"At this rate, neither of us will live long enough for that to matter. Are you sure you want to do this?"

I nodded. Harper shifted her weight, then loaded her pipe with a pinch of the herb. "Nic said it's the strongest non-hallucinogenic stimulant they have. It should take the edge off the pain and make you more alert, but you'll crash hard at the end."

"At least I'll be alive."

"Rose . . ." But Harper didn't say whatever she was thinking. She held the pipe to my lips and gave me a short lecture on proper technique, then lit the bowl. I inhaled, coughed, gagged, and coughed some more.

"How do you feel?"

"Crisped." I coughed again. My throat felt thick and raw, but as I swallowed, my vision cleared, and the headache receded for the first time in weeks. "Oh. Wow."

"What?"

"There aren't two of you anymore."

"You say that like it's a good thing." She flounced her hair, then dropped all pretense of play. "I still can't believe someone tried to kill you."

"I can." I stood, relishing the way the floor didn't sway beneath me and the room held still. Whatever the botanists had done to this strand was working. Cautiously, aware that Harper was watching me, I reached for the ocean.

It felt like wading through the interior of a giant jellyfish. The pressure I pushed against was fibrous and gel-like all at once, and I tried not to think about whether or not that material was the gray matter that made up my brain.

Through it lay true north.

"Rose?"

Harper's hand fell on my shoulder, and she wiped my cheek

with her sleeve. Tears blurred my vision. *North. East. South. West.* The points flooded me, and beyond them, I felt the currents tugging at my alignment. I oriented myself toward north without thinking. It fell on me like sunlight, like warmth, like Miranda's arms around me. *Home.*

"Hey. Talk to me."

The worry in Harper's voice pulled me back. "I'm fine."

I was better than fine. With the ocean in me, I was liquid possibility. I was useful. I was *me.* I hadn't realized how lost I'd felt without it.

"Okay, then. You ready?"

"Yes." It was even true. Together Harper and I left the rooms that had turned into my world and entered the hall.

Walking with Harper was a risk. If someone wanted to take out the Archipelago presence on the ship, all they had to do was corner us. I refused to show my fear. Sailors avoided our eyes even as I sought theirs, looking for answers.

"You're making them nervous," Harper hissed in my ear.

"What?"

She lowered her voice further. "Miranda killed someone yesterday. Nobody wants to be seen as a threat to you, in case she decides to off more of them."

"She wouldn't—"

"The woman carves her mark into people's palms."

"That's—" It wasn't different, my newly cleared mind informed me. Miranda was dangerous and, at times, unpredictable. They were right to be afraid. I recalled the smoothness of her lunge as she'd pulled her knife on my assailant. She struck like an eel. Pirates valued that in a leader until it was turned on them.

"Why?" I asked Harper as another sailor threw her a cautious nod.

"Why what?"

"Why don't they hate you the way they hate me?"

We couldn't look at each other and also keep an eye out for threats as we walked, and so I was spared whatever expression came over her face. Was bluntness a side effect of the drug? Harper had to know how I felt about the crew's lukewarm feelings toward me compared to how they felt about her, but we'd never spoken of it.

"Because I'm not fucking their captain."

"Just her first mate."

"It's different, Rose. And also . . ." she trailed off, and I dared a glance at her. She watched an approaching sailor for a moment before continuing. "Miranda's theirs. Or at least, that's how they feel."

"No shit. She's their captain." The drug was definitely making me blunt. I'd need to watch my tongue.

"That's not what I mean. She's their legend. They pulled her out of the water. They gave her a new life, and she led them to victory. Or she used to anyway. You're part of a different legend, and they don't know what it is. I'm just an engineer to them."

"And Comita's daughter."

"Don't remind me."

"Are we really going to raid a station?"

"I don't know," she said.

Neither of us said anything else about it as we continued on our way. I catalogued everything I could recall from the last few weeks, hoping to sort out new meaning, now that thinking didn't make me feel ill. A ship that managed to avoid sonar. The hatred in the eyes of their captain, right before I lost consciousness. He'd obviously been raided by the sea wolves; what else could explain his reaction to my eyes? That meant they were not only real, but had been close. We could have even sailed right past them without noticing, assuming they had the same technology as the ship that had snuck up on us. How had the sea wolves found that ship? How did the sonar deflection work? And did our attackers use it for raiding, or for protection from the sea wolves? The more I learned about the wolves, the less I wanted to meet them, and the more convinced I became they wouldn't help us even if we did find them. Better to give up and live, assuming Ching didn't kill us.

You elected the wrong bloody captain.

If we didn't do something soon, she wouldn't be a captain at all. I stepped onto the bridge like I belonged there and hadn't been absent for weeks. Miranda looked up, froze, and then nodded as if she'd expected me. Whispers broke out. It all felt so horribly familiar. Harper saluted and then left for engineering, leaving me to face the eyes turned in my direction.

"Our heading's off," I said to Reya.

"You don't even know where we're going." Was that hatred in her voice, or just surprise I was up and walking?

"Aren't we going to Crux?"

Miranda listened from across the room.

"Not . . . that I'm aware of," said Reya. "Captain?"

"Change of plans, Reya."

"Crux it is then." She opened the binder of charts beneath her arm. "Since you're back, plot us a course."

Technically, I supervised her, but I let the command slide and took the charts.

"Is this the most up-to-date?"

"Should be."

I analyzed the approximate coordinates for Crux, wondering. Would things have changed since Ching's attack? We needed intel before we sailed in blind. I didn't trust that the stations had remained where I'd last seen them on a chart. If I were the council—or Comita—I would have moved everything to throw off future attacks. Kraken's spies might know. I approached Miranda. She studied the water beyond the plex with her hands behind her back and an expression that might, charitably, have been called unhappy. Murderous was a better fit.

"Captain?"

"Glad you could join us."

Cold water slid down my spine. We were back to this, then. In my concussed state, I'd managed to partially convince myself we hadn't broken up. "I was hoping to get your opinion on the course."

"Yes, because you value my opinion highly enough to disobey a direct order to stay confined to quarters."

"Should we go to the chart room?" The hum of the ship wasn't loud enough to drown out our argument.

"Fine."

151

Let her be angry. The drug Harper had given me burned away feelings of remorse. She thought she wanted me safe, but she needed me functional, needed me to prove to her crew that I wasn't afraid, that I belonged here.

"What are you doing?" she asked the minute we were alone.

"You're planning a raid. You need me."

"I've raided without you before. In fact, I've never actually raided *with* you, have I?" Her blue eyes looked the way I imagined icebergs might have looked when caught by the sun.

"They'll have moved Crux after Ching's attack. They know they've been compromised. We need—"

"Kraken's on it. I gave you an order, and you disobeyed me."

"With all due respect, *Captain*, if I hide, it will only make things worse. I'm your navigator. We need to remind them of that."

She frowned at me, then put her fingers to my chin and tilted my face up. "You're high. Rose, what did you do?"

I pushed her away. "It's a stimulant."

"Who gave it to you?"

The drug in me ignored the danger in her. "It doesn't matter. It's working."

"Who. Gave. It. To. You." Each word was a threat.

I pulled my chin out of her grip. "I took it. No one gave it to me. This is the first time I've felt good in—"

"You don't know what you're doing."

"I know I'm your navigator. Let me navigate."

"Neptune, I'm trying to keep you alive, and you—" She broke off. "It was Harper, wasn't it? That makes perfect fucking sense. You don't know, either of you, the cost of what you just put into your body."

"I know I'll crash hard."

"We used to use that during raids when the fights lasted more than a few hours. It will keep you going, but when it's done—it can kill you. You could end up in a coma."

"So use me while I'm here."

She looked, for a moment, like she wanted to scream. I hung on to north and let it fill me until I felt the earth's magnetic field wrap around me like an embrace.

"So be it." Miranda pointed at the chart. "What do you need from me?"

"I can get us there undetected. Tell me how close to bring us. If we wait for a storm or a swarm to give us cover, that will help. And I can get us out again."

"Here." She jabbed her finger at the chart, then tore a sheet from the back of her logbook and wrote down my dictated instructions.

"This will bring Comita down on us," I said when I finished.

"She's busy elsewhere."

"But Orion's close by, and they have a big fleet, too."

"They'll be trying to decide whether or not to help Comita with her coup. By the time Crux reports ships missing, we'll be gone."

"Then we shouldn't expect much retaliation." I studied the charts, aware I should be feeling reservations about raiding my former home, but unable to tap into any emotion besides the driving need to act.

"No more."

"What?" I was loath to look up from the charts, but the roughness of Miranda's voice compelled me.

"Don't smoke this again."

"Yes, Captain."

"Now get up. I clearly can't leave you alone, which means you'll be coming with me."

I hadn't reckoned on that outcome. Standing—and enjoying how easily my body managed the feat—I grabbed what I needed and followed her out of the chart room back to the bridge. We lingered there a while and I worked on the floor, charts around me, until Miranda ordered me up.

Next was the vessel bay. Here, Kraken and a crew of engineers looked over the smaller vessels we used for parley, trade, attacks, and, apparently, espionage. Our trawler, *Sea Cat*, bobbed in a far corner. I prayed to gods no one had believed in for centuries we wouldn't need it.

Orca leapt from the deck of a ship and landed in front of us. "Cutter's sharpened. Breaching should be easy. Engines look good, too. This one, though."

Miranda listened as Orca explained the problems with our little fleet. I settled myself on a crate and pulled the charts out again. My mind still felt keen as a whetted knife. Possible courses presented themselves with ease. Avoiding detection while we searched for the station would be simple. Deep swarms offered ample protection, obscuring sonar, and no one was looking for us. Ching had been defeated. The Archipelago probably felt like they'd been granted a reprieve.

"Feeling like bilge water yet?" Miranda asked as we left the docking bay and wound up toward the hydrofarm.

"I feel fine."

"Great. Stay alert, then."

I eyed the rows of piping and the plants growing from them, and then paused by the tanks where we grew nori, eel, squid, and fish. The dark green-brown fronds waved in the pump-circulated water. The motion hypnotized me until Miranda tugged at my sleeve and pulled me onward.

Medicinal plants were grown in a different room, along with the vats of algae. Nic's workers pruned and harvested and examined the plants for disease as Miranda strode through them. Hydrotechs moved out of her way and continued working. That seemed like a good sign; the urge to mutiny hadn't reached these ranks, at least not outwardly, and no one sprang to assassinate me from behind a stalk of kale.

Nic emerged from a tank and pulled off their mask and breathing apparatus, which was nothing more than a long tube connecting to the surface. They hadn't put on a suit, and their wet clothes clung to their body as they shook water out of their eyes.

"How are we on inventory?" Miranda asked without preamble.

"Getting there. They mostly wanted algae, which is recovering. Took all our methane reserves, though. I'm doing what I can with the biofuel strains, but you know how it is. Time."

"I know." Her voice lost its edge. "Make a list of what you'd want me to look out for, if opportunities arise."

"Equipment." Nic listed the equipment the Archipelago had given to us, which the pirates had stolen. Now, we'd steal from Crux—one of the stations that could least afford it.

Don't think like that. We couldn't get through Polaris or Orion's fleet, other pirates didn't have what we needed, and going back to Comita—well. That offered just as many ways to die as this did. Orca and Kraken were right. Miranda needed to distract her crew, and a raid would accomplish that.

I ran my hands over the beds of greens while Miranda consulted with Nic. Tiny leaves pricked my palms. Everything came down to sustenance. Growing things. Fresh water. Purification. The life flowing in all our veins was tied to the sea, and the sea wanted us dead. I settled into the currents and felt them shift around us, massive systems altered by my ancestors, but still adapting, changing, moving ever forward. We needed to be more like that. Maybe I'd been wrong to dismiss Miranda's idealism. We'd remained static for years. Change was overdue.

Don't start giving me hope, I warned the drug in my system. "Rose."

I pulled my hand away from the dark green leaves and followed my captain.

Crew whispered in our wake as Miranda made the rounds of the ship. I channeled all the confidence I could muster into the tilt of my chin, imagining an iron bar in place of my spine, iron filings pointing north and drawing me upright with them. Ching would not send me into hiding. I would not cower behind Miranda's closed doors while Ching reminded the crew who'd given them Miranda in the first place. Let them paint me as the enemy. I knew the truth. The drug burned away my guilt in a swath of glorious fury. I was no more Archipelagean at this point than Miranda, and it had been Ching's sailors who had chased me into the passage. She bore the same blame I did.

The promised crash came after dinner. I walked beside Miranda, aware of the anger still vibrating off her skin, and the door to our quarters—*her* quarters, I reminded myself—spun as I approached. Miranda opened the whirlpool into the room beyond. Gasping, I stepped inside as the currents and the cardinal points and all my courage were stripped away by a howling darkness. When I woke, the pain had returned a thousandfold, and Miranda sat beside me, crying.

East

Captain's Log
Captain Miranda Stillwater
Man o' War
February 25, 2514
11°52′12″N, 4°28′48″W

Raid scheduled to replete lost inventory and restore morale. Mission to Symbiont forestalled at the moment.

[Redacted]

Instructions: The following letter is to be given to Compass Rose in the event of my death.

> Rose, I'm sorry. You were right to ask for time. You should never have given me any of your time. I wanted to protect you. But you're right: that isn't my call. You were naïve, when you came to my ship, but not as naïve as I thought you were—or as you thought you were. You surprised me. You surprised all of us. I'm not half as brave. When Amaryllis found me, I wanted to die. She gave me purpose, and she loved me, Rose, and she trusted me, which was a mistake. But she recognized something in me. It's the same thing I recognized in her, and that I recognized in Comita, and, yes, that I

recognized in you. We're all willing to burn for what we believe in.

I'm not making excuses for her. She's cold. She's brutal. And I loved her, too. Not like I love you. She and I were never like that. But I know what it's like to love someone like me: someone who can be monstrous. And, as I did, you eventually came to your senses and acted according to your principles. I hate that I'm proud of you for that.

The people I love get hurt, Rose. When we first started this, I told myself I wouldn't let you matter to me. That you were just a pretty pair of eyes. I couldn't afford to lose anyone else. But then I got to know you. I saw the rage in you, beneath the surface, and I recognized it. We both know what it is to be tossed away. Because of that, I should have trusted you to understand. You deserve someone who respects you enough to trust you with their failures and their fears, as well as their successes. I wanted to be that person for you. But it was always going to take a long time to work past these scars, if I ever could. Still, I would have selfishly asked for your patience. I would have given you all the time you needed, and I would have been there, waiting, whenever you were ready.

Love,

Miranda

Chapter Nine

A hand shook me awake. I groaned, pain subsuming all other sensation.

"Was it worth it?"

If I squinted, I could make out the blurry shape of Miranda's face. What I could see of it suggested blurriness was preferable. "Huh?"

"You've been out for a full day."

Out . . . where? Automatically, I reached for the currents and the cardinal points. I hit a steel wall. *Right*. My head, the drug, Miranda's anger.

"Mere—"

"Don't."

She pulled away from me and stood. I bullied my body into rising into a sitting position and blinked through my double vision until I could make out her face: fury, anguish, and love.

"You need me functional."

"I need *you*, Rose." The rawness of her voice spoke of fear, and I remembered her warning about the drug's side effects. I remembered, too, how under its influence I'd been able to reach north.

"I'm okay." To prove this, I got up despite the agony of movement and fumbled for my clothing.

"I'll have the charts brought to you. Stay here today."

"No."

"That's an order."

"Can you keep your voice down?"

"Maybe your head wouldn't hurt if you hadn't—"

"Just shut up, Miranda."

She froze. I pulled off my shirt and eased myself into a clean one. When my head broke the hemline, I met her eyes. They flashed with unmistakable temper, but I knew her well enough to see the hurt she couldn't mask.

"Mere—"

"You overstep, navigator."

She left me there.

I contemplated going after her, but I felt too ill. Instead, I slumped back on the bed and stroked Seamus's soft fur.

"Should I tell her what is really wrong with me?" I asked him.

He purred in response.

No. I couldn't. Not with how things currently lay between us. I'd told her I just wanted to be her navigator—and now here I was, unable to navigate when she needed me most. I was not going to let her sail blind with Ching Shih on our ship. Seas only knew where Ching would lead us. My hands didn't shake as I removed the jar from its hiding place in the bottom of my drawer, secreted within the coconut Harper had carved for me long ago. I lit the pipe and inhaled. Clarity was worth it. I refused to analyze anything beyond that. Disobeying Miranda would have consequences, but I feared obeying her could lead to worse.

Walking the halls of my ship felt like swimming through a corridor of squid. Everyone I passed was a potential threat now, and my shoulders tensed as they waited for the sick thud of a knife. Children ran past, shrieking in their games. Adults eyed me. A few nodded in greeting. Others ignored me entirely.

I entered the bridge intact. Miranda wasn't there. The bridge crew looked up from the instruments, and Reya gave me a distracted wave.

"Where are we?"

"Waiting for intel on Crux's shipping routes and trying to stay off fleet radar. Where were you yesterday?"

I tapped my head in answer.

"You've got to get over that. It's been, what, three weeks now?"

Finn had warned me it could take months before I started to feel any real sense of recovery. I didn't have months. As surreptitiously as I could without leaning over her shoulder, I made note of the coordinates on the map beside her and matched it to what my internal compass told me. Close, though I didn't know if the margin of error was on my side or hers. Impossible to say without the stars.

"I'll be in the chart room if you need me."

The chart room—my sanctuary—was occupied. I stared at the woman sitting with her back to me. She didn't turn, and the stubble on her head now measured the length of a finger joint.

"Navigator," she said, though how she knew was beyond me.

I inched backward.

"Stay."

She didn't command me on this ship. I could flee for safety, perhaps pausing to ask Reya why she hadn't warned me—Annie's face flashed in my mind's eye, all smiles until she had cut me loose—without repercussion.

"I won't be killing you today. Sit." The dry humor in her voice would have been disarming coming from anyone else. From her it just raised all the hair on my body. I sat. Ching Shih looked up. Dark circles limned her eyes, and the lines around her mouth were deeper than they'd been when I first met her. The fierce beauty of her plain face was a warning. She commanded attention, even in her diminished state.

"I didn't realize you were here," I said.

"And I was told you wouldn't be here. It would appear I was misinformed."

Sweat prickled as it rose along with my body hair. The drug might have cleared my mind, but it couldn't take the edge off the guilt and terror her presence inspired.

"I warned you to stay close to the shelf. The current's a bitch, but it's safer than the alternative."

"You could have said that."

The look she gave me was cool and almost clinically disinterested. "I am not accustomed to explaining myself to navigators."

Had that been the only reason? Had I misjudged, assuming the worst of her, and gotten *more* people killed? Seas, but I wanted to vomit. Nausea was becoming a lifestyle.

"But since you're here, we might as well make Miranda happy. This is where we're headed, once she's done raiding."

No mention of the fact that Ching was the reason Miranda needed to raid in the first place. She had to know. I looked at the map, because what else could I do? This was my job.

"Symbiont." Her finger stabbed a location nestled in the continent's curving arm. "The capital city. It is closely guarded. You won't make it there without getting picked up by a patrol. What we'll need to do is ensure the patrol doesn't sink us before we have time to make contact."

"Is that a possibility?"

"Potentially. They don't have much use for old tech."

"Old—"

"Everything you have is old to them. And you . . ." she smirked and shook her head, but did not elaborate. Before I could muster the courage to ask, she continued. "The sail itself won't be too challenging unless we need to surface for repairs. Average wave height is fifteen feet, and that's on a calm day. You're looking at a good chance of thirty to sixty, and when I tell you this ship cannot survive a sixty-foot wave, I'm being generous. I've seen waves reach eighty feet, maybe more. They keep detailed records. You bust another valve, and you're dead in the water."

"What about squid?"

"The sizes you're used to."

"The ship that attacked us—they didn't show up on the radar. Will the sea wolves have that technology?"

"They invented that technology. You won't see them coming. But I speak their language."

"So we're dependent on you telling them not to kill us?"

"Essentially." She dropped her attention back to the charts. I tried to take a steadying breath without making it obvious I was doing so. I didn't like this at all. Ching had the advantage, and she wasn't the sort to let advantages pass her by.

"Why did you tell Miranda she wouldn't get what she wanted from the sea wolves?" I asked. With luck, I'd never be alone with Ching again, which meant this was my only opportunity to ask her the questions festering beneath my clavicle.

"Miranda wants something impossible. It will get her killed one day."

"Is that a threat?"

"I have no plans to kill your captain. You should be more concerned about your own life." She mimed throwing a knife. "I hear you nearly had an accident."

"Was that on your orders?"

"I don't need to order your death, Rose. People seem to hate you—or what you stand for—enough all on their own. Though I should apologize for Anemone Dive."

The bottom dropped from my stomach. "Annie?"

"I gave her orders to keep an eye on Miranda, and to protect her from Archipelago influence. It isn't good for her."

The drug couldn't keep up with the assaults on my system. North faded. I spun, again a broken compass. "She was yours."

"Most of Miranda's sailors were, at one point."

And how many still are?

"Did Miranda know?"

The look she gave me was nearly pitying. "I have no idea. She's hotheaded enough to have walked Annie before she gave a full confession, and Annie knew how to keep her mouth shut. She loved Mere."

"She had a pretty fucked-up way of showing it."

"Don't take it personally."

I opened my palm and stared down at the scars tucked in the creases of my skin. Should I be relieved to finally have an answer? I felt nothing. Annie, who had shown me kindness and then left me adrift. Annie, the first to die as a direct result of my existence.

"Why did you let her mark you?" I asked as the jellyfish sigil on my hand stared back up at me.

"I once swore the day I took an order from her would be the day I lost my fleet. I'll admit freely I never expected that day to come. But I keep my word."

I said nothing.

"We're not like your people out here," said Ching. This time there was definite pity in her voice, and I wanted to strangle her with it. "Mere told me you had no idea what your admirals would do to my fleet, and I believe it."

I flinched.

"But," she said, her voice hardening, "ignorance doesn't absolve you. And now here you are, helping pirates raid the people you sacrificed mine to protect. I truly do not understand you."

The judgment in her voice lashed my cheeks. *Get up*, I urged my body, but every limb felt heavy and sullen. Her words pierced the infection of my guilt. It ran hot and thick over my tongue. I deserved this.

Ching wasn't done.

"The biggest irony, as I see it, is that you broke things off with Mere because you somehow, like a child, think you still have the higher moral ground. We're at sea. *There is no ground to stand on.*"

Her voice sharpened from lash to razor.

"If I thought tossing you overboard would do her a lick of good, you'd be dead already. But that's where you and I finally agree: she's too broken to fix."

"I don't think—"

Ching raised her brows in response. This time, my body obeyed my command, and I pushed back from my chair. "We're done here."

"Suit yourself. And remember what I said about the Antarctic. Don't surface. And for fuck's sake, keep us close to the coast until we get there."

Footsteps pounded on the stairs.

"Rose." Miranda's voice was ragged with panic. She crossed the chart room at a run and looked me over, no doubt for evidence of stab wounds. Ching's words echoed in my head: *There is no ground to stand on.* Had I been wrong, not just about Miranda, but about Ching? If she hadn't been leading us astray and really intended to make good on her word to my captain, then what did that make me?

"I'm fine," I said, crossing my arms over my chest in a gesture I knew looked defensive, but I needed the security of arms around me, and couldn't ask Miranda in front of Ching—shouldn't ask Miranda at all, after what I'd told her I needed.

Miranda's gaze passed over me to the table, and she noticed the room's other occupant for the first time. "Where's Nasrin?"

"It's Beck today, and he went to get us food."

"He—" Miranda cut herself off, frustration evident in the click of her teeth as she snapped down on her words. "I thought I made it clear I don't want the two of you in the same room."

"We were just going over the charts. I didn't know she was here," I said. I wasn't defending Ching Shih, but I wanted some control over the situation.

"You should still be resting." Her tone was gentler than it had been when we'd fought earlier that day, but still reproachful.

"She's doing her job," said Ching. "She can rest later. Mere, your charts are horribly out of date."

"And yours are at the bottom of the ocean. This is what we have to work with."

I saw the flash of anger in Ching's eyes at the callous statement. Miranda seemed to have noticed it too, because she tried to backtrack. "Amaryllis—"

"From water we came, and to water we return."

"Water is life, and watery is the grave," said Miranda. The exchange had the rote feel of a call and response, but one I'd never heard before. "You know I didn't mean that."

"I do," said Ching.

"How badly out of date?"

"I've made what corrections I can. And as I've been telling your navigator, you won't be able to surface once you pass the Falklands. The seas down there aren't anything like what you're used to."

"All the more reason to raid for supplies," said Miranda in

what I thought was a brave attempt at pretending the raids were her idea, rather than a response to a stirring mutiny.

"If you say so."

"I do."

"There's still time to change your mind," said Ching.

"You know that won't happen."

Ching shot me a look as if to say, *See? I told you. Broken.*

"I just came to grab some charts," I said, desperate to get out of there.

"Grab them. I'll take you back." Miranda waited while I swiped charts at random, unable to focus. The pounding in my head sounded like drums.

When we were in the stairwell that led from the chart room to the bridge below, she placed a hand on the back of my head to protect it, then leaned me gently against the wall. Her eyes searched mine.

"You swear no one hurt you?"

"I swear it. I was just doing my job."

"Your job—fuck your job. I have other navigators. Do you know what it would do to me if—" She broke off and hauled on her braid, her frustration now violent. With the drug in my system, I could see she was close to breaking. The hand that held her hair was white-knuckled, but the hand cradling my skull remained gentle, and in that dichotomy I saw the stress fractures that ran through her and into the ship. Ching was wrong, however. She wasn't broken beyond repair.

And if she was?

I cupped her face in my hands and kissed her lips. They tasted like rum. She did not respond at first, and my lower lip slid over hers, the curve and softness of it familiar and new each time. The barest suggestion of a whimper escaped her mouth. I kissed her with more urgency. When her lips parted, I pulled her into me, and the wall of our ship held us up while Miranda put all the things I knew she couldn't say into the kiss.

Nothing had changed. I still needed time. But I was worried, so seas-damned worried, that time was the one thing we didn't have.

I undid her braid when she returned me to her quarters. She sat at my feet on the floor while I sat on the bed, and the thick fall of her hair loosened beneath my ministrations. Slowly I worked the knots out of the strands until I could run a comb from her scalp down to the tips. She relaxed against my legs. I pictured each loop of hair as a current while I braided. The clarity granted by the drug wavered once more, and I couldn't tell if the water running through my hands was real or imagined.

"I'm losing my ship." Miranda's voice interrupted my tumbling thoughts. My hands stilled in their work.

"That's not true."

"It is."

I tied off her braid and placed my hands on the tight muscles of her shoulders, kneading them.

"Your crew is loyal to you. We'll distract them with this raid, and then . . ." I hesitated. "Then we find the sea wolves."

"You were right." Her muscles remained rigid beneath my fingers. "The crew doesn't care."

"They care; we—"

"I can see it so clearly, Rose."

With her face turned away, I couldn't see her expression, but the pain in her voice was palpable. "See what?"

"How it could be better. With the right technology there could be enough to at least make this life worth it. I've read the histories. We had a chance to start over out here, and instead we're making the same mistakes, again and again and again. But maybe you're right. Maybe there isn't a better way. Maybe we're just wired to exploit each other."

"You don't exploit your crew."

"No, I just carve my mark into their palms." She laughed without humor. I rested my chin on the top of her head and reached down to take her hands. The scar on her palm matched the scar on mine—ridged, unlike the smooth lines of the jelly scars all over her body.

"How much time do we have?" The warm smell of her hair filled my senses, and it didn't smell like lemon. I held her and the currents tightly to me.

"I'm not sure. If they . . . if they were bold enough to make a move on you in front of me, not long."

"We could go."

"A captain doesn't abandon her ship."

"Then call for a vote."

She laughed again.

"You could," I pressed. "Then, if they choose Ching, you're free."

"I don't even know if they'd elect Ching. She failed them, too."

"Then we run."

"I can't, Rose. I worked—"

"Ching worked hard, too, and look what happened to her. I love your dream. I love that you believe in it. I want to live in that world someday, Miranda, but we can't build it if we're dead." I disentangled myself from her and slid to the ground to face her. She looked tired. She looked beautiful. She looked lost.

"I'm your navigator. I'm supposed to tell you when you're sailing into trouble."

Her thumb brushed the scab on my forehead.

"And I'm your captain. I'm supposed to keep you safe."

Harper lounged on the couch, tossing a lemon into the air and then catching it again. The ship rumbled with the sounds I associated with evening. Laughter and friendly shouts from the day shift filled the halls, and the skeleton crew that oversaw the ship in the evenings trekked to their posts.

"I still say we shouldn't trust her," said Harper.

"I'm not saying we should. I'm just saying—"

"I get it. But you're an idiot if you think this is all your fault."

"How is it not? I took us out from the coast—"

"Because there were active mother-fucking volcanoes."

"Still—"

"And her cryptic 'Stay close to the shelf' hallway exchange?

Dumb. I would have turned us dead into the gyre immediately if she said that to me."

"But—"

"The real issue is that you're trying to navigate at all," said Harper. "Have you told Miranda yet that you can't?"

"What are you talking about?" I turned my head too sharply to stare at her, earning a lance of pain.

"I know you, Rose. I can tell when something is wrong."

For a moment, I considered lying. Revealing this truth would mean facing it, and I wasn't ready—which made me no better than Miranda. A lie was a lie was a lie.

"No," I said. "I haven't told her. I haven't told anyone."

"That's what Orca and I thought."

"Please, Harp. If anyone finds out—"

"You were hit super hard in the head. Of course you're hurt. It will come back."

"You don't know that." My voice cracked, and I stared at the ceiling.

"And you don't know that it won't. But I don't think you should smoke that stuff anymore."

Seeing as I had taken the drug already that morning, I didn't immediately respond. "It's not that simple."

"It is, actually. Rest and recover. Can you even be sure you're okay to navigate high?"

"I verify the coordinates."

"So you're doing twice the work? How does that make sense? Other people can cover for you until you're better. And you were nearly killed the other day. Stay in here and stay safe."

"You sound like Miranda."

"For once I agree with her treatment of you on this." She tossed the lemon and caught it in the same hand. The smack of rind against her palm echoed my heart. *Thunk. Thunk. Thunk.*

"I don't know what to do about her."

"Right now, you don't do anything. You rest. Deal with her when you can think straight." She smirked. "Though maybe 'straight' is the wrong word."

"Funny."

"I know."

The lemon continued its trajectory up, then down.

"My leg still kills me, and it hurts to breathe," Harper continued. "But do you see me running around?"

"You're still working. It's not the same."

"Maybe."

A pause settled between us, punctuated by the lemon. I followed it with unfocused eyes.

"Raiding Crux makes me sick," Harper said eventually.

"I know."

"We could warn them."

I closed my eyes to shut out the thought I'd been suppressing: the choice was the Gulf all over again. "And then what?"

She didn't answer.

"Orca might go with you, if you asked," I said.

"Where would we go? Back to my mom?"

"There are other ships." I pictured Harper living on the *Trench*, engineering her way into yet another new life.

"What about you? Would you come with me?"

"I don't know."

"Miranda?" she asked.

"Miranda."

"You might be able to have something real if she left this ship," said Harper. "A fresh start."

"Is there such a thing?"

The *thunk* of the lemon escalated into a pounding. I blinked, trying to focus my eyes. The lemon wasn't moving, but the sound—

"Speaking of Miranda," said Harper as the door opened.

But it wasn't Miranda.

Armed sailors swarmed us. I recognized a few, including Reya and Nasrin. Wasn't Nasrin supposed to be guarding Ching? My head spun as I struggled to process what was happening. Nasrin didn't meet my eyes as she helped subdue a struggling Harper and bound her wrists behind her back. Another sailor punched Harper in the ribs. She whimpered—they hadn't yet healed fully—and slumped. I hardly even noticed the hands binding my own wrists behind me.

"Harp!" I flung myself toward her, but was restrained with more gentleness than I expected.

"Go easy, and you won't get hurt." I recognized Reya's voice.

Betrayal soured the air in my lungs. Reya. I worked beside her every day. Reya, who I'd thought one of the few people I could trust. It was Annie all over again, just like I'd feared the day I'd found Ching in the chart room. I aimed a kick at her kneecaps. She twisted me closer, knocking me off balance.

"You'll hurt your head if you keep fighting."

My shoulders ached from the binding. I stomped my foot on her toes, and she jerked my arms, straining the joints in their sockets.

"Let's go," said a man I didn't know.

Harper and I were shoved ahead of our attackers and out the door. I stared at it as I was paraded through. The lock hadn't been forced. That didn't make any sense. Only Miranda and I had keys.

"My mother will blow you out of the water," said Harper.

It was the wrong thing to say. Her captor—not gentle Nasrin, unfortunately—slammed her up against the wall of the corridor and cut off her breath with his forearm. She choked, and I writhed in Reya's grasp.

"We don't have time for this," said Nasrin. When the man torturing Harper snarled, she flexed a massive bicep at him in warning, and he lowered Harper back to the ground. She wheezed as we were shoved forward once more.

Captured twice in one month. Not exactly our crowning achievement.

Our progress was slow as both Harper and I fought as best we could. Finally, Reya tripped me. The impact sent stars across my vision. "Get up," she said curtly, but as she knelt to haul me to my feet, she whispered something else. "Cooperate. We have a plan."

I let my head fall against my chest to hide my shock.

They marched us to the brig, which was located in the bowels of the ship, and our captors did not care if we stumbled on the stairs or how many sailors stopped to stare. None intervened, though I saw mutterings and confused expressions. This offered little comfort. Even if half the ship still supported Miranda, they were clearly not the active half. I replayed Reya's words over and over to keep from crying. A plan. They had a plan. We were not all going to die.

Then again, plans failed.

Chapter Ten

The brig smelled like algae and brine. Recent flooding had left grime on the walls, and it was easy to see where the scrubbing crews hadn't gotten around to cleaning yet. Salt encrusted the floor and clung to crevices. The ceilings were even lower here than they were elsewhere. Pipes twisted above us—some filled with biolight, others pumping electric currents. The dried husk of a jellyfish hung from one.

"Get them in," said the sailor guarding the brig hatch. Nasrin opened it, her muscles bulging as she cranked the door, and Reya pushed me through.

The brig had several cells. Two were quarantine cells—one designed for a single occupant, and the other much larger, intended to house small crews. The other cells were uniform in size. Harper's captor unlocked one, then sent her sprawling to its floor. Reya was only slightly gentler with me. I landed half on top of Harper, who groaned as I crushed her ribs.

"Wait—" I called out as the door shut.

Darkness fell. The cell had a small biolight built into the plex of the ceiling—they didn't want us hanging ourselves on exposed pipes—which illuminated little. Harper's face was a kaleidoscope of shadow. I rolled off her, my arms still bound, and absorbed our surroundings. Hard plex walls. Windowless door with a slot for feeding. A bunk. A toilet. Nothing more.

I focused instead on Harper's wheezing breath. "Are you okay?"

"I've been better." She rolled into a sitting position. "What did they tie us with?"

"Hang on." I worked my body through my arms, thanking my flexibility, until my hands were in front of me. "Just rope cuffs."

Easy enough to undo. I freed Harper, who in turn freed me, and we rubbed our shoulders for a few silent minutes.

"We need to get out of here," she said eventually.

"Yeah." I told her what Reya had said.

"No offense to Reya, but she fucking locked us in here, so I'm not going to count on that." She stood, wincing, and hammered on the door. "Hey, shark-dicks, want to tell us why we're in here?"

Nobody responded. Harper kept up a barrage of insults until I stopped her, saying, "You're killing my head."

She slumped beside me on the ground. "I'm not dying in here."

"They don't have the others." *Yet*. I didn't say it, but we both heard the unspoken word.

"Wait." Harper raised her head from my shoulder. "They had a key."

"I know. But how—"

"They must have the captain."

Now it was my turn to surge to my feet and pound on the door. "Miranda," I screamed into the plex. She'd hear me if she was in the brig. No answer came. I continued screaming until my voice faded to a croak and Harper cradled my bruised hands in hers. My head throbbed. The drug was wearing off, and I had no way of getting more.

We fell asleep tangled together on the floor. I held Harper close, burying my face in her curls and tucking her body into mine as we'd done when we were younger. Unlike then, pain hitched our breathing, and there was no promise of morning.

Sounds woke us. My throat was parched and raw from shouting, and I tried to moisten my lips without success. A door opened, then another, and several thuds followed. Bodies. But they had

176

to be alive—we didn't store the dead in the brig. We pressed our faces to the feeding slot, and I tried to make out the few blurred shapes I could see beyond. The footsteps receded.

"Orca?" Harper called out.

A groan answered.

"Miranda?" I tried to speak, but my voice didn't carry. Harper took over.

"Miranda? Kraken?"

"Alive," said a voice that made me want to weep in relief. She was here. She was alive. Nothing else mattered.

"What happened?" Harper asked.

"Mutiny," said Kraken in a defeated rumble. "Ching's captain, now."

I clutched Harper's hand as dread chilled me. *Reya*, I begged, *please*. I didn't know where else to pin my hopes.

"Are you hurt?" Orca's voice was little louder than mine.

"No," Harper answered for us. "You?"

"We'll live."

"Not for long," said a different voice. "Shut the fuck up in there."

"It appears we have a guard," said Harper. "Hey, you barnacle-fucking fuck, can we get some water?"

The guard didn't reply.

Harper banged her fist on the door, once, then subsided. "When we get out of here, he dies first."

My head swam. "How long have we been here?"

"No idea. You were out for a while."

Something clanked, then a flask clattered to the ground beside us. Harper popped the cap and sniffed. "Water. Here." She held it to my lips. I swallowed, then swallowed again, cool water soothing the burn in my throat.

"I'm not going to be much help," I said as she drank her fill. "I feel . . . cracked."

Her hand found my forehead. "Then rest. Nothing else we can do, anyway."

I jolted awake some unquantifiable time later when the door

to our cell opened. My eyes struggled to focus, and I flinched in anticipation of pain as two people entered. One brandished a cudgel.

"Move it, Comita," he said. Harper drew back her fist to hit him. The cudgel hit her first. She collapsed, clutching her half-healed leg, and the second sailor hauled her out of the cell by the back of her shirt. It all happened in the space it took me to draw breath. I rolled off the sleeping nook and crawled to the door, shouting something incomprehensible as the sound of their footsteps faded.

Orca screamed her name for hours. I curled up with my hands over my ears and tried to block out her flayed voice, because it matched the jagged hollow in my chest too closely. *Not Harper*, my mind screamed with her. *Please, not Harper.*

I'd die if Ching killed her. My heart would splinter if her smile broke beneath Ching's cruelty. I loved Miranda—but Harper was home. Harper was the person who knew me best, better even than my mother, and without her I would have no frame of reference for my world. It was inconceivable a world without Harper could even exist. Time stretched in the darkness. I didn't feel hunger or thirst. I floated, suspended by terror, every filament strung out. The ocean was lost to me, but pain offered new coordinates.

"Harper?"

Orca's shout alerted me to noise beyond my cell. My door was unlocked, and then something fell to the ground. I scrambled forward. "Harper. *Harper.*"

She was warm to the touch, and I found the pulse in her neck. "She's alive."

"What did they do to her?"

My hands searched her unconscious body for signs of trauma. No blood matted her hair, and her breathing was steady, so her lungs had not been punctured. No broken arms. No—

I stopped. Her right hand was wrapped in a bandage, and I felt it gingerly. Only a thumb and three fingertips poked out from the wrapping.

"Rose. *What did they do to her?*"

Bile soured my mouth.

"They . . . they cut off a finger."

Orca must have flung herself at her door, judging by the pounding that erupted seconds later. I wanted to do the same. Instead, I pulled Harper's head into my lap and stroked her hair, unsure whether I was glad she was unconscious or desperate for her to wake. Her hands were her life. Engineers needed to be nimble, and while fingers were lost in accidents, Harper was careful. She took care of herself. This would devastate her.

"Rose?" Harper's voice sounded like Orca's: jagged.

"Hey," I said, smoothing my thumb across her forehead. "You're back."

She turned her face into my stomach and sobbed.

We were pulled apart hours later by the same two sailors. This time, I was the one led out. Harper scrabbled at their hold on me, smearing blood across their hands, but we were outmatched. Miranda shouted first for them to let me go, and then for me. Her words faded as fear grayed out my world.

They brought me to my old room. Ching sat on a stool, studying me. She wore Miranda's whip and sword. Two sailors flanked her. One looked away, guilt clouding his expression, but he made no move to help me.

"Isn't this cozy," Ching said.

Fear felt distant. My head was a sick, wet lump on top of my shoulders, and it throbbed with pain. Nausea roiled in my stomach. My system couldn't handle the stimulus. I clung to what I knew: if Ching killed me, my head would stop hurting.

Focus. Salvage what you can. Beg if you have to.

"Harper didn't do anything to you," I said with effort. "You could let her go. I'm the one who—"

"Don't be naïve. It doesn't matter what she did, or what you did. If I have her, I control Comita. And if I have you . . ."

She smiled, and even in my dazed state I could fill in the blanks. If she had me, she controlled Miranda. I wasn't going to die. I was going to be used against the people I loved.

"You're a monster."

How could I have believed, even for a moment, this hadn't been her plan all along?

"Maybe. I'm also captain of this ship. If you eat, you eat by my leave. If I let you live, you live by my leave. And if you want your friends to eat and live with you, you'll tell me exactly what I want to know."

Her eyes—a brown so dark it was nearly black, and framed by short thick lashes—held mine as she leaned forward. I nodded. I would tell her everything, because I knew what she would do if I didn't. I'd sit, bound, while she removed another finger from Harper's hand, or cut the eyes out of Orca's tattoos, or—I couldn't think about what she'd do to Miranda, because I suspected it would involve my own flesh. And Kraken—vast, unshakeable Kraken. What would she do to him?

"Good. I need you to give me the key to fleet code."

I noticed the box beside her for the first time. On a bed of vermillion-stained cloth lay Harper's finger.

"Why?"

"That's irrelevant."

"No. I mean why did you do this?"

She seemed to understand that by "this" I meant betraying Miranda, as she said, unsmiling, "Because she gave me every reason to."

"You swore an oath."

"And I kept it. I did not orchestrate this mutiny. Her crew did that all on their own. As for the rest of that oath, the revenge I'm after has nothing to do with you. Miranda should know that. She also knows that captains earn their position, and that their crew can take it away."

I didn't understand. I was so damn tired of how much it hurt to think.

"What will you do with us?" I asked.

"I'll give Miranda the same choice she gave me. As for you and Comita's spawn, you'll serve your purpose."

Panic should have flooded me. I should have raged against her words. All I felt was empty. Everything about this encounter felt inevitable; revenge was as cyclical as the seasons. When she handed me a pen and paper, I did not even attempt to obfuscate. What did it matter? What did anything matter?

Harper held me in her lap when I was dumped back in the cell an eternity later. I would have sobbed if the neurons in my brain remembered how to fire, but instead I lay still, spinning, spinning, spinning into darkness.

Hours later, another sound woke me. This time it was the grunt of the guard, followed by an odd slither. Harper stiffened. I could feel her straining to listen beside me. Someone cursed under their breath. Then our door swung open.

Nasrin and Reya stood framed by the light of the brig. Nasrin glanced behind us, swore, then grabbed the keys from Reya and fumbled with the next cell.

Reya motioned for us to stand. Weak from hunger, blood loss, and, in my case, my head, we managed to help each other up.

Outside our cell Orca and Kraken waited. They must have been imprisoned together. Harper whimpered as Orca crushed her in a fierce hug, and I looked away.

Miranda was the last to be released. I pushed past Orca and Harper and stumbled into her open arms. The smell of her sweat encompassed me, and I inhaled, willing myself not to cry from exhausted relief. I didn't realize she'd lifted me until she turned and I turned with her. I let her hold me until I felt her arms begin to tremble. Deprivation had weakened her, too. I wriggled free to stand beside her.

Physically she looked unharmed. As I looked into her eyes, however, I saw the damage. They were wide and stunned with betrayal.

"We need to move," Nasrin was saying. "Finn is on the boat. We have an opening of fifteen minutes, tops, and we've just wasted five. Captain, I'm sorry."

"Let's go." Miranda kept her arm around my waist as if

she was afraid if she let me go, I might vanish. I felt the same way about her.

It must have been night. The ship was hushed, as if even the walls slept, and Reya scouted the corridors ahead while Nasrin led our band of exiles. I refused to think about what this meant. Staying alert took all my concentration anyway. Miranda's fingers dug into my waist each time Reya turned a corner or opened a hatch. Discovery was one pair of eyes away.

Ahead, Reya threw up her hand. Nasrin ushered us back and yanked open the door to a supply closet. It was a tight fit, especially with Kraken, but she got us all in before shutting the door in our faces. Voices murmured outside.

Inside, we stank.

Days of fear-sweat and no access to fresh water had taken their toll, and my eyes watered.

At least it isn't lemons.

The thought was so incongruous I nearly laughed—hysteria setting in—before realizing this was the first real sign of improvement I'd seen in myself. Not that it would matter if we were discovered.

Nasrin opened the door a few held breaths later. We trudged after her again. Twice more we were forced to hide before we made it to the hatch into the docking bay.

"This is where it gets tricky," Nasrin said. "I'll go first. Reya, stay here."

Nasrin cranked the hatch. The smell of salt water wafted in, and I took a deep breath. Silence.

"How many—" Miranda asked, but Reya held her finger to her lips. Soft voices, then a thump. Reya winced.

"It was supposed to be clear," she said. "Fuck."

Nasrin reappeared with a strained expression on her face and motioned for us to hurry. The docking bay was a cavernous space. Water filled the lower half, and the blurred outlines of ships bobbed on the surface. Our trawler floated inconspicuously alongside them. Nasrin paused beside the body of a person I vaguely recognized.

"Is she dead?" asked Miranda.

"No." Regret dripped from Nasrin's voice. "But she saw me. I had to knock her out."

Having been knocked out myself, I felt a rush of sympathy for the girl on the floor.

"It's your call," said Miranda.

Nasrin rubbed one of her tattoos. It was too dark to see which one, and I tried to coerce Miranda's words into sense. What was Nasrin's call?

"I can't trust that Dani will forget," said Nasrin.

"I wouldn't ask you to come with us. You'd be giving everything up. As I said, it's your call. I'm no longer captain of this ship."

The kid's face was soft in her forced sleep. She couldn't have been much older than seventeen.

Nasrin nodded to herself before speaking. "I knew the risks."

Reya clasped Nasrin's arm but didn't speak. Maybe she was worried Dani would recall her voice.

"Thank you," Miranda said to Reya. Reya wiped tears from her cheeks with a furious swipe and put her palm to Miranda's. They stood like that for a long moment: Miranda, hair mussed but spine straight, and Reya, fighting her emotions with a trembling lip.

"Come on." Nasrin herded the rest of us toward the trawler. The hatch opened at her knock, and I saw Finn's sober face waiting. Harper descended first. I followed, with Orca and Kraken taking up the rear. Miranda and Nasrin came shortly after.

"Reya will open the seadoor," said Nasrin. "Then we're on our own."

"Rose, navigation. Harper, bridge."

Harper leapt to obey. Miranda helped me down the familiar tight hallway through the cramped common area, small hydrofarm, storage room—and at last, the helm. It could hardly be called a bridge. Just two chairs and clear plex, which currently looked out into black water. Biolights outlined the seadoor.

I sat. Miranda took the wheel and guided the ship toward the door as it creaked open, her face a mask of flickering blue light. The *Sea Cat* blocked our view of *Man o' War* as we sped into the open ocean. I longed to look back anyway. That ship—that *fucking* ship—had given me Miranda, but it had taken more than its share of my blood in return. I hurt everywhere. My head and my throat and my bruised body screamed at me to find the nearest hole and hide so I could at least close my burning eyes.

"Can you get us a heading?" Miranda asked. "We'll need to stay off Ching's radar until we're far enough away to—"

"Miranda." She stopped talking at the flat tone in my voice. I stared out the plex at the fathomless deeps. All that, and for what? "I can't navigate."

"What do you mean, you can't navigate?"

I didn't dare turn to her. My compass spun and spun, unable to settle, unable to align, just like the nightmares that had haunted my childhood. "I haven't been able to since the attack."

Chapter Eleven

"Why didn't you tell me?" Miranda spun my chair—I'd forgotten that feature of the helm—and forced me to look her in the eyes.

"Because I'm your navigator. Your *navigator*, Mere."

"Don't be an idiot."

I stared at my lap. Her hand cupped my chin and tilted it inexorably up. I braced myself for her anger, aware that after all the times I'd accused her of lying to me, I deserved it. Instead, her lips landed on mine, gentle and chapped. I froze in surprise. She pulled away after a moment and settled back in her chair.

"This is my fault."

I made a sound of protest.

"You really think it matters to me, after everything, whether you can navigate?"

"I—"

"Neptune, Rose." She shook her head. "You deserve better than me."

"What?"

The twisted smile on her lips was somber. "I failed you. I failed everyone, but you—I was supposed to protect you, and I've hurt you more ways than I can count."

Dehydrated and exhausted as I was, her words still managed

to break me. "You haven't."

It was a lie—she had hurt me, over and over, and I'd hurt her. This life allowed for little else. Still, the remorse in every line of her body was a balm, and I let it soothe me as we sailed deeper into the night.

"We'll navigate the old-fashioned way. Stars and charts. But you—if I'd lost you—" Her voice broke.

"You didn't."

"I'm so bad at this. At loving you. I want—" She couldn't finish, and her sharp inhale carried an edge of tears.

"You're perfect."

She wasn't. I wasn't. That didn't matter right now as her world collapsed around her. My world remained, because everything and everyone I needed was with me on this ship.

"Fuck. Rose, what am I going to do?" Biolight flickered along the strong curve of her jaw, which she'd clenched so hard I feared she'd crack it.

"We'll figure it out."

"My ship—"

"Is gone." I hadn't intended on being so blunt. My head ached, and my heart ached, and everything had gone so wrong. "But we're alive."

I reached for her hand and wound my fingers through hers. She squeezed them, and I thought about the first time I'd seen her. She'd looked untouchable, and desire had eclipsed me like a summer storm. I thought of all that had happened since. Annie. The Gulf. Orca. Kissing Miranda on the deck of the *Sea Cat* beneath the endless sky. Choosing her, over and over again, regardless of the cost.

"Besides," I said, the words rising from a place beyond the reach of my damaged brain. "I don't think anyone really deserves anything. We take what we can get."

Footsteps sounded in the hall. Days of imprisonment sent a last stab of adrenaline through my body, warning me danger was near, but it was just Nasrin. "Water and some crackers. Kraken's cooking something for later."

We accepted the flasks and the crackers. I softened the over-salted wafers in my mouth with water before swallowing, as my throat was too sore for their rough edges. Sugar hit my blood-stream and some of the haze around my vision cleared. I focused on the water beyond the helm. The small compass on the dash pointed east.

"We should go south," I said, tapping it.

Miranda didn't argue. She adjusted our course and drank her water slowly, probably wishing it was rum.

"Will she send someone after us?" I asked.

"I don't know."

I heard the undercurrents in her voice. She didn't know, because she'd underestimated Ching, and she could never be sure of her again. Her lapse in judgment had cost her everything.

Well, not everything. The trawler hummed, and the sound was familiar and welcome. Something equally familiar brushed against my leg.

"Seamus." Miranda scooped him into her arms and clutched him to her chest, her eyes closing as she buried her face in his ruff. He purred loudly enough to overpower the sounds of the ship. I watched them for a while. Miranda, stroking her cat. Seamus, fat and content, kneading her arm with his large orange paws. His tail flicked periodically.

We were on our own. This trawler was no longer a vessel used for missions, irritating in its claustrophobic confines but convenient for its speed and camouflage, and easily forgotten once we returned to the main ship. Now, it was our world entire, presuming we escaped any boats Ching sent after us. And Nasrin—had she really known the risk of helping us? What about Reya? What would Ching do to her if her role in our escape came to light?

With the ship on autopilot and subbed at a depth I hoped would bring us near a swarm of camouflaging siphonophores, Miranda and I trudged down the hall to the common area at Kraken's summons. I stared at the table. Roaches, boiled and smelling like heaven, sat on beds of seaweed. Orca, Harper, Finn, and Nasrin already sat around the table. Kraken handed me and Miranda plates and motioned for us to squeeze in as best we could.

I fell upon the food like a shark. The roach's meat was tender and sweet and salty, and I cracked the carapace with my hands to suck out the tender flesh. Even Orca dug in with the enthusiasm of the starved. The seaweed crunched between my teeth. Food. Why had I ever taken it for granted?

Kraken poured small measures of rum for everyone but me. When I looked at him, blinking blearily, he tapped his head. "You're in no shape to drink."

"Well," said Finn, finishing his dinner and looking around at us. "Just like old times. You all look like squid shit."

"Thanks," said Orca. Harper remained quiet at her side, holding her injured hand out of the way as she struggled to eat with her left.

It wasn't like old times, though. Jeanine was dead. Finn met my eyes and smiled sadly.

"We all need to rest," said Kraken. "But we'll have to do it in shifts until we're clear. Captain?"

Eyes turned expectantly to Miranda, who ate stolidly, more machine than woman as she chewed.

"I'm stepping down."

"The fuck you are," said Orca.

She chewed, swallowed, and looked up. "Fine. Then here is my last order: elect a new captain from amongst yourselves."

Silence rang around the table, punctuated by the sound of Miranda tossing back the rum and setting her cup down on the chipped surface.

"No," said Orca.

"As first mate, you're acting captain until then."

Orca gaped. I didn't know what to say. Miranda's hand was on my thigh beneath the table, and her grip was steady. She was sure in her decision. Harper nodded slowly, and to my surprise, so did Kraken.

"As you wish," he said. "Orca, arrange the shifts."

"But—" She paused and beseeched Miranda one last time.

Miranda gestured for Kraken to pour more rum.

"Okay. Finn, Nasrin—you're in better shape than the rest of us. Finn, take the helm. Nasrin, you're on call if anything goes wrong."

"I'm a bartender."

"Now you're general crew. Shadow Finn and Harper and learn what they do. Do you have any experience in hydroponics?"

"More than in engineering."

"Then you'll also help Kraken in the grow tanks. The rest of you, get some sleep. What's our heading?"

This last was directed at me. "South."

"Just south?"

"For now, just south, and keep us low."

"I'll clear up," said Nasrin. She stood, and next to Kraken she looked small—despite the fact that her biceps dwarfed my thighs.

The bunks beyond the common room were narrow and designed for one. I made for the berth I'd slept in before, but Miranda caught my arm and pulled me down beside her. Seamus leapt up to make a place for himself between our feet as she tugged the curtain over the alcove.

We still stank. We were still lost. But as she covered us with a light hemp blanket and tucked her arm around my ribs, I felt momentarily anchored.

Life aboard the *Sea Cat* settled into a pattern. By night I checked our progress against the stars and compared it to the charts, my hands clumsy on the tools and my brain still slow to function. I woke in the afternoons with Miranda, who shared the night shift with me, and we took inventory. Kraken's foresight and Nasrin's intervention had supplied us with most of what a small craft needed: breeding pairs of roaches, stable algae stocks, 3-D printer, clothing, rum and a still to make more, grow tanks filled with seaweed, clothing, soap, and, of course, a cat to deal with any furry stowaways.

Harper's wound, however, was a problem. The one thing we didn't have an immediate supply of was antibiotics. She removed the bandage our first full day. It stuck to her skin. Beneath, the red stump of her finger was dark with gore, and I saw bone. I tore my eyes away. I could not plug my ears from her curses. She growled as Kraken washed her finger first with boiled water, then an iodine scrub, but the skin around the site was redder than I thought it should be.

"How long until we have a penicillin culture?" I asked Kraken when we were out of earshot of Harper and Orca.

"At least a week." His expression was grim, and he frowned at the bloody cloth. "And if it gets into her bloodstream, she might not have that long."

"At least we know how to make it, now," I said. He'd wrested the supplies from the main ship over the prior weeks, and I could have kissed him for his foresight.

"Let's hope so."

We were in the small galley kitchen off the common area, which was barely big enough for Kraken, let alone us both. I checked no one was nearby. "Miranda's serious about stepping down."

"I know."

"But she's—"

"Let her be. There are limits to what a person can lose."

"Then who should we vote for?"

"That's up to you." He ruffled my hair and pulled clean boiled bandages out of the water with a pair of tongs. "Just as long as it's not me."

"You'd be a good captain."

"As I said—as long as it's not me."

Ching's ships did not appear behind us, and as the days passed and we saw no one, I began to hope that at least that problem was temporarily resolved. Tending to the trawler required all of our efforts. Miranda worked as hard as the rest of us, scrubbing the floors and the tanks and taking her turn cleaning up, along with assisting me in navigation. She rarely spoke. At night she held me, and while on *Man o' War* she'd slept in my arms, content to be vulnerable only in sleep, I let her cling to me now and clasped her hand in mine over my breast. I knew without asking that her embrace was an apology. *I should have protected you*, it said, *and I failed.*

I knew the feeling. Finn's forced cheer haunted me now as surely as Jeanine's disembodied head had haunted me in the days following her passing.

Sometimes the heat of her stirred a part of me that had been broken with my head wound, but there was something too vulnerable about her lips on my shoulder as she slept. I let the longing pass. Things were not fixed between us yet.

And Harper grew worse.

"Call a vote," Miranda said to Orca over the evening meal, which for me and her was the first of the day.

"Not yet." Orca glanced at Harper, whose eyes had a feverish shine. "I can't focus."

"All the more reason to call a vote."

"She's got a point," said Kraken. "We've had time to think about it, and the sooner we elect a captain, the better for all of us. Harp included."

"How does a vote work?" asked Harper. Was I imagining a scratch in her voice? A catch in her lungs?

"Normally, someone's nominated. But I say we just cast lots. No offense, but no one's going to nominate anyone with you here, Miranda." Finn looked to Miranda for confirmation.

"Lots are fine." Her hands didn't shake. Was she really going to let this happen?

"Great. Here's how it works. Everyone gets ..." he cast around, and then reached for his chopsticks. "A lot. Put it in the cup of the person you want. We'll vote one at a time, privately."

It seemed fair enough. I selected a chopstick and looked

around at my crew, trying to imagine one of them as my new captain. I couldn't. Miranda was my captain. Nobody else had demanded my loyalty in love and blood, though Orca had certainly shed her fair share of it in the ring. Voting for anyone besides Miranda felt wrong on every level. I decided I'd wait to see who the others chose and go with the general consensus.

"Rose, you first," said Orca.

Damn.

The empty common room felt even smaller than normal with its battered table and chairs. Miranda had overturned her cup. I brushed the cool plex of its base with my finger. I both understood her decision and yet didn't. She felt as if she'd failed so completely she no longer deserved the title, but wasn't turning it down a form of surrender? Miranda Stillwater didn't just give up. I refused to believe this had broken her. Fuck Ching. Miranda would be back. In the meantime, I had no choice but to play along. The bamboo chopstick slid over my fingers as I tapped it against my thigh.

Kraken had asked me not to vote for him. Nasrin was a bartender, and while I liked her, she didn't know enough to captain a ship and hadn't planned on coming with us in the first place. Plus, even though she'd freed us, she'd also put us in the brig in the first place. Finn was a brilliant translator, but not commanding, and still wounded from grief. Harper—Harper was a leader. I hesitated, my stick absurdly heavy in my hands. Harper or Orca. My best friend or my . . . whatever Orca was to me.

I'd sailed beneath Orca on this ship before. That, more than anything, settled my mind. My stick landed in her cup with a hushed clatter, and I left the room.

One by one, my crewmates filed in to cast their votes. I toyed with the ring on Miranda's hand. Orca would be chosen. There was no other logical choice, though Kraken was a viable second. It had to be Orca.

Miranda voted last. She pulled her hand free from mine and walked into the common room, shutting the hatch behind her. We waited in the hall.

"I forgot to say, if you elect me, I'm taking away your rum

ration," Kraken said.

"Good thing I didn't vote for you then," said Orca. I wondered who she *had* voted for. Harper? Herself? I'd never asked if that was an option—not that I would have put a lot in my own cup. Only an idiot would elect me, damaged as I was.

"We're done," said Miranda.

I filed in behind Nasrin, and frowned. Had I forgotten the location of my seat? The cup where I thought I'd been sitting had several lots in it, which couldn't be right. I looked to Miranda for guidance, but she was fingering the lots as she made her way around the table, counting.

"Two for Orca," she said, setting the cup back down. "One for Kraken. And . . . four for Rose."

I stood like an imbecile, convinced I was hallucinating. This wasn't real. I'd misheard. My head didn't ache so much as whirl, and, fool that I was, I reached for north.

Nothing. No guiding star, no currents, just the tableau of faces in front of me. Nasrin looked nonplussed. The rest of the crew turned to me, and my brain refused to catalogue the expressions on their faces.

"No," I said.

"No what, Captain?" asked Harper. Her smile was bittersweet.

"I'm a navigator."

"Exactly. We need someone who knows where we're going, for now," said Finn.

"But I don't."

"You'll figure it out," said Kraken. He gave me a reassuring nod.

"But Orca—"

Orca shook her head. "You get to choose your first mate. I'd serve, if you asked, but it's up to you."

"I . . . I need a minute." I cradled my head and sank into my chair, feeling the blood pound in my temples. I wasn't a captain. I'd never wanted to be a captain. I followed orders; I didn't give them.

Though you don't follow them very well, my mind pointed out.

Shut up. There had to be a way out of this. Surely Miranda would see how insane this was and reclaim her position, perhaps with a wicked grin to show it was all a joke. I'd forgive her if she acted soon.

She didn't.

I raised my head and surveyed my crew. Why had they chosen *me* of all people?

"What if I say no?"

"You can," said Miranda. "But think about it first. It's an honor. Don't insult us."

Us. Had Miranda cast her lot for me?

"Then . . . okay. I'll think." *And say no later.* "In the meantime, I guess go about things as usual?"

My crew shrugged and, just like that, it was over. Harper slid into a seat next to me. Her cheeks were flushed, and when she nudged me, her skin burned.

"Hey, Captain."

"You have a fever."

"Just my body fighting off Ching's fuckery. Good thing she left me my middle finger so I can—"

"You should be resting."

"Is that an order, Captain?"

Her tone was joking, but I wasn't. "Yes. Your shift is over anyway. We'll have antibiotics soon, and then—"

"Yes, yes, yes." She waved my concern away. "Don't let power go to your head."

With that, she stretched and padded to her bunk, yanking her curtain shut behind her. Worry grew like a tumor in my gut. Fever meant infection. The penicillin cultures were doing well, according to Kraken, but we were still a few days away from anything that could help her, and there'd been no signs of ships to trade with. Even if I adjusted our course, there was no guarantee we'd find another ship in time, or that Ching wouldn't be waiting.

And they'd made me captain.

I remained sitting at the scratched table, jamming my thumbnail into a crack in the plex, while the crew dispersed. A hand landed softly on my shoulder. I looked up, still numb from shock, and saw Finn. The shock dissipated and was replaced with the now all-too-familiar guilt I felt each time I met his eyes.

"Congratulations," he said.

"I don't want this." The waver in my voice was dangerously reminiscent of tears.

"I know you don't." He propped his hip against the table and looked down at me. "But you'll do it. You know how to make the hard choices."

"What are you talking about? I always choose wrong."

The Gulf. The bodies. Jeanine. If I'd been faster, stronger—

"Not always." He gave me another sad smile. "You were the only one who tried to save her."

"And I failed."

"But you tried." The smile on his face twisted into anguish. "I didn't even know she was in the water."

"Finn—"

"She would have died without you. You gave her a fighting chance."

"But I didn't—"

"I saw her body, Rose. I know what squid are capable of, and even if you'd had an armed team, she still might not have made it."

"I still failed her."

"Do you know what she'd say to you, right now, if she heard you?"

I shook my head.

"'I don't need some jelly saving my ass.' She was tough. Don't dishonor her memory by blaming yourself."

"But you got only three months with her." My voice splintered.

"Yeah."

He didn't say, *But at least I had those months,* or, *Better to have loved and lost than never loved at all,* or some other platitude. Just "Yeah." I felt the chasm of his loss in the inadequacy of that single word.

"Is it hard to be back on this ship?" I asked, immediately

regretting the words. Of course it was hard. I was an idiot.

"I'd rather be here than on *Man o' War*. She didn't die on this ship."

"Finn . . . I'm so sorry."

"Do me a favor." He squeezed my shoulder. "Don't let her haunt you. She wouldn't have wanted that."

"Will you promise the same?"

The eyes he turned on me were as lightless as the caves beneath the sea, but they were kind. "Not yet. But I have the luxury of being haunted. You have work to do, Captain."

"I don't understand," I said to Miranda when we were alone at the helm. "I can't do it."

"Why not?"

"All I know how to do is navigate, and I can't even do that right."

She tucked a knee under her arm and idly turned her chair. "You know how to make tough choices. That's all command really is."

"But Orca—"

"Deferred to you when it mattered, and everyone on this ship—except Nasrin—remembers that."

"That was different." And part of me wished Orca hadn't, now. If we'd never found the channel, we might not be here, exiled.

"Was it?" asked Miranda.

"What about you?" Tears stung my eyes. "I can't be your captain."

She raised an eyebrow. It was the closest she'd come to flirting with me since our fight.

"Seriously, Miranda. I can't."

"You can."

"Then will you be my first mate? I'll do it, if you promise you will be."

"I'm not first mate material."

"You were Ching's."

"And look how that ended."

"It's you or Orca."

Her lips thinned. "Orca's a good first mate. You should ask her."

"I don't *want* Orca. I want *you*."

"I got us into this. Choose someone else."

I glared at her. The scar on my forehead pulled sharply with the motion. "Fine. I order you to be my first mate."

"Or what?"

"See? You can't take orders from me. I can't be your captain."

"I think I'm just as compliant as you were, once upon a time."

"That—" was fair, annoyingly. "If you don't serve as my first mate, I'll assign you dish duty until you die."

"I could live with that."

"Miranda."

"What? I could."

"Please. Don't make me beg you." I was willing to beg. I'd begged her for far less.

"I'm sorry, Rose. I can't." She looked away from me and out the plex at the fading light. Nothing moved in the streaming sea. I thought about screaming at her but didn't want to risk making myself sick.

"Can I at least ask your advice?"

"Always."

It was better than nothing.

Harper's fever rose through the night. Orca stayed up beside her as she tossed and turned and sweated through her clothing. The wound was puffy and inflamed, but no red line crept through her blood vessels toward her heart. We had time. Not much, but some. Kraken and Nasrin pored over the penicillin culture while Finn handled the engines, which were running smoothly anyway and didn't require much of his time.

Meanwhile, I paced in front of Harper's bunk.

"You're disturbing her," Orca said. Dark circles shadowed her eyes. She'd bound her braids back to keep them out of Harper's sleeping face. I'd left Miranda at the helm, and it was just the three of us in the common room.

"I wish I was. She's not even awake." I gestured at her fitful sleep. "What do we do?"

Orca shrugged helplessly. "I don't know."

I knelt beside Harper's bunk, careful not to touch her fevered skin. She needed sleep. It was the only medicine we could give her.

"Ching," I said. I put all my hatred into the word.

"We'll find her, one day. And when we do . . ." She smoothed a damp curl from Harper's forehead.

"You really love her, don't you?" I asked.

Orca met my eyes. "Yeah."

"I'm glad." It was a stupid thing to say, all things considered, but I meant it. "You need someone to keep you in your place."

"So does Miranda."

"I don't think I'm the right person for that job. You should be captain, Orca."

"No." I couldn't tell if there was resentment in her voice, or resignation. "And Miranda shouldn't be, either."

"That's not—"

"You know it's true. She was a good captain, once. But she's fucked up right now."

"So am I," I said.

"Do you know the difference between you and Miranda?" she asked. When I didn't answer, she continued. "You *know* you're fucked up."

"Thanks?"

"No problem. So, Captain. What the hell are we going to do now?" Orca asked the question as if she actually thought I might know the answer.

"I—" I stopped myself from saying I didn't know. I did know. I'd known since I'd told Miranda we were going south, because what other options did we have left?

"We find the sea wolves."

South

Captain's Log
Captain Miranda Stillwater
Man o' War
February 26, 2514
11°52′12″N, 4°28′48″W

Last log as captain of *Man o' War,* written in my cell at the order of Amaryllis. Sorry. Ching Shih. You said you hated that name, but then again, when have you ever told me the full truth?

As you command then.

I remand my ship into the hands of Ching Shih, at the will of my crew, and make no further claims to her decks. All previous contracts will be renegotiated as her new captain sees fit.

May fair seas never find you, my friend.

Miranda Stillwater

Chapter Twelve

Harper lost consciousness on our fifth day of sailing. I returned from the helm as the sun broke the depths to find Orca shaking Harper's shoulders and Kraken kneeling beside her bunk. I dropped beside him. Harper's face and hair were damp with sweat, and the skin on her arm—which Kraken had extended into the light for examination—was mottled and bruised. The discoloration purpled her skin and extended toward her elbow.

"She's going septic," he said.

"Then fucking *do* something," said Orca.

"The antibiotics should be ready today, but . . ." Kraken didn't finish his words. Looking at Harper's eyelids as they twitched in fever dreams, I heard them anyway. Even with antibiotics she'd be lucky to pull through.

"Go see to them," I told him. And then, panicking, added, "Wait."

He paused mid-rise.

"Is there anything we can do? Her fever—should we try to break it?"

"Cold water."

"Okay."

He left to go check on the medicine, and I touched the

inflamed skin around Harper's wrist. It felt tight and hot and sick.

Orca wrestled Harper's pants off, but we left her shirt, not daring to disturb her arm. Orca lifted her gently. Harper's head lolled on Orca's shoulder and I hovered, wanting to help and sensing, too, the protective terror radiating from Orca.

There wasn't really room for the three of us in the head. The restrictive size of the tiny shower, at least, helped keep Harper propped up when Orca settled her down on the floor. I turned on the water. Cold, briny spray misted Harper's curls as the stream soaked her chest. I crouched beside Orca and held Harper's wound out of the water while Orca made sure no water got in Harper's mouth.

Her eyelids fluttered a few minutes in. Orca tensed beside me. I felt all the muscles in her body harden, as by necessity we were squeezed together, and I knew mine had done the same.

"Harp?" I asked.

A slit of pupil answered me. She tried to raise her head.

"Easy, girl," said Orca. "Don't move too much."

The cold water had to be agony on her feverish skin. She groaned and shifted, but did not attempt to escape. I preferred to think of it that way—that she wasn't trying to move, instead of that she *was* trying, but couldn't make her body cooperate.

"How long do we leave her in here?" Orca asked.

"I don't know. I'm not a doctor. Until she cools?"

"Neptune's balls. Look at her."

Harper began to shiver. "Tell ... tell me a story," she said in a rasp through her chattering teeth. Orca glanced at me.

"She's heard all my stories," I said. My heart leapt at the fact she'd been able to speak. "You tell one."

"I'm not a fucking bard."

"Try."

Orca tucked a wet lock behind Harper's ear. Her brow wrinkled as she thought, making her look younger.

"There once was a little—shit. No. Okay. When I was a kid, my da sailed under a man named Davy. I used to think he was Davy Jones himself. This fucker was scary. He wasn't big, like

Kraken, but when he looked at you it was like he could see every bad thought you'd ever had, and he *liked* it. My da kept me away from him, but I served as a runner until I was old enough to work on the other crews. This one time, I was bringing a message from one of the engineers to the first mate. Her name was Ali, and she was just as terrifying, but in a different way. She looks me over and says, 'Take that message to the captain. Then come back to me and tell me what he said.'

"So I go, and I find Davy, and I tell him what the engineer told me, and he looks at me like he knows I'm scared of him and that I'm wishing my da would let me carry a knife. 'What are you scared of, girl?' he says.

"I don't say anything. My da told me not to speak to the captain beyond relaying messages, and eventually he dismisses me with his reply. So, then I go to the first mate and tell her what he said, and she nods. But before I can leave, she says, 'Word of advice, kid. Don't fear death. Fear what comes before, and after.'

"She led a mutiny later that day. I hid with the other kids in one of the creches, and when it was over, my da was dead. I never knew who killed him—her side or his—but she came and found me later. 'Do you understand?' she asked me. I was nine. I was newly orphaned. That was all I understood, and so I said no.

"She adopted me. I moved into her quarters, and by the time I was fifteen I was joining her on raids. We sailed under Ching then. Ali was killed by an Archipelago sailor when I was seventeen, from a wound to the gut. It was messy and awful, and before she lost consciousness, she asked me again if I understood what she'd meant. This time I said yes. I hated watching her suffer. I hated thinking about what would happen after. When death itself came, I wasn't scared of it; she was free. I was the one who suffered. So, you can't die on me."

"Orca," I said, stunned. I'd never asked her life story. I'd thought I knew it—she sailed under Ching, and then she sailed under Miranda, and that was all I'd cared to know. This picture of Orca as a little orphaned girl changed the way light fell across her gray eyes.

"Don't." She flinched away from the hand I put on her shoulder.

"I'm not going to die, assholes."

We both turned to Harper. Her eyes were open wider, and some of the fevered brightness had dissipated.

"Damn straight you're not," I said.

"And you." Harper tried to raise her good hand toward Orca. "You're like a roach."

"What?"

"Hard and spiny on the outside, but sweet and soft underneath."

Orca smiled. The expression on her face as she looked at Harper was radiant, even as she scoffed. "Fuck off."

"Are you her little rumpling?" I said.

"I'll break your face if you ever call me that again. I don't care if you're the new captain."

"Can I get out of the water, now?" asked Harper. She almost sounded like her old self.

"I'll go check on Kraken, see if he has anything," I told them as Orca shut off the water and began the process of drying Harper off.

Miranda stood just past the doorway. I nearly ran into her, and she steadied me with her hands on my shoulders.

"How is she?" Her eyes slid over my shoulder to Harper and Orca.

I shook my head. We walked together to the grow room, and I felt the drag, not of currents, but of Harper's waning smile. I couldn't imagine a world where Harper Comita didn't exist, where her impish grin didn't do its best to convince me to do something stupid, or where her small frame and imposing fists weren't there to thrust themselves between me and trouble. She was more than a friend. She was the rock by which I measured the tides of my life.

Sea Cat's grow room was lit by the morning sun. The thick plex overhead let in the rays that filtered down to our depths, and the tanks lining the walls fluttered with life. Different types of seaweed waved in the filtered current, and roaches prowled the sediment at the bottom, feasting on algae and the snails that crawled along the strands of nori. In the center of the room, greens grew in tiered beds, fed by the pipes winding around the algae vats. Kraken stood beside another vat, which also served as a table for smaller vessels. These were where he cultured our medicines, and the magnifying glass and slides—precious, precious gifts from Polaris—were dwarfed by his hands.

"We've got it," he said when he saw us enter. Relief softened the monstrous tattoos on his face. "I'll have enough to dose her by the afternoon."

I burst into tears.

Miranda rubbed circles on my back while Kraken returned to work. I heaved great sobbing breaths. Harper had a chance. Not a huge one, but a chance.

I slept fitfully, waiting for the sounds that would signify Kraken's arrival with the medicine. Miranda lay awake beside me. Each time I started awake at a sound, I found her lying on her back, one arm around me, her eyes on the plex above us. Her bicep was hard against the back of my neck. I burrowed into her and felt the rigidity of her body soften. *How many sailors have you lost to infection?* I wanted to ask her, but I didn't. One was too many. Harper was healthy and strong, but healthy and strong people died the same as everyone else. I thought of Orca, who had lost most of the people she loved. I thought of Miranda, whose parents had been executed for her crimes.

Save crew members, I'd never lost anyone important to me. My father didn't count—I'd barely known him, and that grief was old. Jeanine, Dev, and Annie were complicated by guilt, but they hadn't felt like family. At least, not yet. Jeanine might have, in a few more months, but we hadn't been granted that luxury—and even so, she haunted me.

I didn't know how to cope with this panic. This helplessness. Part of me wanted to kick Orca away so I could keep these moments with Harper to myself. Another part of me wanted to hide at the opposite end of the ship.

"Try to sleep," Miranda said into my hair.

"Like you are?"

She didn't answer. I rolled onto my other side and studied the curtain.

Long hours later, Kraken's low voice rumbled Harper's name. I tumbled out of my bunk. He'd printed a syringe, and Harper watched as he slid the needle into her vein.

"You're good at that," she said. Orca had propped her up into a sitting position, and one look at her cheeks told me the fever had returned.

"I've had some practice."

"Is there anything you can't do?"

Harper's teasing twisted me from the soles of my feet to the tears prickling again in my eyes. Of course she'd joke. Of course she'd try to lighten this for the rest of us as her body burned itself out.

"And that's it. Anticlimactic, right?" He withdrew the needle and pressed his thumb over the bead of blood. "Hold pressure here."

Orca covered the spot with her own thumb. Our lives were so eager to spill. I wished she'd clamp her whole hand around Harper's arm, stemming the flow and binding her soul to her flesh. I trembled behind Kraken until Harper's glassy eyes found me. "Don't look like such a noodle."

A watery smile was the best I could manage. "Hi, Harp."

"I can still kick your ass. Come here."

Kraken moved out of the way so I could obey. I settled on the ground beside her bunk and hugged my knees to my chest. "As your captain, I could order you to get better."

"Oh yeah?"

I wasn't imagining the rattle in her chest this time.

"Yeah. In fact, Harper Comita, I demand that you recover immediately."

"Sure thing, Cap'n."

"That's right." I squeezed her good hand. "Don't make

me flog you."

"You'd be into it. Don't lie." Her eyes closed as she spoke. "Shh. Rest."

I stayed sitting by her until Miranda touched my shoulder.

"It's sunset. You need to eat something."

I rose reluctantly and followed her into the common area, where Kraken had arranged algae patties on a platter. They filled my mouth, but I didn't taste them. Miranda ate hers with the same methodical precision.

"We'll know if it helped in a few hours. Until then, you're captain, which means not letting it consume you."

"I'm really not. Captain, I mean." I swallowed the last bite of food, hardly noticing the other people in the room. Miranda fielded their questions about Harper's health. Finn patted me on the back as he walked past, and Nasrin grumbled about the things she'd do to Ching, given the chance. Miranda had told me she'd assigned Nasrin to Ching as a guard with the instruction to infiltrate any mutiny, if possible, which explained her role in our imprisonment, but this development was just background noise. I didn't care about anything but Harper.

Only the helm offered relief. Miranda brought the trawler up to the surface whenever possible so I could see the stars. The atmosphere wasn't clear enough to risk going on deck, but few clouds obscured the sky and I could see what I needed to see through the plex. North hovered on the periphery of my senses—closer than it had felt in weeks, but still too far away to touch.

South, then. Ironic that my eyes now sought the Crux constellation, searching for the Southern Cross, when I'd been plotting a course for Crux station only days before. Fatigue ate at my vision. One day I'd have to reckon with the decisions I'd made under duress back on *Man o' War*. But not tonight.

The charts for these seas were largely blank, save for lines of latitude and longitude. No one had plotted common storm patterns or dead zones—those I would have to guess, without any guidance from my internal compass or the currents. I hated it.

This is what it's like for everyone else.

I wasn't everyone else.

Miranda didn't say much as evening wore into night. We surfaced periodically to check our progress against the stars, and I hurt my eyes still further straining to pierce the darkness for swarms and ships. Our sonar didn't pick anything up, but ... well. It hadn't last time we'd come south, either.

"I'll be right back," I told Miranda when my bladder threatened mutiny. I closed my eyes as I walked down the hall, feeling along the rugged plex while my abused eyeballs rested. This stretch of ship was familiar. My feet knew the path, and they led me to the common area and the sleeping quarters.

I paused at Harper's bunk.

"Orca?"

The curtain moved on its track, and Orca's eyes glinted in the low light. "Her fever broke."

"Oh thank Neptune." My knees buckled as relief cut them out from under me. Harper. Harper would live. Harper stood a chance at living. I repeated this to myself as I might have repeated the cardinal points.

"She's due for another dose soon."

"Is she?" My smile threatened to crack my jaw.

"When we find Ching—and we will, that motherfucker—I'm going to cut off her fingers and stick them in a bucket of shit."

"I'll hold the bucket."

"I'll take the shit."

We laughed, and it felt so fucking good I barely felt the wetness on my cheeks.

Chapter Thirteen

"Rose." I sat up, and only Miranda's reflexes saved me from whacking my skull on my bunk and worsening my concussion. Her hand caught my forehead and slowed my ascent.

"Yeah?" I yanked the curtain back and blinked up at Orca. The biolights were bright with daylight, which meant I'd most likely been in the middle of deep sleep.

"Swarm."

I groaned out a series of unintelligible curses and fumbled for my pants.

"Get us out of it," Miranda said to Orca.

Orca and I looked at her.

"I'm on it," I said.

"No. You need to learn to delegate. Orca's fully capable of basic calculations."

Orca glanced between us.

"But—" I said.

"What are you going to do about it that she can't do?" Miranda put no malice into the words, but I winced anyway.

"Right." Orca drew out the word. "So, I guess I'll just . . . go around them?"

"No. Go under. Most fields only extend a few miles." I rubbed

211

sleep from my eyes. "How's Harper?"

"Better."

"That was worth being woken up for then."

"Glad to hear it."

"You're dismissed," said Miranda. Orca nodded and turned on her heel.

"Should you do that?" I asked when the curtain enclosed us once more.

"What, tell her to fuck off in the middle of a REM cycle? I was serious. Learn to delegate."

"Maybe you should be captain then." I shimmied back beneath the blanket. "And while you're at it, take up less space."

"Fine." She rolled over to show me her back.

"Mere—"

"Go to sleep."

I did.

She didn't.

I knew this, because when Orca roused us at the end of her shift, Miranda's face was drawn and the circles beneath her eyes were darker than ever.

Harper joined us at the table for the evening meal.

"Well, look what the cat dragged in," said Nasrin.

"Don't insult Seamus," said Finn. "He's got better taste."

"In honor of your health, I've made poached snails." Groans accompanied Kraken's announcement. "Don't tell me after all your complaints, you've come to appreciate my roasts?"

"Your roaches can fuck themselves for being uglicious." Harper gestured imperiously at the pot and narrowed her eyes at Orca. "Now serve me my snails."

I turned to Miranda to share my amusement, but she was busy moving snails around her own plate and didn't meet my eye.

"A toast?" Nasrin suggested.

"You can take the bartender off the mainship, but you can't . . . wait." Finn tapped his chin. "That joke doesn't really work, does it?"

"You can take the 'specialist' out of 'communications' where you're concerned," said Nasrin. "Now put some rum in that hole of yours and shut up."

She poured a generous round—though I held my hand over my mug, as navigating with a damaged brain was hard enough—and I felt hopeful for the first time since we'd docked at *Trench*.

This was my crew. This had always been my crew. Not *Man o' War,* and not even *North Star*, but these ridiculous, messy, hard-headed fools. I loved each and every one of them.

Miranda knocked back her drink and scooped Seamus, who lurked around our feet in the hopes of discovering dropped snails, into her lap. Her scarred hands ruffled the thick orange and white-tipped fur around his neck.

"I'm so relieved," I said to her as we settled into the helm for the night shift. "I don't think I've ever been this relieved about anything in my life."

"She's not out of the swarm yet."

"But her fever broke and she's lucid."

Miranda shrugged. Anger laced my bloodstream with its poison.

"Can't you even pretend to be happy about that?"

She tossed me a weary look. "I *am* happy she's doing better. But I've seen more cases of sepsis than you have, and when I tell you she's not out of the swarm yet, I mean it."

The memory of her harsh *Go to sleep* stung all over again. I didn't care that she looked exhausted—we'd all lost things. I couldn't navigate without charts, and my head still hurt all the time. Harper had nearly *died.* So what if she'd lost a ship? No one had *asked* her to abdicate her captaincy. *I* certainly hadn't asked to be saddled with it.

"Harper will pull through."

"We'll see."

"Fuck you, Mere."

Her hands gripped the controls tightly, bleaching the scars on the backs of her knuckles, but she didn't respond. I weighed the pros and cons of storming off and decided, with all the regret in the sea, that I couldn't. Captains didn't sulk, and my crew had elected me. I owed them that much, even if I thought they were wrong. I turned my attentions to my charts instead and focused on the memory of Harper's smile at dinner. Miranda didn't know *shit*. Harper would be fine, and I remembered all over again the reasons I'd told Miranda I needed time.

Our stony silence lasted into the night. A cloud of siphonophores billowed beneath us off to port, and I watched their bioluminescent glow until it faded. Miranda didn't apologize. This didn't surprise me. Her apology our first day on the trawler had been shocking enough; Miranda Stillwater didn't like admitting when she was wrong, perhaps because that would mean recognizing she'd erred in the first place. It must be nice inside her brain: everything neatly labeled, black or white, with no confusing middle ground to swallow her whole.

We made better time than *Man o' War*, thanks to our small size and the retrofitted engine. I hoped raiders like the ones who had given me my head injury would be dissuaded by our appearance. Drifter trawlers contained little of value. We weren't worth it.

Unless Ching had put out a reward for our capture.

She wanted Miranda, either for revenge or some other purpose. Was stripping her of rank and ship enough? I didn't know, and so I kept us moving, though what—if anything—we'd find in the south, I didn't know. A heading was a heading. We had nowhere else to go.

Orca pulled me into the storage bay as I made my way back from the helm the next morning. I'd given Miranda a head start. Neither of us had acknowledged our spat, and the silence had only grown in the interim.

"Is Harper okay?" I asked as Orca shut the door. Crates of dry goods like rice and, knowing Kraken, explosives were stacked so tightly around us there was little room to stand without touching.

"She's an idiot."

"Is that a yes?"

"She says she's feeling much better and wants to be reinstated on shift duty." Orca paced as much as the space allowed. "She won't listen to me."

Frustration turned her words into a desperate whine. I sympathized. No one listened to me, either. Pushing the petty thought aside, I raked my hand through my hair and considered our options. Harper returning to work was out of the question, though my heart leapt at her recovery. The real question was how to convince her of this without entrenching her deeper in her position. The woman was almost as stubborn as Miranda. Orca, to her credit, at least respected authority, even if she sometimes punched me in the face. Harper had grown up the daughter of one of the most powerful admirals in the Archipelago. Comita hadn't gone easy on her, but there were things Harper could get away with no one else could.

We weren't on *North Star* anymore, however. Maybe her antipathy to command had lessened without her mother's protection. It was all I had to go on.

"She might if I make you my first mate."

"What?"

"Chief of engineering—not that it means much with a crew this small—ranks below first mate."

"I assumed you'd choose Miranda."

"Well, you thought wrong." I didn't tell her Miranda had refused me. Orca deserved to keep some of her pride, if nothing else.

"You sure?"

"What, do you want me to choose Nasrin?"

"Neptune, no, she'd get off on flogging us once a week. I'll be your first mate. I still don't think Harper will listen to me."

"And you think she'll listen to me? She's been beating me up since we were twelve." I paused. "Why do I surround myself with women who do that?"

"Because you're a masochist. But you're captain. Make her listen."

"As if being captain means anything."

Orca gripped my shoulder. "It won't mean anything if you

215

don't make it mean something."

"I'm the least intimidating person on this ship. The roaches look more authoritative than I do."

"Don't . . . don't talk about them."

"Maybe I should get a roach tattoo around my biceps."

She dropped her hand and edged away from me. "That's fucking nasty."

"You know Kraken would do it."

"Do you really want to go by Rosy the Roach the rest of your life?"

"It's better than jelly."

"Is it, though? Anyway, talk to Harper."

"I will."

"And . . . thanks for making me first mate."

She walked out of the storage room before I could read her expression. I shook my head. Pirates were even more prickly about their pride than Archipelageans.

Miranda cocked an eyebrow when Orca and I entered the common area together. I ignored the judgment in her stare and zeroed in on Harper, who chatted animatedly with Nasrin at the table.

"Orca says you want to be reinstated," I said to Harper.

Harper beamed up at me, all smiles. "Obviously I won't touch anything, but I can monitor systems, and—"

"And no."

"Come on, Rose."

"You were nearly dead less than twenty-four hours ago, and your arm still looks like a wreck."

It did. The redness had receded, but only marginally, and the skin oozed around her bandage.

"I'm bored."

"I've spent most of the last month locked in a room. Don't talk to me about boredom."

"That's different. Your brain got busted. My brain is fine, which is why—"

"I said no, and Orca is my first mate so from now on if she

216

tells you no, you'll listen to her."

I pitched all the authority I could into the words. Harper blinked, and the gathered crew paused. Only Miranda didn't turn to watch. She remained sitting with her back to me at the table, her hands clasped around a mug of rum.

"Who put an eel up your ass?" Harper's eyebrows contracted the way they always did before a fight.

"I mean it. We have a limited supply of antibiotics. I'm not going to waste them on you if you can't be bothered to take care of yourself."

She held up her good hand in a gesture of surrender. "Fine. Easy, Rose. Neptune."

"Orca's your first mate?" Kraken asked. His eyes slid to Miranda, who still hadn't looked up from her rum.

"Yes." It was easier to keep my voice firm this time.

"Consistency is good," he said. "Have something to eat."

I fell on my food, grateful for the excuse to hide my face. Pretending I knew how to be a captain made me feel like squidshit. Miranda's presence didn't help; she dripped authority from her pores. The stark contrast didn't cast me in a good light, and her silence leached my strength.

Cleanup duty fell to me. Soap frothed as I scoured the dishes with salt water, drying them with a hemp towel that had clearly come from a fleet ship once. The constellation for Orion was stitched into one corner.

Harper was better, I told myself as I stacked the dishes in the cupboard. Miranda's dire warnings that she wasn't out of the swarm yet were just that: warnings. They weren't prophecy. Harper would pull through. *Was* pulling through. There was no reason for the dread drying my mouth. A hot tear slid down my cheek and joined the soapy salt water in the sink.

Miranda didn't roll over to accommodate me when I pulled back the curtain. I stared at the curve of her back, frustration coursing through me in waves. I needed her. Not even as a captain, but as a partner or, barring that, a friend. Seamus purred when he saw me, and the smell of rum wafted out of the alcove.

I couldn't handle it. "Sleep well," I said, and clambered onto the empty bunk above her.

Dreams pounced with brutal efficiency. I drowned and watched my friends drown in turn, and all the while Ching traced a knife along Miranda's scars, opening fresh wounds until her skin ran red with blood. My throat ached from screaming.

"Hey."

I woke with a flinch and turned toward the voice, expecting to find Miranda. Kraken's broad hand clasped mine.

"I—I had a nightmare."

"I know."

My fingers stretched to curl around his as I shook off the disorientation of dreams.

"Want something to drink?" he asked. "Water? Rum?"

"I'm okay. Thank you. For waking me up." I would not be like Miranda, dependent on rum to function.

"Anytime, kid." He patted me on the shoulder and left me to lie in the semi-darkness of my bunk. I cried myself back to sleep.

The sound of people arguing woke me up.

"You need to sleep."

"I'm fucking fine."

"Don't try that with me." I recognized Kraken's voice. The other belonged to Miranda. "We need you functional."

"Why? I'm not captain." Her words slurred.

Was she *drunk?* I'd never seen her drunk. Drinking, yes, but not drunk. I listened intently.

"Were you in your bunk at all today?"

"Yes."

"Liar."

"Fuck off."

"She was screaming, Mere. Like you used to. And you weren't there."

Silence.

"Pull yourself together. We've lost everything before, and we're still here. This is no different. You've got an hour till the shift change. Sleep. Please."

I heard the sound of the curtain below me open and then close. It took her breathing a long time to settle into sleep.

"You two look worse than I do," Harper said with glee when Miranda and I stumbled into the common area. Red rimmed Miranda's eyes, and her hair, normally sleek and shiny, was dull and lank in its braid. I smelled rum when she passed close by me, but neither of us acknowledged the other. Harper took this in and wisely shut up.

"How do you feel?" I asked her.

"Like a new person."

I glanced at Orca. Her expression did not carry the same confidence, and, following her eyes, I noticed that the red streaks in Harper's arm had not receded. The antibiotics were holding the worst of it off, but if they couldn't vanquish the infection itself, she was still in trouble. What little appetite I'd woken with vanished.

Miranda showered while I talked with Harper. When she emerged, her hair a wet tangle down her back, she looked slightly more human.

"Ready?" she asked me.

I hugged Harper and led the way to the helm.

"Do we need to talk about this?" I said when we were out of earshot of the rest of the crew.

"About what?"

"Your drinking."

"No, we don't."

"Don't we? You're hiding. You should be captain. I don't want this. And Harper—"

"Rose." Her words cut into mine. "I have cost you everything. If Harper dies . . . I know what she is to you. So tell me. How, exactly, am I supposed to deal with this? I should not be captain, and you were right. I should not be with you. I'm a danger to everyone around me."

I thought of how it often felt like death followed me everywhere

I went. I thought about how easy it would be to blame Miranda and Ching and Comita for every wrong decision I'd made since leaving the *North Star*. I thought about the guilt I felt for Jeanine and Annie and all sailors who'd died in the Gulf, and how it ate at me.

"Kraken's right," I said, hating myself for what I knew I had to do. I couldn't show her tenderness. Not yet. Tenderness would shatter her. "Pull yourself together."

The hurt in her eyes hardened. "You—"

"You think I don't understand? You think I'm going to just let you check out?" I stood, shouting now.

She stood in reply. The scars on her face flushed a darker red in warning. "Don't stress your head, Rose."

"Fuck you." I put all the venom I could into the curse. "All this talk of Miranda Stillwater, the most fearsome sailor the Archipelago ever produced, and look at you. You're pathetic."

"Watch your tone, sailor." Authority snapped out of her like a gale.

I seized the front of her shirt in my hands, relief a tonic in my bloodstream, and pushed her against the wall of the helm. *This* was my captain. Her arms encircled me, first gently, then with urgency as I kissed her hard enough to bruise. Her body was warm and solid. I slid my hands from my grip on her shirt to her neck, and let her turn me so that I was the one against the wall with her hand cradled behind my head to protect it. Her thigh parted mine, demanding. Her lips moved down my jaw to my neck, kissing and biting as we both did our best to make up for lost time.

"Is everything—"

"Not now," I said to whoever stood in the doorway.

I heard a chuckle, which sounded like Nasrin. "Sure thing."

Miranda found the sensitive spot at the base of my neck and rendered further thought incoherent.

"I do want to talk to you," she said when we'd collapsed back into our seats, breathless and sore. My body craved more of her touch, but we were on duty, and these were dangerous waters. "Just not about my drinking. Leave that alone."

"About what then?"

"About us." Her glance skimmed the instrument panel, but I felt the avoidance of her gaze as strongly as if her eyes bore into mine.

"Okay. What about us?"

"I meant what I said. You were right about asking for time."

This wasn't something I knew how to respond to, so I waited.

"And I know things got complicated before we had a chance to talk."

"*Complicated* is one word for it," I said, giving her a half smile.

"Your brain was a giant bruise."

"Still might be." I grimaced, rubbing at the back of my neck. "Why do you think I was right?"

"Do you want the short list or the long?"

"I'm a bruise, remember? Short."

"I don't know how to do what we're doing. The other people I've been with were never ranked officers, or at least not officers serving under me. I have no idea how to treat you half the time. I can't show favoritism, but by trying not to show favoritism, I'm just a saltwater douche to you."

"Thanks for that," I said, clamping my legs shut and shuddering at the visual.

"And I'm so worried someone's going to try to hurt you to get to me, or to get back at the Archipelago, that I can't think."

"You were right to be worried apparently."

"I'm so fucked up, Rose."

I thought about what Orca had said to me. Maybe she was wrong. Miranda *did* know she had some issues. "So am I."

"And you fuck me up most of all."

I looked at her. Both her hands were clenching her chair.

"I cut a crew member's *throat*. I don't—he tried to kill you, I know. I'd do it again. But do you see?"

I did see. And I remembered, also, what Harper had said about a clean slate. I still didn't believe in clean slates, but at least here we were with friends. I'd fallen for her on this tub once before. Perhaps it could happen again. Or perhaps the thing between us had never really stood a chance.

"I know, Mere."

"Keeping things to myself is how I've stayed alive. Lying to you was never my intention." She looked up at last from the instrument panel. "I don't know if I can ever be what you want me to be."

The heaviness that had followed me since Jeanine's death grew still heavier—the pressure at the bottom of an ocean trench, the weight of past and impending loss. I took in her fraying braid and the livid blue of her eyes in the biolight.

"All I've ever asked is that you try," I said. "Can you do that for me?"

Anguish twisted her mouth. "What do you think I've been doing, Rose?"

If that was her best effort, I wanted to say, then we really were doomed.

"I want this to work," I told her instead. "But we can't keep on like we have been."

"No."

"I don't know how to fix it, either."

"Will you give me another chance?" Miranda as supplicant. I'd never heard this particular catch in her voice or seen her eyes so wide and hopeless. My chest constricted with longing. More than anything I wished to say yes. My half-healed brain and my broken heart both yearned to reach for her. But I wasn't as much of a fool for Miranda Stillwater as I'd once been. If we were ever going to be anything to each other, I needed to stand my ground.

"Yes," I said, "but Mere, let's take it slow."

"'Take it slow,' she says, when one of the many things we don't have is time," said Miranda as she touched my cheek.

"You know what I mean."

"I do." Her hand fell back to her side. "Let's start with trust."

I nodded. "How do we do that?"

Her laugh, bitter and self-deprecating, brought an equally twisted smile to my lips as she said, "I have no idea.

"We could start by sharing any secret plots to take down entire civilizations," I suggested.

"*Touché.*"

"You don't have to tell me everything. I just . . . I just want to be a part of your decisions."

"You always are."

"But you choose *for* me. I don't need you to do that."

"That's what a captain does for her crew."

"I know. But I don't want to just be your crew."

"Technically, I'm your crew now."

"You know what I mean."

She reached for my hand and laced our fingers together. "I'll try. That's all I can promise you. But you have to do the same. If you have doubts, tell me before you steal a ship and run."

"I can do that," I said.

"And Rose?"

"Yeah?"

"I'm sorry. For everything."

Days stretched in a tense daze beneath the southern sky. We settled into a routine that was at once familiar and strange. Kraken kept us fed and hydrated, which was an increasingly difficult task as worry for both Harper and our collective future stole away with our appetites. The ocean required my constant attention. While I navigated, Miranda and I spoke tentatively about things we'd never broached before: her time on Gemini, my resentment toward my father, how we might find a mate for Seamus and what we'd name his kittens.

Occasionally someone laughed.

"This is ridiculous," I said on the twelfth day of our sail. Water lapped at the plex as we bobbed between massive waves, and I craned my neck to try to make sense of the stars before we were forced to submerge.

"It's not great," said Miranda. She gripped the controls and did her best to keep us stable. "Do you have a reading?"

"No." I threw the sextant across the room. "Take us under."

"I can give you a few more minutes—oh, fuck."

Something huge and black blotted out the stars. At first, I didn't register what I was seeing. A cloud? A ship? Vague stirrings at the edges of my senses warned me of danger, but I couldn't parse them. The trawler bucked as we hit a deep trough.

Oh.

Ching's warning about surfacing in the Southern Ocean mocked me. Miranda punched the backup accelerant, and the trawler dove beneath the cresting rogue wave. Objects clattered as the undertow tried to catch us up in its tumult, but, growling, she held us steady while the ship's systems did their best to stabilize. Water hissed into the bulkheads.

I emerged from my huddle in my chair when Miranda touched my shoulder.

"You good?" she asked.

"I. Hate. This."

"You're getting better."

"At what, throwing things?" I cast around for the sextant.

"Your brain. You're focusing for longer, and your eyes aren't as glazed as they used to be."

"You say the sweetest things."

"It will come back. Give it time."

"You don't know that." I gave up searching for the sextant and watched the black water churn around us. "What if this is permanent?"

"Then you're going to wish you hadn't chucked that."

I smacked her arm. "You're lucky I don't flog crew."

"You wouldn't know what to do with a whip. Check this out."

She pointed out the plex. I squinted, then gasped. Pale squid jetted around us, too small to pose a risk, but beautiful in their pearlescent whites as they fed below the churning waves.

"What are they eating? I don't see anything."

"We're far enough south there might be krill."

I hadn't thought we were that near the pole yet. "They're almost cute."

"You have questionable taste."

"Oh, I know," I said, throwing her a meaningful look. She grinned and settled farther back in her chair.

"And you didn't even have a head injury back then to blame."

"It's not my fault you're attractive," I said.

"That's a matter of taste."

"Uh, Rose?" Orca stood in the doorway dressed in rumpled clothing, as if she'd just rolled out of bed—which made sense, given the hour.

"Everything okay?" I asked.

She shook her head.

"Sorry about the turbulence," said Miranda.

"It's not that. Harper's fever is back."

All the joy drained out of me.

"What? How long?"

"I'm not sure. I woke up to it."

"But she was getting better."

"She's maxed out our antibiotics," said Miranda.

"What do we do then?" I asked.

"We—"

"What the hell is that?" Orca stumbled back into the hallway.

"Squid," Miranda said dismissively.

Orca shook her head. My skin prickled at the look in her eyes, and I turned back to the helm at the same time as Miranda let out a string of curses.

A ship yawned before us. I'd never seen anything like it: smaller than *Man o' War*, it appeared to undulate through the water as its sides reflected light. No—it *was* undulating. I was so fascinated I didn't even realize Miranda was fighting with the controls.

"What?" I asked when I registered her shout of frustration. "We're about to be—"

She didn't finish as the ship swallowed us. A hole opened in the side of its hull, illuminated briefly by our lights. The edges of the maw were fringed and organic, as if it truly were a mouth, and it leered as it stretched to accommodate our trawler. Miranda slammed the thrusters, but there wasn't time to maneuver. One moment we were in the ocean, transfixed, and the next we were in a steadily draining hold.

"Rouse the crew," Miranda said to Orca.

Orca took off at a sprint. Meanwhile, biolight filtered through the murk of the hold, and I felt our ship shudder as it was moved into a berth by some sort of machinery. I could see people beyond the shrinking water level. Distorted shapes gestured, and then water streamed off the helm as we surfaced.

Before us was a landing bay, but it bore no resemblance to any landing bay in my experience. For one thing, the walls glowed. And for another, the machinery retreating into the wall looked . . . alive.

"I think," I said, my voice sounding very far away, "that we just found the sea wolves."

Chapter Fourteen

The helm was too small to fit our entire crew. We managed anyway. Even Harper crammed herself in, though Orca circled her protectively with her arms to keep anyone from jostling her injury.

"Neptune's balls," said Finn.

I agreed. The water around us glowed bright blue with bioluminescence, and the deck—if it could be called that—glowed too. Some sort of biological material covered it. I didn't think it was algae, but I couldn't be sure. Besides, glowing walls were the least interesting thing about the landing bay. Now that we were above water, I could see the machinery that gripped us, and I pressed back into my chair. It looked like the massive arm of an octopus, right down to the suckers that had suctioned themselves to the side of our trawler. I couldn't tell where it began, but I knew I wasn't alone in scanning the water's surface for a leviathan. My heart beat painfully in my throat. The walls of the bay were covered with more of the growing, glowing substance, and the brightness hurt my eyes. I blinked through the pain until I adjusted, and then I blinked from shock.

The people standing in wait were human in shape, but the similarities between us ended there. Closest to us, a person stood with an octopus draped around their shoulders. It slithered down and crawled across the deck until it could drop into the water, where it then propelled itself toward us and observed our slack-jawed faces with palpable curiosity. The person it had left said something to the person beside them, and I noticed both their skins shifted color, much like the octopus now peering through the plex.

"What the actual fuck," said Harper.

"Are those . . . gills?" said Nasrin.

"Not possible," said Finn, but his words lacked conviction.

The sound of a distant knock on our hatch reminded me that, fascinating as all this was, we could be about to die.

"What do we do?" I asked Miranda.

The look she shot me said *You're the captain*, but she answered anyway. "Lacking a choice, we meet with them and hope they don't kill us on the spot."

"You're such a comfort," said Harper through chattering teeth. Her fever must have been spiking. I turned in my chair to see the sheen of sweat on her forehead. An impossible hope struck me. If the sea wolves were everything I'd been told, perhaps they could save Harper.

"I should go first." *Right?* I didn't voice my last thought, but I sensed Miranda heard it anyway.

She nodded, though it looked like it pained her. "I'll be right behind you."

No point in coming up with a plan of defense. We were out-numbered and out-teched, and completely at the mercy of our captors. I wished I had access to the drug that cleared my head and restored north. I needed clarity. Miranda took a discreet sip from her flask. I glared at her. Now did not seem like the time to broach the subject of her drinking, but I needed one of us fully functional. She ignored me.

My heart beat hard enough I was convinced the people waiting for us could hear it through our hull as I fumbled with the hatch. My fingers, wet with sweat, slipped on the handle, and Miranda climbed up the ladder behind me to assist. Just before the final turn, she kissed my cheek and whispered in my ear.

"I love you. No matter what happens, know that."

Her words gave me enough courage to push the lid of the hatch open.

Two people stood before me. Both had their heads shorn, which made the liquid amber of their eyes even more noticeable. I stared. I'd never seen eyes like mine in another face, and the hot gold of them burned into my skull. Abruptly, I understood why people occasionally recoiled from me. Eyes like that were unsettling as fuck.

The taller figure spoke a few words to their companion in a feminine voice. I didn't recognize the language, but the way they both stared back at me in surprise suggested they were talking about me. I took note of the weapons strapped to their hips. Swords and smaller deadly looking things I thought might be pistols, though I'd never seen one before. What did one say when one's ship had been swallowed? Miranda would have threatened them or offered a biting-yet-disarming remark. I wracked my brain for something neutral but also strong.

"Hello," I said, because my brain was a traitor.

Weapons emerged from their holsters. Miranda pressed into my back, and I absorbed her strength.

The taller one signed something in a series of short, sharp motions, then called out to the deck in their unfamiliar tongue. One of the waiting members detached themselves from the group and hopped across the narrow strip of water onto our deck. She had short hair, though not shaven, and it was the brown of kelp in the blue light. Golden eyes met mine as she spoke.

"Your ship is now the property of the *Moray*. Your supplies and your lives are forfeit. We'll give you five minutes to assemble your crew."

"Wait," I said, aware I sounded desperate. "We came looking for you."

"That was not wise." Her accent was strange, but her enunciation was clear, and the look she gave us was dismissive.

"We sailed with Ching Shih. You might know her as Amaryllis—"

"Stop." The young woman frowned, then called something over her shoulder to her companions. An exchange followed, full of unfamiliar words and odd vowel pairings. After a minute of this, she turned back to me. "Is she on board?"

"Not . . . anymore."

"Then there is nothing to discuss."

"Tell her you've come to claim inheritance to Symbiont," Miranda said in an urgent whisper.

"I've come to claim inheritance to Symbiont." Parroting the words didn't make them coalesce into meaning.

The woman paused, searching my face with those liquid golden eyes. "And your crew?"

I didn't know what to say. My head ached, dull from over-stimulation, and words evaded me. I managed, "They're with me."

"I can see that. Do any of them claim inheritance?"

I didn't know what inheritance was, let alone what it meant for me to claim it. Before I could come up with another painfully inadequate response, however, Miranda spoke low and fast.

"Rose, we're out of options. Inheritance—I don't have time to explain yet. It just means you express the genetic traits of a sea wolf. They'll take you, but if they don't take us, Harper dies. We need their help."

"I know. But—"

"Amaryllis wanted to give them Harper. I said no. But she's a valuable hostage, and she's more valuable alive than dead. She gives them leverage over the Archipelago, which they want."

I recalled a half-heard conversation through a closed door, and Miranda's raised voice.

"We can't," I said, even as I pictured Harper's fever-bright eyes. Why did all the choices given to me have to hurt so seas-damned much?

"Which way do you want to lose her?"

That wasn't a choice at all.

"We have something else to offer in exchange for your help."

"Help?" The woman crossed her arms over her chest and tilted her head.

"One of our crew is sick with sepsis. If you can heal her, we can give you a valuable hostage."

She smiled, and both her cheeks dimpled. I felt a strange pit form in my stomach. There was something oddly familiar about her face. "You should have led with that. Welcome aboard. What's your name?"

"I'm . . . Compass Rose, the captain." It felt like a lie.

"Lia. Ship translator and communications specialist."

The sudden welcome surprised me into bluntness. "You'll help us?"

Lia spoke to her companions. Not for the first time, I reflected that Admiral Comita had erred in selecting me to act as diplomat as well as navigator.

"Provided you cooperate, yes."

"We will cooperate." Relief flooded my words.

"Good. How many are in your crew?"

"Seven."

"Then assemble, Compass Rose, and follow me."

The shaved guards—I assumed they were guards of some sort, sent to remand us as we emerged—made room for us to clamber out of the trawler one by one, until we were all gathered on the *Sea Cat's* small deck. Miranda and Kraken flanked me, and Orca supported Harper behind. Nasrin hulked beside Finn off to starboard. A ramp slid out from the landing deck and stopped when it touched our hull, almost as if it sensed it. I stepped onto the plank. Leaping still required more coordination than my brain could manage, and I needed every ounce of brainpower right now. Miranda's hand on the small of my back kept me steady as I crossed the gap. My feet landed on the bay deck with an odd squish. I balked, necessitating a gentle shove from Miranda, and resisted the urge to kneel and touch the glowing ground.

"Moss," said Lia.

"What?"

"It's moss." She pointed at the ground. "Have you not seen moss before?"

I had—but in the gardens on Polaris, where it grew on rocks

and did not glow. "Not like this."

"I think you will see many things that are new to you." She turned and chattered at the others. They did not all have mottled, shifting skin. Lia didn't, for instance, though I noticed the light fell on her skin with an odd intensity. As she cast a reassuring smile at me over her shoulder, I realized this was because there was bioluminescence *under* her skin. It pulsed along her jaw and down the curve of her neck, disappearing into the collar of her shirt. Only her clothing was familiar: a simple hemp shirt and pants. The sleeves were cut higher than our styles and showed more skin than anything I'd ever wear, but hemp was hemp, and pants were pants. Hers ended in a cuff just above the ankle. She was also barefoot. I looked down at my own boots as they pressed into the moss and thought perhaps that was to preserve the living floor.

"Should we . . ." I gestured at my feet.

She nodded.

"We need to take off our shoes," I told my crew.

"They say that now, but they haven't smelled Kraken's feet," said Finn. I appreciated his effort at humor, though didn't find it particularly appropriate. For all we knew, these people killed jokesters for sport. I kicked my boots off and held them awkwardly in one hand, then, for lack of a better option, crossed back over the plank and tossed them down the trawler hatch. The others did the same.

"Tread carefully," Miranda said under the small commotion caused by removing our shoes.

"Literally or figuratively?"

"Both. There could be toxins in the moss our systems can't handle."

Great. Poisonous moss. Still, it felt pleasantly cool and soft against my toes, and it cushioned my weight. As my feet settled in, my brain struggled to adjust to the boat's movement. Something about it unsettled my compass, damaged though it was. I briefly closed my eyes. The memory of the ship's undulations rose as I matched it to the sensations traveling up my calves. When I opened my eyes again, Lia was studying me.

Right. I was the captain. I had to look like I knew what I was doing. Questions would come later, if there was a later. I nodded, and Lia led the way through a curved doorway and into a hallway.

"What—" Orca broke off, but we were all thinking it. Above us, clear plex contained the water bubbling through a meter-wide tube. Curious octopuses clustered, staring down, and I thought one might have been the octopus that had inspected our ship. Other creatures flitted along the tube. Small, brightly colored fish. Glowing shelled things. Tiny jellyfish. But why? The walls glowed with the same moss as the floor—they didn't need additional illumination. As we walked, minuscule moss fronds waved in our wake, and I reached out a hand to touch them. A dry powder came away on my fingers.

"Don't touch anything," Miranda said in a strained whisper from my side. I remembered her comment about toxins and hurriedly wiped the powder off on my pants.

Lia stopped at a door and placed her hand, fingers spread, on the plex. Or at least, I assumed the material was plex. It slid away, and we trailed her into an oddly shaped room. The walls curved organically, and the ceiling contained a pool where long spiny fish circled. Sunlight filtered through the water and cast rippling shadows on the ground.

An odd clicking assaulted my ears as I looked around. At first I couldn't decipher the source. The room was bare, save for the fish above and the single low chair in its center. But the clicking could not have emanated from the slight man sitting cross-legged with his eyes closed. The sound wasn't human. I covered my ears as it rose in pitch; it left abrasions on my nerves.

"This is our speaker, though I think you'd use the term *captain*," said Lia. "Altan?"

The man opened his eyes. Even after Lia, seeing my eyes in the face of another sent currents of unease through me. Altan's long hair was bound in a knot at the back of his skull, and it drew his skin tightly over his sharp cheekbones. When he spoke, there was an echo to his words, as if I could feel them jostling my atoms.

"Be welcome," Lia translated. He spoke again, and her eyes

speared mine. "He asks what happened to your head."

"Excuse me?"

"There is damage."

"How—"

The sound started again, more shrilly, and I clapped my hands back over my ears.

"He says something has damaged your magnetoreceptors."

"I'm sorry, my *what?*"

"Your ability to navigate." Lia spoke as if the statement was simple—and not part of an answer to a question I'd been asking since birth.

"You know I can navigate?"

"Of course," said Lia, not bothering to translate my words. "It's our most basic skill."

Our most basic skill. Basic, and yet the thing for which I'd been alternately elevated and loathed for my entire life.

Altan spoke. Lia listened intently, a smile forming on her lips. "We should be able to fix you. With the right stimulation, the nerves can be regenerated."

I glanced from Altan to Lia, then back to Altan. The confirmation of my genealogy felt hollow. I did not know these people who held us captive. I did not know what they would do to Harper when I was forced to make good on my word and turn her over, and I sure as Davy Jones's locker did not know what they would do to me. *Our most basic skill.* And the only one I had. The genetic code they seemed to hold in such high esteem was diluted and weak within me. I'd found another place where I only partially belonged. Answers were not worth it. Harper, however, was; and right now her health was the only thing that mattered.

"I received a blow to the head," I said.

Lia frowned, and a lengthy exchange passed between her and Altan before she spoke again. "You have our lineage. The magnetite in your body is only part of the proof; all our expressed genes are linked to lipochrome pigmentation."

"Lipochrome?" My head spun at the onslaught of unfamiliar words.

"Your eyes." She waved away my confusion. "The speaker wishes to know why you have come looking for us."

"We hoped for your aid."

Lia's face twisted in surprise. She relayed my words to the speaker. He rose from his chair and approached me, and only Miranda's hand on my back kept me from retreating. Altan took my measure with eyes I saw every day in the mirror. The lives of my crew hung in the balance of his gaze.

"Aid?" he said in my language.

I blinked and looked at Lia. Her attention, however, was on him.

"And answers. I wish—" I broke off and tried again, telling myself my next words were a calculated response to our situation and not a deeply revealing and pathetic truth. "I wish to know who I am."

Altan held my eyes. "You are a foundling, and now you've been found."

"What—"

He spoke rapidly to Lia, drowning out my question. She addressed me when he finished. "You will be provided with berths, and your injured will be cared for until we get to Symbiont, where your situation will be evaluated. Come."

Altan settled back on his chair and closed his eyes. The strange chittering started again, and, while I was not satisfied with the exchange, I was grateful for an excuse to leave his presence.

"Well done," Miranda said in my ear.

"How? We—"

"We're alive."

The ship curved in patterns that made little sense to my Archipelago-trained eye. The whole thing seemed almost alive, and the subtle undulations acted as a reminder even behind closed eyes. Sea wolves studied us as we filed past. Some, but not all, had shifting skin colors. One very unsettling room contained a tank

235

with children, who parted the water with webbed fingers and breathed through slits in their necks that were undeniably gills. And everywhere, curious octopuses and a few small squid-like creatures peered out at us through the ubiquitous water.

"Here." Lia splayed her fingers on another door, which opened into what I assumed was a medical bay, judging by the beds and antiseptic smell, but that was where the resemblance ended. The beds were not beds so much as shallow tanks. Most were empty, but a nearby tank contained an old man laboring to breathe. Like the children, he had gills, though his seemed . . . vestigial, somehow. His skin flickered from gray to green.

"If you think, for a second, that I am getting into one of those . . ." Harper's voice rasped off into silence.

"Your friend is welcome to abstain, but she will be dead if she does." Lia didn't seem bothered by this prospect. "This is Vi. She will care for her."

A person appeared from behind a curtained tank and swept her eyes over us, settling on Harper. Orca put a protective arm around Harper in response.

"Do as she says," I said. Lia's words sat coldly on my chest. It wasn't a threat. All anyone had to do was look at Harper's haggard face, stripped of its usual roundness by days of fever, to know she spoke the truth.

"I'll stay with her," said Orca.

Lia shook her head. "She will not."

"Like hell—"

"Orca." I snapped at her with all the command I could muster. If Orca didn't realize how tenuous our position was on this ship, then it was up to me to protect her from herself. To Lia, I said, "Will you tell us what will happen to her?"

"It is simple. She will be placed in a nutrient bath and dosed with agents to counter the infection and remove the dead flesh. She'll be asleep, of course. There won't be any pain."

"That's . . . good. But she doesn't speak your language."

"She won't need to speak in the bath."

Harper sagged against Orca, and beneath her bravado I saw

she had reached the end of her strength.

"We don't have a choice," I said, going to her and taking her good hand.

"Just tell them to keep *those* away from me."

I followed her gaze and recoiled. A bath I hadn't noticed contained a small girl. Curled up on her chest, matching her mottled skin tones, rested an octopus.

"It is her companion. You are not so lucky. We will use flesh fish." Lia beckoned Vi to come and take Harper away.

"Rose—" Orca said.

"What choice do you think we have?" I matched glares with my first mate until she released Harper as reluctantly as I'd ever seen her do anything. Vi placed gentle hands on Harper's shoulders and led her toward the curtain.

"We'll go now," said Lia.

I hesitated. Leaving Harper here in this strange place where she couldn't even communicate her most basic needs seemed impossibly cruel, but so did letting her die from infection.

Forgive me, I silently begged her, and let Lia lead us on.

The room that would be ours for as long as it took the *Moray* to decide whether to kill us, help us, or release us was small. Noting its size, however, was like noting the color of a giant squid's mantle as it bore down on you—irrelevant. A plex column of water plunged from the ceiling and into the floor. Sunlight streamed through it, dancing among the jellyfish and squid. The room's walls and floor had the same glowing growth as the rest of the ship, which no longer surprised me, but the bunks—I assumed they were bunks—suspended themselves from the walls like seed pods, almost as if they had been grown, too. Around the central water column, planted in the floor itself, waved ferns. They seemed to curl and dance in the flickering light, and the effect was beautiful and hypnotic. An alcove contained the bathroom. I didn't explore; there was time for that later. My eyes instead fixated on a low curved table containing plates of strange foods. If this was their brig, it was the nicest brig I'd ever heard of.

"Your crew will wait for you here," Lia said to me.

"Wait, what?"

"They will be comfortable and cared for. The speaker wishes your injury healed; this has been arranged."

I swept my eyes over my crew: Miranda, Orca, Kraken, Nasrin, and Finn. How could I trust they would not be harmed?

"Go," said Miranda. Her eyes were on Lia, cold and assessing, but her voice was reassuring. I wished we'd had more time to work things out, and that I could be certain I would see her again.

I wished for a lot of things.

Lia jerked her head toward the door, impatience showing on her dimpled face. I allowed her to lead me back out.

"They will be safe?" I asked.

Lia shrugged off my worries. "Yes. Now, there is so much to discuss. But first . . ."

I assumed she'd lead me back to the infirmary, but instead she descended through a moss-covered hatch and into a room that was mostly tank. A woman swam within, cradling a child on her naked hip. Kelp grew from the tank floor. The woman's gills fluttered as she breathed, and as her child slept, his small pink gills fluttered too.

"This is impossible," I said.

"What is?"

I touched my neck in the places where the woman's gills sat.

"Oh. Not as impossible as you'd think." She tapped the clear wall gently with the pads of her fingers. The woman looked up from her child, shedding the dreamy expression that had occupied her face a moment before, and swam toward the plex pane. Webbing connected her elongated fingers and toes. I glanced down at Lia's feet: normal. No thin membranes of skin, though the faint pulse of bioluminescence lit the beds of her nails a faint pink.

As I studied her, she made a series of whistles and clicks that must have carried through the plex, because the woman nodded and gestured to the ladder on the side of the tank. Fucking ladders. I had a premonition I was not going to like this.

"You'll need to get into the water." Lia reached for a small mask that hung on a disturbingly organic-shaped hook nearby and illustrated how to attach it to my face. "This will allow you to breathe."

I accepted it with sweaty hands. "What is she going to do to me?"

"She is a . . . oh, I don't know how to translate it." She looked like the puzzle intrigued her. "Most of us can echolocate, but—"

"Echolocate?"

"Sonar. That's how the speaker found you. He taps into the ship, and—never mind. It's complicated. She has an unusually well-developed temporal cortex. She can stimulate growth to help regenerate the damaged areas of your brain."

That made even less sense. I wondered if I had a choice or if I'd be forced into the tank, should I refuse. My head ached in response to the overload of new information. Why in all the seas had the crew made *me* captain?

"But I have to get into the water?" I asked, stalling.

"Yes."

"I—" The longing for north sat on my tongue, stopping my words. I'd been willing to risk a coma back on the *Man o' War* to feel north, thanks to the drugs Harper had brought me. How was this any different?

I stripped down to my undergarments, folding them on the soft, mossy ground, and ascended the ladder. When I reached the top, I fixed the mask over my nose and mouth and slipped into the cool water.

My first breath sent bubbles into the tank. Kelp waved, and small fish darted away as I let myself sink. The gilled woman observed me through a cloud of coarse hair. A tiny octopus encircled her ear like jewelry, and her skin changed color with her surroundings, just as the octopus's did. Impossible; and yet, here I was. She extended her hand and held up her webbed fingers in a gesture that reminded me of Lia opening the doors on the ship. Hesitating, I held my smaller hand up to hers. Her skin shifted to match my skin tone. It was oddly comforting. Then she opened her mouth, and I fell into the abyss.

I woke on the mossy ground outside the tank. Lia sat beside

me, clicking to the woman, who sang back. Periodically, they signed. How many forms of communication did these people need? My body felt heavy and damp and chilled, and I instinctively reached for the currents to gauge our location. They coursed through me, stronger than I'd ever experienced, so strong I feared I'd be pulled in and swept away while north pulsed like a beacon in my body. I turned my head to face the cardinal point just to alleviate the pressure.

"You're awake," said Lia, a genuine smile on her lips.

I vomited into the moss.

To my surprise, as I gagged, spit, and gagged again, the moss rippled—and then proceeded to absorb the emptied contents of my stomach at an alarming rate. I wriggled backward, lest I, too, be consumed.

The motion triggered new alarms. Every sense felt raw and heightened. Touch burned. Sound assaulted. Smell, too—no longer lemons, but the pungent scent of growing things, Lia's sweat, and brine. When Lia spoke, her words ricocheted around the room and left patterns across my vision.

"How do you feel?"

"What . . . did . . . you do to me?" Speaking produced more of those bright flashes, as if a pattern lay beneath the world of sight—a fourth dimension of sound.

"She healed you."

"No. I'm . . . this . . . different," I managed.

"You had scarring. Old scarring. She removed it."

I vomited again as her words seared across my vision. Lia frowned and moved to put a hand on my shoulder. I flinched away. My skin felt as if it would slough off if brushed. The sensation of my hands on the moss was too much. I felt *everything*.

"Close your eyes," said Lia.

I was more than happy to obey. I wanted to curl into a ball in this potentially carnivorous moss and die.

Lia clicked. The sound skittered across my brain like water droplets on a hot pan, and my mind glitched. There was no other word for it.

"Make that sound," she said.

It was that or continue vomiting. I touched my tongue to the roof of my mouth and mimicked her—

—And *saw* the room.

My eyes flew open. Lia grinned.

"How?" I asked.

"You're one of us."

"I've never been able to do this before." I spoke carefully, already growing more accustomed to the way my words reverberated and left traces behind as sound waves bounced off walls and objects.

"Like I said. There was scarring."

"From what?"

"That's what I'd like to know, too. She says it was intentional. And old—you would have been a child."

"I don't remember."

"Where were you born?"

I told her. The vibrations of my voice painted the story as I traced myself back to my earliest beginnings. My mother, holding me on her hip. Sleeping curled on our mat looking out the window at the sunlit sea. My father, an average man, with his kind brown eyes and weather-worn skin, lifting me in the air in the years before he vanished. A drifter, bound to the currents, unable to obtain Archipelago citizenship—or so my mother had told me.

"Recessive maybe," said Lia. "But I wonder. May I?"

I held myself still as she touched my head. Her hands were gentle as she probed my skull, and her touch itched in new ways.

"Hmm," Lia hummed. "I'm not as good as she is, but if your father was one of ours, he could have . . . yes. That would explain it."

"Explain what?" I asked as she pulled away.

"He could have had you damaged intentionally, to hide you. To make you like your crew."

"Why would he want to do that?"

"No idea."

"But he wasn't like me."

"Genes are not always expressed, but they can be passed on.

241

If he left us, or if his parents did, he would have taken his genes with him."

"Why would he leave?"

"We do not keep our own against their will. Without any expressed traits, he would have been . . . less."

I leaned into north. My father had known what I was. Known, and denied me the choice of my inheritance. Perhaps he'd told himself he was protecting me by cutting me off from the ocean. He hadn't totally succeeded—my navigational skills were proof of that—but he'd done enough. Did my mother know? More pressingly, would I ever get the chance to ask her?

"I know you have many questions, but you should rest now. Quietly. I will return you to your crew." Lia helped me up and handed me my clothes, which I put back on, and then she offered me a flask of water to rinse out my mouth. When I'd finished, she held out her hand. "It will be best if you let me guide you."

Her hand was warm and her grip was firm and solid. The necessity of the gesture became clear the moment I began walking. North pulsed in my skull and the currents tugged at my blood; meanwhile, sound painted pictures behind my eyes. It was overwhelming, and my head ached, but not in the way that it had. This wasn't the ache of a bruised mind. It was the ache of a child exposed to open air for the first time. I was raw to everything: pleasure, pain, the feeling of air moving across my skin. I clung to Lia until we arrived back at the room where my chosen family waited.

"Rose." Miranda was on me in an instant, snatching my hand out of Lia's and folding me into her arms. I trembled at the touch. Miranda's blood was a current; it sang to mine, and her arms were walls that kept me safe.

"She'll need quiet," Lia said as my crew peppered her with questions. "Let her sleep, and when she wakes, she'll explain. It is late anyway."

I didn't hear the rest of what she said. Miranda picked me up and carried me to a bunk, laying me down on its soft, spongy surface. I reached for her, and she crawled in beside me—then, with a few words to the crew, pressed something that closed the pod around us. In the darkness, I breathed easily at last.

"Are you hurt?"

I shook my head against her chest.

"Then what—"

"I can feel everything," I said, wondering how I could put this into words. "They . . . I can navigate. And more. I can't explain. But—"

Miranda stroked my forehead, and I trembled again. Her touch electrified my skin. Her fingers only stroked my forehead, but I felt them everywhere.

"I'm sorry—" she began.

"It doesn't hurt."

"You need to rest."

"Stay with me?" My hands were curled against her chest, trapped between us, but I touched her jaw with a fingertip and let the vibrations of my voice paint her into being in the darkness.

"I wasn't planning on giving you much choice."

Chapter Fifteen

"About time," said Orca when I emerged from my pod. Orca's voice grated strangely in my ears, but my head no longer ached. In place of pain was an alien mind. My mind. My *real* mind. I braced myself for more sensory overload. Sound and sight had been separate things for all the years of my life. How long would it take to grow accustomed to the layer of sonar skittering over my vision?

"We need to check on Harper," said Orca, who had been sitting with her knees to her chest on the floor. Upon seeing me, she stood.

Harper. A jolt of dread twisted my intestines. She had to be okay. I raced over the memories of the previous day, cursing how blurred the concussion had made even recent events. I wanted to believe she was safe. The rest of us hadn't been harmed, and I was proof the sea wolves had medicine beyond our capabilities, but I needed to see her for myself.

And then we needed to come up with a plan. Now that I could think clearly, the tenuous nature of our survival hit me anew. We knew nothing about this ship or these people. Anything might set them off. Culturally, we were years and oceans apart, and if all that stood between my crew and harm was Altan's interest in my genetic material and the promise of a hostage . . . I shivered. My track record for keeping people alive was less than perfect.

"Eat first," Kraken urged me.

I didn't want to eat. I wanted to find Harper.

"You need every advantage we can give you," Kraken continued, unrelenting. "Low blood sugar will cloud your judgment. Eat."

He was right. I tried not to hate him for it. After a few forced bites of fruit and seaweed cakes, I approached the door.

"Good luck with that. It doesn't open," said Orca.

Ignoring her, I splayed my fingers against the plex the way I'd seen Lia do. Nothing. I shouldn't have expected it to work for me just because I was distantly related to these people. Still, I hesitated. The plex gave slightly beneath my fingertips, unlike the plex I was familiar with. There was an almost rubbery quality to it, like the flesh of a cephalopod.

"I tried everything," said Orca.

"Just let—" As I spoke, sound waves bounced off the door, and I saw it anew. Just off dead center sat a spiraling pattern of intermittent densities. I repositioned my palm in the grooves and gave a slight twist, following the interstitial spaces. The door eased open with a soft shushing sound. I blinked. There must have been a pressure plate beneath the plex. *Or something.* I refused to dwell on what that something might be. Doors weren't alive. Doors didn't have synapses. Doors were refreshingly simple that way.

Silence fell behind me. I stared at the corridor, wondering what would happen to us if we wandered this ship without an escort. Probably nothing good, judging by what had just happened with the door. We had no way of knowing how this ship operated or what risks it posed to those unfamiliar with those parameters. I remembered the fleshy appendages that had maneuvered our ship in the bay and pictured them wrapping around my body.

Harper.

"Do we go, or wait for Lia?" I asked Miranda.

She hadn't risen from our pod. One arm was flung over her eyes, and she lay with her face tilted toward us, listening.

"Your call."

"I know. And I'm asking for your advice. All of your advice." I included the rest of the crew in my words.

"It might help if you tell us what happened to you yesterday," said Nasrin. "You were gone for hours. You must have learned something."

I backed away from the open door before answering. "This ship is impossible. The way it moves, the people . . ."

"The thrice-damned cephalopods." Finn gave a pointed look at the octopus hovering in the water column behind him.

"I think the octopus are pets."

"Don't you mean food?" asked Kraken.

"There was a woman in a tank with a baby—"

"I'm sorry, what?" Nasrin rolled her thick neck from side to side, working out a kink. Tendons swelled.

"She had gills. She's the one who fixed my head. They put me in the tank, and she did something with sound maybe. I don't really remember. But her baby had gills, too, and the woman had an octopus. It was curled around her ear, like an earring almost. Maybe they don't eat them, so let's not make any threatening gestures at eight-limbed creatures."

"Literally nothing you just said makes sense," said Orca. "Let's go find Harper."

"And this moss?" I pointed to our surroundings, trying to get used to the way my voice echoed in my head. "It consumes biomatter."

"Maybe it's how they purify the air," said Kraken. "Might be some fungi worked into it as well. Would explain the biomatter."

Something clicked, and I closed my eyes, letting my senses parse through currents and cardinal points until I could concentrate on the way the ship moved through them. The walls muffled sound, absorbing rather than reflecting. I had the feeling the echoing halls of the ships I was used to would drive me mad, now that sound created shapes behind my eyes. "I think . . . I think the whole ship is alive. Even some of the plex."

Orca crossed her arms. "That's insane."

"I know. But I can feel it. The way the ship moves—I'm not

saying it's sentient, but the component parts are all organic."

"What about the fact that they have fucking gills?" asked Nasrin.

"I have no idea."

"And this is supposed to help Harper somehow?" said Orca.

"Watch your tone," said Miranda.

Orca subsided. Once again, I wished Miranda would reclaim her captaincy. The crew listened to her. We trusted her. At least when she made mistakes, they were for predictable reasons. I had no clue how I was going to screw up, save that I was one hundred percent going to do so soon.

"We need to come up with some sort of strategy," I said.

"Gain Lia's trust," Kraken suggested.

"But don't trust her," said Nasrin. She and Kraken had positioned themselves nearest the door, and there was something endearing about the way they scowled protectively at the rest of us—at least until I remembered how useless muscle was against this ship.

"I'll try. Do you think—"

"Good. You're awake." Lia appeared in the doorway, her short kelp-brown hair damp and the bioluminescence beneath her skin muted. Kraken and Nasrin moved as one to come between her and me.

"It's fine," I told them, though I wasn't sure it was true. Kraken touched my shoulder as he stepped out of the way. The gesture braced me. He had my back. I didn't know if he could help me or what he could really do if they decided we were expendable, but I knew he'd die trying to protect the crew.

"How do you feel?" Lia asked me.

"Fine." Truthfully, I did feel fine, physically. Disoriented from the sonar reinstalled in my head, yes, but that was preferable to pain, and the luxury of thoughts that didn't drag was worth it. My emotional state was another thing entirely. I touched the tender scar above my eye.

Lia quirked an eyebrow. "You will get used to it. Now, I will take you to your friend."

Orca moved forward at the mention of Harper.

"Just you," Lia said to me. She didn't even glance at Orca. The total dismissal narrowed Orca's eyes. She opened her mouth to protest, but Kraken closed a large hand around her arm, cutting her off. I turned to look at Miranda. Her arms were crossed over her chest, and the muscles of her forearms were tight with frustration, but she nodded.

"Why don't you want my crew to come with us?"

Lia shut the door before answering. "It is nothing personal. They are not like us. They will not understand some of what they see, and it is easier this way. For now."

"I'm not sure I understand, either."

Harper remained unconscious when I entered the infirmary. She floated in the bath, naked, with her hair tied out of the way and the stained bandage gone from her hand. The wound still looked angry, but the red streaks and blotches had faded from her skin, and she breathed easily beneath the oxygen mask. My hand hovered over her shoulder, as I was unsure if touching her would rouse her.

The doctor—Vi, I remembered—cleared her throat. I withdrew my hand hastily. Harper's skin no longer bore a feverish sheen. She rested peacefully, and my vision blurred as relieved tears filled my eyes and spilled down my cheeks. She breathed. She was going to live. I wasn't going to be left alone without the closest thing I would ever have to a sister. I swallowed a sob and bit my lip until it stopped trembling.

"She will need another day, at least," said Lia. She spoke a few words in her own language to the doctor while I stared at Harper. Even the pull of the currents faded as I memorized the way her black lashes lay against her cheeks in sleep.

Something darted just past her bound hair. I jumped. "There's something in there."

Lia pointed at Harper's hand. "Flesh fish."

"What are—" I broke off, my gorge rising. Small green fish nibbled at the necrotic tissue around Harper's finger.

"They don't eat healthy tissue."

"What's wrong with a scalpel?" I averted my gaze and took shallow breaths.

"They have analgesic and antibiotic properties in their bite. Our design, of course. They're more efficient; they can find tissue we miss."

"Oh. That . . . that makes sense."

That didn't mean it wasn't fucking disgusting.

"When they're finished, we'll put a flap of viable skin over the site. Whoever cut it off didn't leave much to work with. The bone—"

"That's okay." I didn't want to hear any more details. "But she'll recover?"

"Yes."

"Thank you." Nausea receded, and I met both Lia and the doctor's eyes, trying to convey the depth of my gratitude with a look, because words couldn't even begin to encompass the void her loss would create in my life.

"You're welcome." Lia then translated my words to Vi, who smiled and spoke. Lia relayed the message. "She says your friend is a fighter."

"Yes." More tears pricked my eyes and I wiped them away, too happy to care.

"Would you like to see the rest of the ship?"

"I need to tell my crew Harper is doing well, but yes."

Irritation flickered over Lia's face at the mention of my crew, but she nodded. "Of course."

I ran the short way back to our quarters, my bare feet silent on the moss. Lia didn't say anything when I pressed my hand to the door and opened it without her consent. There would be time to navigate the realities of our situation later. Harper, first.

Orca took one look at my beaming face and slumped against the nearest bunk. Palpable relief seeped from her posture.

"She's—" The rest of my words were cut off by Kraken's hug. My bones creaked as he wrapped his arms around me. Lia stepped out of the way to avoid getting crushed, and though my ears were mostly stoppered by Kraken's arms, I heard Miranda questioning her about Harper's health. I hid my face in Kraken's chest and let his body shield me. He released me when my breathing steadied.

"With respect, while we appreciate your hospitality, traditionally the first mate accompanies her captain," Miranda said to Lia.

"With respect, we follow different traditions."

I blinked my eyes clear of my remaining tears. Both Miranda and Lia kept their voices pleasantly neutral, but there was nothing neutral about the way they looked at each other. Miranda's eyes, by rights, should have sliced Lia to ribbons, and Lia's expression suggested a sea slug had just grown a human mouth and a grasp of language.

"Perhaps you could enlighten us as to those traditions," said Miranda. The scars on her knuckles whitened in warning.

"As I explained to your captain, much of what we are is beyond your comprehension."

"Um—" I started to say.

"I'll give you something to comprehend," said Orca.

"For now, it's best if you all stay here."

"Perhaps—" I tried again.

"Traditionally, prisoners are told they are prisoners," said Orca.

"Hardly. The best prisons are built on the illusion of freedom, don't you think?" Lia dropped all pretense of neutrality. Light pulsed in her neck. "We are not the same, which is why, again, it is best you stay here until your captain can explain the situation in ways you can understand."

This time, I managed to get the words out. "My crew is perfectly capable of understanding anything I can."

"You haven't seen enough of our ship yet to make that call," said Lia.

"And if I refuse?"

Lia's dimples vanished. "Then it will not be our fault if something happens to them."

"Is that a threat?" asked Orca.

"Parts of this ship will eat you alive. Literally."

I thought of the way the moss had absorbed my vomit. My initial outrage faded. The way she addressed my crew was unacceptable, but perhaps there was a rationale guiding her words.

"That's impossible," said Nasrin.

"It . . . might not be." I avoided looking at Miranda as I spoke. "I don't like it, but Lia might be right. For now."

"Good. Let's go. The speaker wishes to see you again."

Miranda scoffed, but did not argue. I half wished she would. It wasn't right; she should be the one negotiating. A surge of anger at her flared. She should be the one handling this situation, not me. I didn't have the training or the temperament. Finding the sea wolves had been her damn idea, not mine. I followed Lia with the relief from moments ago draining away.

"You don't like my crew," I said, keeping one eye on her and the other on the walls, which I did not touch. Could moss be carnivorous? Anything was possible if people could have gills and glow.

"I neither like nor dislike them. Though that woman—the one who seems to think she is the captain—"

"Miranda. She was the captain until recently."

"She lacks respect."

"You can't hurt her."

"I meant what I said. This ship is not safe for them. It is only safe for you because you're with me. I will tell you what you need to know to navigate it safely. Understand, it is unusual for us to bring others onboard. You claimed inheritance, which is different."

"What is usual, then?"

Lia raised an eyebrow. "I think our reputation precedes us?"

Legends. Nightmares. The hatred on the face of the pirate who had nearly split my skull.

Two women emerged from a doorway. Both had the mottled, shifting skin I'd noticed on some of the other sea wolves, and both stared at me out of golden eyes. *Lipochrome*, Lia had called it. Linked genes. Genes my father had tried to suppress in me as best he could, for reasons I would never understand, because he'd vanished forever from my life when I was five.

I expected her to bring me back to the room where we'd first been received by Altan. Instead, we descended a hatch to what I guessed was the common area. People lounged on mossy couches, some balancing bowls of food, others engaged in board games I didn't recognize. A few children chased each other around the perimeter. With the exception of the ubiquitous moss and the tanks of curious octopuses, it felt much like any other common room I'd set foot in.

Then I saw the center of the floor.

Ringed by couches lay a pool, its surface disturbed by a number of gilled humans—though I wasn't quite sure the label "human" applied. They lounged at the edges, submerging to breathe in between signing with the people nearby.

"Our engineers," Lia said when she caught me staring.

I'd been exhausted and overwhelmed when she had brought me to the tank for healing. Now, I was fully conscious and alert, and the chatter in the room created an overlay of sonic patterns in my perception. Perhaps they signed to reduce the sheer volume of noise the human tongue produced.

I asked the only question I could think of: "How?"

"Genetic manipulation. It's not my field, but from what I understand, it's a matter of finding old codes in DNA and flipping them on. We emerged from the oceans once. Why not go back?"

"Because the water's toxic most of the time?"

"We're working on that, too."

She spoke with such assurance that its meaning took a moment to find me. "What do you mean, you're working on that?"

"You'll see." She pulled me toward a corner. The speaker, Altan, sat alone with a mug of something warm in his hands. Steam wreathed his smooth face and broke like clouds on his cheekbones.

"Altan," Lia said.

He looked up and smiled. "Join me."

We sat.

"Are you comfortable?" he asked.

"Yes, thank you. And thank you for seeing to my crew."

"How are you adjusting?" He tapped his head to indicate his meaning.

"It's confusing," I admitted.

"Altan's sonar is the most developed on the ship," said Lia.

"Does this noise bother you?" I waved at the common area.

"I have learned to sort through it. Much like visual stimuli."

"And you speak my language."

"We are the only ones on the ship who do," said Lia.

"We raid equatorially enough to merit it," said Altan.

"There was a ship that intercepted ours before we came south," I began, unsure of how to finish. "They'd been raided."

"Are you asking if that was us?" said Lia.

"It's possible." Altan set his cup down. "Friends of yours?"

I touched the scar on my forehead. "No. But they didn't show up on our sonar."

Altan nodded as if this made sense. "Everything adapts."

"I'm not sure I understand."

"Evasion. They've learned how to avoid basic sonography waves. Not that it often helps them. Displaced water has its own signature."

"Oh."

"You have also been displaced," he said.

The shift in conversation took me by surprise. I wished I had tea of my own so that I had something to do with my hands.

"We've worked hard to preserve our bloodlines. Too much is at stake, which is why we have inheritance rights."

"My parents never mentioned anything. My father—he had to be the one—vanished when I was young. He was a drifter." I glanced down at my unwebbed hands. "He had brown eyes."

"How did you come to work with Amaryllis?"

"It's . . . complicated."

"Uncomplicate it for me." He spoke gently, but I wasn't fooled. I was treading squid-infested waters.

"I actually worked against her. I'm Archipelagean. Or I was." In halting sentences, I gave him an abbreviated version of the events that had led us to flee *Man o' War*. I didn't know what to keep secret, so I skipped what I could and hoped I wasn't damning us. When I finished, Altan watched me from above those severe cheekbones.

"Do you know how we came into being?"

This was not the follow-up question I'd been expecting. I shook my head.

"The Archipelago is just one of many installations designed by our ancestors. Some have been more successful than others. Yours, for instance, has merely managed to survive. We Symbionts seek more than that. We were founded by scientists, and the spirit of inquiry lives on in all of us. 'What if?' This is the first question our children learn to ask."

"What if?"

"What if we could breathe water? What if we could seed the seas with bacteria to combat the dead zones? What if we could see sound, feel north, live as the creatures of the seas have always lived?"

What if Miranda had killed Ching? What if Comita hadn't betrayed my trust? What if my father hadn't left me with more questions than memories? I had 'what if's' enough already.

"The dead zones are getting larger," I said, trying and failing to keep the accusation out of my words.

"But not as large as they would have without intervention. If you want proof of more obvious success, consider our ships. Can you feel the difference?"

"Yes. But—"

"They're composed of living material. Cells send messages, and they move and breathe and respond. Just as plants bend to the light, so our ships move. More efficient than your dated solar tech."

"The ships really are alive then."

"Of course. Sentience is debated, but it is a moot point. All living things are sentient in their own way. Granted, we don't think the ship as a whole is sentient, merely a collection of smaller selves. The moss is separate from the algae plex, though the relationship is symbiotic, and the fungal components live their own little lives beneath the rest." He smiled, as if this were a joke. I couldn't smile back.

"But why raid?"

"Ah." Altan exchanged a glance with Lia before continuing.

"I will be transparent. We do not raid for material gain."

"Then why? What other reason is there?"

"Would you knowingly sail into territory patrolled by ships stronger, faster, and deadlier than yours?"

"She did," said Lia.

Altan ceded the point with a nod. "Not the best analogy. But you were seeking us out. Most don't."

I remembered the revelation I'd had while looking at our charts: Archipelago territory was bound by more than temperature extremes and dead zones. Our ships avoided the poles for a reason, a reason that now sat across this small table from me.

"You're protecting your territory."

"More than that. We're protecting our cities."

Cities were drowned things—the jagged, broken teeth of civilizations lost to time and waves. Perhaps it was an error in translation. "Cities? Are those like stations?"

"Approximately. We're heading to Symbiont, our capital, as we speak. The commission will assess your case, as I told you."

My heart stumbled. Our case, and the hostage I'd promised them. But Harper was alive: I clung to this fact. A living hostage could be rescued.

"What assurances do I have my crew won't be harmed?"

"What assurances do we have that you did not come here intending harm?" Altan countered. Then, still watching me with those amber eyes, he said, "They will not be harmed without cause. See that they do not give it."

"I will."

"Good."

I needed to find out what claiming inheritance meant, but I was afraid to ask, as it would reveal the depth of my ignorance. There was one question, however, I could not repress.

"My father . . . if he was a Symbiont . . ." *Symbiont.* That was what Altan had called himself. Not a sea wolf, but a name synonymous with equilibrium.

"The commission will check our records. You may have other family, too."

The sharp stab of hope almost made me gasp. It was a child's hope, and traitorous. I did not have time to search for relatives my father had actively tried to prevent me from ever finding. And yet, how could I not yearn for answers?

Chapter Sixteen

"Well? Do you think you can explain things in ways we can comprehend?" Orca said when I returned.

"No, because I don't understand any of it."

"News that surprises no one."

"They fed us while you were gone. Hungry?" Kraken gestured to the table, perhaps hoping to offset Orca's bickering. Her scowl implied she was not deterred, but I approached the table, mind reeling from the last few hours. The food consisted of a platter of sweet round fruits, crispy wafers, and a gelatinous substance that tasted significantly better than it looked. I took bites in between filling my crew in on the conversation I'd had with Altan and Lia.

"What is the name of this city? Symbiont? That's a little . . . obvious . . . don't you think?" said Finn.

"Not any more obvious than naming stations after constellations or a ship after the jellyfish that fucked up its captain," said Kraken.

"Can we please get back to the part about the gills?" said Nasrin.

"She said they were the engineers."

"Implying the engine is underwater?"

"I'm not sure there is an engine, at least not like we're used to."

"They would have had to breed selectively," Kraken said, his rumbling voice darkly speculative.

"Eugenics always ends badly." Despite her words, Miranda sounded thoughtful, rather than alarmed. "That explains a few things."

"Like what?" I asked.

"Like you."

I reached for another fruit. Lia's dimples stuck in my mind like sonar ripples. The familiarity I felt in her presence haunted my thoughts when I needed them clear, and old memories gnawed: a nondescript man I loved with all my childish heart, his arms around my mother; large, warm hands keeping mine safe; good-bye after good-bye until one day he didn't return. Lost at sea. Gone. I'd been too young to understand, and young enough to adapt to life without him; and as I'd grown, I'd asked after him less and less. He was the reason I was mocked. He was the reason my mother was lonely. We both avoided the subject and the pain it raised. In Lia, I saw the life I might have had, and it seethed beneath my skin like bioluminescence.

"I need to get back to the trawler. Our stocks will die, and that hell beast needs feeding," said Kraken.

"Seamus." I'd forgotten about Miranda's cat. "I'll say something. Maybe we can stay there instead of here."

"Check this out."

We turned to Nasrin. She had her hand pressed to the plex column. Inside, a small blue octopus matched her fingers with five of its eight limbs. When she moved, so did it.

"Do you really think they don't eat them?" she asked.

"We haven't been served any," said Kraken.

"I don't think they do." A new idea occurred to me. "Maybe they're not pets after all. I think they might study them. That's why some of them have skin like an octopus, though I don't know why that would be beneficial."

"Maybe it's just decorative," said Miranda. "We're assuming everything they do is utilitarian. That could be a mistake."

Her hands trembled as she reached for her flask. She gave it a shake, then returned it to her belt. It must have been empty. A spasm of an unnamable emotion crossed her face. I studied the twist of her mouth and swallowed my dread.

Lia didn't return for me again that day. By my estimation of evening Miranda's shaking had worsened, and she lay on the bunk with sweat pouring off her skin. I sat beside her and stroked her clammy forehead.

"What's wrong with her?" I asked Kraken.

"I'm fine," Miranda said.

"Is it an infection?" All I could think about was Harper, lying unconscious while fish ate the dead flesh from her hand.

"It's not an infection." Kraken crouched before Miranda and took one of her hands in his. Her scars and his tattoos complemented each other, and I remembered him telling me she'd been the one to ink him. He had been the first sailor she'd marked, though ink was a kindness she hadn't shown the rest of us.

My brutal, beautiful, broken love.

"It's nothing." She struggled into a sitting position. Strands of lank hair clung to her face. "It will pass."

"Kraken—" I said.

"She's right. It will pass." He held Miranda's eyes, and the look they shared shut me out entirely.

"Go find Lia," said Miranda. "See about our ship."

"I'm not leaving you."

"I told you. I'll be fine."

"Miranda—"

"Fucking *go*."

Stunned, I jerked away from her. She closed her eyes and leaned back against the wall of the pod, her hand still bound with Kraken's.

"Fine."

"Don't give me attitude, Rose. Just do your job."

As if *I* was the one with the attitude. I stood and headed for the door, pausing only long enough to beckon Orca to come with me.

"Breaking rules already?" she said as she stood with a clink of shells.

"You're my first mate. They can deal with that or they can kick us off their ship."

Orca grinned at the anger in my tone. "Whatever you say, Captain."

Once in the hall with the door sealed behind us, I realized my first problem: I had no idea how to find Lia, and I did not speak the Symbiont language. Instead of admitting this, I snapped at Orca, whose grin widened each time my temper flared. "Let's see Harper. And don't touch anything."

Orca walked in step with me down the mossy hall. The light from the moss showed me her face in profile—jaw set, eyes wary, ready to take on the ship itself. I was suddenly glad she was my first mate. By all rights she should be furious with me. I'd ascended to captaincy after only a few months on her ship, whereas she'd served for years, and I'd come between her and that same captain. Yet she'd taken it in stride. I hadn't been in any condition to predict her reaction at the time, but in retrospect I was surprised. She'd just lost her ship, too, but unlike certain others who would not be named, she wasn't trying to drink herself into a coma.

We didn't pass anyone on the short walk to the infirmary, nor were we eaten by the walls. I pressed my palm against the plex door. It slid open. I tried not to think about the conversation I'd had with Altan regarding sentience. A door was a door. Plex was plex. Algae were algae.

Orca pushed past me and ran to Harper's side. She remained unconscious, but her face had regained some of its usual firmness. I hadn't realized how much flesh the fever had leeched from her bones. Orca stroked her wet hair and I turned away to give her privacy.

The child in the tank with the octopus caught my attention. She curled around it like it was a cat; its tentacles entwined around her fingers and wrist. Moving closer, I crouched to study them. Tight, short curls crowned her head. Her eyes were closed, and her lashes brushed round, childishly plump cheeks. She couldn't have been more than four. The octopus changed colors with her breathing, shifting from blue to purple to green. The shifts soothed the ache in my chest left by Miranda's harsh words; they were innocence suspended.

The child's eyes opened slowly, and she blinked. Gold pierced the water. Her gills flared, and though the organs unsettled me, there was something about the motion that felt like a human gesture. The octopus woke, too, and tightened its grip on her hand. Her other hand formed a series of languid signs. Not knowing their sign language, I didn't know how to respond beyond a small wave. She smiled, revealing small white teeth, and waved back. I wondered why she was here. Nothing appeared visibly wrong with her, but then again, what did I know about what was normal for a gilled child? I put my hand against the plex. She mirrored the gesture, and the octopus extended a tentacle. A tiny sucker fixed itself to my thumbprint. It was such a contrast to the last sucker I'd had directed my way.

"Making friends?" Orca asked from Harper's side.

I nodded.

A voice spoke in Symbiont. I didn't understand, but the reprimand was clear. I looked up from the child to see Vi enter the infirmary. She strode across the floor and yanked me upright by my left arm, speaking rapidly. I shook my head in an attempt to communicate my confusion. Her brows contracted in frustration. Finally, she pointed at me, then Orca, and then the door.

"I think we're being kicked out," I told Orca.

Orca kissed Harper's forehead. Vi growled something. Orca ignored her and, with a lingering touch to the tank, joined me at the infirmary door. The last thing I saw of Vi was her frown as the plex slid shut.

"She looks so much better," said Orca.

"I know. Except for the flesh fish."

"Excuse me?"

I filled her in on Symbiont medicine as we followed the curve of the ship past closed plex doors. Several sailors frowned as they passed us, their expressions identical to Vi's, and I guessed it was only a matter of time before word got back to Lia. Good. I needed to talk to her.

"Check this out." Orca paused by an open door. Within, coils of fleshy tubes emitted faint pulses of bioluminescence. She moved to investigate, but I pulled her back.

"Lia wasn't kidding about the ship being dangerous. I watched moss eat my vomit."

"When did you vomit?"

"When they fixed my head."

"Fucking gross."

"What are you doing?" Lia approached at a dead run, her face wide with horror as she saw the room beyond us. Bioluminescence pulsed along her skin in staccato bursts.

"Looking for you," I said.

"You should not be out here. Especially not her."

"This is my first mate, Orca." The anger I felt at Miranda spilled over into my voice. "We were looking for you."

She caught her breath and straightened. "What did you need?"

"We would like to return to our ship."

"You are not authorized to leave." More pulses of light glimmered beneath her skin. I wondered if they bore any correlation to her emotional state. Was that why their clothing was so damn revealing?

"We have no intention of leaving, but the ship requires maintenance, and my crew would feel more comfortable in their own quarters."

Lia's eyes flickered over Orca before returning to me. "Would they stay put?"

"Hey, now—" Orca bristled at the implication she required containment.

"We will."

"Then I will talk to Altan. Is there anything else I can do for you?" Her tone suggested the only valid answer was *Please take us back to our quarters and lock us in.*

"It's been nice to stretch my legs," said Orca.

"You are lucky to still have them." Lia glanced once more at the room Orca had nearly entered. Was I imagining one of the tubes had inched closer? I tugged Orca away.

262

"Remind you of something?" Orca said.

"Yeah." The massive squid we'd battled several months ago had possessed tentacles of a similar size. The comparison felt like a premonition. This ship seemed poised to swallow us all.

Lia herded us back to our room. When I turned to seal the door behind us, she caught my arm. "I am serious. There is danger here. More than you know."

I gave her a fake smile and stepped away, doing my best to look sobered by her words instead of infuriated. I was so fucking sick of cryptic warnings. Comita, Miranda, Ching, and now these Symbionts—could no one just spell things out clearly? Maybe this was why the world had collapsed: nobody knew how to communicate. The Symbionts should add *that* into their genetic coding.

Orca clasped my shoulder and drew my attention to the rest of the crew. "We need to get to the ship," she said to me in a strained voice. "Miranda's in withdrawal."

Before me, Miranda crouched on her hands, dry heaving into the moss. Kraken supported her with a steady hand on her back and murmured something I couldn't hear while Finn and Nasrin played a game of dice at the table, using fruit as chips.

Cardinal points skittered around my compass. I knew Miranda drank too much. Her flask was always handy, but she was never *drunk*—until recently. Once or twice I'd even wished she would tip herself over that edge, if only to see her lose control. She wasn't in control now. She'd stripped down to her undershirt, and the muscles in her shoulders bunched as she shook.

"Neptune," she groaned, and my anger dissipated at the pain in the line of her bowed neck.

"I know," said Kraken. Kraken, who'd been Miranda's confidante for years. He, of course, would have known about Miranda's drinking. She'd promised me no more secrets. But this . . . The sounds of dice rolled around my head, disturbing my thoughts. How could the crew just sit there, pretending this wasn't happening? Nasrin felt my glare and looked up. The grim set of her mouth told me more than words. She wasn't ignoring Miranda. If she was sitting there, it was for a reason.

I thought back to all the times I'd seen Miranda sipping from her flask. She'd been drinking more of late. That much, at least, I'd noticed. The pit of anger in my stomach stirred anew. We couldn't afford her to collapse. I needed her to be strong and stable, as she'd been since I met her.

Had she been strong, though?

Ching had told me Miranda was broken. I'd seen the cracks in her façade, but cracks could be smoothed over. Resealed. I'd thought her stable despite the fault lines. Now, standing in the doorway as I watched her heave, I felt a lens shift. The sound of her moans rippled across my newly sensitive mind and revealed patterns I'd been blind to previously. Patterns I wished I couldn't see.

Miranda, carving her mark in my palm. Miranda, striking me with her whip. Miranda, walking Annie, walking Andre, slicing that man's throat right in front of me, while betrayal after betrayal left its own mark on her body.

Miranda, lying.

I'd mistaken her cruelty for strength, and her tyranny for command.

She'd told me, right before our capture, that she knew what it was to love someone like her: someone brutal and damaged and scarred. Of course I'd known the scars on her body were more than skin deep, but that knowing had been different from understanding. I pictured how she must have looked when Ching pulled her out of the water: her skin necrotic, her joints swollen, her muscles twitching and aching and alive with pain. It would have been months before she could move comfortably, and months before the wounds healed to the scars I saw today. The deepest wounds, the ones on the backs of her legs, still pained her. I'd seen her rubbing them after a long day on her feet. How naïve I'd been to have ever thought them superficial—or healed.

Seconds passed.

I did not know what it said about me that I loved this woman, or that I'd been willing to sacrifice so much to stay at her side. At least the deaths I'd caused had been accidental. I'd never set knife to throat and drenched my ship with blood.

I hovered on this precipice, there on a foreign ship in waters I'd sailed into not because I shared Miranda's twisted idealism, but because I'd had few other choices, and wondered which way I'd fall. To one side lay a path I wished I wanted, where I steeled my heart and will and pursued a life without Miranda in the hopes I could one day balance my ledger against the damage I'd done while in her orbit. In that life, I found a way to escape the Symbionts with Harper and returned her to Polaris, but there my imagination balked. Polaris was no longer my home. I had seen the Archipelago for what it was, and I harbored no illusions about my place within its walls.

On the other side of the knife's edge lay the path I still ached to follow. In this life, Miranda learned to respect me as her partner, and together we brought down the systems that had shaped and alienated and cast us out, no matter the cost. But to take that path I'd have to accept the side of me Miranda claimed to recognize, which was, in its own way, just as brutal as she was—the part of me that burned beneath the cardinal points, simmering, magmatic, and furious; the part of me that had once longed to break the nose of a boy named Maddox in the *North Star* training room; the part of me that put off seeing my mother because I could not hide the truth: that despite the sacrifices she'd made to give me a better life, I was just as adrift as I'd been at birth.

I felt the blade with my bare feet and knew where I'd fall. I could not keep pretending to be someone I wasn't. Perhaps that was why I'd been drawn to Miranda. It wasn't that I had a thing for dangerous women. It was that I wanted permission to become one. I would never fully belong anywhere. Even if I found family in Symbiont, or if we reclaimed *Man o' War*, I would always be a chimera. It was time to stop trying to belong and to be what I was—whatever shape that took.

I crossed the room and made my choice.

"No," Miranda said when I knelt before her. "Rose, please go."

"I'm not leaving you."

She didn't raise her head. Kraken held her braid out of the

way of the puddle of sick, which, I noticed with a jolt of unease, was already vanishing into the moss.

"I don't want you seeing me like this."

I touched the curve of her ear. Her skin was clammy and cold, and she smelled of sour sweat.

"Fuck," she swore again. Her body shook as something wracked it, and her nails dug into the mossy floor, gouging tracks in the sporophytes. I put a hand on her shoulder. She flinched.

"Don't touch her right now," said Kraken.

I pulled away. Kraken saw me staring at his hand on Miranda's back, and grimaced before amending his statement. "Touch her as little as possible."

"Mere?"

"Neptune." She lay her head on the moss, heedless of her bile, and screamed. I recoiled from the raw agony in the sound as it grated on all my senses.

"Is this normal for withdrawal?" I asked him. I longed to reach for Miranda, but when I touched her arm, she screamed again.

"For her, yes." Kraken's lips jerked downward as Miranda's screams went on, and I longed to cover my ears and block out the sound. Sonar sliced like a knife across my vision. Pulses of the world ricocheted back, blurred and fractured. She sounded like she was being torn apart. I inched closer.

"This is why she drinks," he said in the next pause.

My hand hovered over the back of Miranda's head without settling. Quietly, I put into words what I'd only recently understood. "You pulled her out of the water, but the pain never stopped."

Her scars gleamed in the blue light as he acknowledged the truth in my statement. I thought of my captain floating in a sea of man o' war, tentacles trailing across her body and stinging her over and over and over, their bladders keeping her afloat even as she tried to drown herself. The ocean hadn't let her die—nor had it let her forget.

The ocean never let any of us forget.

"What can we do?" I asked.

Kraken shook his head.

"There has to be *something*," I said, my voice rising. "We can't let her live like this."

"The withdrawal will pass in another few hours." Kraken moved Miranda's braid as she heaved again. "She'll manage."

"I'll talk to Lia. There's rum on the trawler, and they have to have something—"

"No," said Miranda. Sweat dripped from her skin. Heedless, I bowed my head to rest beside hers. She pressed our cheeks together. Her ragged breathing vibrated against my forehead where it rested on her shoulder. "No, Rose."

The tremors shaking her body intensified, and she gasped.

"I'm here," I said.

"I didn't. Want you. To see me like this."

"Tell me what to do to help you."

"Nothing." She groaned and stifled another scream.

"Maybe they can fix you like they did me and Harper. A detox—"

She shook her head against mine. "Better this way."

"How is this better?"

Her chest heaved. Sweat trickled between her breasts, illuminated by the glowing floor. She didn't answer.

"How is this better, Miranda?"

Her hand seized mine. Moss was embedded beneath her nails, and her knuckles whitened as she clenched my fingers. I braced myself against the pain of the bones in my hand grinding against each other, grateful to share some of it. My palm itched where she'd carved her mark.

"Because I'm trying to deserve you."

"Oh, Mere." I took her braid from Kraken and adjusted my position so that she could lean into me instead. Kraken nodded and stood. I wiped her streaming eyes with my shirt. I'd thought of the two of us, I was the masochist—but maybe I'd been wrong about that, too. I also suspected the real reason she refused Symbiont help was her fear of showing weakness. She'd rather suffer like this than let them know she had a vulnerability they could exploit. The part of me that hated seeing her hurting railed against this, but the larger part, the part that was now captain, agreed. We couldn't afford to give them any more leverage against us than they already had, and there was only so much rum currently distilled on the trawler. Without access to our beets and the still, we had no way of making more.

"Though drowning would be preferable," she said in a lull between tremors. Her ribs dug into my thigh, where she'd collapsed, and her words were spoken to the moss.

"I'd rather you didn't."

"If wishes were fishes . . ." She trailed off with a groan.

"Shh." I cupped her skull, careful to apply steady pressure and not to brush her hypersensitive skin as I would normally. "Just try to breathe."

The fact that she complied told me a great deal. We sat, Miranda curled half in my lap, half on the ground, in the waning sunlight of the south, while the rest of the crew cast us anxious glances and periodically brought water for me to raise to her chapped lips. My mind wandered as she shuddered and retched, traveling down familiar corridors with new eyes. *You pulled her out of the water, but the pain never stopped.*

It had taken me less than a month to turn to drugs in order to function after my head injury. How long had Miranda held out after her ordeal before turning to liquid solace? And how could I have ever let myself judge her for it? I chewed the inside of my lip to keep from clutching her to me and weeping. I could be strong for her, even as it ripped me open to see her crumble.

Chapter Seventeen

A splutter and a gasp announced Harper's return to conscious-ness. She sat up, aided by Vi, and coughed. Water streamed from her hair and down her body. It didn't stop me from throwing my arms around her.

"It's not like I died," she said into my armpit.

"You almost did."

She wriggled free and examined her hand. A new flap of skin stretched over the stump of her forefinger, and while the area looked tender, it was no longer inflamed, and her arm lacked all signs of blood poisoning.

"I'm going to kill her," Harper said, and the venom in her voice told me she meant Ching Shih.

"That would require getting close to her, and I don't ever want that to happen again." I meant every word. Twice now I'd escaped Ching Shih by the skin of my teeth. I doubted I'd be so lucky a third time.

Harper wrenched her eyes away from the wound and stared at her surroundings. "Where the hell are we?"

I wasn't surprised she had no memory of our arrival, given the state she'd been in. "You've been out for two days. I'll explain everything later."

Harper was able to walk with my support. Days of fever had weakened her considerably, and she struggled to catch her breath as we hobbled together down the hall after Lia.

"She glows," Harper said in a whisper. Ahead, Lia stiffened, though she couldn't possibly have heard.

"She's the most normal one here."

"Just think." Harper paused and panted for a few seconds before resuming. "Right now we could be back on *North Star*, plotting how to beat up Maddox."

"Less talking, more walking."

I relinquished my hold on Harper only when Lia opened the door, and Orca swept her into an embrace which hurt to look at. I shared too much of Orca's relief, and I did not want to think ever again about how close we'd come to losing Harper. The long days of her illness would haunt me as surely as Jeanine had haunted me following her death.

"Altan has denied your request to return to your ship," said Lia. I snapped my attention back to her.

"What? Why?"

"You may send someone to see to the ship under guard, but we've inspected it. We know you carry weapons."

"Then I will send someone with you now."

"Good. And we arrive at Symbiont tonight. You will join me so you can see it for yourself."

"And my crew?"

"Will remain contained."

I nodded. This was not the time to make demands. I motioned for Kraken to come closer and whispered my orders. "Get the cat and do what you can to put the ship in stasis. And . . . get rid of the rum."

He held my gaze for a full count of cardinal points. I didn't know if he approved or disapproved, but he didn't argue. The decision churned my stomach. I ignored the cramping. I'd let my digestive tract make too many choices in the past. I no longer trusted my fickle gut.

As the crew filled Harper in on events, I sank onto the bunk I shared with Miranda. She slept fitfully, her skin still damp with sweat. The withdrawal had passed over the course of the night, but she still shivered with pain.

"Mere?"

She cracked open her eyelids.

"Lia said we'll be at Symbiont later today."

"Lia is a barnacle's cunt."

"Kraken's getting your monster for you," I told her. "He's going to freak out over all these fish."

She managed a smile at the mention of her cat, but it faded as she tried to sit up, winced, and then lay back down. Her eyes closed once more. "Is he bringing anything else?"

I'd been dreading this question. She hadn't quite been able to hide the hint of pleading in her voice as her resolve wavered.

"No," I said.

Her face contorted, and for a moment I thought she might scream at me. Her chest rose and fell in a rapid succession of deep breaths. I waited. She steadied herself, and the lines eased around her mouth.

"Good call." She didn't sound like she believed it.

"I need you to work through this before we get to Symbiont. I have no idea what to do. This is your plan, Mere."

"Not sure it was a good one."

"It's a bit late for second guessing. Can you keep it together?" I asked, forcing myself to speak with authority.

The door opened and her attention focused on a spot over my shoulder.

"Monster," she said as Seamus wriggled free from Kraken's grip, drawing blood in the process, and bolted toward us. He landed on Miranda's chest with a disgruntled hiss and stared around the room with wide green eyes. She stroked his head. I, meanwhile, did my best not to attract his rancor. His bushy tail lashed Miranda's hips.

271

"Ship's in good shape," Kraken said.

Lia had entered behind him, and her eyes remained fixed on Seamus in frank fascination.

"Never seen a pussy before?" said Finn.

"A what?"

I prayed the translation overlooked the double entendre.

"A cat," said Nasrin. "Furry mammal, eats rodents . . ."

Lia shook her head.

"I wouldn't recommend touching it," said Kraken. He examined the claw marks raking his arm. Blood trickled down his inked skin.

"We do not have such things."

"No, you have those things." He gestured at the octopus eyeing us.

"Did you check the engine?" I asked him.

"She's fine. Everything's fine, though it could use some sunlight."

"This can be arranged," Lia said, still watching Seamus. The cat had his claws sunk into Miranda's chest. One had punctured the skin, and blood beaded on her shirt. She didn't seem to notice. Her blue eyes softened as she ran her nails along his head. Gradually, his low growl subsided, and while he didn't purr, his wary crouch relaxed into a huddle and his claws retracted. I still didn't dare touch him.

"Do you have more of these?" asked Lia.

"Not with us, but yes."

"Fascinating."

So fascinating, she forgot to sneer as she peppered my crew with questions. Miranda ignored all but the most direct. Her head rested on my thigh, which was still the most contact her skin could bear. Seamus, however, seemed to be an exception.

"It is yours?" Lia asked Miranda.

"As much as he is anyone's," she said. Her voice was still hoarse. Periodically, she twitched as her muscles spasmed.

"Fascinating," Lia said again. Her fingers flexed as if she was restraining herself from asking to touch him.

"Dunno how you can live in a world without cats." Orca looked horrified at the prospect. She sat on the floor with Harper curled up next to her.

"Can it sign?" asked Lia.

"As in sign language?" asked Orca.

"Yes."

"In their own way," said Kraken. "You learn to read their body language."

Lia chewed on her lip. Curiosity was clearly vying with her inherent disdain for my crew. "We bond with an octopus in the birthing tanks. It teaches those of us with mutable pigmentation how to use color to communicate, and those of us without learn—"

"That's why that kid had one?" interrupted Harper. "I was afraid it was like those fish."

"Octopuses are clever. Highly intelligent, but not like us. It is important to recognize other ways of thinking. Ingenuity leads to adaptation."

It had the rote sound of something taught. I considered pointing out that Lia didn't seem to recognize my crew as intelligent, but thought better of it. Pissing her off right before we arrived at a foreign city with Miranda incapacitated seemed like a bad idea.

"What happens to those who can't adapt?" I asked Lia.

"Same thing that always does," said Miranda. She forced herself into a sitting position to glare at Lia, who shrugged.

"The fossil record is full of species who failed to change in time. There is no malice in it."

"The dead might disagree," said Miranda. I considered reminding her later that finding the sea wolves had been her idea, and that alienating them over semantics wasn't the best way to achieve her goals.

"The dead aren't here." Lia looked Miranda up and down. "Be grateful you are not one of them."

Miranda stumbled to her feet with a snarl. The rest of the crew snapped to wary attention, hands on missing weapons.

"Is that a threat?"

"A threat?" Lia tilted her head. "Why would I want to kill

you? You're doing such a good job of it yourselves."

"Lia—" I positioned myself between the two of them. The hand I placed on Miranda's shoulder wasn't just to stop her. I'd seen her sway, still weak from her sickness.

"It's true. That's why you're here, isn't it?" There was such genuine confusion in Lia's voice that I paused in the act of replying. Lia took advantage of the silence to continue. "We'll be at Symbiont soon. Come."

With a pained look at Miranda, I followed.

"Why do you treat them like that?" I asked when we were out in the hall. "Like you hate them."

"I do not hate your crew."

"You don't like them."

"It is not that." Lia chewed on her lip.

"Then what is it?"

She examined her hands before answering. "We have more in common than you think, Compass Rose."

"What does that mean?"

"It means I know what your people are capable of, and I don't trust them."

"You don't even know them."

"I do not need to."

"Your people are the ones who raid." We raided, too, but I didn't feel like being fair.

"We raid to protect our cities. What we're doing— you can't understand until you see it."

"Your ships outgun ours in every way," I said.

"A defense mechanism, along with our reputation. *Your* people want to exploit that. That woman, Miranda. She—"

"She doesn't want to exploit you. She wants to find a way to bring balance to our side of the ocean. We're dying out there."

"And we're trying to save you."

"What—"

"I am not authorized to answer these questions. Will you just come with me?" Her voice rose in frustration, and abruptly I realized she was young: perhaps even younger than I.

274

"Am I the first person you've met who's claimed inheritance?" I asked.

She glanced at me sidelong. "You're the first we've picked up while I was on board, but I've met some back home."

That explained a few things, including her lack of diplomacy. She made me look like a Sagittarian ambassador.

"How old are you?"

"Twenty," she said.

"You're lying." I said it gently, and she gave me another irritated glance through her eyelashes.

"I'm seventeen."

I'd been seventeen only five years ago, but it felt like a decade.

"Is that young? For your job, I mean."

"Yes."

"Is this what you want to do? Translate?" I gave myself a mental pat on the back. If I could keep her talking and draw her out, she might tell me something useful.

"Yes."

"How many languages do you speak?"

"Seven. But I sign in two."

I spoke only one language, and not even very well half the time. "Are all Symbionts multilingual?"

"Of course not. They don't need to be."

"Right. Because you make sure no one gets to them."

"Exactly."

"I thought maybe it was part of . . ." I gestured at her skin, which emitted purple pulses.

"No. I worked hard."

"I believe you," I said, raising a hand to forestall the indignation in her eyes.

"Lia." A harsh voice penetrated our argument. I looked up to see Vi, who had emerged from the infirmary with a stern expression. She spoke several curt sentences in their language. By the time she finished, Lia's glare had smoothed into a pretension of neutrality.

"Apparently, we are disturbing the infirmary," she said when

Vi stormed away.

"Tell me something," I said more quietly. "What will happen to my crew if your commission decides they can't stay?"

"Worst-case scenario, they'll probably be sent to the colony."

"The *what*?"

"Shh. They'll like it there."

"What the fuck is the colony?"

"It's fine. And they probably won't get sent anywhere. I'm only telling you so you stop shouting at me. What matters is they're not going to be killed or marooned or whatever you're afraid of. Besides, one of them is a hostage, right?"

"Yes, but—" A low throb vibrated through my feet and up into my chest. "What was that?"

"It means we're there. Come on."

Nonplussed, I walked beside her down the curving, living hallway, trying not to visualize it as a monster's gullet, until we came to a room I hadn't seen before. Clear plex covered the space, and I realized it must be the bridge, though I saw few instruments and fewer sailors. The strangest thing was the floor, which was bare of moss. This puzzled me until I remembered what light did to eyes straining for the stars.

My observations were cut short by the sight looming in the distance.

Archipelago stations were large. Circular, with deep keels, they held all we needed to survive and were unflappable in even the worst storms. Symbiont was nothing like a station. It spread as far as I could see, a vast network of organic shapes, some of which were easily as large as several stations combined. Ships darted around them, moving with the same languid motions as the *Moray*. The turbulent Southern Ocean should have tossed them together like flotsam. Instead, each ship kept its distance. Strands of some thin, flickering substance glimmered around them. The strands reminded me of jellyfish tentacles, or cilia. And beyond, far out of sight, I sensed something solid.

"We're near land."

"The continental shelf. Look." She pointed, and I reached

out and grabbed her arm as a pod of creatures I'd only ever seen in illustrations swam past.

"Are those dolphins?"

"Yes."

Further speech evaded me. The pod clicked and whistled at each other as they torpedoed through the water, their bodies made for swimming. I dropped my hold on Lia and walked to the plex, standing so close my breath fogged the surface. Fish swam in shoals around the city. The word *city* fit after all. Stations were city-states. This was a city in the old sense of the word, more like the drowned things I'd sailed over in the Gulf than my home. I couldn't see the end of it.

Whatever force guided the ship—Altan, I suspected—took us into the mass of floating structures. They rose above and below us, some the spherical or oblong shapes ships were supposed to be, others looking like they'd been grown in a petri dish with their odd protrusions and twists. Up close, the strands of cilia were delicate, and whenever we brushed against them, they recoiled. The ships attached to them edged away, too. *Sensors.*

But the city couldn't hold my eyes for long. Life pulsed around it. Corals grew on some of the structures, and fish schooled, hunted by dolphins and larger fish. Seaweed grew on the lower ships, forming beds of kelp that rose in columns. Octopus and other animals prowled their green shadows. I even saw the jagged edges of what might have been shellfish. A spotted animal slightly larger than a human paused in its swim to turn a whiskered face toward us. The word *seal* rose to my lips. Impossible things. Impossible creatures. They were extinct, and yet . . .

Something tickled my nose. I wiped my face and found it wet.

"How?" I managed to say.

"Science."

A seadoor opened in the structure directly ahead of us, cutting off my questions. I wanted to stay out here, observing. The Symbiont's ships might be incredible, but I'd seen ships before. I'd never seen dolphins.

"Just a minute longer," I whispered, my breath fogging the plex.

We sailed into the seadoor despite my plea. Bioluminescence lined the docking bay as the larger ship forced water out. Blue light dripped from the walls. Unsurprisingly, they were covered with the same moss as the *Moray*. Except . . . I squinted. It wasn't moss. It was seaweed. Which made sense—so much more sense, in a way, than our light tubes, though I wondered how the seaweed absorbed the sun's rays. My speculation was cut short as Lia tugged me away from the plex.

"You may choose one member of your crew to accompany you," she said, grudgingly.

"Miranda."

Perhaps I should have chosen Orca. She was, after all, my first mate, but this was Miranda's dream. I couldn't deny her this opportunity—though I prayed to all the seas she could stay standing.

Chapter Eighteen

Miranda splashed water onto her face, which was sallow despite her light brown complexion, and pulled her shirt back on. The rest of the crew grumbled about staying behind, especially when I mentioned the dolphins, but protocol was protocol. I slipped my hand into Miranda's as we walked. She tolerated the gesture of affection. That, more than her clenched jaw, told me how poorly she still felt.

"What now?" I asked her as we followed Lia.

"We wait and see." More quietly, she added, "We need to tread carefully. Amaryllis didn't tell me what they'd want with Harper."

Other members of the *Moray* joined us in the halls. Their skins shifted as they spoke with one another—some laughing, others arguing—and the vestigial gills on their necks held my gaze. The red flesh within the slits looked like wounds.

We exited the ship in a queue. Lia beckoned us to stay close as we filed onto the dock, which, despite being covered in more of the glowing seaweed, was not slippery beneath my bare feet. More of the strange undulating ships occupied the other berths, held in place by the same fleshy arms that secured our trawler within the *Moray*. I craned my neck to investigate the apparatus more closely. Had they simply modeled plex on cephalopod anatomy, or was something stranger at work?

The hatch into the bay opened with a sucking sound. No door, here. The hatch was more like a sphincter. It widened to let us pass, and as I edged through it, it quivered. I watched it over my shoulder. At a touch, it shut with a biological squelch that made me deeply uncomfortable.

"Did that . . ." I said to Miranda, whose eyes were as wide with horror as my own.

"Remind me of something? Yes. Let's never speak of it again." Her lip twitched in a shadow of a smile. My face cracked open in response. Her smile was all the light I needed.

The hall beyond the hatch resembled the halls on the *Moray*: glowing moss, plex tubes. The difference lay in scope: this hallway was broader, and the plex water tubes were wide enough to allow for human traffic. People swam, signing at one another with deft motions. Water passed through their gills. I stared until my eyes felt dry and itchy, not caring if it was rude.

We passed through several more sphincter-hatches down winding corridors lined with doors and branching halls. I was again reminded of the sensation that the ship itself was alive, and Altan's philosophizing on sentience, combined with the periodic shift beneath my feet, led me to conclusions I could no longer ignore. They'd figured out how to grow their own ships. In a way, it made more sense than mining and harvesting old plastic, and we were doing something similar with our bioplastic production, just on a much smaller scale. Here, though, biological material seemed to replenish itself, purifying the air and working symbiotically to stabilize living conditions while also providing a flexible structure. Our scientists would cut off both their legs for the opportunity to study this.

As for the gills, the explanation was stranger. The idea of returning to the sea in this literal sense through forced evolution made the skin on my neck prickle with fear. Was this their end game? To abandon air entirely? It would save us from the risks of surface toxicity and drowning, but our bodies were not equipped for life underwater. Surely our skin would slough off, oversaturated and pruney.

This tech was not going to help the Archipelago or the rest of the ocean. We needed air. So, it seemed, did at least half of the Symbionts. What status did the gilled sailors hold? Higher? Lower? The lack of cultural context made negotiations daunting in the extreme, and it took all my self-control to keep from hyperventilating.

The hall widened the farther we went. I sensed a great open space ahead, and sure enough, the walls flared to reveal a vast chamber. It encompassed the center of the ship almost entirely, from the plex dome atop to the water beneath the plex at our feet. In the middle, suspended, climbed pillars of vines. Flowers grew on twining tendrils, and the roots descended into the water, where fish and eels and children played. People lounged about on the plex, occasionally talking to the swimmers in strategically placed surfacing pools. It reminded me of Seraphina's garden, as well as the gardens on Polaris, but there were a few key differences beyond the presence of what I could only term "mermaids."

Birds—birds!—flew about the ceiling. Moss flourished on the walls, along with plants blooming in brilliant shades of colors. The air was warm and humid and smelled like life. We passed a group of young people working on lap looms with bundles of soft hemp fiber beside them. Curious octopus and fish gathered beneath, and a young woman changed colors to match the octopus hovering directly beneath her. Mimicry? Communication? I listened to the echoes of their voices across my sonar and saw the room in too many dimensions.

Lia walked with purpose. She did not pause to explain or point out details of our surroundings, and the stiffness in her spine suggested tension. Almost every pair of eyes I saw matched mine. I'd adjusted to this new status quo so thoroughly that the first pair of brown eyes took me by surprise. A child raced past, laughing, and her large dark irises arrested me. The child chasing her had eyes the yellow of sunset, and I wondered if the brown-eyed girl felt as I had—alone. Would it kill us as a species, I thought with a depth of bitterness that startled me, to find a way to live with difference?

Miranda squeezed my hand, and I felt the comfort she offered through her fingers. Her scars drew attention from the passersby. Several heads turned, and while I couldn't understand their language, the low murmur of speculation was universal enough.

Lia led us through yet another sphincter. *Hatch*, I decided. I would call them hatches, despite their resemblance to anatomy, because it disturbed me to do otherwise.

A slim pier extended into a pool in the room beyond. The room, I quickly realized, was mostly water. Only the strip of mossy plex and a round platform at its center offered familiarity. Lia walked down the strip and waited in the center of the room, motioning for us to follow. Glowing fish and cephalopods pulsed in the dark water. The walls dripped with moss above and seaweed below, and a clever skylight let in light—though it didn't penetrate the water very far. I wondered with a shudder how deep it went.

"What are we doing here?" I asked.

"Waiting for the commission."

"Who, exactly, are the commission?" asked Miranda.

"You would call them a trade commission, maybe, though that isn't exactly right."

"What kind of government do you have?" Miranda sounded clearer than she had in days. Perhaps moving around had helped, rather than hurt.

"The kind that works."

Miranda and I both scoffed.

"I'll believe that when I see it," Miranda said.

"You're about to." Lia pointed to the water.

Heads surfaced. Five people in total, of varying ages over thirty. Some had mottled, mutable skin; others, tones more like my own people, but all had gills. These were not vestigial. They passed water through them, though they seemed to also be able to breathe air, at least in enough quantities to speak. The eldest among them had a feminine face and tightly braided hair. The thin braids formed patterns over her skull, and a few strands of black streaked the whites and grays. She swam close to the platform, her webbed hands cutting gracefully through the water. Looking down on her felt wrong. Lia, however, did not seat herself. Instead, she struck a respectful pose with her head slightly bowed and her posture unthreatening. I followed suit. Miranda widened her stance, taking up the space we'd relinquished.

"Greetings," said the woman. She had a gravelly voice, and I felt it shiver over my skin.

"I bring you the sailors from the North Atlantic," said Lia.

"One of them is a foundling, I see. Like you." The woman smiled at Lia with affection. Her peers grouped behind her and fixed their golden eyes on me. Too much gold. Assembled like this, I noted slight variations in their eye colors. Some were the hot, burnished gold of metal, others deepened into amber, and some had hints of green. "You've come to claim inheritance?"

"I believe my father carried the genes," I said at Lia's encouraging nod. "He was lost at sea when I was young."

"Know, first, that we embrace our own."

"I thank you for your courtesy." I clasped my hands behind my back and waited for the interrogation to begin.

"Why else did you seek us out?" asked the woman.

I wished Miranda could answer for me. She could rally a crowd or convince a commission. The last time I'd had to make a public case for something was before the Archipelago council, and the memory, while the least of my nightmares, remained unpleasant.

"I was born on an Archipelago station in the Atlantic called Cassiopeia, like the constellation. I became a navigator, and eventually left the Archipelago to sail with Miranda, who was my captain. We were working with a woman named Ching Shih after destabilizing events in—"

"Ching?" The woman's gray brows furrowed.

"You know her as Amaryllis," said Miranda.

A pause ensued. "She is still alive?"

"Yes," I said.

The commission broke into a heated conversation in their language. Lia followed it with raised eyebrows, and I wished she would translate. She didn't.

"Explain," said the woman.

I explained as best I could the events that had led up to Ching's supposed death, and her current circumstances, leaving out my part in her fleet's destruction. I wanted to ask how Ching fit into this ever-expanding puzzle, but this wasn't the time.

"But she is not with you now."

"No," I said, that particular memory still sharp. "We had . . . ideological differences."

"Unsurprising," said another member of the commission in a tone I could only call *sotto voce*.

"News of her survival is indeed worth something. And your crew: I understand you've brought a hostage as an offering of goodwill, but in exchange for what?"

This was the moment I needed to maneuver with utmost caution. I took a moment to gather my thoughts.

"Things are unstable. Oceanic conditions worsen, and everyone is struggling. We . . ." I took a deep breath. "We came here because we'd heard you had another way. Perhaps a better way. We are willing to come to an agreement on your terms if you will consider lending aid."

"Aid." The woman's smile was less friendly, this time. "What kind of aid did you have in mind?"

"Your ships aren't like anything I've seen. The technology alone—"

"Was earned. Your people chose their path, and we chose ours. The divergence was too long ago to mend."

"But—"

"Look around you. Would your people thrive here? What could we give you that your bodies could handle?"

"With time—"

"The Archipelago was charged with carbon absorption; did you know that?" She moved her arms lazily as she tread water. Her skin wasn't wrinkled. Perhaps a life submerged prevented the worst of gravity's ravishes.

"The project failed," said Miranda, quoting the textbook response. The stations had been built as tenement hous-

284

ing-turned-bioengineering project, but the latter hadn't lived up to its potential.

"It did not need to. The people failed. Machinery could have been repaired, but no one was willing to experiment. You turned inward, for survival. Whereas here . . ." As if she'd commanded its presence, a seal surfaced. Its sleek head bobbed beside hers before it dove once more. "We've turned our focus toward adaptation. Not just of ourselves—but of the ocean's children. The algae we seed into the sea will, over time, help stabilize the climate. It will not go back to the way it was. But we will thrive regardless. The projects we have underway are all designed with that aim in mind, though it may take many more generations. Your people have nothing to offer us. Perhaps I sound cold, but consider this: we have changed our very genetic code. Some among us argue we are no longer the same species. Your people would suffer here, and only their children's children's children, with careful selection on our part, would find themselves at home. We are the future. We cannot look back."

Her words reverberated over the water and sent ripples through sonic space. I did not know what to say. What *could* I say?

"There is the reclamation project," said a man with skin the blue-black of deep ocean.

The woman nodded, thoughtful now, as she considered me. "True. The southern continent is promising. Forests grow again along the coasts. The winters are mostly unsurvivable, and the volcanoes are imposing, but there is potential. We have an experimental colony close by."

"On land?" My voice squeaked on the last word. *This* was the colony Lia had mentioned? "You say you're seeding the sea. We could work to develop strains that counter blooms—"

"We have them."

"Then if we could—"

"Why should we part with what we've developed over generations?"

"You say you wish to restore the ocean—"

"We do." The subtext of her statement sharpened her eyes.

But not for you.

I twisted my fingers together hard enough to crack the knuckles. Silence settled over the assembly.

"There's always the mission Amaryllis failed to finish," said the *sotto voce* man.

The woman's eyes narrowed in thought, but I didn't wait to hear her conclusions. Currents swirled. In them, I saw the shape of something monstrous.

"Amaryllis's project?" Miranda asked in a voice so flat and calm I almost didn't recognize it.

"She was tasked with bringing the Archipelago to the bargaining table, or, if that failed, to heel. But she managed to do neither." *North. South. East. West.*

Past the buzzing in my ears, the commission continued. "Who is the hostage?"

No, I wanted to scream. There was no way I could turn Harper over to these people, even if they had healed her. I turned to Miranda. Her face betrayed little, but her tell, the twitching muscle in her jaw, told me that she, too, was reeling.

The sea wolves, Miranda's last hope for redemption, were behind everything.

Time stretched in the liquid way of revelations. I was aware of the room in all its dimensions, and the expectant eyes of the commission, and Miranda, who still had not taken a breath, beside me, and I was aware, too, of Harper back on the *Moray*. Ching had taken a finger. What would these people take?

I searched for any option besides the ones before me. Giving Harper up wasn't one. Couldn't be one. I'd panicked before, too terrified of losing her to think clearly, but there had to be a way out.

"We need assurances any hostage won't be harmed," said Miranda. I knew she was buying us time. *North, south, eastwest-northwestsouth*—any course but this.

"What assurances could we give you that you would believe?"

said the woman.

What would happen if I refused to give them anyone? Would we be allowed to leave? Could I claim it had been a trick to get medical assistance? I knew so little about how these people worked, and I could not afford to guess wrong about their reactions.

"None," said Miranda. She stepped past me and squared her broad shoulders. "I submit myself as hostage."

"Miranda—" I began, but silenced my outburst at her sharp hand gesture. This couldn't be happening. I couldn't let this happen.

"And why would we want you?"

"I can give you leverage over Josephine Comita, admiral of Polaris Station, who I know for a fact is planning a coup."

The commissioner swam closer. "What kind of leverage?"

"She and I worked together. My past history with the Archipelago is complicated. I am a criminal. You can undermine her hold on power by exposing her relationship with me."

"What was your crime?"

"Mutiny."

"Mutiny?"

"I incited a station into rebellion."

"And do you have proof of your relationship with the admiral?"

Miranda hesitated. I didn't know what proof she might have had, but with another spike of dread, I suspected that proof remained on *Man o' War*. My hands twitched as I longed to reach for her. *Thank you*, I wanted to tell her. *Thank you, and damn you*, because how was I supposed to choose between my best friend and my lover?

"I do," said Miranda.

"What is the proof?"

"I am," I said.

Miranda whirled. *You are not the only one who can make sacrifices*, I told her with a look.

"You?"

"I served as navigator for Admiral Comita. The Archipelago Council knows my face, and they know I served as a spy. I can corroborate any reports."

"A mutineer and a navigator," said Mr. Sotto Voce. "Now there's a story."

You have no idea.

The commission spoke amongst themselves long enough for my racing heart to somewhat calm. They were considering it, which meant that maybe, just maybe, we'd spared Harper—as well as making ourselves more valuable alive than dead.

"We shall consider your case," said the commissioner with a nod to Lia. "Take them to Kole. He'll weigh their evidence."

"You really didn't know?" I asked Miranda as Lia led us out of the room. Miranda shook her head, looking as stunned as I felt.

"Of course I didn't know."

Ching hadn't told Miranda everything, then. That was a small comfort. If Miranda had lied to me about this . . . but she hadn't, and the problem before us was much larger than Ching's predictable deception. Harper's parentage had to remain a secret. If only I could store the knowledge in a chest and drop that chest into Davy Jones's locker or, better yet, the Mariana Trench.

"They can never find out," I said in a whisper too low for Lia to hear—I hoped.

"I know."

I wished, too, that we'd been given time to get our story straight. I'd already betrayed the Archipelago on more than one occasion. I'd even been willing to plot a raid against Crux's supply lines. This, though—this was different. We'd been dropped in the middle of a game where we did not know the rules. I was shaking as badly as Miranda had in the worst of her withdrawal. The sea wolves—Symbionts—were not the solution. They weren't even potential allies. They'd been willing to set a butcher on my people, and for what? My bare feet sank into the moss, and each step felt like drowning.

The room Lia led us to overlooked the central chamber. I could see the vines and the birds through the wide plex on the far wall. The effect was soothing, had I been in any state to be soothed. My thoughts tumbled over each other. Harper. Ching. Comita. Later, I'd have time to consider the effect this news had had on Miranda. Later. After I'd secured Harper's safety. I'd failed Jeanine, but I would not fail Harper.

In the middle of the room, his head resting against a tank filled with tiny octopus, sat a man. He looked to be in his fifties, with the leathery, sun-darkened skin of a drifter. His thick, curly hair thinned at the temples. Gray laced the black. Someone had broken his nose at least once. It leaned crookedly to the right, and a divot in his upper lip suggested he'd lost more skin in that fight than his face belied. Wide shoulders. Waist thickening with age. Lean legs, bare from the knee down to reveal feet with the same high arch as mine. Deep lines in his cheeks. And his eyes—

Miranda tightened her hold on me as I slumped. Lia said a few words in their language to the man, her back to me, unaware I'd partially collapsed. He nodded, but his eyes remained fused to my face. He stared at me, drinking me in like a shriveled root.

Eyes the warm brown of sunlit kelp, with the barest hint of gold.

I should not have recognized him. Too much time had passed. He'd left when I was five, and what I remembered most were his large callused hands and the way his shoulders felt beneath my small thighs.

"Rose?" His voice traveled back through time and undid everything.

I ran. The door opened at my touch and my feet flew down the halls, skimming over the sucking moss. People leapt out of my way. I vaulted over a series of small pools, scaring several children swimming below the surface. Leaves whipped my face. Moss brushed my arms. I stopped only when the vines towered above me and I could force my way into the tight grove at the base. There, I huddled on a tangle of roots, feeling the pull of water up through the vines into the mangrove forest and north swirling all around me. I pressed my back into the roots hard enough to bruise my spine. I couldn't do this. I *wouldn't* do this.

It was too much. Everything was too damn much, and I hadn't asked for any of it.

Miranda found me. She crouched outside the grove and peered into my hiding place. I shook my head, unable to speak. Wave upon wave of tight, hot anger rocked me, and beneath the anger swam shoals of shame. Moving past this scant security was unthinkable. Here, I was just a nodule on a mangrove root, poised between water and sky. She edged in. One of her feet slipped on the net of roots crisscrossing the surface. She caught herself. There was barely room for both of us in the shade of leaves and smooth bark. Her hand reached out for mine. I fell into her, shaking so hard my teeth rattled.

"I'm so sorry, Rose."

Fish glittered in rays of sunlight. A child laughed nearby. The rattle of my teeth painted sound patterns across my eyelids.

My father was alive.

"I want to leave," I said.

"I know you do."

"He's dead. That man is dead. I don't know him." She stroked my back. I placed my tongue between my teeth to stop the rattling and tasted blood. "It's getting more and more complicated."

Miranda took my face between her hands and wiped my tears away with her thumbs. She, too, was a shell.

"He . . ." I couldn't say the rest.

"You need answers. I can't give them to you."

"I don't want to know."

"You're not a coward." Her fingers pressed into my jaw, forcing me to face her. "You're a navigator. A captain. *Mine.* And I don't tolerate cowards."

"Mere—"

"I'm so sorry. I'm so, so sorry, but you have to face this. I'll be right beside you."

"I can't," I said, but I took her offered hands and crawled out of the mangrove, blinking at the bright light because she was right. I had to face this. My crew depended on it.

The walk back to the room seemed to take less time than my

flight, for all that we walked slowly. This was time I knew we should be using to plan, but I couldn't. I couldn't think at all, except to ask the same series of questions: how, why, and why again.

Raised voices greeted us at the door. Miranda put an arm around my waist and pulled me slightly behind her as we paused to listen. Lia shouted something at the man—my father—in their language, her voice breaking as it rose in pitch. His voice rumbled beneath hers in the baritone I remembered.

They broke off their argument, for I didn't need to speak their language to know they were fighting, when they noticed us. Lia made to push past Miranda to leave, but he spoke a sharp word, and she halted. Tears glittered on her cheeks. She wiped at them furiously.

"What's happened?" asked Miranda, holding even more tightly to me.

Lia threw a poisonous glare over her shoulder at the man waiting for me and refused to answer.

He stood. One of his legs buckled as he attempted to rise, but he steadied himself.

"You were born facing due north," he said to me. My mother's words: the story she'd told me on nights I had trouble falling asleep. I wanted to cover my ears with my hands, and I wanted to throw myself into his arms, as I had so often as a girl. Instead I clung to Miranda. Her arm enveloped my shoulders, holding me close. She couldn't protect me from this the way she'd shielded me from other dangers. This was no pirate ship or duplicitous crew. This was betrayal on a level so deep I couldn't have plumbed the depths if I'd wanted to.

"How do you know that?" I asked. I had to ask. I had to be sure, and I had to hear him say it.

"Rose, what are you doing here?" He looked at me like his heart was breaking. Good. Let it break, as my mother's had. As mine had. I didn't owe him answers.

"Your name wasn't Kole when you were my father."

"I can explain, if you'll let me."

"Does my mother know?"

He shook his head and closed his eyes.

"You were never a drifter." Years of ridicule, of wondering, of searching drifter tubs for a familiar face. All for nothing.

"I was."

"It was his cover. If you're going to tell the story, tell all of it," Lia said. A bloody red line marred her lower lip where she'd chewed it raw, and bioluminescence pulsed along her neck in shades of red almost as violent. Her reaction didn't add up, but I couldn't process any emotions other than my own.

"The work I did for Symbiont required access—"

"My mother was *access?*" I struggled free of Miranda and took a step toward him, though what I intended to do wasn't clear even to me.

"No." His face crumpled. "I loved her. I still do."

"You *left her.* We thought you were dead!"

"I make no excuses. What is done is done. But Rose—"

I remembered, suddenly, the last time I'd seen my father. He'd kissed my forehead and bade me to be good, and I woke the next morning with a terrible headache. My mother had bathed my forehead with cool cloths and sang to me until it passed. That must have been when he'd made the alterations. Then, he'd left us forever.

"Why didn't you take us with you?" I wished I sounded like Miranda: cold and commanding, not petulant and hurt.

"You had a good life. You were safe."

It was true. My mother loved me, and we'd been happy. I didn't want to have been raised by this man instead, but things might have been so different, had I known the truth. "Is that why you messed with my head? To keep me *safe?*"

"Never let it be said he doesn't learn from his mistakes," said Lia.

"Lia-lee—" he began.

"Oh, shit," said Miranda beneath her breath. I looked at her, but she was staring at Lia with something like horror.

"What?" I asked her.

She shook her head and squeezed me.

"Are you going to tell her, or should I?" Lia continued.

"Tell me what?"

Kole cleared his throat and, with a heavy glance at Lia, began to speak. "I met your mother two years before you were born, Rose. I was on a reconnaissance mission. Symbiont has been keeping tabs on the Archipelago since the beginning."

"No one looks twice at a drifter tub," said Miranda. How many times had we relied on that very sentiment over the last few months? Drifter anonymity had saved our lives. I locked my knees to prevent them from giving out on me while I struggled to parse through the maelstrom of emotions to the facts beneath.

"And you are?" He took in the protective curve of the arm she'd placed around me.

My life. My heart. My broken, angry ocean.

"Miranda Stillwater," she said.

Kole rocked back on his heels in surprise.

"So, you've heard of me?"

"You caused quite a stir," he said.

"You're getting off topic," said Lia.

"The Archipelago had a duty, and they failed." He cleared his throat and searched my face, as if he wished he were saying something different. "The finest geoengineering minds built us both. The Archipelago was supposed to work with us to reverse what we could of the damage to the climate so that the oceans, at least, would remain livable."

"What does that have to do with my mother?"

"He was a spy," said Miranda.

"Did she know you were using her?"

"I never used her. She had nothing to do with my mission."

"Which was?" I asked.

"I cannot tell you." Regret flavored his words so thickly I could almost taste it. "Believe me, if I—"

"Why didn't you come back? Can you at least tell me that?"

"My cover was exposed. You would not have been safe. If someone had linked me to you—"

"Brief 182C," Miranda said. "Seas. That was you?"

293

"What?" I said.

"There was a brief I found in an old ship log on my first ship. I didn't understand half of it then, just that a drifter man had kidnapped a kid from Gemini. The admiralty wanted that kid back. Badly. I remember it because the wording was odd. There was something about the mother, too—"

"She died," said Lia. "After trying to drown me."

My mother had dated only one person since my father had vanished: a woman named Kit, who worked with her in the kelp beds. Sometimes Kit had dinner with us. Occasionally she stayed the night. I never got the sense it was serious for either of them, but I liked Kit well enough. She never got between me and my mother, and she made my mother smile. There hadn't been anyone else, before or after, that I knew of. Despite my father's long absences, she'd remained faithful to him—or perhaps she simply hadn't craved companionship. She'd never told me whether or not she and my father had spoken of commitment or monogamy, and I had never asked. For all I knew, she'd given him her blessing to be with as many other people as he wanted.

This was different. Slowly, I peeled my eyes from my father's face to look at Lia. "Drown you?"

"She thought I was radioactive because I came out glowing."

I'd been five years old when Lia was born. Five years old. The same age as when my father left us forever one August morning.

"Of course I couldn't drown because I had baby gills." She touched the skin on her neck. No gills broke the surface, but that angry red still pulsed. "She didn't know that, though. She'd already slit her wrists."

"Oh," I said, an involuntary gasp of pain for the girl standing with her arms wrapped around herself.

"What's funny is my father always told me he didn't know his genes would pass it on. He said," and here she glared again at Kole, "he came from three generations of Symbionts who hadn't expressed, which was why he made such a good spy. He used to tell me that if he'd known, he would have warned my mother. But you did know, didn't you?"

This last was directed at Kole.

"Lia—"

"Because he already had another child, and she'd been born facing due north with eyes the color of a fucking star."

The message my brain had been trying to nudge my way finally penetrated my shock: Lia was my half sister.

"I couldn't tell you," said Kole. "Not without jeopardizing Rose."

"Who you protected with a *lobotomy*." The accusation she flung at him stuck its landing, and he flinched. "Have you ever spoken a single word that wasn't a lie?"

"Enough," he said.

But Lia wasn't done, nor was she going to listen to him, no matter how firm he made his tone. "*You* can go talk to the commission and explain to them why you were not able to validate their evidence today. I'm done."

"Lia!"

She stormed out of the room, tears clinging to the lashes around her golden eyes.

"Rose, you should sit," said Miranda. She pointed to a chair. I obeyed, feeling dizzy. Then she turned to Kole. "She will speak to you when she's ready. Until then, I have a few questions."

He stared out the plex window, perhaps hoping to catch a glimpse of Lia's retreating form.

"Did you work with Amaryllis?" she asked.

His head whipped back around. "How do you know that name?"

"Used to sail with her."

"She told you her real name?"

"She did. Left out a few other things, though, like how your people financed her attack on the Archipelago."

"Before you judge, consider this: once we are in possession of the stations, we will reintroduce the protocols that should have

295

been in place all along. It will take time. Generations. Our innovations might be able to keep us alive as a species long enough to benefit. Without intervention, we'll be dead within the next millennia. We had no choice."

"What about negotiations? Did you think about talking to us before you decided to wipe us out?" I said.

"Repeatedly." His mouth twisted bitterly. "For decades. For *generations*. Each attempt has been rebuffed by your council."

I recalled my own experience with Archipelago politics. It had taken the threat of immediate annihilation to get them to act on Ching. Cold pervaded me as I realized he might speak truth. The Archipelago responded slowly, if at all.

"Now, will you tell me why my daughter is here?" he asked Miranda.

"Because I am a fool. And no. You will never touch her again. In fact, you—"

"Miranda," I said, catching the hem of her shirt as she advanced on Kole. "He doesn't matter."

Kole—I would not call him Father again—looked at me with that same heartbreak.

"We came here with Amaryllis because the Atlantic order is crumbling, and we'd hoped to broker a trade alliance, or at least . . . something. On the way, we had a falling out."

"She would not have wanted to return empty-handed," he said. I filed the information away for later, as I had to do with all the emotions currently putting themselves through an engine turbine in my chest.

"Then one of our crew got an infection, and we had nowhere else to go so we stuck to the course. We did not know you were behind the attack on the mines. If we had, we would never have come. But I guess it's all the same, in the end. You want order. Comita wants order. Who the fuck knows what Ching wanted. We came looking for answers, and now we have them, and I wish we didn't."

"Rose—" Miranda began.

"You say you want to stabilize the ocean," I said.

He nodded.

"Convince me you'll find a place for everyone else, and we'll tell you everything we know."

"Your mother will be safe. I promise—"

"I'm sorry if I wasn't clear. By everyone else, I meant the Archipelago. Pirates. Drifters. Everyone you seem to think matters less than you. And when I said convince me, I didn't mean you, personally. Get your commission to make us an offer."

We were in no place to make demands. I knew this, but I was gambling on the stricken look in his eyes and a prayer he was human enough to feel guilt.

"You look so much like your mother," he said. His arms hung limply at his sides.

"Thank the seas for that," was all I could manage before turning and walking out of the room. I would not give him the privilege of seeing me cry.

Chapter Nineteen

Somehow, we made it back to our room. Miranda led the way, and I was dimly impressed, as I could tell by the clammy feel of her skin that withdrawal still had her in its grip. I was in no mood to navigate. Some things were just too big to process.

Kole.

Lia.

I visualized the chest I'd wanted to put Harper's identity in and added my own burdens, then mentally dropped it overboard. I couldn't. I just couldn't do this. Not if we were going to survive.

"We need a plan," I said, standing outside the closed plex door.

"You need a minute to breathe."

"We don't have a minute."

She leaned against the wall, then, noting the moss, straightened. Haggard wasn't a word I'd ever thought could be accurately applied to Miranda Stillwater, but then again, I'd just learned I had a half sister whose mother had tried to drown her before killing herself, as well as a spy for a father who was also, wait for it, *not fucking dead*.

"We need to convince them we're on their side, and we need to find out everything we possibly can."

"No. It's over, Rose. All we can do is try to survive right now."

"You're not the captain."

Her shocked expression, under different circumstances, might have been gratifying. "Okay, Captain. What did you have in mind?"

"I'm not sure yet."

But that wasn't true. One course did remain.

Orca broke the uneasy silence. "Now what?"

I glanced at Miranda. Her eyes remained on Lia, who slumped against the far wall, where she'd apparently been for some time. I'd expected her to be anywhere but here. Her presence suggested she'd been ordered to keep a watch on us by an authority she could not flout. What did it say that they thought we posed so little threat a teenager could guard us?

A teenager who was my sister.

No. I would break down over everything later. Right now, Lia's presence was an unexpected gift. If I could orchestrate a performance that looked genuine, she might pass it along.

"We don't really have much choice," I said. "Ching was working for them all along."

"Wait, what?" said Orca.

Kraken didn't look surprised, but he did look annoyed; perhaps his pride was injured. As a spy, knowing things like this was his job.

A spy. Like my father.

No.

"Then we need to warn my mo—"

"How?" Miranda said, cutting Harper off before she gave herself away in front of Lia. "We have no ship, no plan, and no navy."

"They'll wipe out the Archipelago." Harper half rose in her anger. An algae cake oozed through her clenched fist and dripped down the back of her hand.

"Just like the Archipelago wiped out Ching's fleet?" said Orca. Harper stared at her as if she'd received a knife to her gut. Orca wavered beneath the onslaught of those eyes but held her ground. "Objectively, they should be aware of the risks of retaliation—"

"Retaliation from *pirates*, not this barnacle-fucking biohazard of an armada." Harper's voice rose with each word. By the last, she was shouting, and Lia raised her head from her hands to blink in confusion. She was right to be concerned. Harper liked to hit things when she got angry.

"Fine. How, exactly, do you plan on getting out of here?" Orca's temper flared to match. My body had absorbed enough of her punches to testify she, too, liked hitting.

"I don't know, yet, but at least I'm willing to try," said Harper.

"What do you think we've been doing? Everything we've tried has backfired. Aren't you tired?"

"No! And you—"

"Harper," I broke in.

She rounded on me. "You can't seriously be considering this."

"Miranda's right. We're done. There's nothing we can do."

Several noises escaped her throat. None were words, but all sprang from fury. She finally managed to say, "My mother."

Who could be anyone, I reminded myself as I hid a wince. Her words had not been incriminating.

"Mine, too."

Her eyes searched mine. "Do you really hate us that much?"

"What? No—"

"I thought you left because of her." She jabbed a thumb at Miranda. "But honestly, Rose, I'm not so sure anymore. Maybe this is what you wanted all along. Payback."

"How could you think that?"

"How could I not?"

"Because you know me!"

"Do I?"

"Harper—"

"You're the captain, and even if you weren't, it's clear where the rest of you stand. But I'm leaving."

"No, you're not. I will order Kraken to tie you down if you try. They'll hurt you. And then you won't save anyone. It's over."

My soul crumbled as she stormed to her sleeping pod and closed herself inside. Orca tried to follow, but a blistering barrage of curses erupted from the pod. Kraken didn't offer any input. He studied me from beneath his tattooed brows.

"Lia," I said, wanting to get this over with as soon as possible so I could talk with Harper. "Can you take Finn back to our ship? I need all our communication records. As soon as possible."

She stood, as eager for an excuse to leave as I'd hoped she'd be, but hesitated as she stared at me. Whatever she wanted to say, however, she thought better of it, and exited.

Later. Later I'd think about what all this meant, and how I was supposed to live with it.

I ran to Harper's pod as soon as the plex door shut on Lia. "Harp, I need to talk to you."

Silence.

"Harper."

More silence.

"Open the damn pod."

The pod opened. I crouched to speak to her and reeled as her fist collided with my nose. Orca caught me as I stumbled back, and she positioned herself between me and a whirlwind of black curls and knuckles. Harper didn't scream as she fought. Each blow carried her characteristic focus, but there was murder in her eyes. Orca blocked her as best she could. I scuttled backward.

"Enough." Giant arms closed around Harper and lifted her in the air. She flailed, feet pounding on Kraken's thighs, but the tentacles inked on his skin might have been real tentacles for all they loosened. I observed through streaming eyes as she slowly calmed, though that could have been a result of the forearm cutting off her air. Blood trickled into my mouth. Miranda's hand touched my shoulder.

"You okay?"

"Yeah." My voice sounded nasally and clogged. "Is it broken?"

"It doesn't look like it."

She helped me up. I approached Harper warily. Kraken held her arms, but she still had legs and teeth.

"Listen to me," I said. "We have to act like we've given up. They won't let us out of here any other way."

"Wait, what?" said Orca.

Kraken answered for me. "Think, Harper. Lia was in the room. We can't help anyone if we're prisoners. Or dead. They're right about one thing: the only way to survive is to adapt. We become what we need to be, which, right now, is whatever they want us to be."

Rage bled slowly out of Harper's eyes. My nose, however, showed no signs of clotting. Each word grated on the cartilage, but I had to speak. "Trust me."

"You don't think we deserve to be wiped out?" Seas, but she sounded like she'd actually believed this was a possibility.

"Neptune, no." I wiped a fresh gout of blood onto my sleeve and swallowed more of the coppery stuff. "But I couldn't say that in front of Lia."

"Oh." Her brows lowered, and I stepped hastily back. Embarrassed Harper also liked to hit things, and she redirected her gaze to Orca, who glared back.

"Well, I meant what I said," said my suicidal first mate.

"Then I hope you like sleeping alone."

I interrupted their brewing argument. "And another thing. Nobody can know who you are, Harp. Nobody."

The pod closed around me and Miranda, blocking out the blue light. I lay on my back and let out the shuddering sobs I'd been keeping locked behind my ribs.

"What do I do? About him?" I asked her.

"Whatever you want. He doesn't have to mean anything to you if you don't want him to."

"But we need him."

"We don't. You've gotten this far without a father."

"No, I mean we need him on our side." I felt sick at the thought. I never wanted to see him again. Lia's words kept repeating in my head. *Tried to drown me. Lobotomy.* The man I'd built my father up to be in his absence was nothing like Kole.

"I'd prefer Lia, all things considered. Which is saying something." She stroked my hair as she spoke.

"We probably need her, too."

"First, we both need a nap."

"Almost." I propped myself up on an elbow. She couldn't see me, but I could see her in waves of sound. "Why didn't you tell me about your drinking? You promised no more secrets."

"There are secrets and there are secrets. Would you have told me about your drug use if I hadn't called you out?"

"That was different. It was medicine."

"Why the fuck do you think I drink, Rose? Rum isn't the problem. It's the solution."

"The solution to—" But I didn't finish. I knew why Miranda Stillwater drank: pain, betrayal, and loss. "Then promise me something."

"Almost anything," she said, rubbing her thumb over the scar on my palm.

"If it ever is too much—"

"I can control myself."

"No. I mean if the *problems* ever get to be too much, Miranda Stillwater, you *tell me* before you throw yourself off my ship."

"Your ship?" she said as she kissed my hair. The comment sounded reflexive, and I basked in the semblance of normalcy.

"Please."

"I won't throw myself overboard," she said dismissively.

I pulled away from her and glared at her, though she couldn't see it. "You know what I mean."

"I'm not going to kill myself."

"Really? What about your liver?"

"My liver is fine."

"There are other ways you could be dealing with this. I've seen your hydrofarms, Mere. You had plenty of alternatives, and I'd bet some are more effective than rum."

"Less fun, though."

I let her comment go. She could deflect, but I suspected part of the appeal of drinking herself to death was the morbid end result.

"I want to thank you," I said.

"For what?"

"For what you did for Harper. For not turning her over."

"You don't need to thank me for that. She's family."

"And one more thing."

"Is it a nap?"

"In a second." I curled against her and rested my head on her shoulder. Her arms closed around me. "I love you. We're going to figure this out."

"By this—"

"I mean us, yes. We're probably all going to die, but you and I—"

"I love you, too, Compass Rose."

Two tense days later, the commission finally came to a decision to let us stay, and we were moved out of our room into new quarters on Symbiont. If we had to be prisoners, I reminded the crew, then at least these conditions were better than on *Man o' War*. For example, no one had attempted to hack off any of our body parts. I ignored Harper's darkly murmured, "so far."

I also ignored Kole's attempts to speak with me. Lia, who seemed determined never to speak of our shared heritage, aided me in this by denying any and all summonses containing a whiff of his presence. I was grateful. Perhaps one day I'd be ready to talk to Lia and Kole about the blood and lies that bound us, but that day was as distant as the equator. For now, Lia and I circled each other like cats forced to share a storeroom.

The new suite of rooms assigned to us overlooked a massive garden on one side and deep ocean on the other. Moss covered all the walls. Here, though, the architect had designed or bred the moss to grow in different shades of color, from green to a brilliant red, forming geometric patterns that soothed the eye. Comfortable couches littered the common area, and there was a pool that presumably connected to the rest of the ship's tubes.

Small fish swam in and out through a grated port. There was another common space on the far side, but here the seating area faced the sea. Seamus took to this room at once. He lounged in shafts of sunlight and pricked his ears and whiskers toward the sea life swimming beyond.

Each of us had a room to ourselves. I shared with Miranda, but Harper gave Orca a flaying look when she suggested they, too, could bunk together. Kraken found the kitchen while the rest of us sorted out sleeping quarters. "There's a tank for our roasts," he said, a grin on his face when I joined him. "We'll have to get them transferred here, and look at this." He showed me the private hydrogarden provided for our culinary use. No one had yet explained how we were supposed to get rations, but I figured there was time. I wished I shared his enthusiasm.

A shriek disrupted our tour. We both ran toward the sound, and when I skidded to a halt in the observatory, all the breath left my lungs. Harper and Orca stood transfixed by the plex. Miranda, too, hung slack from a doorway as three large shapes swam past. Their vast bodies were black, but white spots circled their eyes and marked their fins and what I could see of their bellies. The only difference between them and the tattoos on Orca's arms was their eyes. These creatures' eyes were black, not red, and full of an intelligence that hurt to behold.

"Is that . . ." I whispered to Kraken.

"That's a whale."

Out of the corner of my eye I saw Harper clutch Orca's hand in repressed excitement, their rift forgotten in light of the impossible. The whales circled, once, pausing to stare in at us before moving on into the shifting light of the autumn sea. I heard them singing as they went.

My cheeks were not the only ones wet with tears. Kraken sniffed unashamedly as he wiped his eyes. Orca blinked furiously, a counterpart to Harper, who made no effort to hide her weeping. Even Miranda's eyes caught the light oddly, glittering with unshed salt.

"I had no idea they were so beautiful," Orca repeated to herself as she touched her tattoos.

The whale song lasted long after the orca pod disappeared. I held the notes in my mind, wishing I could share it with my crew, heartbroken they'd never feel it swell against their spine or fill the hollows in their bones as I did. Let the sea wolves kill us; I could die, now, because a loneliness I'd never realized filled the empty ocean had been eased.

"We've been looking for answers in the wrong places," I said, loath to disturb the lingering echoes of song but possessed with a sudden clarity I needed to voice before my courage failed me.

"What do you mean?" Harper pulled her hand out of Orca's as she spoke. The spell cast by the whales was breaking.

I turned from her to meet Miranda's blue eyes. She watched me with a levelness she'd been missing since Ching's reappearance, waiting. She was still my captain. She would always be my captain. But right now, she needed me to pull that weight while she put herself back together. I could do that.

I *would* do that.

"We're not Archipelagean or pirates or fucking sea wolves. *Those* are sea wolves." I pointed in the direction the whales had gone. "We've been waiting for someone else to provide us with answers to the problems we created."

"I didn't create this," said Orca. Behind Kraken I saw Finn emerge from his room and give me an encouraging smile.

"We're each a microcosm of everything that's wrong with the ocean. Drifter. Pirate. Fleeter. Wolf." I pointed at each of us in turn.

"Just because *we* all get along doesn't mean these assholes will want to try cooperating," said Harper. "Or my mother."

"We won't ask them to."

"I'm not following," said Orca.

Miranda, however, wore a faint smile of approval to match Finn's. She moved to stand beside me. "Rose is right. Fuck them. It's time to build something new."

Captain's Log
Captain Ching Shih
Man o' War
April 4, 2514
8°11'18"N, 26°22'57"W

I've sent an emissary to Josephine Comita with a special gift. It's fitting to think that by taking everything from me, she lost her daughter—and that as I take back what is mine, I will be the one to return her.

In pieces.

It doesn't matter that Harper has temporarily evaded us. Her mother will recognize the finger. I made sure to select one with a prominent childhood scar. Recognizing it, she will not question the pieces that follow. Reya shall pay for her role in their escape. They share a similar complexion, and a similar appetite for revolution.

We'll see how cold Comita is when it's her daughter's feet on the plank.

Epilogue

Josephine Comita stared at the box on her desk. It had come in on the tide, carried by a witless drifter who even now languished in the brig. She'd detain him as long as necessary. Forever. Because whether he knew it or not, the news he'd brought had damned every ship in the ocean not under her command. She would sink them all until she found her.

Her daughter.

Mija. The endearment, passed to her from her mother and her mother's mother and down the maternal line since the collapse, burned in her throat. How had she let her go? How could she have believed her safe in the hands of that—that—

Words failed her. She cupped the box, not daring to open it again but unable to dispose of the gruesome talisman inside. Her daughter. Her headstrong, brilliant, beautiful daughter, who was everything she'd raised her to be and more. She'd thought by letting her go, she'd given her a chance for seasoning. She'd hoped Harper would return wiser. Perhaps a trifle more levelheaded. Certainly, more aware of the forces ranged against them.

Instead, they'd both been deceived.

The note that had accompanied the box lay smoothed across the polished desk, though creases from when she'd crumpled the hemp paper in her fist remained. She longed to burn it, shred it, eat it, anything to destroy what had been written, but she'd need the evidence to make her case.

The words had etched themselves into her retinas.

Dearest Josephine,

Find enclosed a token of my respect. If you are half the woman your daughter is, I find defeat easier to bear. Know I will take great pleasure in taking her apart. More soon.

Yours,

Ching Shih

She would drain the ocean.

Her hand did not shake as she pulled a pad of paper from a drawer and scrawled a message of her own for later transmission to Leticia Gonzalez, admiral of Aries Station.

Leticia,

We've been betrayed. Ching Shih is alive, and she has my daughter. If this is not proof that mercy is weakness, I do not know what is. I should not have spared Stillwater. Once a traitor, always a traitor, and now Harper pays for my mistakes. They sent me her finger—

Her hand seized on the pen and ripped the paper. No matter. Nothing mattered except Harper.

We've been lenient. We've pandered where we should have conquered or destroyed. Drifter, pirate—anyone who isn't us is a threat. I know we'd planned

310

to wait before we finished things, but the time for patience is past.

She crossed the last line out. Too diplomatic.

Leticia, I will sink them all. Are you with me?

Yours,

Josephine

Acknowledgments

This book, for lack of a better phrase, kicked my ass. I would not have finished it without the continued support I received from you, dear readers. Thank you for loving Rose and her crew, and for waiting patiently for this next installment.

Big thanks, too, to the team at Bywater Books, who turn Word docs into books through some sort of sorcery, and to my cover designer, Ann McMan, who dresses up my stories and saves them from the embarrassment of wandering naked through the wilderness.

Rey and Shauntel rescued this book from itself more times than I care to admit, and occasionally rescued me from myself after receiving escalating "everything is awful and the book must die" messages. May every writer have such writer friends.

In the chaos and uncertainty that was 2020, my Patreon Patrons brought me not a ray of sunshine, but a whole damn star. This book is for you. I cannot express my gratitude deeply enough, both for your support and for the community we've built together.

And last but never least, Tiffany, thank you for being you.

About the Author

Anna Burke enjoys all things nautical and generally prefers animals to people. When she isn't writing, she can usually be found walking in the woods with her dogs or drinking too much tea, which she prefers hot and strong—just like her protagonists. She is the award-winning author of *Compass Rose*, *Thorn*, *Nottingham*, *Spindrift*, and *Night Tide*.

Follow Anna Burke here:

Twitter | @annaburkeauthor
Instagram | @annaburkeauthor
Facebook | facebook.com/annaburkeauthor/
Patreon | patreon.com/annaburkeauthor/

At Bywater, we love good books by and about women, just like you do. And we're committed to bringing the best of contemporary literature to an expanding community of readers. Our editorial team is dedicated to finding and developing outstanding writers who create books you won't want to put down.

For more information about Bywater Books, our authors, and our titles, please visit our website.

www.bywaterbooks.com